Thomas U. Brocklehurst

Mexico To-Day

A country with a great future, and a glance at the prehistoric remains and

antiquities of the Montezumas

Thomas U. Brocklehurst

Mexico To-Day
A country with a great future, and a glance at the prehistoric remains and antiquities of the Montezumas

ISBN/EAN: 9783337227982

Printed in Europe, USA, Canada, Australia, Japan

Cover: Foto ©Andreas Hilbeck / pixelio.de

More available books at **www.hansebooks.com**

MEXICO TO-DAY:

A

COUNTRY WITH A GREAT FUTURE,

AND A GLANCE AT THE

PREHISTORIC REMAINS AND ANTIQUITIES
OF THE MONTEZUMAS.

By THOMAS UNETT BROCKLEHURST.

WITH COLOURED PLATES AND ILLUSTRATIONS FROM
SKETCHES BY THE AUTHOR.

LONDON:
JOHN MURRAY, ALBEMARLE STREET.
1883.

In Memoriam Meorum

PREFACE.

I SHALL be sorry if the title of this book has led the reader to look for a full account of the recent history of the Republic of Mexico, and of the present social and political condition of the people over the whole extent of its territory.

That more complete accounts of Mexico will soon be published, I have no doubt, as the resources of the country are now being rapidly developed, and foreigners are visiting it in great numbers, either for amusement, or to see what encouragement is offered for the extension of commerce.

In my own work I have little more to offer than extracts from a daily journal, kept during a residence of seven months in the City of Mexico; I have included, however, a few notes of excursions to neighbouring cities and places of interest.

How far I am justified in making general comments upon the condition and character of a 'people with whom my acquaintance is so slight, is a matter of which the Mexicans themselves will be the best judges. I may have seen many things *couleur de rose*, because during my residence in the country I enjoyed perfect health, was introduced to most agreeable society, and enjoyed opportunities of seeing something of the home life of various classes of the people, besides all the ordinary objects of interest presented by a great capital. I entered the hovels of the poor as often as the palaces of the rich, my desire being to lose no opportunity of enlarging my observations. What I saw was generally noted down during the two hours of rest which it was prudent to take in the middle of every day. Now that the journal has been condensed into chapters, and the notes relating to the several subjects have been arranged under their proper heads, I can only hope that some portions of the work may so far interest my readers as to make them more willing to take up fuller accounts of Mexico hereafter. The additional interest which Mr. Whymper and Mr. Vincent Brooks have given to my book by their artistic and yet accurate reproduction of my sketches may further warrant my offering it to the public, instead of confining it, as was my first intention, to private circulation.

Englishmen have taken little interest in Mexican affairs since the French intervention, and the withdrawal of the British Minister in 1860. The unpaid debt on the English loans may have disgusted many. But if I have been able to convey to the reader my conviction that a bright future is awaiting Mexico—if I can induce any of my countrymen to secure to 'themselves a share of the prosperity that is undoubtedly coming upon this latterly much distracted and suffering country—my venture will not have been altogether in vain.

CONTENTS.

CHAPTER I.

WASHINGTON TO MEXICO.

CHAPTER II.

FIRST IMPRESSIONS OF MEXICO.

CHAPTER III.

HOTELS.

CHAPTER IV.

STREET SCENES.

CHAPTER V.

PUBLIC INSTITUTIONS.

CHAPTER VI.

THE PALACE—THE MONTE DE PIEDAD.

CHAPTER VII.

PUBLIC INSTITUTIONS—*continued.*

CHAPTER VIII.

CHURCHES.

CHAPTER IX.

PROTESTANT CHURCHES.

CHAPTER X.

RIDES ABOUT MEXICO.

CHAPTER XI.

ESCANDON HACIENDA AND THE MAKING OF PULQUE.

CHAPTER XII.
SHRINE OF GUADALUPE.

CHAPTER XIII.
GENERAL CHAPTER ON MEXICO.

CHAPTER XIV.
POPOCATAPETL.

CHAPTER XV.
POPOCATAPETL.

CHAPTER XVI.
PACHUCA AND ITS SILVER MINES.

CHAPTER XVII.
HACIENDA, OR MEXICAN FARM.

CHAPTER XVIII.
DRAINAGE OF THE CITY AND VALLEY OF MEXICO.

CHAPTER XIX.

CHINAMPAS, OR FLOATING GARDENS.

CHAPTER XX.

RUINS OF ANCIENT CITIES IN MEXICO.

CHAPTER XXI.

MEXICAN ANTIQUITIES.

CHAPTER XXII.

INNER LIFE.

CHAPTER XXIII.

AMUSEMENTS.

CHAPTER XXIV.

COURTS OF JUSTICE.

CHAPTER XXV.

VISITS TO NEIGHBOURING CITIES AND OTHER PLACES.

CHAPTER XXVI.

RAILWAYS.

CHAPTER XXVII.

COINAGE, INSURANCE AND OTHER MATTERS.

CHAPTER XXVIII.

FAREWELL.

CHAPTER XXIX.

CONCLUSION.

LIST OF ILLUSTRATIONS.

ERRATA.

Page 2, line 15, *for* " was that, owing" *read* " was, that owing."
Page 8, line 10, *for* "lonely " *read* "lovely."
Page 65, line 21, *for* "they might" *read* " may they."
Page 73, line 4 (heading), *for* " Mulino del Key " *read* "Molino del Rey."
Page 99, line 13, *for* " young plants in full ear" *read* " young plants, in full ear."
Page 116, line 16, *for* " skirts of the base" *read* " skirts the base."
Page 137, line 20, *for* "*burros*, the country," *read* "*burros* of the country."
Page 146, line 6, *for* " Pulancingo " *read* " Tulancingo."
Page 150, line 34, *for* " joy " *read* " boy."
Page 161, line 15, *for* " win " *read* " wring."
Page 162, end of line 26, take out comma after " meat."
Page 162, line 31, *for* " Estrella " *read* " religious."
Page 172, line 27, *for* " Analhuac " *read* " Anahuac."
Page 173, line 2, *for* " Teotihuachan " *read* "Teotihuacan."

MEXICO TO-DAY:

A COUNTRY WITH A GREAT FUTURE.

CHAPTER I.

WASHINGTON TO MEXICO.

Montgomery—New Orleans—Morgan City—Gulf of Mexico—Vera Cruz—Yellow
Fever—Railway to Mexico—Tropical Vegetation—Orizaba.

WHEN, in the autumn of 1879, I left England with Edward
Massie of Chester for a tour round the world, Mexico was not
included in the list of countries it was my purpose to visit.
After seeing something of India, Japan, and other parts of the
Old World, we arrived at San Francisco, and after a visit to
the Yosemite Valley, the Yellowstone River and Niagara, my
companion returned home for the Christmas of 1880.

All that I saw in the New World interested me so deeply,
and, according to first impressions, was so different to the quiet,
plodding progress of things in England, that I resolved on
prolonging my stay in the United States, and also on visiting
Canada. While in Washington, for the purpose of witnessing the
inaugural ceremonies of poor President Garfield, March 4th, 1881,
I learned that my friend Mr. George Neyt, the Belgian Minister,
had just been appointed from his post at Washington to represent
his king and country at Mexico; and as he and his family were
to leave Washington for the "Halls of the Montezumas" on
Tuesday, the 8th of March, I was only too glad to seize upon so

favourable an opportunity for visiting a country of which I had heard so little and had read so much.

The route by rail from Washington to New Orleans is not by any means through an interesting line of country; we broke the journey of three hundred miles by resting a night at Montgomery,* the capital of Alabama, and once the capital of the Southern Confederacy, and another night at Mobile, arriving at New Orleans on Friday evening, the 11th of March.

During the journey we passed from the cold weather of the North to the most delightful spring temperature; blossoms of apple, peach and pear were succeeded by lilacs and other beautiful shrubs, and tropical plants greeted us as we advanced farther south. As I never tire of gazing out of the window on the surrounding country, the time passed very rapidly, while the journey was enlivened by three episodes. The first was that, owing to the bursting of a boiler pipe, our train was detained for several mid-day hours in a fragrant pine-forest in Alabama. The second was the upsetting and smashing of the train by the cars " jumping the track." It was night; we were in the sleeping-car and all in

---

* Events proved it would have been better to have continued the journey, as Montgomery happened to be very crowded; the Assizes were going on, also some races in the neighbourhood. At supper there was only one dish out of the dozen placed before me by the darkey that I could eat. I supposed it to be a salmi of prairie hen, or some bird, and helped myself a second time; on being told it was squirrel, I had to rush to the bar at the end of the room for a *petit verre*, or * * * At night we were doubled up two in a bed, and four in a room; this was bad enough, but, to make matters worse, one of the "strangers" in the other bed was very drunk, and gave us a hottish *quart d'heure* of it before he settled down, when he began to spit all over the room, high and low, far and near. I had put all my clothes, including my boots, under my end of the bolster, and, when called in the morning, I put on my boots and carried my clothes out into the passage, where I performed a hasty toilet, knowing that I should soon find a comfortable dressing-carriage in the train, where I could "fix myself up" properly before entering the drawing-room car. Travellers' experiences are various; better take things as you find them if you cannot alter them. This was the only occasion that I was ever really inconvenienced during many months of travel in the States.

FOREST ON FIRE, ALABAMA

bed, and although pretty well knocked about by the accident, no one was hurt, with the exception of the conductor, whose wrist was perforated by a bullet from a pistol, the property of nobody knows who. The third episode occurred after we emerged from the thick woods into the open country, on the borders of the Alabama River. The forest on our left to the extent of several miles was on fire; the bright flames, intermingled with occasional dense masses of black smoke, shot luridly high above the tops of the trees. To add to the awful and picturesque effect, a large steamer came gliding down the river, and some of the passengers in the cars excitedly laid bets as to her chances of escaping from the advancing and devouring flames.

I thank my stars that my lot in life has not been cast in the city of New Orleans, which is built on a low mud-bank, two or three feet below the level of the splendid river that is the cause of the city's existence. Had a more fortunate site been selected, where the commerce of the Mississippi, the Gulf of Mexico (the Mediterranean of America), and the tropical regions of the western hemisphere could have been carried on and developed without the scourge of unhealthiness and yellow fever, New Orleans would eventually have become the greatest commercial emporium in the world. As it is, New Orleans contains some fine streets and public buildings. The Saint Charles's Hotel is a palace, and perfect in every respect save in the matter of the *cuisine*, which to a European is, to say the least of it, unpalatable. I can recommend a sanded-floored French restaurant, "Moreau's," where we obtained food almost Parisian in its excellence. We heard 'Rigoletto' at the Opera, 'Stabat Mater' at the Jesuit Church of the Immaculate Conception; we drove out to lake Ponchartrain, also to the Jockey Club grounds; we took a bird's-eye view of the city from the roof of the St. Charles's Hotel; and on Tuesday, the 16th, at noon, we went by rail to Morgan City, about eighty miles distant from New Orleans, a journey of two hours, over a stretch of marshes extending as far as the eye can reach, and literally teeming with duck and fresh-water fowl of every description. We looked for alligators, which are said to be equally abundant, but we failed to see any.

It is a tedious journey of a hundred miles, following the windings of the Mississippi from New Orleans to the mouth of the river; to avoid this the Morgan Company run their steamships to Vera Cruz, from the head of the estuary of Atchafalaya. The steamer *Whitney*, in which we crossed the gulf, is a small vessel of four or five hundred tons. She is very comfortable, well appointed, and the food is passable. There were forty cabin passengers, the fare being ten pounds, or fifty dollars, per head, including the railway journey to Morgan City. The voyage to Vera Cruz occupies from four to five days, according to the condition of the weather. We were lucky in having four days of a fairly calm sea, and arrived under the sparkling domes and towers of the city of the True Cross on the morning of Sunday, the 20th.

The harbour of Vera Cruz is so unfitted for shipping that several neighbouring parts of the coast have been surveyed with a view to discovering safer anchorage. The harbour is exposed to the violence of the north winds, the bottom is too rocky for vessels to anchor in safety, nor can they approach within half a mile of the shore when north winds drive across the bay. In the autumn and winter months ships often have to put out to sea. The city is low, ill-drained, and subject to *vomito* all through the summer months, but the first strong north wind, so dreaded by sea captains, at once clears off the yellow fever, of which little more is heard till the following summer. This terrible scourge visits all the shores of the Gulf of Mexico and the neighbouring West India Islands, but is unknown on the Pacific coast in the same latitude. Scientific investigations into its cause are being strenuously carried on both by the Mexican and the United States Governments, and during my visit to the country I frequently saw notices in the papers respecting it, the cause being

BIRD'S-EYE VIEW OF VERA CRUZ.

[page 4

generally assigned to the putrefaction of innumerable small animalculæ, molluscs, or worms on the shore. Whatever the cause, during my summer's stay in Mexico I knew of several cases in which personal acquaintances succumbed to the disease, and M——, a fine young man who left Mexico City for a lucrative employment on the railway at Vera Cruz, returned in a month so yellow and shattered by the disease that I did not recognise him until after he had spoken to me.

The landing at Vera Cruz by little boats from the steamer is not an agreeable experience, especially when you are bewildered by the noise and shouts of the strange-looking boatmen who clamour for your patronage and your fare; while the anxiety to prevent your baggage from being wetted or lost almost prevents your enjoying the strange scene. At a distance of about half a mile from the main land lay fort San Juan d'Ulloa, grim, hoary, dented, the bayonets of the sentries flashing in the glorious tropical sunlight. The fort built on the island is used as a prison, and it is here that Hernando Cortes landed on the 21st of April, 1519, a date destined to become memorable in the annals of Mexico.

Vera Cruz, baked to a dull pink, confronted us out from behind a tawny sand bank; clean cut against a keen, full, blue sky stood church towers and domes surmounted by burnished crosses; here and there stately palms might be perceived *en silhouette*, while snow-white houses, adorned with coloured Venetian blinds, peeped over walls and fortifications ragged and jagged as the outer surface of a rough oyster-shell. On the right a feathery column of white smoke indicated the direction of the railway, and on the extreme left stretched a dull, dead plain of sand, all without a break save the dust raised by a train of passing donkeys, till it met the sky-line. Dim and shadowy spectres filled the back-ground, mountains jealously enshrouded in a mantle of clouds. What a scene! There is no time to take notes; our copper-coloured boatmen in ever so white drawers, cut away at the knee, scanty tunics and straw sombréros, are nearing our boat to the shore; such flashing teeth, glittering eyes, and blue-black hair; if they were rascals they were very handsome, and they brought us safely to the slippery steps. The mole or pier was literally swarming with human beings; caballeros in full *charro* jostled aguadores (water-carriers) dressed in little more than leather aprons; Indian flower-girls offered gigantic bouquets; military officers fiercely puffing cigarettes chatted gaily with civilians who seemed to wear the tightest of pantaloons, save at the instep, where they bellied out wider than a would-be sailor's in 'Her Majesty's Ship *Pinafore;*' vendors of strange-looking sweetmeats and still stranger-looking fruits pestered us with their wares; porters, black as the ace of spades, and a few showily caparisoned mules and donkeys added to the general hubbub and dazzle of this novel scene. In a few minutes we were within the grim-looking fortified gate of the custom-house, where the officers are most searching in their investigations. Happily my luggage was passed unopened, along with that of the Belgian Minister, as I was presumed to be an attaché of his Excellency's party. We repaired to the Hotel Diligencias in the square, as the train for Mexico did not leave till midnight.

The mosquitoes gave us so warm a reception that I had to rise from the couch on which I was trying to rest and move to the open staircase of the hotel, where there seemed to be a draught of air too strong for the delicate organisation of this most pestilent insect; fleas and their numerous relations may swarm upon me without causing any special irritation, but a single mosquito-bite has occasionally necessitated my having to send for a doctor! As we did not care to venture into the town for fear of yellow fever, we were lucky in obtaining a superb view into the Plaza from the balcony of the hotel. A broad paved walk ran round the outside of the Plaza, the interior space being laid out with walks, grass, and beautiful trees. A fine Doric church with dome and campanile stood on the right, a colonnade of shops and imposing buildings on the left, while the municipal palace, with an exquisite open-worked tower, faced the hotel. Every building had on its roof or pinnacle a flock of *zapilotes* or large black buzzards, which swoop down to the ground to pick up any tit-bit their quick eyes may discern; they act in the necessary and useful capacity of street scavengers; possessing the freedom of the city, they perch where they like, and take no notice of anybody. Woe to him who lays profane hands on any one of their number! You cannot take a feather out of one without having to make your choice between fine and imprisonment. What if the black vomito does carry off a few hundred Vera Cruzians every year with its pestilential breath? These zapilotes * have had the city scavenging since the time of Cortes, and who would alter a system rendered as sacred by antiquity as that of the London Corporation?

It was the third Sunday in Lent. The square was crowded all the afternoon and during the entire evening with pedestrians, many of whom wore masks and some few were attired in masquerade dresses.

A little before midnight on the same day we packed ourselves as comfortably as might be in the railway carriages for a nineteen hours' journey to the city of Mexico, a distance of 264¼ miles, including an ascent of 7600 feet.

This railway was constructed by an English company, and the

---

* In a book on the birds of the United States by Alexander Wilson, published in 1813, this bird is named *Vultur aura* (turkey buzzard), and *Tzopilotl* is given as the Aztec name. It is two feet and a half in length, six feet from tip to tip of the wings, and the bill is two and a half inches long. The plumage is black, and the head and neck are covered with black wrinkled skin. The female does not make any nest, but lays two to four eggs of a dull dirty white colour on the stump or bough of a hollow tree, the male bird closely watching the female while sitting. If not disturbed, they occupy the same breeding place for several years. The young are covered with a whitish down similar to that which covers young goslings. This bird is found in all parts of North and South America, but in the greatest numbers near the equator, where it is most useful; it has all the characteristics of the vulture tribe, and is disgustingly filthy in its habits.

whole line opened on the 1st of January, 1873. The construction of the line occupied thirty-six years, under forty Presidents and an Emperor; and cost \$40,000,000 or £8,000,000, an average of £30,303 per mile. The railway is a very marvel of engineering, and reminded me of the Indian line from Bombay to Poonah; of the 7600 feet of ascent, 4000 are done in twenty-five miles. The road spans ravines, scales precipices, gets higher and higher by loops, plunges through the heart of the mountain, and then up it goes into cloud-land, and, in the teeth of almost insurmountable difficulties, passes into a lonely plain and winds into the capital near the celebrated shrine of Our Lady of Guadalupe.

The carriages are arranged in compartments after the English fashion. The locomotive which was destined to haul us up the 7600 feet was a very formidable-looking monster, built expressly for the work by Fairlie of Manchester; it resembled two engines locked together, back to back; the chimney at the end, the wood for fuel in the middle.

There are several dangers to be encountered on the journey. First come the robbers, who might throw the train off the track and murder the passengers. The traveller is supposed to be guarded against these gentry by an escort consisting of an officer and fifty soldiers who occupy the rear carriage of the train. Next come the dangerous curves and trestle bridges round and over some of the ravines of the mountains; this danger is avoided by starting the train at midnight so as to pass the shaky portions of the line by daylight. The third peril arises from cattle, which stray upon the track; of this latter we had ample experience.

We had not been travelling more than half an hour, when, near Tejeria, the engine was thrown off the rail, and the train brought to a standstill. Some cows had gone to sleep on the line, and the engine had jumped over them; the first two carriages, being empty and light, were flung off the rails and smashed, and the third carriage, in which we were sitting, after a series of bumpings and jumpings, came to a dead stop; the last carriage, containing the soldiers, suffered nothing from the shock. After some delay an engine came up from Vera Cruz, and hauled us back into the station, and there we were compelled to remain in the carriages till 12 o'clock the next day, when the line was reported open for travel. We were not allowed to leave the carriages, as the officials declared they did not know at what moment the train would start. The tedium of the detention was however much relieved by the satisfaction we felt at the escape from what might have proved a very serious accident, and we were all as merry as crickets, especially Mr. Neyt's little daughter, when we sped slowly out of the station, passed the crumbling walls of Vera Cruz, out on to the tawny sands, speckled with scant and mangy vegetation, never a palm or banana, nothing but patches of jungle, and stunted cacti.

At Paso del Macho, 500 feet above the level of the coast, we were still in a thirsty, gritty country, sprinkled with gaunt shapes of rock; wild copper-coloured Indians, in scanty white garments, waved us onwards as we passed the huts and stations.* We were now on the very threshold of the beauties of the line; at forty-seven miles from Vera Cruz aromatic odours borne by gentle breezes saluted our nostrils; rich vegetation took the place of dreary, desolate, sandy wastes; and, as the train reached the bridge of San Alejo a perfectly tropical scenery burst upon me. The bridge, an iron cobweb, springs from a bed of verdure so rich and varied, it seemed a very couch for Titania herself; reds and yellows, blues and greens, lichens and mosses,

---

* Professor Oliver Hubbard, of New York, told me the following tale in reference to this road. Before the railway was opened, a New Hampshire man from Gilmantown ran coaches from Vera Cruz to Mexico, and arranged with the robbers to leave the travellers always sufficient money to complete the journey comfortably. When General Scott invaded Mexico in 1847, and wanted a purveyor for the army, he made this same man commissary-general, and his old friends, the robbers, supplied him with as many cattle as he wanted.

ferns and orchids, drove me wild with desire to jump from the
train, and revel in their beauties.   But there is one drawback to
the scene; I am always more or less saddened and disappointed
with tropical vegetation, from the number of broken and decayed
trees, seemingly in nearly equal proportion to the fresh-leaved
striplings which are succeeding them in growth.   It is as
though the trees hastened to maturity, and then rendered up
their lives to the net-work of flowering creepers; these web them
over and prey upon them, like as in the insect kingdom the
spider spreads his web to catch the fly.

The bright gleam of the coffee plantations, dotted with scarlet
hibiscus, succeeded the sugar plantations of the lower ground,
until the lovely cerro or mountain of the Chiquihuite was reached,
where a cascade, starting from a rift in the rock, falls sixty feet
like a cotton thread; and we "slowed" into the Barranca de
Metlac, over a bridge 350 feet long, and 90 feet in height
from the bottom of the ravine.   In twenty minutes we reached
Orizaba, eighty-two miles from Vera Cruz, the city whither
Cortes and his desperadoes hastened in the hope of looting its
treasures and riches, of which the Aztecs had given so glowing a
description.   It was evening; the moon, only a few days past its
full, lit up the snow-capped peak of the extinct volcano, 16,000
feet in the air, which glittered like a sugar loaf against the
darkened sky.

Orizaba stands 4027 feet above the level of the sea, and the
average temperature is 72° Fahr.   The town is an old, noiseless
place, with irregular streets and quaint houses, whose eaves
stretch out until they almost meet those of their opposite neighbours, and one can walk from one end of the place to the other
during the rainy season without an umbrella, and at noon without
a parasol.

On the western side of the town stands a mount, El Borrego,
known in the annals of the French invasion as the point where
the Mexicans, 5000 strong, were routed by a hundred zouaves,

who scaled its steep sides under cover of night. A rude wooden cross marks the spot on the summit where two of the gallant baggy-breeched veterans "fighting fell!" It was at Orizaba that Marshal Bazaine in 1866 took leave of the ill-fated Maximilian, a ghostly shadow over the future of both.

I missed the wondrous beauties of the line of railway from Orizaba to the capital on my up-night journey, but, *gracias á Dios!* I lost nothing of their glories on my return, and I will endeavour to give a slight description of them in this portion of my narrative, in order to complete the chain while somewhat reversing the order of things.

Orizaba is situated on the top of verdure-clad hills. A few miles, and the train reaches the Barranca del Infernillo, or "Little Hell"—a chasm that divides the craggy steeps, whose depths I could scarcely measure by my eye. I felt actually dizzy while gazing down into it, and the Indians in passing through keep muttering their prayers and devoutly crossing themselves, some of them wrapping their heads in their sarapes in order to shut out the grim yet superb sight. Bridges span rifts and gulfs and yawning chasms, while tunnels pierce opposing mountains and rocky promontories. A nut, a bolt, a rivet out of place, and what a crash! There is no trace of vegetation, not a tree, not a shrub, not so much as a vagrant fern on the oozy black rock. What a leap into light, as we emerge from the Dantesque horrors of the past into the plains of La Joya— the joy! On your right—I am taking the reader up to the capital—stand mountains dappled with bright-hued flowers and crowned by a foliage of forest trees. To the left, extending itself to the horizon, the valley, which is as rich in colour as a Turkey carpet; in its midst a silvery stream in a bed of yellow sand, while the glacial-capped Orizaba, flaunting its white mantle in delicate relief against a sky of Italian blueness, stands silent sentinel over the many ranges of Sierras below it.

At Maltrata, the first train to arrive awaits that which comes from the opposite direction. The train from Mexico appears to the travellers from Vera Cruz, if they happen to reach Maltrata first, like a child's toy, high in air; it slowly passes along the summit of the mountain, alternately appearing and re-appearing before it zigzags into the station with its dusty passengers. We now rise 3600 feet in about an hour and a quarter, and come to Bocca del Monte, 107 miles from Vera Cruz, and 7922 feet above it. Here an extra wrap is desirable by night or day ; we are in the *tierra fria*, for we have quitted the *tierra templada* and have struck the country of the aloe, or maguey (*Agave Americana*). After several stations Apizaco is struck. It is the junction from which a line branches to Puebla, and it may be noted as having an excellent refreshment table, where a hot meal is offered for fifty cents, or two shillings. A first-class imitation Bass is also procurable at three shillings per pint bottle; some of our party on the way up indulged in fruit, peaches and bananas included, such as had been refused with horror at Vera Cruz. Apam, the plains of which are covered with maguey and haciendas for the making of pulque, is seventy-five and a half miles from Mexico, and is the only other station I will mention ; from this point the track goes down a gentle decline to the city.

We are in the valley of Mexico, as the plain is called, 8000 feet above the level of the sea, and from the carriage windows rows upon rows of aloes are the only things visible in the shape of vegetation.

All this I saw on my downward journey; the up-journey over this part of this line ended by our gliding, under the silver beams of a brilliant moon, into the station at Mexico at four A.M. on Tuesday morning, the 22nd of March, 1881. We had been twenty-eight hours in the train, ten of which had been spent in the carriages at the station in Vera Cruz, as mentioned at the commencement of the chapter. The Belgian Consul and some friends met their minister, Mr. Neyt, at the station of Buena Vista, and having put Mrs. Neyt and her daughter and the

domestics into a carriage, we men walked to the hotel, only too
delighted to stretch our legs after the tiresome confinement in
the train.   It proved a walk of a mile and a half to the Gillow
Hotel, where rooms had been prepared for us, and some greasy
tepid soup was improvised for our refreshment.   The city appeared to be well lighted with gas, and the public gardens, the
palatial-looking buildings which lined the streets, and the
churches, gave a promise of something well worth seeing by
daylight.

CHAPTER II.

FIRST IMPRESSIONS OF MEXICO.

Native Dress—Longevity of the People—Horses—Newspapers—Police—College for
Girls—Hospitals—Clubs.

I HAD scarcely been a day in the city of Mexico when I sallied
forth for the purpose of purchasing a map, a guide-book, and a
pocket dictionary in Spanish and English, imagining I had
nothing to do but enter the first book-store, pay my money, and
take my choice. No such thing. I wandered from one shop to
another, invariably asking the same question, and invariably receiving the same reply. "No, señor, the Americans have bought
every guide-book and Spanish and English dictionary in the city.
We have written to Europe, and expect a fresh supply in six or
eight weeks."

I never tired of strolling through the streets, each turn revealing something strange, something new; everything full of
fascination and colour. The natives are picturesque. The men
—I speak of the lower classes—dress in white cotton shirt,
jacket and trousers, seldom wear guaraches, sandals, or shoes of
any description, and their head-covering is a straw sombréro.
They carry a gaily-coloured woollen blanket, called a "sarape,"
over their left shoulder, or wear it in loose folds around the
throat, and scarcely ever cease smoking very formidable-looking
coarse cigars. The women, when very young, are comely, their
blue-black hair, bright, dark eyes and white teeth rendering
them attractive enough. Their dress is a calico print, short as a
Boulogne fishwife's; a "reboso chiquita," or small scarf of silk or

cotton, is wrapped round the head and shoulders, its long knotted fringe falling down the back. This reboso has very often double duty; it is used as a cradle for the baby, the black-eyed, chubby infant being suspended by it on the woman's back. But the women soon become wan and haggard, and bear evident traces of very hard work; for when I have met them on the country roads carrying loads that would test the vertebræ of Barclay and Perkins's draymen, their busy hands were engaged in knitting or in plucking one of the fowls they were taking to market. Both men and women have a peculiar gait; it is not a walk, neither is it a run: it comes between both, and the pace is not that of a Piccadilly or Fifth Avenue lounger.*

In the city of Mexico everything has a Spanish look, and is as

---

* Humboldt in his description says: " The 'natives enjoy one great physical advantage, which is undoubtedly owing to the great simplicity in which their ancestors lived for thousands of years. They are subject to hardly any deformity—I never saw a hunchbacked Indian; and it is extremely rare to see any of them who squint or are lame in arm or leg. They do not suffer from *goitre*; their hair seldom becomes grey, nor is their skin subject to wrinkles; and it is by no means uncommon to see in Mexico natives, and especially women, reach one hundred years of age !

" We can have no doubt, then, that the absence of natural deformities among them is the effect of their mode of life and the constitution peculiar to their race. We are inclined to believe that the Arab-European race possesses a greater flexibility of organisation, and that it is more easily modified by a great number of exterior causes, such as variety of aliments, climates and habits, and consequently has a greater tendency to deviate from its original model.

" When the kingdom of New Spain shall enjoy an administration favourable to knowledge, political arithmetic will then furnish data of infinite importance, both for statistics in general, and for the physical history of man in particular. How many problems there are to be solved in a mountainous country, which exhibits in the same latitude the greatest variety of climates, inhabitants of three or four primitive races, and a mixture of those races in all the combinations imaginable? How many researches to be made regarding the fecundity and longevity of the species? The latter is greater or less according to the elevation and temperature of the places, according to the variety of the races, and finally, according to the difference of food in provinces where the banana, the jatropha, rice, maize, wheat, and potatoes grow together in a narrow space."

These remarks of Humboldt are fully corroborated by all one sees to-day, and different from what one sees in the United States, even at New Orleans, as Italy or Spain is from England. The sun is hot, too hot from ten to four to walk much, except in the shade; so horses are recommended. In Mexico no one who can afford to buy a horse of any kind ever goes on foot. Mr. Neyt and I went to some stables and picked up a horse apiece that turned out all we could desire.

The horses are mustangs, small, fourteen or fifteen hands, the price being from $80 to $150 (£16 to £30), but good horses are occasionally to be had at half this price. I saw the Rev. John Patterson buy five or six one day for the use of his missionary preachers, at an average of $15 (£3) each; they appeared perfectly sound and well broken, and looked as if they had lots of work in them. Horses are seldom shod; they are taught to work and canter perfectly; their mouths are so fine that they answer to the slightest movement of the bit. On my first canter down the paseo I slightly checked my horse on approaching some rough stone; he stopped dead short, and so suddenly, so unexpectedly, that I still marvel how I kept my seat.

From whatever point of view the city is seen, be it from the top of the cathedral towers, the hill of Guadalupe, the porphyry rock on the summit of which stands the castle of Chapultepec, or the distant Ajusco mountains, it is as beautiful as Humboldt has described it as being. Its domes and towers reminded me of Florence, but instead of the Arno the wide and silvery lake of Texcoco washed its eastern side. At the time of the conquest it was the Venice of the west: it had canals for streets, and was joined to the mainland by a road or causeway, along which

in reference to age, several men and women were pointed out to me as known to be over a hundred years of age; and Mr. S. F. Winston, President of the Mutual Life Insurance Company of New York, stated he had met a Mexican woman one hundred and thirty-two years old, that he had seen her again when she was one hundred and thirty-four years, and that her age was attested by church register!

Cortes and his small army had to fight their way during the sad, sad hours of the Noche Triste, when he imagined his reverses were irretrievable.

Had Prescott, before his eyesight failed him, but visited Mexico, and inspected the localities of Cortes's most marvellous adventures, how very much more interesting to the Mexican traveller his "Conquest" would have been. As it is, one has the greatest possible difficulty in realising his most telling incidents from the want of matter whereby to localise them.

One morning while discussing the matter in a walk with General Grant (who was in Mexico on railway matters), the ex-President said, "Ah! your Bulwer Lytton wrote romance but made it history, and our Prescott has written history but has made it romance." I may here mention that General Grant, who in society seems so silent and shy, is a most agreeable walking companion. I seized upon every occasion that offered for walking with him, for the sole pleasure of listening to his conversation. One evening, at his rooms in the "Iturbide," I told him I had been compelled by my friends, very much against my will, as I had no subject to speak upon, simply to shake hands with him on three separate public occasions in New York, during the previous winter. Mrs. Grant, who was present, promptly remarked, "I wish many people were like you; the General's arm is often paralysed by prolonged hand-shaking."

One thing that strikes a stranger in the streets is that many of the buildings are sunk and distorted, on account of the foundations sinking by reason of the spongy nature of the ground.

Most of the church towers have settled out of the perpendicular; so have also many of the public buildings, notably the "Mineria," or school of mines, whose magnificent façade is, owing to this, more of a wavy than of a straight line. In some streets the handsome doorways of the houses have sunk a foot or two below the pathway, and the head must be lowered on entering. I noticed that the foundations of all new buildings are left level with the ground for a year or two, to enable them to settle before the superstructure is added.

Earthquakes do occasional damage, and the last one, some forty years back, destroyed several churches. It is for this reason that the palace and most of the houses are only built two stories high, and all the principal buildings appear sufficiently massive and solidly built to withstand ordinary shocks of earthquake. All the houses in the streets are very quaint and picturesque, many of them enriched with stone carvings, stucco ornaments, bright colouring, and large striped sunshades or blinds to the windows and balconies, from behind which the young ladies of all degrees puff cigarettes, and make eyes at their beaux in the street.

The streets are at right angles to each other, from north to south and from east to west. They are perfectly straight, there is not a curve in any of them, but the monotony is relieved by squares and gardens; some of the cross streets are very short.

Mexican newspapers have rather a continental character, official announcements, and novels or other light reading being a prominent feature. There are twelve scientific, twenty-five political, four religious, and three literary newspapers published in the city. Many of the political journals appear daily, the type and the paper being fairly good. All newspapers are printed in Spanish, except the *Two Republics*, which is in English for circulation amongst English and Americans, and two papers which are published in French. That there may not be wanting a supply of readers in the next generation the municipality sustains thirty-five day schools for boys, and forty-five for girls, besides many night schools; some of these I visited, and found the course of instruction similar to what is given in other countries.

There is one feature of the city which will probably, ere long, be a thing of the past, viz., the arched aqueducts, with their fountains and sculptured tablets, portions of which have already been taken down where they interfered with street traffic, or the formation of new streets. They were originally constructed by the Spaniards, and are such handsome and striking pieces of architecture that it is almost to be regretted that necessity compels their removal from within the area occupied by the streets.

The city is to the Republic what Paris is to France, being the seat of government, the centre of a rapidly growing railway system, the mart of commerce, and the abode of nearly all the wealthy landowners of the Republic. Life and property are perfectly safe, though I one day saw a large knife taken from under the cloak of a countryman when he was searched at the city gates. Police are stationed about one hundred yards apart all over the city, they are well dressed, and paid $1 per day. They do not appear to move far from their posts, and at night they place a lamp on the ground in the centre of the street to indicate their whereabouts. These lamps have a most curious effect. Imagine bright lamps on the ground one hundred yards apart along the centre of Oxford Street or the Strand, and the drivers of vehicles of any kind subject to heavy fines for upsetting them.

There are several things that strike a stranger favourably in the streets of the city. The people move about politely, without crushing or crowding. Ladies and children can return from the theatres, cafés, or the *zocalo* at late hours of the night without molestation, or such offences as might cross their path in London ; and what has been accomplished in a city of 300,000 inhabitants is being extended to the neighbouring cities and country districts with every prospect of soon rendering all parts of the country as safe to travel in by day or night as is the city of Mexico itself.

CHAPTER III.

HOTELS.

The Emperor Iturbide—Hotel Prices—Mode of spending the Day—
Mexican *Menu*.

THE Mexican world keeps early hours. Chocolate about seven
A.M.; a heavy " square meal " called *almuerzo*, it may be breakfast, luncheon, or dinner, between eleven and two; in the evening,
chocolate, ices, or some light refreshment followed by the opera,
theatres, or, what to me was far preferable, an excellent band of
music in the gardens of the Plaza. I broke through the
restaurant rules to some extent by demanding dinner at six or
seven; and, when I had succeeded in making the waiters
understand my wants, was very pleasantly and civilly supplied
with " quelque chose réchauffée."

The Hotel Gillow is on the handsome new street Cinco de
Mayo; it seemed to be managed by two or three Spaniards, and
the rooms were not so clean as we English are accustomed to
desire. There was no woman throughout the whole establishment, or certain little matters might have been better attended
to. I made a visit of inspection to the other hotels to ascertain
if I could improve my quarters, having friends staying at most
of them, and, after hearing the remarks of *mis amigos* I found a
change might only lead "out of the frying pan into the fire.'
So after I got Santiago to take the dirty old carpets and
gorgeous, but rickety, chairs out of my rooms, and paid something extra to have the floors washed with good strong soap and

THE PLAZA, MEXICO CITY.

[page 20.

soda, I made up my mind that my little parlour and bedroom were about as clean as they looked; and when, after a struggle I was provided with a hip bath, I did not begrudge the three Mexican dollars per night that I was compelled to pay for this palatial accommodation; the hotel people probably considered me mad, but that was of little consequence; it only prepared them for my future vagaries.

The hotel and boarding-house accommodation of the city is barely sufficient for the present influx of American visitors; and should a gentleman desire to visit the city with his wife and family, it would be well to secure rooms beforehand by telegram or letter. The principal hotel is the Iturbide, an immense four-storied palace, with three or four *patios* or courts. It is in the Street of San Francisco, and takes its name from having been the private residence of the Emperor Iturbide, who ruled in 1822.

Up to a certain point in his career, Iturbide was a mild form of patriot; but the fiery curse of ambition led him to accept the imperial crown, and he fell.

On the 24th of August, 1821, he achieved the independence of his country from the yoke of Spain, passing over to the Mexican revolutionists, whose leader, the Cura Hidalgo, had been shot by the Spaniards in 1811. He entered Mexico at the head of a Mexican army, carrying the "Trigarante," green, red, and white—the national colours; but he broke faith with the leaders, both of the Spanish and the native population, and after reigning for a year was banished the country on parole never to return; however, he disregarded his pledge, arriving from Europe in 1824, contrary to the promise given to Santa Anna, who, by order of the then president, General Victoria, caused him to be seized on landing at Vera Cruz, and on the 19th of July of the same year to be shot as a traitor.

I saw the old flint guns that did the bloody deed; they are gracefully hung against the wall in the armoury of the governor's palace, and on the same wall are the seven rifles, whose deadly bullets chilled for ever the life blood of the hapless Maximilian. The remains of the latter were restored to his " kin beyond the sea ; " those of Iturbide lie encoffined in a crystal urn in the cathedral at Mexico. The portraits of both these men, which are seen in various places in the capital, represent them as handsome, but with a weak vacillating expression ; no man with the mouth and chin of Maximilian could rule a turbulent country ; Iturbide's face is equally weak, and his gorgeous uniform and his orders are perhaps an indication of his vanity and selfishness. I give this brief notice of poor Iturbide, in order to account for his palace having been turned into a caravansary.

The other principal hotels are the " Comonfort," the " Bazar," the " San Cárlos," the " Nacional " and the " Bella Union. These hotels are palatial in size, with large open courts, and a common staircase leading to all the floors, upon each of which are stationed " muchachos," men who take charge of the keys of the rooms, which vary in price from one to three dollars per night. You can obtain handsome suites of rooms at fluctuating prices. During my stay General and Mrs. Grant and party occupied a fine suite of apartments at the " Iturbide," probably costing twenty or more dollars per night. General Ochoa also had nice rooms *au quatrième.*

To all these hotels are attached restaurants, the proprietors of which charge for what food you consume, independently of the hotel. I always breakfasted at the Gillow restaurant about ten o'clock, after returning from my morning's ride ; and having at first tried all the varieties of the dishes of the *cuisine,* I invariably afterwards made my breakfast of two sweet limes (as preferable to oranges) chocolate, omelette and a dish of " frijoles," without which no Mexican meal is considered complete.

My day usually went in this way: an early ride on horseback, till nine or ten, bath, breakfast, rest during the hot noon hours in my own room, and from then till my dinner-time visiting the

HOTEL ITURBIDE, CALLE SAN FRANCISCO.   [page 22.

various institutions and sights in the city and neighbourhood. It is the custom in Mexico for all the banks and business houses to be closed for two or three hours from noon, when every one goes to *almuerzo.* After this the day seemed somehow disjointed, as there was no certainty of finding any one at business again.

If I ordered a private dinner at the " Concordia " in an upstairs room for half-a-dozen or more friends, it was not badly served. Let me give a *menu* in full; not that the chef of an English club or Paris restaurant would like to imitate it.

Potages.

Ratioles á la Mexicana.   Arroz á la Parisana.

Relevés.

Filetta á la Criolla.   Hauchinango á la Holandesa.
Barcalas á la Vizcaina.   Carnarones frescos.

Entrées.

Vol-au-vent à la Financière.
Cordonius à la Provençale.   Foies Gras.
Patos á la Veracruzana.   Croquetas á la Duquesa.
Punch à la Romaine.

Légumes.

Esparragos.

Rôtis.

Roast Beef.   Ensalada.

Entremets.

Gelatiues.   Puddings.   Cremas.   Helados.

Dessert.

Queso.   Frutas.   Pasteles.
Dulces surtidos á la Mexicana.
Café de Uruapan.   Té.

The wines were Clicquot, Château Lafitte, and Xerez. The liqueurs, Pulque compuesto and brandy.

I found that the young English and Mexicans engaged in the railway offices generally arranged by the month for two square meals a day and a cup of chocolate in the early morning, at one of the restaurants; the payment ranging from about twenty to thirty dollars per month. I noticed that they invariably changed their restaurant at the end of the month, in the hope of improving their fare. After a round of trials they said they generally returned to "La Bella Union," at $25 per month, or to the Café Italien, at $20 per month, according to the state of their pockets. They paid extra for beer and wine, and I heard no complaint of the food, except as to the tea and coffee. There were lower class hotels of every degree, down to a shed in a back yard, where the poor Mexican and his family might spread their mat, and huddle under a blanket till the morning. I never saw any one sleeping all night in the streets or public gardens.

CHAPTER IV.

Early Mass—Father Gillow—Origin of the City of Mexico—Lotteries—Flowers—
Rural Guards—School of Arts and Trades—Blind People—German Club.

A ROSE-PINK light crept into my apartment, robbing me of at
least fifteen of my last forty winks; with the light came the
clang, clang, of the harsh and discordant bell attached to the
little belfry on the Professa church, my next door neighbour; on
gazing out of my window I found the main street thronged with
pedestrians all *en route* for six o'clock Mass, the ladies in veil,
mantilla and high comb, as it is *de rigueur* to attend early service
in this most graceful of costumes. Later in the day, however,
the señoras and señoritas don gaudy and singularly unbecoming
French fashions, of which more anon.

The hotel where I am staying is " run " by a Catholic clergy-
man of immense wealth, whose name it bears. His career is a
romance. His father came to Mexico in the early part of the
century, engaged in business, and amassed riches. He married a
Spanish lady of *sangre azul* and vast property, her ancestral
estate being known jocularly as " Quito Calzones." Señor
Gillow converted this estate by his skill into one of the most
valuable in the country. He added estate to estate, and managed
all so well that on his death he left his son five magnificent
haciendas, on which are used the best and most improved agricultural implements, both American and European, and his
estates are noted as examples of the highest Mexican cultivation.
He built the Hotel Gillow, and, in addition to having an

eye to the main chance, promoted several enterprises of public improvement. His son, Eulogio, my landlord, studied for the priesthood, and in due time was ordained. While at Rome he attracted the attention of Pius IX., who manifested the warmest friendship for the young ecclesiastic, and finally honoured him with the rank of domestic prelate.

Padre Gillow it was who preached the celebrated sermon at St. Peter's, on Papal Infallibility, which gave so powerful an impetus to the movement that resulted in the Œcumenical Council. On the death of his father, Padre Gillow returned to Mexico, to find his large property in apparently inextricable confusion. Acting on sound legal advice, he applied himself resolutely to putting his affairs in order. In time his labours were crowned with success, and he is now one of the most influential citizens in the Mexican Republic. He owns and cultivates estates. He has a palatial residence in the Mexican capital, and his *hacienda* at Cholula, in the state of Puebla, which I visited, is one of the show places in this wonderful country.

The Mexican hotels are good for lodging only, and your meals must be eaten at the restaurant attached, or elsewhere, as fancy or chance may suggest. Directly opposite the "Gillow" stands the Café Concordia, the Durand of Paris, the Delmonico of New York. It stands at the corner of the San Francisco Street, and its large windows command a good view of Mexican street life. In Maximilian's time it was the great rendezvous of French and Austrian officers, and many a dispute raised within its gilded and mirrored walls has led to a meeting and the crossing of small swords behind the grey walls of the Belem aqueduct, or beneath the cypress-shaded glades of lordly Chapultepec.

To the Café Concordia I wended my way for a cup of chocolate and a large spongy bun in the early morning, but I soon gave up this practice, and ever afterwards breakfasted at the restaurant attached to the Gillow Hotel, between ten and eleven, on returning from my early ride with Mr. Neyt.

The city of Mexico of to-day ranks amongst the largest cities of the western hemisphere, and, with all its steeples, towers and domes, presents, from whatever direction it is approached, a magnificent and striking appearance.

The valley in which it stands is forty-five miles long by thirty broad, mostly level, and contains 700,000 inhabitants, the city itself mustering near upon 300,000. Its climate is temperate, never exceeding 70° or going below 50° Fahr. The streets are at right angles from north to south and east to west. Each line of streets has for a background the mountains which surround the valley, and in the early morning, or when the sun is sinking behind the western ridge, they appear to rise abruptly at the end of the street, instead of being from twenty to forty miles away.* The valley contains the lakes Texcoco, Chalco, San Cristóbal, Zumpango, Xaltocan, and Xochimilco, six lakes covering an area of fifty miles. The lake Texcoco, nearest the city, though possessing all the appearance of a sheet of deep water, is but a shallow lagoon, and men can be seen pushing or drawing boats on it a mile from the land, the water not reaching above their knees.

The ancient name for Mexico was "Anhuac," "by the waters," from its topographical position. The Aztecs, after their migration from the north, wandered a considerable time in Mexico, till, in 1325, they halted on the shores of lake Texcoco, and there beheld an eagle perched upon a nopal, or cactus, engaged in devouring a serpent. This omen was pronounced auspicious, and here they forthwith founded the "Tenochticlan," the nopal on a stone. This device with the eagle has since been

---

* "The contours of the mountains appear so much the more marked as the air, through which the eye receives the rays, is more rare and transparent. The snow on the volcanoes is of a most extraordinary brilliancy, particularly when it descends from a sky of which the blue is always deeper than that of the sky which we see from our plains on the temperate zones. The observer finds himself in the city of Mexico in a strata of air, whose barometrical pressure is only 585 millimetres, or nearly twenty-three inches. It is easy to conceive that the extinction of light must be very trifling in an atmosphere so little condensed." (Humboldt's ' New Spain.')

borne on the national banner of the country. The city was subsequently called Mexico, from the god Mexitli. Towards the middle of the fifteenth century a city of stone and lime succeeded reeds and rushes, and when on the evening of the 7th of November, 1519, its long lines of glittering edifices first met the eyes of Cortes and his followers, it looked, says Prescott, "like a thing of fairy creation rather than the work of mortal hands." The city was nine miles in circumference, the number of its houses 60,000, and of its inhabitants 500,000.

I shall now return to 1881. This rarified atmosphere, 7416 feet above the sea level, tells upon new-comers, especially while ascending stairs. Young ladies, until acclimatised, discover that waltzing is out of the question, and gentlemen lodged *au quatrième* do not go up and down stairs oftener than they can avoid; such things as lifts or elevators are unknown. I induced Mr. Bishop, who had a room at the top of the Iturbide Hotel, to tie a red handkerchief to the iron rail of his balcony as a signal when he was in; the terrible flights of stone stairs in the hotel were almost as hard to climb as Popocatapetl.

The street called San Francisco Street, prolonged by Il Plataros, nearly a mile in length, and running from the Plaza Mayo to the beautiful gardens of the Almeda, is from its position and excellent shops the most attractive and fashionable street in the city. The new street of the Cinco de Mayo, from the Teatro Nacional to the cathedral, is partly under construction; it will be a noble street when completed, and the avenue of trees continued its whole length; but unless it is lined with shops it will not compete, from a business point of view, with San Francisco Street, which is the great thoroughfare of the city. When the ladies are not in church or in the gardens they are shopping. The shops in this street have a perky Parisian appearance, not that of the palatial establishments on the boulevards, but rather that of the third-class streets of Paris. I may mention that, though the foreign element is numerically of no account, its influence is paramount. France comes first; then, in order, Germany, Italy, Spain, America, England, Switzerland and Austria. The English residents cling to banking and money matters, and seem to be making a good thing of it. France caters for the ladies, the shops for their amusement and adornment having French names over them. Germans appear to monopolise the sale of all other European commodities, save and except arms and ironmongery, which are always advertised as American. The mercery and millinery shops are so crowded with customers all day long that the ladies who come to them in their carriages invariably have the goods brought to them for inspection, and the street, always crowded, is doubly blocked by the shop attendants carrying piles of goods to and from the carriages.

Though I have only mentioned two streets, there are a dozen others that might claim equality with them in many respects; all are crowded from morning to night; move gently! for it is difficult to pass along, especially in arcades under which, in addition to the shops, you find large cupboard-like stalls for the sale of trinkets, knicknacks, sweetmeats, toys, and cigars. The three most prominent types in every street are the boys who sell feather ornaments or cards, those who sell lottery tickets, . and those who are selling or delivering bouquets of flowers.

Feather ornamentation is a Mexican industry from the earliest period. Montezuma's cloak and shield, preserved in the National Museum, are ornamented with very fine feather work; and in one or two of the curio shops I was shown scarves, serapas, and long pieces of canvas, ornamented with feathers, and represented as genuine old articles. The street vendors offer cards with outlines of birds drawn on them, filled in with brilliant feathers from the plumage of the humming-bird; they will produce you any design you suggest; large cards with half-a-dozen birds upon them to be framed as a picture for the wall, down to *menu* or small visiting cards. The feathers are stuck on to the card by a waxen composition, each feather being separately applied ; they never use any portion of the bird's skin, or the feathers would soon drop out. It is a marvel how they do the work so neatly and keep the cards so clean, considering the dirty smoky huts in which they often manufacture them.

The appeals of the dealers in lottery tickets are most persistent; each offers to sell the number that is to win at the drawing of the next day, and flourishes a bundle of tickets before you, that you may take your own choice if you disbelieve his assertion. All the lotteries are regulated by special laws and are only conceded to certain privileged corporations. They are conducted with the utmost fairness, and the poor *peon* for his *peso* may buy a ticket that will make a rich man of him for the rest of his life. The big plums are few and far between, but they occasionally fall into lucky mouths. I had pointed out to me two men in the city of Mexico, one of whom had won $10,000, and the other $8000, in the great national drawing. The drawings take place in public, and the numbers are pulled out of the ballot-box by boys, pupils out of some one of the institutions for the blind.

I was present at the drawing of a grand lottery in the national theatre on the 5th of May, and when a prize number was announced there were great exclamations, followed by a lively tune from the orchestra ; nor was the opportunity lost, for we were entertained by the delivery of a pompous recitation by some smart young boy connected with the managers of the lottery. To give an idea of the sum realised by the sale of lottery tickets, I may mention that in the year 1880, the receipts were $2,632,004 (£530,000), the expenses being $532,460, and the premiums $1,620,292, leaving as profits the handsome sum of $479,252. Everybody more or less takes a turn at fortune, and, as everybody cannot win, the lucky people are regarded with considerable envy, and that there *are* lucky people, a vast *hacienda* not a hundred miles from Manzanillo will attest, Señor Manuel Gracia having plucked the big plum at three successive, or nearly successive drawings. For myself I can only say that though I tried my luck several times, dame Fortune did not smile upon me; on one occasion indeed, the number of my ticket was next to the winning number, and so I saved my stake.

Fresh flowers seem in Mexico to be a daily necessity; in addition to the bouquets alluded to, the *pulquerias*, the street stalls for the sale of lemonade and such like beverages, are often partly concealed by screens of fresh made green wreaths ornamented with flowers. During Lent the extra *pulquerias* erected in the square near the cathedral were walled in three or four feet high with soft clay, on which were arranged devices in fresh flowers every morning, in the same manner I have occasionally seen at the pretty well dressings in Derbyshire. As to the bouquets, the flowers are gathered on the *chinampas* or floating gardens, and brought into the city at early morning down the Viga canal. They are made into bouquets in the markets or at the flower kiosk in the Plaza Mayor, and thence disseminated over the city; some of them are of Brogdignagian proportions. I measured one twenty-four inches high and thirty inches in diameter. I saw many every day equally large, and the price was a shilling. Roses of all sorts form the base of most of these bouquets; and it is a curious fact that these and all sorts of flowers, lovely as they are in shape and colour, possess little or no perfume, by reason of the rarity of the air.

The sellers of crucifixes, rosaries, and pictures of the Virgin of Guadalupe have their throng of clients. The strolling shopman is here with his tray, offering combs and knives and mirrors and all that line of commerce. Very prominent were the sellers of slippers and knitted socks, also of men's neckties of every description. The *portales* were much obstructed by stands laden with sweetmeats and toys; what strange toys too! Little bulls made out of untanned cowhide were the most comical and attractive I saw; nor could I ever pass an old street book-store without looking for a musty vellum-bound volume, something of the sixteenth century, in black and red letter and coloured capitals.

If you wish to purchase, always offer half what is demanded ; should the vendor ask "*dos pesos*," offer him "Uno" or one; this is both a golden and a silver rule.

The city swarms with soldiers, and the sound of the trumpet call startles the ear at all hours of the day, and in the most unexpected places. The soldiers are generally seen walking about loosely in large groups, under the charge of an officer or of the serjeant—this for fear of their absconding. They are soldierly little men, and fairly well dressed. But the Rural Guard carries off the palm. These men are fine smart fellows, and wear a most picturesque uniform of soft buff leather, scarlet silk necktie and waist-sash, grey felt *sombréro*, richly laced with silver, gauntlet gloves, and buff high boots with spurs—the rowels the size of cheese plates—carbine, revolvers, and sword. Their horses are highly bred, and so exquisitely trained that they obey the pressure of the knee, the rein being seldom if ever used. A troop of twenty to thirty of these picturesque-looking fellows, filing past, escorting a diligence or accompaning our Saturday pay cavalcade down the railway line, is one of the prettiest sights of the city of Mexico.

An officer of the general army with whom I became acquainted gave me an idea of the pay of the officers in the different branches of the army.

	Cavalry.	Infantry.
General of the Division	$500 per month.	
General of Brigade	375 „	
Colonel	$225	$208 per month.
Lieut.-Colonel	150	137 „
Major	130	122 „
Captain	95	80 „
Lieutenant	65	60 „
2nd Lieutenant	60	57 „

The pay of the Rural Guards is $160 for the officers and $55 for the men per month.

PLATE VI.

THE PLAZA OF SAN DOMINGO.

[page 32.

CHAPTER V.

Records of the Inquisition—Old Store Shops—School of Arts and Trades—
Blind People.

THE city lions have to be visited on foot, and it requires a little
management to keep the shady sides of the streets; I often
gladly turned into a cool, dark church for a few minutes' respite
from the outside glare. The old church of San Domingo, with its
pink walls, quaint entablatures, peculiar portals, and glittering,
tiled dome, is at an easy distance from the hotel. The garden
and plaza in front possess several attractive features, and the
square is generally filled with carts and mules, the carts loaded
with hay and other farm products exposed for sale. On the
east stands the School of Medicine; the course of study lasts
seven long years. I was shown over the interior, and saw more
than I cared for. This building was formerly the tribunal of
the Inquisition, which was established in Mexico on the 4th of
November, 1571, and suppressed by a decree of the Spanish
Cortes on the 22nd of February, 1813. It was then converted
into a state prison, and the notable yard of the orange-trees
thus brought within the Mexican Bastille.

It has since served as a lottery office, a barrack, and a House
of Congress; in 1854 it was adapted to its present purposes,
having been purchased for $50,286, or £10,000.

Not far from this stands the old church of the Jesuits, its
tower falling into ruins. The interior—the gilding still clings

D

to the roof and frescoes cover the walls—is used as a custom house store, and is full of bales and merchandise; a tablet in one of the corridors at the rear, now almost obliterated, indicates the spot where some dungeons of the Inquisition formerly existed.

Many records of the Inquisition are preserved in the archives of the government, and not a few have found their way into private hands. Mr. Hope very kindly gave me two original MSS. that had for a long time been preserved in the family of his father-in-law, Señor Tejira. They are interesting from the fact that one is dated Mexico, the 9th of April, 1573, two years after the Inquisition was founded; the other is dated the 1st of July, 1772, two hundred years later. The early manuscript is a statement of proceedings taken by the Holy Inquisition against Juan Viscayno, native of Spain, for not fulfilling his religious duties, and for having two wives.

The later manuscript refers to the Inquisition proceedings against the chaplain of the Bethelmitas for misconduct. So far as I can make out the writing, the proceedings seem something after the manner of a court-martial at home, denunciations being repeated and corroborated by various witnesses; the signatures of the executives to different portions of the manuscripts indicating by the dates that the culprit was brought before them on different occasions for a period extending over a year. I give a facsimile of the first page of the earlier manuscript on which proceedings are noted down in detail, including the preliminary arrangements, the accusation, the torture in the prison, and the final judgment. The place of execution for those that were executed by order of this tribunal was at the end of the Alameda, near the spot where the buildings of the present American Legation stand; and I was told by several persons that most of the bodies of the sufferers were buried in the Alameda, and this was assigned as a reason for the luxuriant growth of the trees. It requires fine reasoning to decide whether the human sacrifices

Guadalax.ᵃ ⸻ 1576.

Proçesso confra,

Joan Viƶcayno, llamado, Joanes de Galarraga
natural de Vrnieta. aldea de S. Seuaſtian en la
prouinçia de Guipuƶcoa, Serzero, &ᵗ.º En la v.ᵃ de
Llerena. minas del Sombrerete, Obp.ᵃᵈ de Guadalaxᵃ

~ Jnformacion,
~ Man.ᵗᵒ de Captura,
~ Priſsion
~ Moniçiones.1.ᵃ z.ᵃ
~ Acuſsacion
~ apruena,
~ Suelto Laciudad
  Por Carcel
~ buelta a Reclusi
~ Publica.ᵒⁿ
~ q deffiniᵃm

Caſado dos Yezes ~
nº 3 ...
~ Abogᵈᵒ.

~ el licᵈᵒ Auacos

Votado Aperi.ᵃ pu. 200. açotᵉ q
deſtie Porpetuo de las yndias

~ Secha en la cin. 24 y 25. de dos vezes

Letra T. leg.º 2.º

by the Aztec priests on the Teocali were not equalled in cruelty
by those of the Holy Inquisition.

That terror to importers, the Custom House, occupies nearly
an entire side of the square; and it is equally terrible to
exporters. I had to spend many hours within its walls, dancing
attendance on the officials, in order to get my boxes of curios
despatched to England. By a regulation, the wisdom of which
I fully commend, nothing of archæological or national interest is
permitted to leave the country without special permission from
government. After I had presented two or three petitions to
Señor Montez, the minister for Hacienda, he very kindly gave me
an order to have my collection examined in Mexico, fastened
with red tape and sealed with many government stamps, in order
that the boxes might not be reopened by the custom-house
authorities at Vera Cruz.

On the west of the square is a long, wide arcade, under which
people, whom, for want of a better name, I must designate junk
dealers, expose broken odds and ends of all sorts on the stone
pavement for sale. It was my frequent lounge, as I was led
thither by the hope of picking up a few curios. A general
glance at the things suggested pieces of joiners' tools, odd
stirrups, spurs and bits, knives, nails, buttons, broken military
ornaments, and glass bottle stoppers. One evening, at a dance
at the American Legation, Mrs. Aymé, the wife of the consul at
Merida, showed me a magnificent old Spanish fan, worth $60,
for which a lady present had paid but $1 in this very arcade; it
was in a broken condition and minus a rib when she bought it.
I was led into purchasing several old Spanish iron locks; I found
also a St. Joseph and Child painted on copper, not badly finished,
for which a few days afterwards I had twenty times its cost
offered me. Under the same arcade, behind little screens,
perch elderly scriveners of cadaverous aspect, who for a *medio*
(or five cents) will indite love-letters or cartels, invitations or
invoices.

D 2

The fountain in the centre of the Plaza has its place in the history of the bloody annals of civil and internal strife. Many hundreds of patriots, rebels, call them what you will, with their backs to the old church, the golden beams of the risen sun on their blanched features, have leaned against the stone-coping of the fountain till the gentle splashing of its waters was drowned in the roar of musketry that put an end to their sufferings. It is the favourite resort of *aguadores*, or water-carriers, who repair thither for the *agua dulce*, or pure water; their picturesque dresses—consisting of a leather helmet, a leather doublet, open like a herald's tabard, with flowing white drawers and *guaraches*, or sandals—imparted a quaint animation to the scene. I counted as many as twenty of these itinerant water vendors round the fountain at one time, their red earthenware vessels glittering in the dazzling sunlight.

Close to the Church of the Jesuits is the School of Arts, an institution of which I must make mention, as, after visiting it on several occasions, I arrived at the conclusion that the work which it performed was singularly beneficial. Some years ago the artisans of the city founded a society in which the members who were temporarily out of employment could obtain *ad interim* work at small wages; the excellent results eventually brought the institution under the notice of government, which granted the society a large disused convent and adjoining buildings for their workshops, with the proviso that the society should take a number of boys from the orphanages, industrial schools, and kindred institutions of the city, and thoroughly instruct them in some trade. The place is now an immense workshop, including iron and brass foundries, carriage and cart mending, building and masonry, various branches of joinery and upholstery work, and silk and cotton hand-weaving. Workmen are paid wages a trifle lower than the market price, and they have the advantage of instruction in their trade, schools, reading rooms, recreation rooms, and fixtures appertaining to a workmen's club.

This institution interested me so much that I gave a donation to the library, sufficient to constitute me a life member; the whole affair is so admirable that it would repay adoption in any country.

If a government or country may gain credit for the excellence of its philanthropic institutions, I would rank Mexico, under its new *régime*, as high as any country I visited; education is compulsory between the ages of five and fourteen; waifs, strays and neglected children are swept into reformatories; and the establishment for teaching the deaf and dumb enables its inmates to talk a language of their own.

A stranger cannot avoid noticing the number of blind people in the streets, and at the doors of the churches; they sell lottery tickets, matches and trifles. They are not allowed to beg, but, without soliciting alms, they carry a begging box—this refers to middle-aged and old people, who however appeared well clad. The young people who are blind are cared for and taught in institutions, and the establishment for their higher education in music in the Calle de la Encarnacion, is on the same principle as that at Norwood, near London. But I found its useful work was so little known amongst the society in which I had the pleasure of visiting in Mexico, that I hired an extensive suite of rooms for a day or two at the Hotel Gillow, in which I gave a large afternoon party and dance, and secured a number of blind boys from the school to perform on various instruments in the corridors and the salons. As most of the diplomatic circle and a large contingent of Mexican families attended the reception, the blind boys advertised themselves thoroughly; when not engaged in playing their harps and trumpets they contrived to get into everybody's way at the refreshment tables, and the ladies and gentlemen assisted me in leading them back to their places. I was afterwards amused at seeing notices of the entertainment in the local papers, and a statement that "El Señor B. mostró mucho solicitud por los muchachos ciegos," or, as the

English papers had it, "the pupils were the object of Mr. B.'s special attention." *

There are several other public or government institutions situated in the streets running out of the Plaza San Agustin, which I visited in company with Bishop Riley, Mr. Henry Hope, or some other able cicerone. I will merely note the Escuela Preparatoria de San Ildefonso, a sort of university, in which young men have to undergo a curriculum of three years before they can enter any of the learned professions.

The bishop also took me to a government college, where there is a free education for girls and young ladies who have satisfactorily passed minor examinations at other schools; secular instruction only is afforded, but this is of the very highest order. We were unmercifully delayed here one day, while some enthusiastic professors searched for some difficult music to be played by half-a-dozen of their favourite pupils on pianos at the same time; the sewer in the street was being repaired just under our noses; the windows were all open on the balcony; no reference was made to the rank compound of villainous smells,

---

* I see by entry in my note-book, in reference to this school, that it was originally founded by Señor Ignacio Trigueras and friends in 1870, and soon after adopted by Congress as a national institution. There are at present forty boys and as many girls within the building. The sexes are separated; the course of instruction is industrial and musical; indeed, a thorough education is secured. No pupils are admitted over fourteen years of age, and the course of training extends over eight years. There was a little English girl in the establishment, named Catherine Hollis, whose blindness was caused by an accidental blow on the head when she was five years old. Her little heart quite overflowed when she found a person addressing her in her own language; nothing seemed to be known of her parentage. Both boys and girls are allowed to make paper cigarettes during recreation hours, for which they are paid a small sum for pocket money. I was told that many of the old people had become blind from suffering and exposure to heat and cold during the revolutions in the period from 1840 to 1860, the bright sun and the rarity of the air contributing to this result. In the young people it was partly hereditary, and partly from sickness; some of it may be due to smallpox; but I noticed very few blind either in the schools or in the streets who were in any way disfigured by this terrible malady.

though it quite sickened me; since the sewers, running down the centre of all the streets, are but a few inches below the surface, on account of want of fall, and are continually getting blocked up and put under repair, the people probably get accustomed to the nuisance.

The large majority of all the institutions of the city have their local habitations in handsome quadrangled buildings, most of which were originally constructed for conventual or ecclesiastical purposes; open *porte-cochères*, or trellised iron gates, lead into them from the streets; the quadrangles are filled with palm trees, flowering shrubs, and lovely creepers; the gateways of the larger private houses exhibit similarly decorated courts and corridors. When the government, after the establishment of the Republic, confiscated ecclesiastical buildings, they handed them over for secular purposes or sold them to private companies or societies; not a few were divided up and converted into dwelling-houses and stores. Towards the end of Spanish rule, the city had become little more than a pile of ecclesiastical buildings. The handsome streets of the present day have been formed through the midst of them, a fact occasionally demonstrated by the remnants of an enormous wall coming to the face of the street at an irregular angle.

A categorical description of the minor institutions would but weary the reader, yet I have a word to say for the military and municipal hospitals, whose ventilation and cleanliness are unexceptionable. The military hospital of San Lucas, in the San Pablo quarter, was particularly noticeable for its cleanliness. The rooms are lofty and the windows open wide, while in some cases they are altogether dispensed with, thus enabling the authorities to place the beds closer together in the dormitories; how different from the shut-in hospital at home!—but it is the climate.

The theatres and tivolis, the clubs, the gardens and lounges of the city, claim to be equal to those of any other city of the same size. The seats in the public gardens were always filled.

I enjoyed the hospitalities of the French, German, and Spanish clubs. The German club formerly belonged to the convent of the Colegio de Niñas, and occupies the whole of a magnificent quadrangle; it contains a ball-room, a concert-room, and a library, in addition to all the other adjuncts of a first-class club, and it was a treat to go occasionally to the private practices of the German glee club in the concert-room, where the singers always received me kindly. During the dry season the members of this club occasionally had a paper hunt early on a Sunday morning, which was really capital fun. Some twenty or thirty horsemen assembled at one or other of the tivolis outside of the city at seven A.M., and spent half-an-hour over coffee and refreshments, while one or two of the party, ably assisted by the master of the riding school, were out laying the trail. All Mexican horses can jump, but they hate getting fast amongst the aloes or magueys, the spikes of which are as sharp as a spur on their tender flanks. When the paper trail was lost, and I happened to find it, I shouted Tally-ho, yo-hoik, and nobody paid any attention. When the Germans took up the scent they yelled *schnitzen*, in reference to the strips of paper, and I soon learned their cry. The hunt lasted about three hours, and was not ended before several men had come to grief, generally in the wide water ditches which have treacherous banks. Of course the hunt ended at Chapultepec, or some rendezvous where a cavalcade of carriages filled with ladies and a few gentlemen disinclined to severe exercise in the saddle awaited our arrival, and the fair occupants assisted us in the enjoyment of a bountiful and *recherché* breakfast, spread out on tables; all had been brought to the spot in the club waggon, and was arranged by the club servants. On returning to the city it was a matter of good taste, and enjoined by the authorities of the club, that the party should break up into small detachments, and present no indications of the morning's amusement.

CHAPTER VI.

National Pawn-Shop—Pearls—Out-of-door Music—Rooms in the Palace—Portraits
of the Presidents—Relics of the Patriot Hidalgo.

ONE of the most remarkable institutions in Mexico, the Monte de
Piedad, or national pawn shop—answering to the Mont de Piété
of Paris—is well worthy of a visit. It stands in the Calle
Empedradillo, almost facing the celebrated Aztec Calendar, which
is so well placed in the wall of one of the cathedral towers. The
Monte is one of the oldest edifices in the capital, having been built
immediately after the conquest for the private residence of Cortes,
and from time to time subsequently used as the official quarters of
the viceroys. It is a building of considerable dimensions, and,
happily for the tourist of the nineteenth century, has not been
modernised or improved. Its doors, windows, staircases, ceilings,
patios and balconies, are just as when the haughty hidalgos flitted
in and out, attired in all the bravery of velvet and lace, and com-
mented upon the progress made in the construction of the opposite cathedral when it was rising upon the site of the former
Aztec temple. In 1744 this building was utilised for the Monte
de Piedad, whose founder was the Count de Regla Don Pedro
Terreros, who endowed the institution with \$300,000 out of his
private fortune; nor did he rest until he had organised and
matured the plan upon which the institution is at the present
moment being worked. His object was philanthropic to the last
degree; his wish was to relieve the poor and those in bitter

financial straits from the usury of the *empēnos*, or pawn-shops, as well as to lend a helping hand to persons in a comfortable condition, but who might be pressed for money on some sudden or unexpected emergency; as a matter of fact, this class of person in Mexico is more numerous than we probably imagine.

The rules and regulations permit the lending of money on most liberal terms; the depositor gets about one-third of the value of the goods deposited; the rate of interest never goes lower than 3 per cent. or higher than $12\frac{1}{2}$ per cent. per annum, and the tickets have to be renewed every eight months.

When the depositor ceases to pay the interest on the loan advanced, his pledges, whatever they may be, are retained in the bank for seven months; they are then carefully appraised by paid and expert officials, and are offered for sale at the appraiser's valuation for one month. If after the expiration of one month they remain unsold, they are again valued, this time at a lower figure, and again deposited for sale in the sale-rooms on the lower floor. For six months this process goes on, after which, if still unsold, the goods are knocked down at public auction to the highest bidder. If the goods bring less than the value set upon them by the appraisers, the latter must themselves make up the deficit to the bank.

Mexico is famous for pearls; they are found in the Gulf of California, but the fishery is very dangerous, as every diver that goes down has to be accompanied by a man to defend him from the sharks, which abound in the gulf and are of great size. I saw three large pear-shaped unset pearls in the Monte, which I was desirous of purchasing to present to a lady in England; I watched the price rebated upon them for three months, then made my investment, and was much pleased with my bargain. On certain days in each month certain kinds of goods are sold; for example, on one day clothes will be sold, on the next jewels, on the third flotsam and jetsam—all sorts of odds and ends.

Don Pedro Terreros' portrait holds an honoured place in the

building; his name is venerated and respected all over the country. If his soul is not pretty safe, it is a sad thing to contemplate, for all the profit of the institution for seventy years went for masses for its repose. The surplus funds are now devoted to the establishment of branch banks all over the country.

I visited the great vault, and stood in a veritable Aladdin's cave; around me in bags, made of the fibre of the maguey plant, were upwards of $7,000,000, the funds of the bank, in solid silver and solid gold, a mine of wealth. From this vault I was led to the picture, silver plate, candelabra, timepiece and bric-à-brac rooms, and I will close the sketch with the jewelry department, one of the richest and rarest collections, perhaps, in the entire world. Such pearls, rubies, emeralds and diamonds; heirlooms descended from the times when loot was an institution in the country; some handed down from the date of the Conquest, and at various periods deposited here, partly for safety and partly for the consideration of hard cash.

The machine seems to work with marvellous precision, and the order is simply admirable. The sale-room is generally crowded, and it is no humiliation to have a little transaction at the Monte de Piedad! It is a banking affair, and everybody hies thither as to a bank, the dealings being as confidential as in Coutts's or any other London bank. It is needless to say that the Monte de Piedad is probably "fire-proof," and strongly guarded by night and by day.

Crossing from this admirable institution, and passing by the cathedral, you find yourself before the National Palace. It overlooks the " *Zocalo* " in the centre of the Plaza, a garden planted with umbrageous trees always in leaf, below which are beds of glorious flowers, marble seats and sparkling fountains. An elevated stand occupies a central position, and here bands, which the spirit of Jullien might like to conduct, discourse every afternoon and evening Beethoven, Wagner and Suppé, stepping from the sublime to the bouffe, from the sonata to the fandango.

The National Palace was erected in 1693, in place of one in which Cortes and the Spanish viceroys had resided until it was destroyed by fire in 1692.* It occupies the extreme length of the eastern side of the Plaza, and measures 2867 feet. On its north side are several public institutions, the Post-Office and Museum to wit, of which more anon. The President's private apartments are also situated in the north wing, but the Chief of the State only uses them officially; he is supposed to reside in his own private house. This palace contains the presidential offices, the cabinets of the ministers, the headquarters of the military commanders, the treasury, the archives of the nation, the offices of the meteorological department, and a large room, the chapel of Maximilian's time, but at present used as the chamber of senators, while the *patios* or courts would seem to be the happy hunting grounds of parasites, lobbyists, and hangers-on. Here the Mexican Micawber waits for something to turn up. The structure is only two stories high, but the central tower over the gateway, with illuminated clock, and the bronze angels or other ethereal beings on the façades which flank it, have a very good effect. The palace and all the buildings round the square, being low, allow the height and magnificent proportions of the cathedral to show themselves to the greatest advantage.

I had several opportunities of visiting General Ochoa, the chief of military engineers, who had apartments in the front of the palace, also Señor Marischal, the minister for foreign affairs, whose bureau is at the south end. In passing through the corridors to these apartments there seemed to be as many rooms as there were Arabian Nights' Entertainments, some

---

* After the destruction of the Mexican city, Charles V. placed this site at the disposal of Cortes; and in the first lordly dwelling-house erected by the intrepid desperado, was a single apartment capable of containing three thousand persons. The King of Spain, according to papers still extant in Madrid, paid $33,000 for it to the family of Cortes, on the 19th of January, 1562.

gaudily and some poorly furnished; and the corridors are constantly filled with persons of all classes seeking interviews with ministers or the members of their respective staffs. Señor Marischal's anteroom gave but little indication of the magnificent furniture of his official reception-room. The apartment in which the President and his Council assemble for business is furnished in the style of the most splendid days of Napoleon the Third. On an oval table in the centre of the room I noticed that the blotting-books were arranged for the members of the cabinet in the following order from the right hand of the President: Foreign Affairs, Finance, Home, War, Justice, and Public Works. A scarlet silken cord, hanging from the ceiling to the President's portfolio, serves to summon the guard. In an equally fine room adjoining was a small iron bedstead, for the use of the President if required.

There are two fine rooms fronting the Plaza, fitted up with dais and throne in regal style. The first room is the *salle de Iturbide;* the walls are hung in crimson damask, with large Venetian mirrors, the Mexican arms, the eagle and serpent, together with the motto, *Equidad en la Justicia,* in gold letters, being freely sprinkled about. This apartment and the adjoining corridors lead by doors into the hall of the ambassadors, a room imposing for its great length. At the farther end of the room is a large picture, twenty-five feet long, and ten feet high, painted by Miranda, of the battle field of the Cinco de Mayo, 1862; it is badly painted, but probably suggests a very correct plan of the battle at the moment that the regiment of half-clothed Indians from Zacapoaxtla, State of Oaxaca, were wheeled into line and turned the tide of fortune against the gallant, but thoroughly beaten, French. Having been over the field at Puebla, where the battle was fought, I recognised in the picture the positions that were pointed out to me on the actual ground, a matter of more importance than the lack of any excellence in painting. On the entire length of the walls, opposite the windows of this apartment, hang full length portraits of the Mexican presidents, including Hidalgo, Morelos, Guerrero, Bravo, Juarez, Arista, Matamoras, and Iturbide. The portrait of the ex-President Diaz, painted by a Mexican artist, is admirable in likeness, tone and finish. He is in uniform—dark grey—with a raised collar worked in gold, grey waistcoat, with blue waist-sash, ornamented with gold braid. He grasps in his hand a telescope.

There is one other apartment worth mentioning, viz., the corner room of the north end of the palace : it has two windows, one looking upon the square and one upon the street in which is the great market. It was a favourite room of poor Maximilian ; he could see two ways at once, though not the way to hold his throne; at present the room contains a few relics of the patriot Hidalgo, also the banner which he bore, and which is annually brought out on the 16th of September, and carried to the national theatre, amidst great military display and firing of cannon. I was lucky enough to occupy a box with some friends on the anniversary. I heard long patriotic speeches, and saw the President wave the flag three times at the front of the stage, to a roar of " *Viva la República*," which might have raised the roof of the building. This ceremony is always performed at exactly eleven o'clock at night, the hour at which Hidalgo tore the flag down from his church in 1810, and rushed into the street uttering the cry of independence. Poor Hidalgo! when you were shot by the Spaniards as a rebel on the 21st of July, 1811, you little thought your old tattered banner would be so venerated, nor could you have dreamed of the scene that presented itself in the theatre ! The boxes of the dress circle and other parts of the house were filled with ladies in brilliant evening costume, resplendent in diamonds and jewels, while the orchestra performed national airs when the interludes between the national speeches afforded them an opportunity.

CHAPTER VII.

MEXICO is not behindhand in the fine arts; sculpture, painting and music, wherever the Latin races are in the ascendant, would seem to be naturally allied to fine climates and blue skies. The native Mexican in bygone times had an appreciation of the beautiful, as is testified by the imposing magnificence of his ritual, and the remains of the sculptures and vases, gold work and feather work, which bear record of his art. Of course when the Spaniard came into the country, his hidalgoship built churches and palaces equal to what he had at home, and adorned them with the works of Murillo, Velazquez, and all the most renowned painters of the land of his birth.

The national picture gallery of San Cárlos and the art schools connected with it are not unworthy of Mexico, and of course much better than anything to be seen in any other part of America.

There are three large rooms in the building, one devoted to old masters, in which are fair originals by Leonardo da Vinci, Zurbaran, Murillo, Rubens, Correggio, Velazquez and Carreno; and some fine pictures of the Florentine and Flemish schools. One room is dedicated to old Mexican masters, probably Spaniards born in the country; the names being Baltasar de Echave, Juarez, Ibarra, etc.; the pictures in another room are the productions of the pupils of the academy. These indicate talent, if not perfect finish. The principal of these latter works are by Rebul, Pina, Sagnedo, Ramirez, Cordero, Flores, Parra, Monroy, Urruchi, Velasco, and many others. There is one large picture in this gallery which no one who has ever seen it can possibly forget. It would be impressed upon his mind as much as the St. Cecilia at Bologna, or the Descent from the Cross at Antwerp, or other well-known pictures. I refer to the large picture of the good Spanish priest, Las Casas, imploring Providence to shield the poor Mexicans from Spanish cruelty. The priest stands on the steps of a Mexican Teocalli, at his feet a murdered Mexican chief, whose wife is grasping the Padre's robe in overwhelming grief. This painting is by Felix Parra, and holds the place of honour in the gallery. The artist painted it before he had seen any country but his own, and was awarded the Grand Prix by the Academy at Rome on account of its merit; no wonder; it fascinated me more than any picture I have seen; it is simply perfect in sentiment, grouping and colour; I did my best to make a coloured sketch of it.*

The sculpture gallery on the basement floor of the academy

---

* Bartolomeo de las Casas was a Spanish prelate, distinguished for his generous and constant, though unavailing, exertions in favour of the natives of the Spanish colonies. He was born in 1474, and he sailed with Columbus to the West Indies. He seems to have been greatly shocked by the cruelty of the Spaniards to the native Indians, and twelve times he crossed the ocean to plead their cause at the foot of the Spanish throne. His fervent eloquence moved the Emperor, Charles V., to attempt the redress of some of the wrongs which the Indians were suffering, from the avarice and cruelty of their conquerors. Prescott frequently mentions Las Casas, especially where the bishop risked his life, and he gives a long note at the end of the first volume, with details of the most eventful periods in the good man's life. The Spanish Government promoted him, at the age of seventy, to the bishopric of Cuzco, one of the richest sees in the colonies; but the disinterested soul of the missionary did not covet riches or preferment. He rejected the proffered dignity and accepted the bishopric of Chiapas, a country which, from the poverty and ignorance of its inhabitants, offered a good field for spiritual labours. Las Casas died after a short illness, July 1566, in his Dominican monastery of Atocha at Madrid, at the great age of ninety-two.

THE LAS CASAS PICTURE IN THE ACADEMY, MEXICO

BY FELIX PARRA

contains copies of most of the best known subjects, and a few statues by Tenerani, Pradier and Sola; also some works by the students of the school. In looking at the noble copy in marble of the group of Laocoon, and other well-known large Greek statues, the visitor wonders how such heavy masses were conveyed over the steep mountain roads between the coast and the city, and that the Spanish viceroys had time and inclination to obtain these works of art, either for their own pride and pleasure, or the instruction and enlightenment of the people of the city.

The National Museum, which, with the Post Office adjoining it, appears to be a portion of the National Palace, is at present in process of transformation and rearrangement, and will be a handsome building. It is divided into two sections, that of natural history, and that of Mexican antiquities. The former is a very small collection, but exhibited to the best possible advantage, while the gallery of Mexican archæology is being developed into a rich and valuable collection. Señor Mendoza has charge of this department, which is not at present open to the public, and he very kindly received me on several occasions, producing his rarest treasures for my inspection. Some of those I have described in the chapter on Mexican antiquities. Another public institution, to which the visitor will hear constant reference, is the Mineria, or school of mines; a most necessary institution for a country which possesses such wealth beneath her soil.

I have mentioned the exterior appearance of the building as exhibiting curious wavy lines in its architecture, from the sinking and settling of its foundations, but I was told it is quite safe. The lower and back rooms of the building are occupied by lecture-rooms, class-rooms and laboratories. In the large upper apartments are a fine collection of minerals and geological specimens. I was shown the fossil skeleton of a horse three feet high, an animal pretty common in the country in the Pleistocene period, but since extinct, no horses having been found in the country by the

Spanish invaders, and the present stock having originated entirely from what was imported.

On Wednesday, the 5th of October, the spacious court-yard of this building was draped in black and ornamented with military equipments for the lying in state of the remains of General Arista, who was President of the Republic in the stirring times of 1852, and who afterwards retired to Portugal and died there in 1855. In front of a catafalque, surrounded with flaming lamps, was placed a small wooden box containing the former President's bones. The highest officers of the army stood guard in various parts of the *patio* or quadrangle, which was ornamented with cannon, cannon balls, piled arms, and other military devices. Several bands discoursed operatic music, and for the entire two days and two nights countless multitudes of people streamed up the staircase and round the corridors, gazing down upon the gorgeous and impressive scene below, and behaving in a most orderly manner. Arista, after doing his country good service, had retired altogether from Mexico at the end of his presidential career, in order to prevent his partisans from pressing him into any opposition to his successor. The bones were removed to the cemetery of Dolores on the third day with all the pomp and military parade the government could provide.

In addition to the large cemetery above mentioned, the English, French, and American colonies here have all their separate cemeteries, which are kept in beautiful order. Several of these are passed on the road to La Piedad, and the tramcar companies have special carriages, very nicely arranged, for funeral purposes.

Amongst the scientific societies in the city, I would not willingly omit that of Geography and Statistics, as being amongst the first of its kind established in the world. Humboldt was admitted a member whilst he was resident in Mexico. The meteorological department is worthy of the highest praise, and the manner in which it gets up its charts and maps has won the warmest culogy from meteorologists in all parts of the world. The late General Meyer, chief of the United States signal service bureau, has declared that the charts and reports coming from Mexico were more satisfactory than those he received from any other country. The observatory is attached to the National Palace.

The public libraries in Mexico and in other cities of the Republic are not difficult to find. They are held in sequestrated churches which have in the last few years been specially adapted to receive books and made convenient for the reading public. The new National Library, which is being arranged in what was once the church of San Agustin, will be as handsome as any to be found in an European capital. The exterior of this old church is being sufficiently altered to give it a secular appearance, and this secularisation has been carried so far into the interior as to hide the fine dome by continuing the vaulted roof of the nave.

I was very fortunate in making the acquaintance of Señor Vigil, the chief librarian, and through his instrumentality and assistance the government allowed me to take away eight large volumes of old Catholic chant-books and services, on replacing them by standard English works of equal value for the use of the library. The chant-books were all of vellum, and dated 1600; they had formerly belonged to this church, but had been thrown into an outhouse, and allowed to become so decayed that out of fifty I could only select eight ponderous tomes which I considered worth sending home. The books are similar to those still used in the choir of the cathedral, and some of the other churches in Mexico. The illuminated borders, headings, and capital letters in several of the volumes are very good.

Curious old Spanish books are occasionally to be picked up at the book-stalls. The Spaniards introduced the printing press into Mexico soon after the Conquest. Señor Izcalbazeta showed me several books printed in Mexico about the date 1550; the type evidencing that the Spaniards were in no way behind other European nations at that date. Books in the Aztec language, too, are to be occasionally found, the words being jaw-breakers, like some German words we wot of.

South of the National Palace is the principal market of the city; and in the early mornings, indeed, all day, the adjoining streets are scarcely passable from the crowds of people pressing to and from its attractive portals. It is enclosed by a high wall, and on the right the whole is overshadowed by a still higher wall of some old convent. Against this are a lot of shanties and booths where old clothes and old everythings are exhibited in the greatest abundance. The market is provided with four gates, each gate giving upon a street. Around the walls, inside the enclosure, are shops and projecting piazzas, the remainder of the space being occupied by stalls and booths, which are protected by framework covered with matting, in the shape of gigantic umbrellas. A portion of the market has a zinc roof. The space literally swarms with human beings, from the *dueña*, or housekeeper, of some swell Mexican family, to the Indian woman with the inevitable child strapped across her back in her *rebozo*. Each class of article exposed for sale has its own quarter in the market—meat, fruit, fish, vegetables being in separate places. Vendors who are not the possessors of stands spread out their wares on mats, utterly regardless of space; and you will find yourself treading on the stock-in-trade (the owner uttering shrill cries of warning) unless you keep a pretty good look out. Indian women stretched on mats indolently watch their wares, red and green pepper pods, *granadas*, melons, *papaya, camote, chirimoya, chico zapote, chiote* (fruit resembling a hedgehog), *jicami,* and fifty other Mexican fruits, whose names I could not note down; the omission, however, is not of grave importance, for very few of those I have mentioned are worth eating. Dealers in fried meats dole out their commodities to hungry customers. *Tortilla* venders do a roaring business. Indian

THE MARKET. [page 52.

maidens, with great coops of chickens on their backs, and a dozen live fowls hanging with their heads downwards from their waist-belts, jostle past you, while a donkey places his pointed, unshod foot on your favourite corn. The *dueñas* drive hard bargains in the shrillest possible tones. *Rancheros*, in gay and gaudy *sarapes* or *ponchos*, whiff cigarettes, while huckstering over some desired object, which they will hang on the saddle pommel of their mustangs, patiently waiting for them at the gates. Look out for the sticks that support the awnings covering the stalls, or they will poke you in the eye; look out for the merchandise spread beneath your feet; look out for a peck from the beak of some half-strangled turkey; look out for the fat little happy Indian babies, mixed up with everything; look out for discarded, but still lighted, ends of cigarettes which are thrown carelessly about; and don't look out for the bad smells.

Most things are extraordinarily cheap. A Mexican lady gave me a list of the following prices, which she said her housekeeper never exceeded:

Turkeys	6 to 8 reals, or 3s. to 4s. each.
Large fowl	2½ to 3 reals, or 1s. 3d. each.
Small fowl	2 reals, or 1s. each.
Beef, according to cut	1 to 1½ reals, or 6d. to 9d. a pound.
Rabbits	1 to 2 reals, or 6d. to 1s. each.
Lake ducks	¾ to 1 real, or 4½d. to 6d. each.
Eggs, about 8 for	1 real, or 6d., all the year round.

Another part of the market interested me very much, it was the space devoted to the sale of coarse earthenware, the forms of which were generally beautiful. The ware is of a soft red clay, apparently not very hard baked, or I would have risked sending a few large dishes home. Some of them are prettily marked with black or deep brown geometrical figures, and on many of them are painted the names of the purposes for which they are used, or they are marked with Christian names, saints' names, and days of the week; some are highly glazed. Many of them are two to three feet in diameter, and are used over charcoal fires for cooking. The jugs and jars are of all sizes, and made on the same pattern as those used by the water carriers, with bulging sides, small necks and mouthpieces, and broad short handles, a well-known shape in Spain and most eastern countries.

The next interesting point is the piazza, on the branch of the Viga Canal, to which the boatmen bring the fruit, vegetables and flowers, from the Chinampas. There are some old, rather dilapidated houses with stone balconies on the opposite bank; Mr. Terry, a very able artist, whose agreeable acquaintance I made on my first arrival, showed me a clever oil painting he had made of this spot before I visited it, and I at once supposed it to be a view in Venice; many people who have seen Venice would have been equally misled, especially if the boatmen had cast aside their *sombreros*, the only striking point of difference. It is a lively scene, every boatman endeavouring to get the prow of his boat against the steps, so that he may be first to unload his cargo; a boat-load of red tomatoes flanked on either side by boats laden with green vegetables and beautiful flowers is a pretty sight.

The high-arched, white-washed bridge close by is crowded with lounging boatmen and market people. They have done their work, and have had their drink of pulque, and are chaffing the men unloading below. The water in the canal, as you may suppose, is not of the clearest, nor are the surroundings altogether savoury; it is the picture that is worth the money. As is generally the case near a market, there are rag-and-bone shops in the immediate neighbourhood, and if no better way of spending time presented itself, Bishop and I used to pass an hour or two in searching amongst them for curios. One day he dropped upon a very fairly painted old picture of St. Dominic, and I tried hard to match a silver-mounted spur, eventually succeeding. But a vast deal of rubbish has to be overhauled before anything worth carrying away is discovered. The proprietors of these shops were as civil and polite as possible, and begged you to turn their trash over and over again with the hope "que el caballero encontraria algo á su gusto." While on the market topic, I should mention the large quantity of butcher's meat consumed in the city. I did not notice much exposed for sale in the market, but butcher's shops are innumerable. The animals are all slaughtered in rastros or abattoirs on the outskirts of the city. I frequently looked into a very large one on an open square on the way to La Viga, in which the arrangements for cleanliness, etc., seemed to be all that could be desired.

The shops for the sale of meat are without windows, and are shaded from the sun by clean-looking red and white curtains. The number of customers seen in these shops, and the quantity of meat served at mid-day and evening meals, both in public and private establishments, gives a visitor an idea that the population is decidedly carnivorous. This was not always the case, but is partly the result of European civilisation, and the rarity of the air probably accelerates digestion. The beef is very good; I cannot say so much for the mutton, but kid dressed *á la Concordia* is not to be despised. There is a restaurant in the Calle Refugio kept by a Mr. Naylor, an Englishman originally from Manchester. He came over to this country years ago to assist in a cotton factory, and, after realising a competency, settled down to his present occupation; he only serves beef, potatoes, apple tart and plum pudding, and he prides himself that these viands cannot be surpassed in excellence anywhere in the world. Every Englishman and most Americans pay him an early visit. I dined there once or twice, and, on his discovering I knew something of Manchester and the Lancashire districts, he rather overpowered me with conversation. His Manchester was the Manchester of forty years ago, nor could he realise the changes which have made it what it is at the present hour. One day I saw Mr. Naylor in the market; he was selecting potatoes, no doubt upon the same principle on which he selects his prime cuts of beef, for I noticed that he was difficult to please, and only chose the finest and nicest-looking tubers on the mats.

I walked through the markets in every town I visited; all were well-supplied, busy and amusing places. All were very similar, being mostly open to the sky, the stalls shaded by improvised mats. The market at Puebla was the most interesting, inasmuch as it was by far the cleanest; the market women wore a peculiar costume—a white chemisette, ornamented with bands of very pretty bead work, of which I procured samples. I saw nothing else of the kind so pretty in Mexico.

An hour inside the market, followed by an hour outside the market, is quite enough; and you retrace your steps to the "Concordia" for whatever you think will most refresh the wearied frame.

Early trains arrive in Mexico at four or five o'clock every morning, laden entirely with milk and pulque. The milk is quite new and excellent; it is retailed all over the city in milk carts at a real, or sixpence, a quart. Butter is good, but scarce, and costs two and a-half to three reals per pound. Cream is not procurable. I made several efforts to obtain it, giving three or four days' notice, but to no purpose. Vegetables and fruit are very cheap; fine strawberries are to be had all the year round, at sixpence or ninepence a pound. Mexican bacon is bad, at two and a half reals, or one shilling and threepence per pound. Bread is cheap and delicious. Foreign wines—champagne, hocks, claret, sherries—are obtainable at the restaurants, also beer and porter; there are several breweries of lager in the city, but I did not like it; the only English beer procurable was Tennant's, which is imported in cask and bottled in the country; we were glad to pay seventy-five cents., or three shillings, a pint bottle for it. How is it Mr. Bass has not tried this market? We made many inquiries for his brew, and would gladly have paid a dollar, or four shillings, a pint for it. Mexico was the only place in my journey round the world where Bass's beer was not to be had.

CHAPTER VIII.

CHURCHES.

I HAD the good fortune to be in the city of Mexico during Lent, Holy Week, and Easter. Religious sights and ceremonies were mingled with considerable gaiety and amusement; much more amusement than I could have imagined the Catholic Church would have allowed was indulged in by the entire population.

When Cortes conquered the country, he had instructions from Ferdinand and Isabella, from Charles V., and from Pope Alexander IV., to Christianise it; and this part of his duty, with the help of his army of priests and the formidable terrors of the Inquisition, he accomplished all too zealously. The successive Spanish Viceroys completed the work in the spirit of their age; indeed, in such a manner, that when the books are opened and the last seal broken, the cries of the heathen will most probably drown the anthems of the saints. The Old Testament injunction, "Thou shalt utterly destroy the heathen from amongst you," without a single gleam from the brightness of the Sermon from the Mount, has under no circumstances been more rigorously enforced than by Spain in Mexico and Peru; and what remains of her glories, but the bitterest of bitter feeling in Mexico, and the hatred of her Cuban subjects?

In the Conquest of Mexico it was the rule to destroy all the high places and all vestiges of the ancient worship. The Teocalli or temples were levelled to the ground; crosses were set up and churches built on their sites. The magnificent cathedral of Mexico stands over the spot where the high altar of Montezuma and his predecessors once ran with the blood of human sacrifices. The first church on this site, after the destruction of the Teocalli, was founded by Charles V. His successor, Philip, ordered it to be pulled down, and commenced the erection of the present structure in 1573. It was not finished and dedicated until the 22nd of December, 1657. It has a fine dome and two open towers, each 218 feet high, in which are large bells exposed to view. The length of the building is 426 feet; the architecture is Doric; the railings of the choir, and the passage to the high altar, were made of *tumbago*, manufactured at Macao in China, and weighing twenty-six tons. It is a brassy-looking metal, composed of silver, gold, and copper, but containing so much gold, that an offer has been made to replace it with pure silver, and give many thousand dollars in addition. The cost of the cathedral, that is, of the walls alone, was over $2,000,000. The interior of the building forms a Greek cross, and is divided into five naves. On either side of the main nave are wide chapels, elaborately adorned and enclosed by bronze gates; the walls are clothed with pictures in rich old Spanish gold frames; and at one time a Murillo stood over the high altar, but the present archbishop, wise in his generation, after the robbery of a famous picture from a church in Spain, caused it to be removed to the archiepiscopal palace, where it now hangs. There is no stained glass in the windows, and there are no such luxuries as pews; Indian and Hildago, Aztec and Spaniard, peon and peasant, kneel on the bare boards. One rude bench is reserved for the old and infirm.

The choir is one mass of elaborate carving; the choir books, dating from 1620, are of vellum, and painted in black letters. Close to the choir is a magnificent altar, supported by green

INTERIOR OF THE CATHEDRAL.

marble columns resembling malachite. A rich balustrade of
tumbago connects the altar and the choir. The picture of the
Virgin, in the central nave, was painted by Cabrena in 1700, and
a St. Sebastian, in one of the chapels, by Balthasor de Echavi
in 1645. The glory of the cupola was painted by Simeno de
Planes; on the first plane are placed the ancient patriarchs and
the celebrated women of the Old Testament, the colours being as
vivid at this moment as when laid in. The balustrade surrounding the grand altar is also of *tumbago*, as are the sixty-two
statues which serve as chandeliers. The high altar is approached
by seven steps, the tabernacle is supported by eight ranges of
pillars in the form of a colonnade, on the first of which stand the
statues of the apostles and the evangelists, while those of
numerous saints occupy the second range. On the third appear
groups of angels, and, rising from the midst, the Mother of God.

The sacristy is fitted up with oak, black as ebony from age,
with several large pictures. I often looked into it, and one day
I found two or three priests indulging in a quiet chat after Mass,
while the attendants folded away the rich vestments. A padre,
seeing I was a stranger, offered to show me the magnificent set
of vestments worked for the cathedral by command of Isabella of
Spain; they are of cloth of gold, encrusted with gems, and in
panels passages from Holy Writ are worked exquisitely in silk,
so as to have the effect of the finest painting; it is only on close
inspection that I could discover the traces of the needle. These
gorgeous vestments are useless for practical purposes, for they
are so heavy that no man of ordinary dimensions could sustain
their immense weight for more than a few minutes. Saying
Mass, or even pronouncing the benediction in them, is out of
the question. By the kindness of the padre I was also permitted to view the great council chamber, part and parcel of
the cathedral, in which the councils of the bishops were held,
the Archbishop of Mexico presiding on a great gilded throne.
This is indeed a noble apartment; it has an open groined roof,

and around the walls are portraits of suffragan bishops of Mexico —copies only, for the originals are hung in a sort of secret chamber, to which I was subsequently conducted. This chamber was approached through the gates of a side altar, and the cicerone touched a—to me—invisible spring; a door of maximum thickness slowly opened to admit us to a sort of crypt, with formidably barred windows, around which hang the original portraits of the bishops from first to last, in splendid preservation. In this apartment was a massive oaken table, with a sort of funnel in the middle of it. It is on this table that the offerings of the faithful, after a collection, are deposited, counted, and dropped through the funnel into huge, grim-looking, iron-bound boxes, which stood about the room.

During my stay in Mexico excavations were being made in front of the cathedral to convert the paved ground into a garden, and but a few feet below the surface some octagonal columns of the first church were discovered; also two heads of large stone serpents, some ten feet long, and five feet in depth and in thickness; the carving of the feathered ornaments on the heads was perfect; they had originally been the capitals to the door-posts of the pagan temple of Montezuma, and these interesting fragments of both temple and primitive church were conveyed with much labour and care to the National Museum. An additional hall is at present being built there for the reception of the large Aztec archæological remains which are unearthed from day to day.

I must not conclude this rather long account without mentioning the large stone on which the marvellous Aztec Calendar is engraved, and which is appropriately placed in the base of the left-hand tower, though I shall describe it fully in a future chapter.

In addition to the cathedral there are forty-six churches in the city, all large, lofty, and ornamented with towers and domes. The Profesa adjoins the Hotel Gillow; this is the church in favour with the upper classes of society, and during Lent it was crowded with all the rank and fashion of the city. Black dresses were at that season *de rigueur* for the ladies. How preferable this style to the Parisian fashion of the day, in which the ladies appeared a few hours later at the shops in the Calle de Plateros. San Fernando is near the cemetery containing the graves and monuments of most of the noted men of the Republic, including that erected to the memory of President Juarez—the tombs of Generals Miramon and Mejia, who were shot in company with the ill-fated Maximilian, are also here; San Diego, Santa Teresa, the Jesus, founded by Cortes—under the altar of which rest the ashes of the conqueror, brought hither from Spain, where he died—are interesting. Nor must I omit the Sagrario, the church with the rich carved façades adjoining the cathedral, with which it connects by a large door, and in effect seems to form a portion of the larger edifice, as the congregations crowd in and out of either church to visit their favourite shrines and altars. There are thirteen large parish churches. In every case it seemed to me that the fine proportions of the buildings were somewhat dwarfed by the tawdry tinsel ornaments hung all over the walls.

There are also six Protestant churches, all beautiful buildings, either originally Catholic churches with groined roofs, or parts of convents converted to their present uses. Bishop Riley has a large Episcopal cathedral in the Calle San Francisco, with a lovely garden approach to it. The Rev. John Butler has roofed in the quadrangle of an old convent in the Calle de Gante for the Methodist Episcopal congregation, and the Rev. Mr. Patterson has two large groined-roofed apartments devoted to the services of the Presbyterian church. But the work of the Protestant churches merits a separate chapter.

The Catholic churches at Puebla, Pachuca, Tula, Tulancingo, and other towns I visited, are relatively as large and impressive as those in the city of Mexico.

From the church on the top of the pyramid of Cholula—some six or eight miles from Puebla—I counted thirty-four sacred edifices, some eight or ten at the foot of the pyramid, the towers and domes of the others dotting the adjacent country. There is scarcely a church anywhere from the portals of which you cannot see four or five other churches.

In our early morning rides from the city of Mexico Mr. Neyt frequently proposed a dash across country from church to church, this being perfectly practicable, as our horses would jump anything, and the only danger being from soft, treacherous ground on the banks of some of the deep watercourses. From the high ground behind Tacubaya we discovered several routes back to the city, these routes leading from chapel to church, and none of them roads.

It is rather difficult for a Protestant to describe faithfully the ceremonies, the changes of decoration, the music and the ordinary incidents which are daily to be witnessed in the churches during Lent, without offending the tender consciences of enlightened Catholics, the very last thing I should wish to do.

When the Catholic religion was first introduced into the country, the ceremonies were probably arranged to attract the sympathies and feelings of the Pagan natives; and, sad to say, after three hundred years of complete rule and guidance, the people have not been instructed nor elevated in religious thought in any way. The Christian doctrine of the New Testament is exhibited to the nation in a realistic rather than a spiritual manner; for instance, in the church of San Domingo during Holy Week I saw a medium-sized household bed placed in the centre of the floor, and, on it, partly concealed by bed-clothes, was a most ghastly representation of a Christ carved of wood, the flesh torn and discoloured; over it stood a figure of the Mater Dolorosa, clothed in rich black velvet, with an embroidered lace pocket-handkerchief in her hand, probably the offering of some lady for the occasion. The Virgin's dress was changed every day;

BISHOP RILEY'S PROTESTANT CATHEDRAL.
CALLE SAN FRANCISCO

some days it was black satin or lace; life-sized figures of weeping angels and of the apostles were occasionally added to the group.

In other churches I noticed equally realistic representations of the Crucifixion, and details of that terrible tragedy which in various ways affects us all so deeply.

Hundreds of people of the lower class knelt for hours round and before these representations of sacred scenes, while Mass was being celebrated at the altar; and in the large music gallery, which is found at the west end of all sacred edifices, an orchestra of some twenty instruments would render the airs of a favourite opera, to which parts of the service had been set. In fact, the Church seems to allow any description of music in its services. One or more grand pianos always stood in the large choirs, and this was the only instrument used in many of the country churches. At Toluca I heard the music of "Madame Angot," including the Conspirators' March, also the music of "La Favorita," during the celebration of a Mass which was attended by several hundred young men and boys from the college and school adjoining the cathedral.

Some of the city and many of the country churches are in a very dilapidated condition, and are used only on special fête-days, when the congregation are endangered by the falling of a brick or two from the roof. All the roofs are vaulted with brick; I never saw a timbered roof covered with slate or stone, as at home.

Until the year 1860 nearly one half of the city of Mexico consisted of convents and ecclesiastical buildings, which the governments of the Republic have confiscated and partly pulled down for city improvements. Several of the old churches, as I have already mentioned, have been utilised for public libraries. The new National Library in the church of San Agustin, at present being organised under the head librarian, Señor Vigil, promises to be in every respect a magnificent institution.

Old ecclesiastical buildings are also convertible into excellent stables and storehouses. I kept my horse in a large livery stable, sometime the refectory of a convent, and Mr. Neyt's horses were stabled in a similar building. One word more about the churches; I never contemplated any of these magnificent buildings without thinking of the amount of misery and death entailed on the poor Mexican Indians employed in their construction. Called forth by their conquerors by thousands, they were compelled to work for the bare dole of food that would sustain life. Some of these edifices, notably the cathedrals of Mexico and Puebla and the church at Tula, are constructed of large blocks of stone, most neatly and accurately laid and jointed, evidencing that the natives were not only well instructed, but that they were ably overlooked as to their work. A majority of the churches were built of rough, partly-dressed stone, thickly stuccoed and ornamented with cement—a cement which seems to stand the ravages of the wet season more stoutly than does the woodwork of the windows.

The Church of Mexico has been all-powerful from its commencement; it may be said to be the government, the magistracy, the army and, the master of the homes. Everything in Mexico has been subservient to its dictadura. The priesthood has been entirely free from the national courts of law, they have had courts of their own, and the *fueros,* or privileges and prerogatives of the ecclesiastics, placed them entirely beyond the reach of secular power. They levied taxes and tithes of everybody and everything they had a mind to. The extent to which the clergy accumulated wealth is almost incredible; they are said to have possessed three-fourths of the whole property of the country, consisting of lands and other real estate, rents, mortgages, conventual buildings and church ornaments. Moreover, there were no bankers in Mexico, except the clergy, so they had complete power over the estates as well as the souls of the people.

As the priesthood, the military officers, the Spanish nobility, and the wealthy generally, acted in concert, their despotism over the people must have been absolute.

In 1850 Señor Lerdo de Tejara, Ministro de Fomento, or Minister of Public Works, published a statistical account of the revenues and endowments of the Church, with the numbers of the clergy, monks, nuns and servants connected with the religious establishments; the details he gives, like the evidence of the existing churches, and the remains of the disused ones all over the country, quite support his statement that the Church was possessed of three-fourths of the property of the State.

Now, from the spiritual point of view, what is there to show for all this power and wealth? Are the people better off, better housed, more comfortable, happier, better mentally and physically than they were in the days of Montezuma? Undoubtedly they are; but until lately the change has been little, owing to the darkness and thraldom in which they had been kept by the Spanish Church and rule; it was lucky for the Mexican people that the spark of patriotism and liberty burst into the flame which freed them from their oppressors; thenceforward, responsible before God and the world, they might prove their capacity for making themselves a thriving and respected nationality.

CHAPTER IX.

PROTESTANT CHURCHES.

Persecution of Protestants—Bishop Riley's and other Protestant Churches—
Experiences of Mission Work at Tula—Sufferings of Country Ministers—
Missionaries.

AT the present time, both in England and in America, a great
deal of interest is felt in the development of Protestant Churches
in Mexico. By the law of the land religious liberty is granted
to all, even to the Mormons, whose missionary bishop I, had the
pleasure of meeting several times; and the liberal government of
the Republic not unwillingly assists and quietly encourages the
development of Protestantism as a set-off to the aggressive
attitude of the Catholic Church.*

In Mexico City and the other principal towns of the country
Protestant congregations can hold their services, and their schools
can be conducted without molestation; but it is not so in the
small towns and country districts, where the Catholic priests
excite their congregations to annoy the Protestants in every
way in their power.

Very soon after my arrival in Mexico I made the acquaintance

* After the Republic became established, the civil authorities confiscated the
various religious houses of the Franciscans and Dominicans, and the churches
attached to them, and, indeed, all the property of the religious orders. This step
was positively necessary for the security of the Republic, as the ecclesiastics of the
Roman Church, the Jesuits, the inmates of the convents and monasteries, even the
servitors and dependents of the ecclesiastical establishments, had allied themselves
to the party opposed to the Republic and in favour of Imperial rule.

of Dr. Riley, who has devoted the greater part of his life and fortune to furthering the work and extension of the Episcopal Church.

He has obtained by purchase from the government two or more magnificent old churches, notably one in the Street of San Francisco; and he has established excellent schools, and an embryo college for the education of young men destined for the ministry. There is also an orphanage for young girls, under the management of Mrs. Hooper, which is attached to Bishop Riley's communion.

He kindly devoted as much time as he could spare from his duties in showing me this and kindred institutions under his charge. We occasionally rode out on horseback together on the *paséo*, when the conversation generally turned to the work in which he is so much interested.

Close to Bishop Riley's cathedral, and in buildings that once formed part of the convent attached to it, the Rev. John Butler, of the American Methodist Episcopal denomination, has roofed over the *patio* or court of the convent as a place of worship, which, with several large halls and rooms, and a pretty entrance way from the Callé de Gante, affords him space for schools and an orphanage, which seem to be ably managed by Miss Elliot.

There is another large Protestant congregation under the name of Union Protestant, or Presbyterian, of which the Rev. J. Patterson is the pastor; and, finally, the name of a fourth congregation—that of the Southern Methodists—bears evidence of its origin in a secession from the Northern Methodists at the time of the late Civil War in the United States; but now, as the strong antagonistic feelings engendered by the war are happily fast dying out, the two bodies are again working in harmony.

The three reverend gentlemen I have named were very agreeable, superior men, and, as the two latter were married and blessed with charming wives, who gave excellent afternoon teas,

I was an occasional visitor at their houses, and heard a great deal of their doings.

All these clergymen stated that the writings and pamphlets of Dr. Ryle, the Bishop of Liverpool, which had been disseminated through the country, had been the principal means of extending Protestantism there; and where I visited the schools, or was introduced to the local missionaries, Bishop Ryle's name was always uppermost, and I was requested, whenever I had an opportunity, to convey to him the blessings and thanks of one and all.

These gentlemen had to pay frequent visits to the country districts. It was with Mr. Patterson that I went to Tula, where he had a congregation on the ground floor of a house on the Plaza. On the Sunday morning a native minister conducted the usual Presbyterian form of service, in the Spanish language, with a congregation of some thirty or forty persons; several hymns were sung to the accompaniment of a harmonium. There was a crowded market being held at the time some twenty yards from the windows, and a number of young fellows were attracted to the windows by the music, and jeered and extracted great amusement from what was going on. One or two of the merriest-looking young market-men got rather excited and threatening, and, though I was behind the iron bars of the open windows, I had some misgivings that I was risking more than was called for in attending the service, especially as we had from twenty to thirty miles to ride the next day, over an unfrequented piece of country; and I knew from previous experience that Mr. Patterson would distribute Protestant tracts to every one he met.

The persecutions of Protestants in country districts was real enough; some eight or ten people were killed during my stay. They were worshipping in a small chapel, and were set upon by a violent mob, and killed. When the government sent to make inquiry into the circumstance, the Jefe Politico, or chief magistrate of the district, who sympathised with the mob, suggested that the ringleaders should absent themselves from the district for a time; consequently no one was brought to justice.

On Monday, the 20th of June, 1881, Mr. Ober and I accompanied the Rev. John Butler to Texcoco. We wanted to see the ruins and the archæological discoveries lately made there. Mr. Butler had another object. One of his local native preachers, Camilo Ariata, in the town of San Vicente Chicolopam, had been thrown into prison.

The report was that he had taken a Protestant child a few months old for burial in the Catholic cemetery, which by law is open to all denominations, but the priest and his people had objected and raised a tumult, and some shots were fired at the preacher; the shots, as he reported, apparently coming from a group of women who were very much excited. Some hours later he was arrested on the plea of having fired at them, and he was taken to the prison at Texcoco, some five or six miles distant.

We visited the man in the prison; he was a fine-looking elderly man, but had lost an eye. In the midst of the rascals with whom he was incarcerated he seemed very quiet and perfectly self-possessed; he assured us he had never carried or fired a pistol in his life. His trial was going on in another part of the building, where the local judge and his secretary were hearing what the witnesses on both sides had to say, the prisoner himself not being present nor knowing anything of the proceedings.

Mr. Butler waited on the magistrate and presented a letter he had brought from the Minister of Justice, begging that the case might be adjudicated upon with as little delay as possible; and we returned home in the evening.

I frequently afterwards asked Mr. Butler how the case had ended. Ariata was kept in prison three weeks and then liberated; in the meantime the Jefe Politico had conciliated the Church party by drafting off several men of Ariata's congregation as soldiers; this was quite unlawful, the men in question being married, respectable householders with families.

During the whole period of Ariata's three weeks of incarceration, two of his congregation by turns had kept watch and never lost sight of the prison door, fearing the plan might be adopted of removing him to another prison, when the probability was that the pistol of one of the guards would go off accidentally (?) on the road, and Ariata would be heard of no more.

At the risk of wearying the reader, I have given this rather prolonged account, because while in Mexico I continually heard of such cases of persecution, and this one came directly under my own observation.

I saw Ariata after his release: he said he feared further persecution, and he asked Mr. Butler whether it would not be well for the sake of the congregation that he should be removed to another district; at the same time he said he was prepared to do his duty anywhere.

On our way to Texcoco we had stopped for breakfast at Ariata's chapel at San Vicente Chicolopam; his wife had provided us with an excellent meal in the school-house, and some dozen children who were present repeated to us some hymns and selections they had learned; they appeared as orderly and well-behaved as if Ariata's eye were upon them.

The chapel and school-house had been built at the sole expense of some American gentleman, and as it was in too confined a space to be well photographed, I endeavoured to make a traveller's sketch of it to be sent by Mr. Butler to the founder, who had asked for a picture of the edifice.

Mr. Morgan, the United States Minister, told me that cases of persecution in country districts were frequently brought under his notice, and all he could do was to forward the particulars to the Minister of Justice. Missionary work, whether in civilised or uncivilised communities, must bear its cross. I have, at every opportunity in my journey round the world, investigated as far

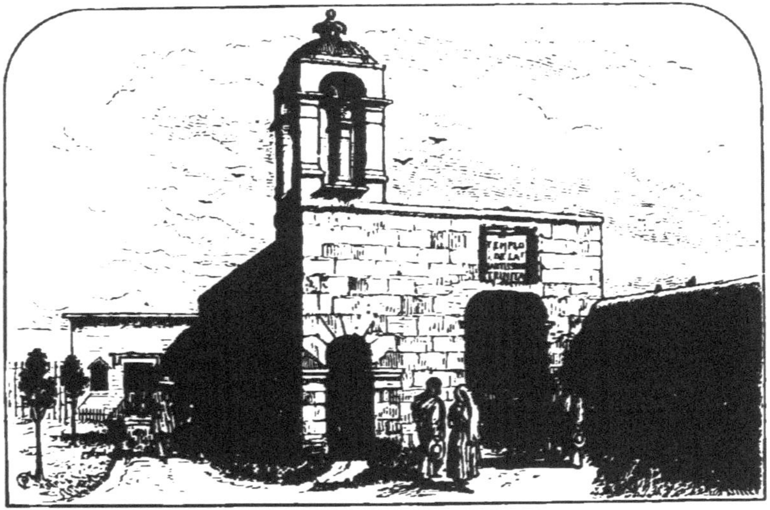

ABIATA'S METHODIST CHAPEL AT SAN VICENTE CHICOLOPAM.

as I was able the work and operations of missions; my investigations have led me to the conclusion that many missionaries are inadequately instructed for their noble work. I can cite cases in India and Japan where positive harm is being done; the money would be better spent in our crowded cities at home.

I am sure that many well-meaning and truly Christian people, who give largely to foreign missions, would agree with me, if they saw the very small amount of good that results from the inexperience and utter want of tact of a majority of the missionaries.

The services in Bishop Riley's cathedral are in Spanish, as the congregation is composed of Spaniards and Mexicans. It is a very interesting form of service, being a judicious modification of the services of the English and American Episcopal churches. The singing of the choir and children sounds wonderfully well in the spacious cathedral. There were about 200 persons present at the Sunday services, and a fair number at the weekly morning services. One thing was particularly noticeable in all the Protestant places of worship: the people were as quiet and devout in outward appearance as they are in the Catholic churches. Moreover, they were exceedingly clean and neat. The women's hair was beautifully braided, as could be seen when they slipped off the light shawl which they wore mantilla fashion.

The services in all the other Protestant churches in the city were generally in Spanish, sometimes in English, and both the gentlemen and ladies of the congregations seemed to do their duty very fairly in the schools and at the Bible-classes.

An Episcopal service in English was held every Sunday morning in a large, quaint room in the Callé de la Independencia, supported by a few American and English families, residents of the city; and in the same room, every Monday evening, Bishop Riley presided over a school entertainment where music, recitations, and good management brought together several hundred people, Catholic as well as Protestant.

I am sorry to say that the Protestant community in Mexico, to whose labours I wish every success, is not free from ecclesiastical prejudices. Bishop Riley is, I am convinced, a very good man; but his attitude towards the other Protestant denominations is not a kindly one.

There was a most melancholy exhibition of this on the occasion of the funeral service of the lamented President Garfield, which had to be held in the church of the Rev. John Butler, and was attended by all the Corps Diplomatique, and every American and Englishman in the city; the members of the German musical club, greatly to their honour, coming in a large body to sing several appropriate pieces of music. This service was held in Mr. Butler's church because the bishop would not associate himself with the other ministers in his own, nor did he assist in Mr. Butler's. The result was altogether most unfortunate, because it nearly broke up the little English Episcopal service, the American minister and several prominent families absenting themselves from it during the remainder of my stay.

The co-existence of several small communities of differing Protestants exhibiting feelings of animosity towards each other in a purely Catholic country is a source of great weakness, as it affords the Catholic priests an opportunity of cautioning their flocks against joining a body which is so divided in itself.

CHAPTER X.

Gay appearance of the Streets—The Paséo de la Viga during Lent—Catching Cattle with the Lasso—The large Trees at Chapultepec—The Battle of Mulino del Rey.

IF I were endowed with the power to paint in words my walks and rides about the city of Mexico and its environs, as Mr. Augustus Hare has described Rome and excursions from it, the result would be eminently satisfactory to the reader.

A clear, unclouded atmosphere at an elevation of 8000 feet above the level of the sea in the tropics puts everything *couleur de rose*. There is no heat, no cold; the average temperature is about 60°, and the atmosphere is so clear that when you see the mountains at the ends of the streets they appear close at hand, instead of being from twenty to forty miles distant.

All the houses in the city have a gay appearance; such as are not white or light yellow or green are tinted with various shades of red, and many of the churches may be pronounced pink; three or four hundred yards of a street in pink has a pretty effect, especially if continued in pale green; a house in grey stone adjoining another faced with blue encaustic tiles is, to say the least, pleasing to the eye of any one who for months past has only gazed upon dwellings of dull-red brick. As you get into the outskirts of the city the houses are meaner, but many of them are festooned with flowers and wreaths, so the appearance of beauty is maintained, even if on close inspection it is found delusive.

One of the three principal rides out of the city is the Paséo

de la Reforma, three miles in length, leading to the castle of
Chapultepec; here the gay world disports itself from seven
to nine in the morning on horseback, and from six to seven
in the evening in carriages; but it is deserted during Lent for
the Paséo de la Viga, where three or four military bands discourse
excellent music; the wide canal of Chalco, which runs along
the roadside, is gay with boats; and during the *fiesta* it requires
many mounted police to keep the crowd of carriages, equestrians
and pedestrians on their respective lines. The Thursdays are
red-letter days on this paséo; they are regular carnivals, and the
gentlemen indulge in the vanities of silver mountings of every
description on their clothes and horse trappings. I saw some
saddles and embroidered saddle-cloths worth from one to two
thousand dollars apiece. It afforded me intense pleasure to see
the poor people come out, as well as the rich, and enjoy the
scene; they were seated in crowds under the trees on both sides of
the way. It is the custom for this beautiful avenue, ornamented
with the fine bust of the Aztec hero, Guatemotzin, and a pretty
lodge and bridge at the end of the drive, to be thronged daily
during Lent, and virtually deserted for the remainder of the year.

The road to Guadalupe, which is the third of the principal
rides, is less frequented than the road to Tacuba, and to the
"Noche Triste" tree. But it is a charming gallop of three miles,
and one on which I very frequently took a breather. The tramcars on the roadside, carrying people out to the shrine of Guadalupe, may prove a nuisance to the *beau monde*.

Mr. Neyt assisted me during our morning rides in exploring
the picturesque and well-constructed roads, lined with superb
trees, which run in all directions out of the city. The Spaniards
have left their best mark in the making of these fine causeways,
which in some places are carried high and dry above lands
submerged in water during the rainy season. When we discovered a new road, we usually declared it finer than anything
we had seen before. The magnificent trees on either side of

these roads are fair indications that these causeways had been constructed two or three hundred years.

Upon one occasion on our way to Tacubaya we saw a man on horseback trying to lasso three bulls which had strayed from their pastures. It was as wild and amusing a chase as if they had been on the open prairie, indeed, more so, on account of jumping of ditches, and bolting through fences; we joined in the chase, and witnessed the whole operation. The manner in which the rider's horse understands when the bull is lassoed is marvellous; he sticks out his feet and stands as firm as a post, while the lariat or rope is tightened on the pommel of the saddle. A bull that has once been lassoed knows on a second occasion that he is a prisoner, and after a few efforts to release himself submits quietly to his fate.

The principal ride is to the castle of Chapultepec, and as it is the first ride every visitor is sure to take, he will be interested to learn that the building on the summit of the porphyry rock, visible from all parts of the valley, stands on the site of the palace of Montezuma; * it is known as the Hill of the Grasshopper in old Aztec charts, and is always drawn on their hieroglyphics as a mound, with a grasshopper as large as the mound itself on the top of it.

Nothing remains of the grandeur which marked the place in Montezuma's time except the avenues of enormous cypress trees (*Cupressus distica*) beneath whose shades were the gardens where he loved to wander, even after his beloved capital had fallen into the rude hands of the invading Spaniards.

I measured the girth of several of these trees, and found three or four of the largest to vary from thirty-five to forty feet at five

---

* Humboldt says that the hill of Chapultepec was chosen by the young Viceroy Galvez as the site of a villa (Château de Plaisance) for himself and his successors. The castle has been finished externally, but the apartments are not yet furnished. This building cost the king £62,000. The Court of Madrid disapproved of the expense, but, as usual, after it was laid out. The plan of this edifice is very singular. The common opinion at Mexico is that the house of the viceroy at Chapultepec is a disguised fortress.

feet above the ground. Their height was proportionately grand, 100 to 120 feet, and the trees are well shaped. Long festoons of a greyish Spanish moss hang from their branches; this moss is supposed to add to the beauty of the groves, but it gives me an idea of decay.

In Prescott's fourth book there is a graphic account of Montezuma's town and country palaces of barbaric splendour; his armouries, his granaries, his strange collection of human monsters and dwarfs, his menageries, and the aviary, which alone required three hundred attendants; the royal household is described, and in proof of the luxury of the royal table, it is mentioned that there were runners stationed every twenty miles the whole distance from Vera Cruz to Mexico, that the red mullets might be placed fresh and sweet upon his table; it is said that the runners brought up these delicacies from the coast in quicker time than the present railway can accomplish.* No one can doubt the truth of the description of his magnificence who has beheld the trees that are still standing along the avenues of what was once his royal garden. From the terrace in front of his palace he saw the snow-capped mountains Popocatapetl and Ixtaccihuatl, and the city of Mexico, entirely surrounded by the waters of Lake Texcoco, glittering at his feet; the Pinion de los Baños, Pinion del Marques, Santa Catharina, and San Nicholas, all small craters or volcanic cones; and to the right the hill called Estrella, on which the sacred fire was always burning, till the 26th of December, every fifty-second year.

At these intervals the fire of every temple and house was extinguished, and the people, abandoning themselves to despair, tore their garments and destroyed their furniture, as their priests taught them that it was probable that the world would be destroyed. The ceremony was terrible; a noble victim was

---

* For the rapid conveyance of news, towers were erected at intervals of six miles along the high roads, where couriers were always in waiting for dispatches, which were transferred from hand to hand at each stage.

sacrificed, and it was not till after midnight, when the constellation Pleiades had passed the zenith, that the priests announced
that the world was again saved. The sacred fire kindled by the
friction of sticks placed in the wounded breast of the victim was
conveyed to the altar, when the blaze of the funeral pyre
announced the glad tidings of joy to the countless multitudes
looking on from every part of the valley; these thereupon gave
themselves up to transports of delight, and kept the Carnival or
national jubilee, which lasted twelve or thirteen days. New fire
was then carried by fleet runners from the altar of Estrella to
every part of the kingdom.

There is an idea of stability in the Scriptural phrase " everlasting hills." The " everlasting hills " are before me; the aspect of
the valley has been changed. Lake Texcoco has been withdrawn
a mile or two from the city; the domes and spires of the city are
different from the Teocalli and palace of Montezuma; and the
palace of Chapultepec, in front of which I am standing, has been
rebuilt several times by Spanish Viceroys. The present building
was erected so lately as 1785; it is a kind of gilt pagoda on a
castellated basement, and the rooms were decorated by Maximilian,
its last occupant, with coarse Pompeian arabesques. These are
changes, but Popocatapetl and Ixtaccihuatl rear their snow-capped
heads as they did before man counted time.

At the back of the castle, looking over the large cypress-trees
on the pleasaunce below, is seen the high ground on which the
battle of Molino del Rey (the king's mill) was fought in
August, 1847, between the American army under General Scott
and the Mexican army under General Santa Anna. The large
flour mill and other buildings bear marks of shot and shell, and
the centre of the battlefield is indicated by a square marble
pedestal, on which are inscribed the names of the Mexican officers
who fell on the field.

This was the last battle of the war which arose out of the
secession of the territory of Texas from Mexico in order to become

one of the North American States.　General Scott being victorious over the Mexicans, the treaty of peace—known as the treaty of Guadalupe Hidalgo—was ratified in the early part of 1848, by which the Americans obtained the territories of Texas, New Mexico and Upper California.　Arizona was subsequently bought from Santa Anna by the treaty of Messilla for $10,000,000.

On the left of Chapultepec lies the pretty suburban village of Tacubaya, in which are situated the summer residences of the wealthy inhabitants of the city; there is a pretty residence built by Mr. Jameson, a rich Englishman, now the property of Don Antonio Mier y Celis; but the two principal houses are those of Messrs. Baron and Escandon, which, with their treasures of art, are occasionally thrown open to the public.　I had a letter of introduction to the Escandon family, and the two young gentlemen, Don Miquel and Don Pablo, showed me polite attention. Don Pablo's great pleasure lies in horses and the handling of them; morning noon and night he was to be seen in the saddle or on wheels, and he appeared to be always breaking in new horses.

On the third day after my arrival he drove me out from the city to their villa at Tacubaya, where, after spending a pleasant afternoon, we returned in the dusk of the evening, outside a four-in-hand, with several friends.　Between Tacubaya and Chapultepec we were fired upon by some miscreants at the road-side.　I was sitting on the seat behind the driver, and some of our party said they heard the whiz of the bullets close to our heads.　As there were four servants on the back seats of the coach armed to the teeth, I naturally asked why they did not fire back, to which Don Pablo replied, "Oh, we have escaped; nobody is hurt; and it is wiser not to return the fire; they are probably drunken people and don't know what they are doing."　I did not feel the slightest alarm, and, strange to say, during my seven months' residence in the country this was the only occasion upon which I was in any way attacked; and I presume I owed this attack to being in such well-known wealthy company.

CHAPTER XI.

Pulque, or Mexican Beer—The Cultivation of the Maguey or Mexican Aloe—Fermentation of the Juice—Intoxicating Spirit—The Unveiling of a Monument by the President—The Noche Triste—Village Fêtes.

A FEW days after the escape mentioned in the last chapter, Don Pablo took me out in an open carriage and pair to one of their large haciendas and initiated me into some of the mysteries of Mexican farming. A coachman drove; Don Pablo, Mr. Killion, and I rode inside, each having a loaded rifle and a brace of pistols, and Don Pablo exhibiting evident symptoms of anxiety while we passed through several villages. As the family are the wealthiest bankers and proprietors in the country, the only reason I could assign for so much precaution was that a member of the family might be kidnapped for the sake of the heavy ransom which the relatives were sure to pay for his release. The road we were travelling was crowded with Escandon carts, loaded mules and workpeople. Don Pablo assured me there was an impression made by exhibiting firearms which increased our safety; it would probably prevent any intended attack.

The estate is several miles in extent, and produces Indian corn, barley, wheat, vetches (several crops annually of these last, under a system of irrigation), various kinds of beans, magueys, or Mexican aloes, and building stone of excellent quality. The farm buildings are very extensive and enclosed within high walls, with large, massive doors.

The hacienda is to some extent fortified, and there are

sentinels posted on the roof night and day. All the details of the farm were most interesting, but as I must give a special chapter on Mexican farming later on, I will now confine myself to the production and preparation of pulque, as I devoted my attention to this more than to other matters on the farm, on this, the first opportunity I had of seeing it.

Pulque is made from the maguey, or Mexican aloe (*Agave Mexicana*), and is the national beverage of the country. In appearance it resembles thin buttermilk; it has a sourish taste, with just a suspicion of spirituous flavour, and more than a suspicion of Harrowgate water. It is consumed out of wooden vessels scrupulously clean, shaped somewhat like a pint or quart measure, and is tossed off like beer or XX. The taste for it is an acquired one, and foreigners are broken in on "pulque compresto," that is, pulque with a dash of raspberry, strawberry, banana, or some other fruit juice introduced.

Pulque affords an enormous revenue to the government. Two special pulque trains arrive in the city each day from the direction of Apam, where the best pulque is said to be produced.

On arriving at the hacienda, my host took me at once into the maguey fields, where it became necessary to be very careful of the great scimitar-blade-shaped leaves of the plant, which stood in some portions of the ground as high as ten and fifteen feet, with bayonet-like thorns confronting me on all sides.

We were accompanied by a *tlachiquero*, a man whose business it is to suck up the *agua miel*, or juice of the aloe, through a siphon made of a large gourd with a cow's horn at the end of it, and called *acajete ;* this acajete, together with a raspador—a sort of harpoon-shaped knife, with a scoop in the blade—is attached by a chain to the belt of the *tlachiquero*. Behind, trudges a brace of donkeys, their backs laden with the *corambe,* or sheep skins, into which the *agua miel* is poured, after being sucked up into the siphons. The plant is prevented from flowering at ten years of age, the date at which it yields pulque, and during its growth it throws out shoots or young plants which are removed from the parent plant when about three feet high, that is, after two years' growth. These are planted out at distances of a yard apart; later also transplanting takes place according to the condition of the plant.

The *tlachiquero* goes periodically amongst his vegetable cows, and marks those fit for milking by cutting a cross on the top of the highest stalk of each plant. When the maguey is fit for milking, the *tlachiquero*, dexterously thrusting aside the spiky stalks, cuts out the *meyolote* or central spike, leaving a *cajete*, or cavity, which he visits after the expiration of eight days to find it full of *agua miel*. The plants only begin to yield the juice (called *agua miel* on account of the saccharine principle in which it abounds) when the flower stalk is on the point of its development. It is on this account of the greatest importance for the cultivator to know exactly the period of efflorescence.

Humboldt says this is discovered by the direction of the radical leaves, which are observed by the natives with much attention. These leaves which are till then inclined towards the earth, rise all of a sudden, and endeavour to form a junction, to cover the flower spike which is on the point of formation. The bundle of central leaves becomes at the same time of a clearer green. The *tlachiquero* is never deceived by these signs, but there are others of no less importance, which cannot be precisely described, because they have merely a reference to the carriage of the plant. The cultivator, or his *tlachiquero* must go daily through the maguey plantations to mark those plants which approach efflorescence.

I watched the process with considerable interest; the sight was novel and intensely picturesque. The *tlachiquero*, with his dark skin and white dress, his immense straw *sombréro*, his leather apron, and the implements of his profession hanging by his side, sucked up the juice into the gourd, and poured it into the sheepskins upon the back of the patient donkey at his side. These sheepskins last only about two months; they cost twelve reals, or about six shillings each. Here is a chance for an inventor; why not introduce indiarubber, or some less perishable material?

The maguey, after the expiration of eight days, is milked regularly three times a day, viz. at three A.M., seven A.M., and three P.M., it yields over a gallon a day, and is milked for three months, each plant producing in round numbers about 120 gallons before it dies. This abundance of juice is so much the more astonishing as the maguey plantations are in the most arid ground, and frequently on banks of rocks hardly covered with vegetable earth. Humboldt says the cultivation of the maguey has real advantage over the cultivation of maize, grain and potatoes. The plant, with firm and vigorous leaves, is neither affected by drought nor by hail, nor by occasional severe frosts, which destroy the less hardy crops.

We proceeded from plant to plant until the sheepskins on the donkeys' backs were filled; then we returned to the *tinacal*, or place where the "pulque" is made—a large fine barn, the earthen floor clean as the deck of a man-of-war. It was filled with square wooden frames, on which were stretched cowhides, shaped like vats, the hairy sides upwards. The liquid seemed to curdle in process of fermentation, and smelt very badly. The cowhides with their frames are called "tinas." The rotten curds are fed three times a day—in other words, after each milking—with *agua miel*, this ferments for about three hours, and from the tina is drawn into barrels for the pulquerias, or gaudily adorned public-houses where pulque is sold, and which are to be found at the corners of almost every street in Mexico. In many cases it is carried about the country in sheepskins, on the stalwart shoulders of peripatetic pedlars.

We entered the *tinacal* in a sort of procession, each one on entering exclaiming "Alabo á Dios;" "I praise God," as he reverently removed his hat. The donkeys remained on the

PULQUE TLACHIQUERO.   [page 82.

threshold, and the agua-miel-laden sheepskins were carefully brought in on the backs of Indians one by one. When the orifice of the sheepskin was opened and the liquor ready for pouring out, the *tlaqualero*, or "boss" pulque maker, of the *tinacal* took the *meneador*, a long stake or switch from the corner, and, making the sign of the cross in the rotten curds, reverently exclaimed, "Ave Maria purísima," to which the Indian devoutly responded, "Alabado sea Dios y la Santísima Trinidad." Then the Indian proceeded to pour the contents of his sheepskin into a great vessel held over the "tina" by a man who cries, "Uno! dos! tres!" etc., as he turns the contents into the "tina."

On a large hacienda like this, the rocky dry lands which are unfit for cultivation and the hedgerows are appropriated to the maguey plant; on a thousand acres a million plants of all ages may be flourishing, of which 300,000 will be maturing plants, five to six years old; 15,000 will yield pulque annually, 4000 of them producing daily an average of 3500 gallons, worth, at seven cents a gallon, $24·5.

Apam, a city at the edge of the plain, produces the best pulque, and in great quantities. They can sell, in the city of Mexico, fifty quarts for a dollar, say eight cents a gallon.

The government receives a thousand dollars daily in duty on pulque brought into the city of Mexico, and the railway companies a similar sum in freight. I made several attempts to drink it, but it was impossible. A mixture of sour buttermilk and Harrogate water would be preferable; and I am not alone in my dislike, as Humboldt describes it as a vinous beverage resembling cider, with an odour of putrid meat, extremely disagreeable. The Indians are passionately fond of it, they throng the *pulquerias* on Sundays and holidays, and consume it to excess. Some few get intoxicated and lose the use of their legs; the spirit does not rise to the head to do any harm, beyond making them merry, but a man seems to lose all control over his legs, and has to sit down in the street or at the roadside until he regains their use. I never saw them brawling or fighting, but if they get the fiery spirit called "mescal"—distilled from a different kind of maguey—I am told it renders them wild and furious, and is as bad in its effects on them as "Jersey lightning" is on an American, or vitriolised gin in our own country. If they get really drunk and quarrel, they have it out with their knives ; wrapping the *zarepa* tightly around the left arm, the combatant takes his *sombréro* in his left hand, and whirls it about so as to dazzle and bewilder his opponent, the *macheta*, or knife, gleaming in his right hand.

After a long morning's experience of pulque-making, and an inspection of the fat cattle in the yards, I asked to see the labourers' cottages, which are in lines beyond the farm buildings. Each family, large or small, had a room some sixteen feet square, which seemed to be equally shared in by the family, the poultry and the pig ; luckily the climate enables them to live mostly out of doors. I was rather amused by my young host saying the *hacienda* really belonged to a lady member of the family, who, when she came to visit the estate, was most interested to see that all the *peons* (labourers) attended Mass in the beautiful chapel in the *hacienda*, but he thought she had never been to look at the labourers' homes. How easy it is to form good resolutions when one is a long way from the scene of duty ! I remember many cottages I had seen in England on large estates that were hardly what they ought to be, though sometimes within a stone's throw was the palace of the landlord. I think I have one or two, which I then and there resolved I would at once visit if ever I reached home again. Our new English system of sanitary inspection of labourers' cottages has done good work in bringing some few evils into notice.

I will turn from the cottages and their surroundings to the garden in the courtyard of the *hacienda*, where stood two towering cypress trees, whose mark on the clear azure sky was visible from every part of the estate, and with a little whitewashed belfry below them, looking like a pearl on blue satin, reminded me of something similar I had seen under an Italian sky.

If the choice of roads was left to me in our early morning rides, I generally chose a direction which would bring us out upon the high ground at the back of Chapultepec. There was always a breeze on these hills, or the air seemed fresher than that on the plain : we often found more open galloping ground, and the view extended to the greater portion of the valley, the distant lakes beyond the city glittering in the sunshine. If possible, we struck Tacubaya either going or returning.

There is a large military school there, in a building that was once an archiepiscopal palace, and in riding past it we were certain at any hour to see batteries of artillery, regiments of cavalry, cadets exercising, trains of baggage waggons, and all the paraphernalia of grim-visaged war.

As we returned early one morning, the President and a distinguished suite came to Chapultepec to uncover and inaugurate a handsome monument, raised to the memory of the cadets who had fallen at the battle of Molino del Rey, in defending the castle from the attack of the Americans. After many speeches had been delivered, and President Gonzales had placed a number of immortelles on the monument, he walked to his carrriage between a double line of cadets, who were ordered to face about, thus presenting their backs to the President, while they fired several *feux de joie ;* no doubt this was safer for the President and his friends, but it had an unmilitary, if not a ludicrous, effect.

The President is a wise man, for though I saw him on this and several other public occasions, I never heard him speak or utter a word, except when he opened the sessions of the legislature, and read his annual message from under a canopied throne. He always allows others to do the speechifying.

President Gonzales' appearance is prepossessing ; an open

broad countenance with black hair and thick black beard, middle height, and broad pair of shoulders. He usually wears plain civilian dress, with a broad red and green ribbon of the Republic across his expansive chest. He has but one arm, having lost the other in action. To an outside spectator he appears to make himself very genial and agreeable to his suite, maintaining at the same time quite a commanding dignity.

We had seen preparations making for the inauguration of the monument several days previously, but could not learn when the ceremony would take place, so that we were lucky in taking that morning's ride in that direction.

One of our favourite rides was across some open country which eventually landed us near Tacuba, and so on to Popotla, for the sake of looking at the celebrated tree of the "Noche Triste," under which Cortes rested some time at the end of the memorable night in 1520 when he had to evacuate his position in the capital, and save himself and his few followers, by a retreat effected under circumstances for deaths, distress, and dangers, unparalleled in the annals of his Conquest. Chapter III. of Prescott's fifth book is headed:—"Council of war—Spaniards evacuate the city—Noche Triste, or the melancholy night—Terrible slaughter—Halt for the night—Amount of losses."

The tree under which Cortes halted to watch the remnant of his followers pass by is a fine old cypress, similar to those at Chapultepec. It is preserved from depredation by an iron railing, as the tree was once set on fire by the natives, as a mark of detestation of their Spanish rulers. Prescott, in the chapter just referred to, gives a graphic description of this, the most noted episode of the Conquest. I again regret that the learned historian had never the opportunity of visiting and seeing the places he describes. It is so difficult, under the present changed aspect of the famous causeway, to find the spots where the greatest feats or most terrible sufferings took place. There were three temporary bridges on the causeway to be crossed, or rather the gaps

THE TREE OF THE NOCHE TRISTE.

[page 88.

where the bridges should have been; that over which Alvarado made the almost incredible leap is still commemorated by his name, though it is now merely a gutter or drain under the road. This and other famous places in the locality now take hours of research to find, whereas a note or two given by Prescott might have clearly indicated them. From this tree Cortes went on a mile farther to Tacuba, or Tlacopam, as it was then called, where he endeavoured to reform his disorganised battalion, and bring them to something like order. Here is still to be seen a portion of a large pyramid, on the top of which stood probably the *teocalli*, or temple, which he used as a refuge for his exhausted troops. The pyramid is being rapidly destroyed by brickmakers, who are working up the old material into new bricks.

A Sir John Lubbock's Ancient Monuments Preservation Bill is much wanted in Mexico; I myself added to the destruction of the mound by turning over several spadefuls of earth, in which I found some broken pieces of pottery and bits of obsidian, possibly bits that may have been in whole condition and in use on this very eventful night. I have given a drawing of the tree; it stands on an open green in front of a church, and seems to be the favourite perching-place for some large crows, who kept a sharp look-out on the fondas, or halting-places of the village below them; it was occasionally worth their while to swoop down upon a morsel of bread or meat, which the chattering wayfarers had dropped on the way to their mouths; there was much broken garbage on the road through the village, as it was the last rendezvous and resting-place for the muleteers on their way from the mountains to the city of Mexico with their supplies of charcoal and farm produce.

The interesting rides from the city of Mexico are numerous, and in all directions; every village, every church, has some attractions in the way of Aztec or Spanish archæological remains which repay inspection. For ladies, and those who do not care to ride on horseback, horse-car tramways are available every hour from the great Plaza. Do not hire carriages; they are expensive, and the jolting on some parts of the roads detracts from the pleasure of carriage exercise. Fêtes are generally going on in one or other of these villages; church fêtes, flower fêtes, bull-fight fêtes, and gambling fêtes, which you will find announced by placards in the streets. The people cannot live without fêtes, and every fête has a speciality of its own. Don't be annoyed if the tramcars are overcrowded; every one is so polite that no inconvenience is experienced but that which may occasionally arise from too much cigar-smoke. The dryness of the climate prevents even this from being disagreeable, and your clothes never seem to have a taint of tobacco; the thin blue smoke is lost in the air as soon as it is emitted from the cigar.

If you lay your plans for seeing everything, and cast in your lot with the pleasure-seekers of the hour, you may have a "good time" of it. And what traveller repairs to Mexico, but to see and learn, and enjoy all he can? If an Englishman, by his inoffensive demeanour and behaviour, commends himself to the people of the country, the nation he represents will be respected and appreciated accordingly.

The names of some of the villages are difficult to read at first sight; the tramcar with AZCOPOTZALCO upon it requires close scrutiny as it passes, in order to distinguish it from JXACALCO, a village in an opposite direction; and a stranger might easily make a mistake between Mixcoac Tacubaya and Popotla Tacuba, as the cars pass rapidly along the street.

CHAPTER XII.

SHRINE OF GUADALUPE.

Tramcars—The appearance of the Virgin to the Shepherd at Guadalupe—Description of the Shrine and the Picture of the Virgin.

IF the visitor wishes to inspect anything particular in the neighbouring villages, it is better to exchange his hack for the cars which run from the Plaza Mayo every half-hour to all the outlying districts. Take a first-class car if you can, for there are two classes, the second being used by the Indians and often overcrowded. The tramcars in Mexico are all drawn by mules; the rails are four feet eight and a-half inches in gauge; and when you get outside the city boundary the mules go at a fierce gallop to their destination, the fare-collectors leaping on board at a given point of the route. The conductors are smartly clad in blue cloth tunics, high boots, and *sombréros* of grey felt, and are provided with a horn, which they sound at street-crossings, or as a signal to the driver to pull up.

One day I took a car to pay a visit to the shrine of Guadalupe, which is situated three miles from the city, and is a great point of attraction both to residents and visitors.

The old road from the city to Guadalupe, with its handsome wayside shrines, was given up to the Vera Cruz Railway, and a new road for tramcars and traffic has been made alongside of it. As soon as we had passed the gates and the aduana, "crack, crack, hi, hi, hi!" and off we went at a hand gallop past adobe houses and *pulquerias*, the snow-capped giant Popocatapetl lifting his white head to the azure on the right, and soon, through the avenue of trees, the little church on the hill Tepeyac, erected where the Virgin appeared to the peasant Juan Diego, and the cathedral at its foot, with its flat façade flanked by low towers, were both visible in the distance.

The cars came to a standstill in front of the cathedral, and a motley crowd of loungers watched us alight.

The houses are one-storied and old, the windows barred after the fashion introduced by the Moors into Spain; behind the bars stood village maidens and matrons who signalled and saluted their male acquaintances by holding up the left hand, the fingers extended, which they wriggled to and fro about half-a-dozen times; this is their mode of salutation, possibly it means "we have fruit and entertainment to offer."

The church of Nuestra Señora de Guadalupe is the most famous of all the churches in the country, owing its notoriety to the legend that, on the 12th of December, 1531, the Virgin Mary appeared to a poor Mexican shepherd in that neighbourhood; he reported the vision to the priests, who asked him to substantiate his statement by proofs. The Virgin showed herself to him on five different occasions, and finally stamped her image on his blanket; this mark was accepted; our Lady of Guadalupe was officially proclaimed the patron saint of Mexico by the authority of Pope Clement VII., and thereby the influence of the Catholic religion was greatly extended, it being asserted that, by her graciously appearing to a native, all natives were taken under her special protection. A shrine was erected on the top of the hill where the vision appeared. At its foot rose a magnificent cathedral, which at one time was very rich in gold and silver ornaments, the offerings of the faithful; but many of these were confiscated and coined into money by order of President Benito Juarez in 1860, and have since been replaced by inferior metal.

The name of Guadalupe was combined with that of Hidalgo,

the Mexican priest who in 1810 raised the cry of independence from the Spanish yoke. He had painted on his standard the image of the Virgin of Guadalupe, which greatly helped to excite the patriotism of the natives ; more than 100,000 of them rallied round him ; but they were so badly armed that they could not compete with the Spanish forces, who, curious to say, fought under the banner of the Virgin Los Remedios.

Poor Hidalgo was captured by the Spaniards and shot in 1811 ; but his followers, in whom he had aroused much enthusiasm, continued the war, and, after eleven years' hard fighting, independence was accomplished, in 1821, under Iturbide ; and Spanish Viceroys and their rule were abolished. Mexican presidents, nominated every four years by the plebiscite of the nation, took their place.

There is not much to see in the cathedral, which has been despoiled of its silver and valuables (the golden frame of the Virgin was taken, but returned) ; so I made the ascent by a zigzag road to the shrine at the top of the hill.

Before entering the chapel, stop to look at the view; it will repay any amount of trouble taken in mounting the steep steps. The city, the lake and Chapultepec are within the range of a camera, if it could so be fixed as to avoid the roof of the cathedral below you. Turn and enter the shrine: at a little altar on the right are rude daubs of pictures representing miracles worked through the intervention of the Virgin—pious offerings in commemoration of a child saved from fire, a husband from lightning, a wife from a runaway train, a lady and gentleman from an overturn of a carriage, people rising from a bed of sickness, and such like—some of them with the paint hardly dry.

The altar railing is of solid silver ; this railing was, of all the sumptuous church fixtures throughout the land, alone spared by the Liberals. Its value must be immense ; pious Mexicans do not like to appraise it, for reasons best known to themselves. The great gem however of this church is the image of the Virgin of

Guadalupe, which she herself imprinted—according to the legend
—upon the *tilma*, or garment, of Juan Diego, the poor peasant, as
a proof that she had appeared to him ; this relic is hung over the
high altar, in a wrought-iron case, and is only exposed on rare
holidays. By especial grace I obtained a view of it. The *tilma*
is a very coarse piece of woollen fabric; the colouring of the
image is distinct, and may have been touched up from time
to time. On a table at the door are copies of the picture in all
sizes, and you see them in every Indian hut, every wayside shrine,
in all the public offices, in every church—indeed in every place
in the land, appropriate or inappropriate, as the case may be.

In an adjoining churchyard are some pretty tombs, and great
prices are paid for interment in this sacred spot. Santa Anna
rests here, and the names of the leading families of Mexico could
be read on the marble in all directions.

After descending from the hill I visited the miraculous sulphur
spring, said to cure everything; the church or dome which covers
it was being redecorated at great expense at the time of my visit.
The legend says that this spring of sulphur hydrogen gushed
forth from a spot touched by one of the Virgin's feet. On the
12th of December every year (the anniversary of the apparition)
thousands of natives from all parts of the country visit this shrine
and the church of Guadalupe. The name is familiar to many
people as that of a town between Toledo and Trujillo in Spain,
where there is a famous shrine to the Virgin ; there is always a
longing in the minds of colonists to perpetuate the names of the
country of their birth, and Guadalupe is no doubt an instance of
this patriotic feeling on the part of the Spaniards ; the Geronomite
convent in Spain was at the time of the Conquest the richest and
most venerated shrine in the old country, its celebrated figure of
the Virgin being believed to have been carved by St. Luke
himself, and it was given by Pope Gregory the Great to San
Leandro for putting down Arianism. The figure was hidden and
miraculously preserved during six centuries of Moorish invasion,

and when brought to light was so venerated by the whole Spanish nation that the settlers in New Spain would delight in perpetuating the name of the shrine in their new home.

At the conclusion of the ceremonies there is an exhibition of fireworks in front of the church, at which the high dignitaries are present, in all the paraphernalia of pomp, and afterwards the natives are allowed to dance the *mitate* in one of the halls adjoining the church, in their presence, and with their sanction. I was told the *mitate* is a native Indian dance, representing very questionable antics, and, from the description given me, it is probably a dance similar to one I several times saw performed at night in front of Queen Emma's residence at Honolulu during the month that the body of her mother, who was a native princess of the old dynasty, and much respected, was lying in state in her daughter's house previous to burial. The gardens at Queen Emma's were lit up and crowded by natives who had come long distances and from other islands to the obsequies, after the old native fashion of the Sandwich Islanders; the men and women performers were mostly professional, and the dances alternated with wailings, and songs of a gross character: the exhibition lasted all night long, the most extraordinary thing being that Queen Emma herself and her attendants, in deep mourning and with large black fans, sat in the balcony overlooking the scene. Dr. Willis, the Bishop of the Islands, told me these old customs occasionally cropped out, though the funeral at the end of the time of mourning would be conducted by himself with Christian rites. It is impossible rapidly to convert Pagan natives and abolish at once all old associations, and this *mitate* dance is a remnant of the Aztec ceremonies which, amongst other things, the Catholic priesthood incorporated with the occasional services of the Church in Mexico, but ought now, after three centuries, to be discontinued.

On my return journey I stood by the driver of the tramcar, and thoroughly enjoyed the gallop to the city boundary.

CHAPTER XIII.

GENERAL CHAPTER ON MEXICO : PRODUCE, STATISTICS OF IMPORTS AND EXPORTS—COFFEE.

So very little is generally known of Mexico that I am not afraid to offer the following information to my readers. It is a Confederate Republic of twenty-seven. states, one territory (Lower California), and one federal district, that of Mexico City. It has taken the form of government of the United States for its model. Its territorial area comprehends 741,800 square miles, an area greater than that of the combined territories of France, Spain, and the entire German Empire, with Great Britain and Ireland into the bargain. The population of Mexico is over nine and a-half millions; it is therefore a little more populous than the two kingdoms of Holland and Belgium.

The old popular impression that they are "pronouncing" every other day in Mexico is, to use an Americanism, "played out;" the iron road and the telegraph wire have killed all that sort of thing. There is far less political disturbance to-day in Mexico than in Russia, and Mr. Gladstone and his Ministry would have a bed of roses to lie upon if Ireland were but half or a quarter as tranquil. The last presidential election, the occasion on which a row might have been fairly expected, was as peaceful as the coronation of Queen Victoria. Mexico is on the direct water highway between Europe and Asia. Eighty years ago Humboldt called it "el puente del comercio del mundo"—" the bridge of the commerce of the world."

The City of Mexico, with its 300,000 inhabitants, has about the same population as Rome (305,000), and nearly equal to Baltimore (332,000). San Luis Potosi, with 65,000, is about as large as Geneva (68,000); Puebla and Guadalajara, with 75,000 each, are exactly on a par with Plymouth and Wolverhampton. Leon, with 132,000, is larger than Antwerp (125,000) or Genoa (130,000). Silao, with 38,000, is equal to Metz (38,000); Guanajuato, with 63,400, is larger than Verona (60,000). Such comparisons might be multiplied, but what I have stated may suffice to give an idea of the size of the cities and of the trade that might be done; at one port on the Pacific, Manzanillo, during the freighting season, six hundred donkeys and mules leave every day for the interior. All this old-fashioned traffic will now be superseded by the railway which is just opened to this seaport, and has connected it with the central lines of the country.

The ten million Mexicans, with their cities and states, and all the wants of civilised life, inhabit a country of unparalleled resources and wealth. What did Humboldt say, in his day? "This vast empire under careful cultivation would alone produce all that commerce collects together from the rest of the globe." I spent a long morning with Consul Aymé in the Museum of the Mineria or School of Mines. He was an expert in minerals, and he told me there was not a mineral known except *cryolite* (whatever it may be) that is not found in Mexico. After all, her mineral wealth has been her bane, rather than her benefit; for it she has neglected the produce of her soil, her cereals and fruits, her sugar, rice and cotton, her tobacco, her dyewoods, and whole classes of purely tropical products. Mexico also produces Coffee, Indigo, Cocoa, Cocoa-nuts, Caoutchouc, the Indiarubber tree, Vanilla, Chili, Cochineal, Mahogany, Rose-wood, Ebony, Lemons, Limes, Pineapples, Jalap (so called from the town Jalapa), Salts, Vegetable Waxes, Medicinal Gums, Cinchona, Bark, and Aniseed, Mexcal on the lower ground, and

Pulque on the plateaux (to this latter I have given a special chapter), Sissal Hemp, Madder, Ramie, Hennequin, and many kinds of vegetable dyes, nuts, oils of commerce and for the table, fine cabinet woods, and, in a word, every variety of produce known in the temperate or the torrid zone. In reference to her cereals—her wheat is the finest in the world after that of Egypt; Indian corn, maize and barley are of excellent quality, and one of her specialities is beans (frijoles) of all kinds and colours, varying from black to white.

The beautiful marbles and transparent alabasters from Puebla are seen in all the churches, and shops are filled with small ornaments made from them.

Large beds of coal have been opened near Laredo, and also on the *Banderas* near Manzanillo; excellent coal abounds in the state of Michoacan. At the very doors of Mexico is the greatest market of the future for all these products—the United States.

The following table will prove of interest, as it shows the imports of some of the staple productions of Mexico into the United States for the ten years ending the 30th of June, 1880:—

			Value.
Sugar	lbs.	1,731,405,439	$74,717,935
Coffee	„	446,850,727	60,360,769
Crude india-rubber and gutta-percha	„	16,826,099	9,606,239
Molasses	galls.	38,008,930	8,705,243
Tobacco	lbs.	10,411,757	7,315,898
Indigo	„	2,625,240	2,752,900
Gums	„	17,842,086	2,444,302
Rice	„	51,943,609	1,316,132
Cocoa	„	7,403,643	1,306,239
Cochineal	„	1,364,285	890,168
Total value of ten articles			$169,415,825

Or about £34,000,000.

In reference to the production of coffee, for which certain portions of Mexico seem specially adapted, the only plantations

I saw were at *Cordoba*, on the railway between Vera Cruz and Mexico City, but the Hon. J. W. Foster, late Minister to Mexico for the United States, and since Minister to Russia, reports: "It may be an unknown fact to Americans, that at our very doors—in Mexico, our neighbouring Republic—there exists the agricultural capacity to produce all the coffee that can be consumed in the United States of America of a quality equal to the best grain in any country." And I was told the berry generally is superior to the coarse berry from Brazil. I only wish the American Government would take the coffee business in hand, and see that its own country is properly supplied with this delicious beverage, for, with the exception of the coffee served in a few first-class hotels and restaurants, what is supplied under this name generally, in both the United States and Canada, is probably little more than burnt toast.

The coffee production of Mexico has hitherto been almost entirely limited to supplying the home demand, but it is now creating a considerable foreign trade, as shown by the statistics I have given. The tree is grown chiefly in the states of Vera Cruz, Oxaca, Tabasco, and Colima, on the Sierra. The produce is classed either as coast or mountain coffee, the distinguishing features of which are, that while the berry of coast coffee is light and spongy, that of the mountain plantation is hard and flinty. Mexican coffee is known in the market as Tabasco, Jalapa, Cordoba, and Oxaca. The first named is coast coffee, and of poor quality. Jalapa has a small, yellowish bean, rather short and wide, but irregular in size. Cordoba furnishes a larger and longer bean—this coffee is often polished and used as a substitute for Rio, to which really it is infinitely superior. Oxaca is a rough green mountain coffee; were this coffee properly cleaned and carefully assorted, it would, on the authority of Mr. Francis B. Thurber, of New York, a most renowned coffeologist, rival in appearance and flavour almost any upland coffee cultivated in Costa Rica and Jamaica.

France takes a large part of the Mexican coffee crop, which is usually shipped in grass bales, weighing from 220 to 260 lbs.

In the southern part of Mexico, coffee grows wild; the natives do not even take the trouble of gathering this free gift from the bountiful hand of Nature; we cannot expect that they should, as at present they have no roads, and they have a weakness for chocolate; but, without any stimulus from the interior, their export to the United States has in seven years increased threefold.

Mexico yields two crops of maize every year, each crop about sixty bushels to the acre. This cereal forms the staple food of the people. It is not ground into flour, but mashed up into a paste, as described in the making of *tortillas*.

Humboldt (vol. ii. p. 307, of his ' New Spain '), says that "maize is a true American grain, and that the old continent received it from the new. On the discovery of America by the Europeans, the *zea mays* (*tlaolli*, in the Aztec language), was cultivated from the most southern part of Chili to Pennsylvania. According to a tradition of the Aztec people, the Toltecs, in the seventh century of our era, were the first who introduced into Mexico the cultivation of maize and cotton. It might happen, however, that these two different branches of agriculture existed before the Toltecs, and that this nation, the great civilisation of which has been celebrated by all historians, merely extended them successfully. Hernandez informs us that the Otomites even, who were only a wandering and barbarous people near the Rio Grande, planted maize.

"Maize, when introduced into the north of Europe, suffers from cold wherever the mean temperature does not reach 44° or 46° Fahrenheit. It is commonly believed that this plant was the only species of grain known by the Americans before the arrival of Europeans. In the climate of Mexico the fecundity of the tlaolli, or Mexican maize, is beyond anything that can be imagined in Europe."

a. MAIZE, OR INDIAN CORN.
b. MALE FLOWER.
c. FEMALE FLOWER AND CORN-POD.
d. STALK ROOTS.
[page 98.

I noticed that maize was very unequal in its growth. In the same field there would be patches of high stalks, each stalk with at least three large ears of grain upon it, and in other places patches of dwarfed unhealthy stalks without any ears. Various causes were assigned for this irregularity, as cold draughts of air, humidity, and slight variations in the soil; but there is seldom any general damage done to the crop, except from want of rain or premature frost. If there is a general failure of the crop, it results in a famine to man, cattle, pigs, and poultry, as it is the food of them all.

During the summer months that I spent in Mexico, from March to October, the maize crops seemed to be in every state of growth, including young plants in full ear, and short old stubbles upon which pigs were feeding.

Rice is second only to maize in production and utility. One single sowing will yield successively two crops without the slightest additional labour. A general rule of plantation farming in the *tierras calientes* for nearly all crops is, one crop a year from the natural rains, and another crop from irrigation. One year only is required for maturing the first crop of sugar-cane, after which two crops can be obtained in fifteen months; once started, the cane will yield prolifically for twenty years without re-planting.

Now about the soil. What would the reader think about a soil that requires no manuring? The volcanic ridges of the hills are strewed with potashes and other rich chemical substances. The continuous gentle rains in the summer months wash these down into the valleys, hence the replenishing of the soil is absolutely automatic. This district of the *tierras calientes* in the south was visited by some of my friends during my stay. They made a journey too laborious and fatiguing for me, visiting the ruins of Mitla and Palenque; they described the Indians of this district as lazy and indolent; but why need they work? Nature has done everything for them, they have only to raise sufficient for their daily wants, and there are neither roads nor means of transporting the surplus produce to distant markets; but this will soon be altered. Railway routes are now being surveyed to run through their midst, and there is no reason to suppose the peons will not work as hard and steadily as the population on the plateau, when they find they can be remunerated for their labour. I can speak from actual observation of the hard work which the natives of this elevated section of Mexico performed. The navvies on the railway works seem to labour without lagging; and the people in the cotton factories and print works I visited were too busy to notice the intrusion of strangers.

There are ten or twelve iron-works in the City of Mexico, and forty reduction works in the state of that name. Leon, the Manchester of Mexico, has her whole population very busy, and the workpeople troop out of the workshops at six o'clock in the evening just as they do at home.

The Aztecs, by universal testimony, were a hard-working, thrifty people, and those who make any statement to the contrary of their descendants have not visited the workshops, but judged of the people from the few idlers and loafers in the streets. Three-fourths or more of the present population of Mexico are of Aztec descent; the other fourth is of Spanish descent. I am of opinion that all that Mexico wants is a chance; that chance she is getting now—a new era is dawning upon her. *Esto perpetua!*

And now as regards the standing of Mexico as a nation —there is also considerable misconception on this point. Fixed and traditional error makes her out to be a hopeless bankrupt, not able to offer a farthing in the pound. But what are the facts? The national debt of Mexico, distributed over the population who must pay it, is $22 per head; that of the United States, $52·56; that of France $127·53; that of Italy, $71·94; and that of our own Great Britain, $114·62. Mexico has the resources to even increase her debt and repay every penny of it. At the present time the large sums she offers as concessions to the railway

companies on the completion of every fifty miles of their roads
are paid most regularly. The government grant for this purpose
in the year 1881 was $4,000,000, and every penny was duly paid.

Mexico's only foreign debt is that held by English bond-
holders, and this amounts to less than $100,000,000, to which
has to be added, however, unpaid interest; and a balance of about
$2,000,000 (two millions) is owing to American citizens, as per
settlement made by the British minister, Sir Edward Thornton,
formely in Washington, now our ambassador at St. Petersburg,
when he acted as arbitrator between Mexico and the United States.
Her French debt she has repudiated, owing to the war, and when
the settlement was made, so that a French minister could come
to Mexico, it was distinctly understood that France should not
press her claim.

As a traveller I was disappointed to find that the English
Government had no minister nor representative in Mexico. Mr.
Ashton Forbes, till then our minister, was recalled from Mexico
in December 1861, the English Government very properly with-
drawing from assisting Napoleon in his French intervention; and
since that time diplomatic relations have never been renewed.
Mr. Morgan, the American minister, uses his kindly offices (I
believe by arrangement with the home government) in rendering
assistance in every way to any English subject who applies to
him. He told me that most of the English residents had left
the country since the withdrawal of the English minister, but
that there was still a sufficient number remaining, generally in
places of great responsibility, in banks, mines, cotton factories,
machine shops, and in breweries; while the increase of arrivals
in the country was causing an addition to his work. In support
of the claim which this question has upon the English Government for further consideration, I may mention that I visited more
or less in the families of the ministers and attachés of the French,
German, Italian, and Belgian embassies, and they all regretted
that there was no English Legation in their circle; and I may add

that Mr. Marischal, the Mexican Minister of Foreign Affairs, whom I had the honour of occasionally meeting, deeply deplored that the English had not seen their way to entering into friendly relations with his country. I gathered from him that the chief obstacle lay in the English Government's claiming certain guaranties as to the payment of the Mexican-English debt, but as the continental countries had resumed friendly relations without reference to unpaid debts, they could not open negotiations with England except on similar terms. To a man not versed in the mysteries of diplomacy, and looking at matters from an ordinary business point of view, it certainly appears more probable that the debts to England would be paid if England had a representative residing in the country and in a position to further its claims upon the government, especially as Mr. Marischal assured me this, and he allowed me to report, that the Mexican Government had in no way repudiated their debts to England, but up to the present time had been totally unequal to meeting them. There are such evidences of progress and development all over the country, seen in railways, a network of telegraph lines, new buildings, factories, compulsory education, and improved farming and mining operations, as to more than warrant the supposition that the country has done with its *pronunciamientos*, and is turning its attention to developing its resources in every possible way.

The numbers of the population vary in accordance with the fertility of a district. On the arid bare lands, where only the maguey grows, or on the rocky barren slopes of the hills, the population is very thin as compared with that of the more fertile valleys and the mining districts; as distributed over the whole soil, it is 13·50 to the square mile, the population of the entire United States being 13·91 to the square mile.

The revenue is most inefficiently collected, yet it amounted in the year 1880 to 18,000,000 dollars. It is a rapidly increasing revenue; the customs at the port of Vera Cruz, for instance, in

February 1881 were three times as large as those for the same month in the previous year. All these figures tell the story of a country just commencing a system of thorough internal communication by a network of railways.

Of course I am principally interested in the relations of commerce between Mexico and my own country, and from the Mexican Blue Book, which was kindly furnished me by Señor Don Matias Romero, I conclude the chapter with the following statistics of exports and imports between the two countries :—

Years.	Imports of British Home Produce into Mexico.	Exports from Mexico to Great Britain.
1871	£1,049,013	£397,334
1872	843,186	443,524
1873	1,194,124	499,532
1874	1,124,613	546,651
1875	884,901	721,097
1876	502,224	662,132
1877	995,510	798,857
1878	773,331	507,082
1879	693,123	582,759
1880	1,225,567	628,071

CHAPTER XIV.

POPOCATAPETL; OR, THE MOUNTAIN THAT SMOKES.

WITH Englishmen it seems to be a natural impulse to shoot anything they can shoot, and to climb anything that they can climb. Who could possibly remain long in the city of Mexico, and gaze daily upon the snow-capped peak of Popocatapetl, without being filled with a burning desire to see how the country looked from such an altitude? Moreover, to have ascended a peak 5000 feet higher than the summit of Mont Blanc would be something to think of at a future day.

Day after day I asked, first one friend, and then another, to attempt the ascent with me, till it finally came to pass that Mr. W. H. Bishop, correspondent of *Harper's Monthly Magazine*, and Mr. A. K. Owen, an American civil engineer engaged in making plans for the draining of the Valley of Mexico, arranged to form a trio with me for the climb.

The mountain and the sulphur-works in the crater belong to General Gaspar Sanchez Ochoa. He is chief of the military engineering department of the Republic, and we waited upon him at his rooms in the National Palace, to ask permission to remain for a night at the rancho of Tlamacas, half-way up the mountain, where his sulphur-works are situated. We were very kindly received by him; he seemed interested in our proposal, and ordered his agent, Señor Domingo Zela, who luckily happened to be in Mexico at the time, to place himself at our disposal, and render us all the assistance that lay in his power.

ASCENT OF POPOCATAPETL

General Ochoa, a remarkably fine intellectual man, probably forty-five years of age, holds the rank of brigadier-general. He rendered eminent service to the Republic at the time of the French intervention, and his portrait, which hangs on the wall of his room, is decorated with several medals, granted for special personal bravery. One of our party remarked to him that the expression of the portrait was too severe, when he laughingly replied, " Oh, that is my war face, but I now wear my civilian smile."

In reply to our inquiries as to how he became originally possessed of the crater, he told us that when he was a student in the mineralogical department of the Military Academy, some twenty-five years ago, his tutor, Señor Andres del Rio, a friend of Baron Humboldt's, and who had heard from the Baron of the great purity and value of the sulphur in the crater, recommended his pupil to apply to the government for permission to work the sulphur deposit. This was granted, together with permission to operate on the side of the mountain down to the line of vegetation. The General afterwards added a rancho by purchase, on which he erected sulphur-works, where the crude sulphur is sublimated, and put into a marketable state. He spent some months himself in the crater, and is now occupied in extending the operations by means of scientific machinery, as he explained that, although the specimens of sulphur he exhibited at the Philadelphia Exposition were purer than any other, he is undersold in the market at the distant coast towns by sulphur brought from the Mediterranean.

On Wednesday, the 11th of May, we left Mexico by the 7 A.M. train for the town of Ameca-ameca, under the charge of Señor Zela. At Ameca-ameca we went to General Ochoa's country house, and were served with a capital breakfast. While Señor Zela was arranging to hire horses for us, we repaired to the market, where we purchased provisions to last three days; we also went to a shop and provided ourselves with leather sandals, calico for " leggings," and one or two things we had not had time to obtain in Mexico.　As anything of the shape of an alpenstock is unknown in these parts we were unable to buy one.

The bargaining for the use of the horses for three days was a lengthy affair; it was finally settled at $2½ per day for a horse and attendant groom, the owner of the horses to accompany us at extra pay.

It was three o'clock before we left Ameca-ameca for a ride of fifteen up-hill miles to the rancho of Tlamacas, where the first night had to be spent.　For an hour or more we passed through a lovely country, abounding in barley ready for reaping; Indian corn on its high stalks, and beans of velvety green, while the roadside was bordered with some of our home greenhouse flowers. At five o'clock we had got above the rich vegetation, and were on grass lands and in woods.　At six, the grass land had been passed and it was all wood, principally fir; at seven, it became dark, and we had another hour's march, through a pathless, undulating wood, keeping the party together by continual shouting.　This was a very unpleasant experience, and very trying to both horse and man, for in some places there was an undergrowth of brushwood which lashed us pretty severely, and sometimes caused the horses to lose the trail; our guides seemed to trust entirely to the leading horse, and if we came to a dead halt he was urged to make a fresh start in any direction he liked to take.　Soon after eight we struck General Ochoa's sulphur ranche at Tlamacas, and we found it was a sulphur ranche and nothing else.　There was a large yard with a railing on one side, opposite to which stood a long building, with some brick furnaces in it for melting the sulphur.　The other two sides were occupied by a barn, the roof open at both ends, and Señor Zela's cabin and a mule shed lay on the left.　The cabin was just large enough to accommodate a smithy fireplace and the señor's bed.　We proceeded to make ourselves happy.　We blew up the smithy fire and cooked the beef, the onions, and the eggs; we boiled the coffee and the milk, topping up with something stronger and cigars; and it was not till ten o'clock that we thought of arranging for a place in which to lie down. We could not intrude on the señor's bed, so we turned out into the yard to see what shelter the other buildings offered. Our attendants had lit a fire in the centre of the barn, round which they were asleep on the ground, the horses close to them. We entered the sulphur building, where two men were keeping up the furnace fires; and as there were a number of bass mats in the place used to pack the sulphur in, we made beds of them and lay down. Warmth was the only compensation for the discomforts of this place. The men made such a disturbance in stirring up the fires, and such whiffs of sulphur came to stifle us, that first one and then another got up and joined the men and horses in the barn; sleep was out of the question, the cold from the open roof chilling every part of the body that was more than a few inches from the fire; this was not to be wondered at, since we were at an altitude of 12,995 feet.

Every soul of us was astir before sunrise, and, after some breakfast cooked on the smithy fire, we mounted our horses for the ascent. Up! up! up! over broken scoriæ and cinders we rode, to within 200 yards of the snow-line. For some time the horses had such difficulty in getting their breath that they did not proceed more than twenty yards at a time without stopping and evincing signs of great distress. We had been told to be sure and make them carry us as far as the snow-line, but after passing the rocks called Las Cruces the scoriæ became so fine and deep, and the ascent so steep, that we were obliged to dismount and leave the horses with their *mozos.*

Before we started from the rancho we had abandoned our shoes, bandaged our legs with cotton cloth, and fastened on our sandals by long leather thongs, after the manner of the Roman peasants on the Campagna. The snow-line is at 14,000 feet, and was reached at one o'clock. From this point to the crater the ascent was decidedly laborious, but there is no danger—we found no crevasses, no clefts, no chasms and no avalanches. The smooth cone-like summit of the mountain is covered with a cake of snow which, by alternate freezing by night and thawing at noon, is as slippery as glass, and would be insurmountable were it not that where the guide takes you it is thickly covered over with upright blocks or small columns of snow-ice. When you slip you only slide a foot or two till you are brought to a stand by one or more of these pillars of ice. The edges of these pillars, large and small, are sharp as razors. I luckily had on a thick pair of woollen gloves, and escaped scathless, but the gloveless hands of my companions were so badly cut that our ascent might have been traced by their blood on the snow.

The weather was perfect, without a cloud in the sky; Ixtaccihuatl, the sister mountain, though 15,705 feet above the sea, appeared to lie at our feet, its summit having the appearance of boundless plains of snow.

There was a clean sweep of country to the mountain of Malinché; the peak of Orizaba showed itself like a little sugar loaf on the sky-line; and further to the east lay the valley of Puebla, with a dim outline of something in its centre that we took to be the city.

At half-past two o'clock we were at the lip of the crater. Owen was the first to shout "Eureka!" he and Bishop were fine young athletes, and as I was double their age I was not in the least chagrined at following ten minutes behind. Had I not felt that it was both important not to lag far behind them nor lose sight of them, owing to the pillars of snow, I should have taken more time in the ascent, and have rested oftener, under pretext of admiring the view. When I arrived at the crater, though not overheated, I was glad to wrap myself up in a warm *serape*. The crater is very similar to that of Vesuvius, only about three times the size, and is silent. There is a pool of melted snow at one corner of it. I called the crater silent, but there is a slight fizzing sound from the several solfeterras, which I perceived were emitting a thin blue smoke from various crevices of the crater. The large solfeterra at the bottom of the crater, 1800 feet below us, emits a jet of vapour with a force of twenty horse power, and over it General Ochoa proposes to put a turbine wheel by which to hoist the sulphur he gets from the bottom to the top of the crater, instead of having it carried upon men's backs, as at present. The supply of sulphur is said to be inexhaustible, for if a ton is picked out one day another ton oozes out by the next.

The edge of the crater, according to General Ochoa's latest survey, is 19,000 feet above sea-level; but this is not the top of the mountain, on the west of it rises the peak, calculated to be 1000 feet higher; but nobody has ever been able to scale it. General Ochoa told us he had offered any of his workmen, who were continually ascending and descending the mountain, $50 if they would accomplish the feat, but none had claimed the reward.

I afterwards met several American gentlemen who declared they knew people who had been at the top, and when I asked if they had proved it by claiming the reward, they said it would not be worth claiming, as it was under $500.

We had not been more than a quarter of an hour on the edge of the crater before a tremendous roar of thunder announced an approaching snowstorm, and the snow-flakes began to fall fast and thick. What at first appeared to be a misfortune proved to be no misfortune at all, as it afforded us an opportunity of witnessing a curious phenomenon. When it snows the crater becomes very dark in its hollows, and the solfeterras show themselves to great advantage, exhibiting red and blue flames; we could also distinguish a light in one of the workmen's huts at the bottom of the crater.

Out of the hundred men employed on the mountain, some thirty remain about twenty-eight days at a time in the crater.

We were told they did not seem to suffer from the effects of the sulphur fumes, except that their teeth wear down and their clothes rot; these ills are counterbalanced by the extra amount of pay they receive.

The descent was fatiguing, though rapid; walking down the slippery snow was impossible. I improvised a seat out of my woollen *zarape,* and slid *à la toboggon*, from column to column of snow until, after much bruising and banging, I arrived at the edge of the snow-line about the same time as my companions, who had each descended after a fashion of their own, their hands being cut in a worse manner by the sharp snow-ice than when ascending.

We got to the rancho at six o'clock, and it was pronounced too late to return to Ameca-ameca, so we were doomed to another night in our old quarters; but we managed better than on the previous night.

Señor Zela arranged that we should occupy the floor of the smithy and a cabin he had improvised for the occasion, he himself kindly insisting on giving up his bed to one of the party who was rather exhausted with fatigue.

An early hour the next morning found us on horseback, retracing our steps through the woods (the first wood being the one in which we were lost in darkness on the ascent) and then through the fields to Ameca-ameca. As we had the day before us, we halted several times on the high land, while Señor Zela pointed out to us the route by which Cortes entered the plain of Mexico.

It was over the lower spur of Popocatapetl and between that volcano and the volcano of Ixtaccihuatl that Cortes and his soldiers originally crossed and caught their first glimpse of the city, then called Tenochtitlan or Mexitli.

The distant view then, no doubt, appeared more beautiful than at present, beautiful as it still is, on account of the larger sheets of water which at that time surrounded the city.

Prescott's researches into the archives of Spain have brought to light many letters of the conquerors, in which it is probable they exaggerated some of their achievements. For instance, at page 46 of vol. ii. there is an account of an eruption of Popocatapetl copied from a letter of Diego Ordaz, one of Cortes' captains, and apparently the special correspondent of the expedition. In this letter to the authorities in Spain, Ordaz describes an eruption of Popocatapetl so graphically that his family were granted permission by the Emperor Charles the Fifth to bear a burning mountain on their escutcheon. General Ochoa tells me that all geologists who have reached the crater, or to whom he has sent specimens of its lignite and other minerals, assure him that it must be at least ten thousand years since any eruption or volcanic action could have taken place. It is possible that a terrific thunderstorm upon the summit of the mountain at the time of Cortes' passing under it might have led Ordaz into error. My own experience of the storm at the crater suggests to me this apology for him; but surely Prescott should have added a foot-note to his account, stating facts, and not have allowed his readers to imagine there was really an eruption in 1521.

About half-way down the hill, on a turn of the road near Zumpango, we stopped to rest before a wooden cross erected under an open rustic chapel; the pine-trees at the back of the shrine were magnificent, and reminded me of trees in the Yosemite Valley. On the cross was the following inscription, "Uno sudario por el alma de Felipe Bartolo Flores, que fue víctima el dia cinco de Octubre 1875." The guides told us that this unfortunate man was a merchant who, being on his way from Puebla to Mexico city, with $200 in his saddle-bags, had incautiously let it be known he was so laden, and a gang of robbers could not resist the temptation. One of them was afterwards taken and shot by order of the authorities close to the same spot, and a cross marks the place where he paid the penalty of his crime. The peons say a prayer before both crosses.

These memorials of murder and untimely death, so frequently seen by the roadside, cause the wary traveller to put his hand on his pistol to assure himself that his means of defence are all right in case of an attack ; but the pistol of the peaceful traveller would be of little service, for a murderer would be sure to get the first shot, and if this were not effective, its failure might probably induce him to slink away before his fire could be returned. The great safeguard in carrying a pistol is to have it prominently in view, and handy for whipping out. It is a caution to ruffians and ill-conditioned people, who might attack you in a lonely place if they thought you had no means of defence.

We found it hot and dusty as we neared Ameca-ameca, the cool breezes of the hills having been left behind; and to shorten the journey we put our horses into a gallop and arrived in time for a welcome and hospitable luncheon at General Ochoa's house, before leaving for the train at half-past three for Mexico.

In the ascent, none of us suffered from any oppression of the chest, or difficulty in breathing. With spiked sandals, good alpen-stocks, and favourable weather, there is no reason why even ladies might not make the ascent, as one or two American ladies are reported to have done.

Mr. Owen carried an aneroid which indicated the heights pretty accurately. Tight woollen clothes and a cap with ear covers are all that is necessary, as the exertion of continual climb-ing keeps one warm. If you rest during the ascent for a few minutes, and also during the time you spend at the crater, it is not only wise but necessary to use an extra wrap. I was only too glad to get my head through the hole of a large poncho, or Mexican blanket, which my guide, for a trifle, had carried up for me.

On our return to Mexico, we waited on General Ochoa to thank him for the great attentions we had received from his agent,

Señor Zela, who, as Americans would say, had been "real kind." On parting with Señor Zela I gave him as a souvenir a pocket-knife. Weeks afterwards, happening to meet in the Plaza Mayo of Mexico, he clasped me in his arms, in good Mexican fashion, crying out, "*Bueno, bueno, el cuchillo.*" Nothing is so useful for a small present, where money cannot be offered, as a good English pocket-knife, with a corkscrew, &c., in it. I gave such knives away in various parts of world, and I have no doubt they are much treasured and used, and the donor kindly remembered. Should I again ever come across one of the recipients of my knives, I feel sure that the American proverb—"*Cast thy bread on the waters, and it shall come back to thee buttered toast*"—would be fully realised.

CHAPTER XV.

AN ACCOUNT OF POPOCATAPETL BY AN AMERICAN.

Mr. Frederick Ober,* an American ornithologist and naturalist, from Beverly, near Boston, whose book on the Carabee Islands is delightful reading, was in Mexico at the same time as myself, and I made several excursions with him. He had ascended Popocatapetl a week previous to our ascent, and he wrote an account of his experiences to *The New York Herald*, which, with his permission, I now add to my own.

Mr. John Bright once said that a well-written newspaper was the best reading any man could have, and Mr. Ober's account, trimmed up with capitals to suit American taste, is, I must admit, a masterpiece of its kind.

POPOCATAPETL.

HOW A 'HERALD' MAN ASCENDED THE "SMOKING MOUNTAIN."—SLIDING FROM ZONE TO ZONE, AND FROM PEAK TO PINE.—A SNOW-STORM EIGHTEEN THOUSAND FEET ABOVE THE SEA.

Ten thousand feet above the valley of Mexico rises the peak of Popocatapetl, covered with perpetual snow. At its side a sister volcano—Ixtaccihuatl—flashes the sun from her crest at an altitude of 2000 feet lower, yet she, too, wears the robe of the upper regions. They are the first objects that greet and enchain the traveller's eye as he enters the Mexican valley—the first he seeks in the morning, the last he loves to look upon at evening. The higher peak towers above every other volcano in

* See note on page 135.

North America save one; one of the mightiest of that "girdle of burning mountains" that surrounds the Pacific, reaching an altitude of 17,800 feet! It is called an "active" volcano, yet has emitted nothing but sulphur fumes within the memory of man. Yet it may be at present only resting, for old historians affirm that it was active in the first years of the Conquest, and its very name—Popocatapetl—signifies the "smoking mountain."

Volcanoes take their rest like human beings, and we have but to turn to the history of Vesuvius to confirm this. In 1631, for instance, "that mountain had been so long dormant, that it was forgotten that it had ever been in eruption; the walls of the crater were clothed with forests, harbouring the wild boar and other game; its bottom had grassy plains, in which cattle quietly grazed." But that year witnessed an eruption that overwhelmed three cities. The formation of the volcano of Jorullo, in Mexico, in 1759 is another example, when, from a fertile and highly cultivated plain, were thrown up six volcanoes, the central one rising to a height of 1600 feet. Yes, Popocatapetl, may be called an "active volcano," and just now may be taking a rest. Hardly a visitor to Mexico looks upon the peaks of these everlasting hills without being filled with an unquenchable desire to place them beneath his feet; hardly a visitor does so, though many attempt it.

THE SUMMIT OF POPOCATAPETL.

They said I couldn't reach it, but I did. Men, high in authority here, warned me not to attempt the ascent alone, and assured me that only my skill as a pistol-shot could save me from extermination. Very fortunately, I was not called upon to give an exhibition of my skill, and have not added—nor have I been the means of adding—another of those black crosses to the large number that line the waysides all over the country. Giving heed to the warnings of my friends, I attired myself in my oldest clothes, donned a Mexican serape and sombréro, girt myself about with a belt stuffed full of cartridges, and containing a dirk and revolver, and travelled for the station. The disguise was so perfect that an acquaintance met me in the Plaza, and was about to pass without a recognition.

"Oh, don't mention it," said I, "but, tell me, do you see about me any evidence of wealth?"

"No," said he, "I'm blessed if I do."

Then I allowed him to pass on. At the station the agent confirmed me in the belief that I would pass for a ruffian, by giving me a third-class ticket. This made me happy, for I then knew that I appeared thoroughly disreputable, and that no robber would murder me with the expectation of getting anything for his pains.

The Morelos railroad runs in a south-easterly direction from Mexico for one hundred miles, crossing the marshes between Lake Texcoco and Chalco, the dry plains at the foot hills of the volcano Ixtaccihuatl, and skirts of the base of Popocatapetl. Forty miles from Mexico it passes through Ameca-ameca, the largest town on its line, and the point whence the ascent of the volcano commences. In Mexico I had procured a letter from General Ochoa—who owns the crater of the volcano, and works it for the sulphur—to his major domo, Don Domingo Zela, but Don Domingo was absent from Ameca-ameca, and I was thrown upon my own resources. After reducing the station agent and all the assembled multitude of Mexicans to a state of despair by the manner in which I murdered the Castilian of the academy, it occurred to me to ask if there were a person in the town who could speak English.

"Sí, señor, one man and only one."

"Then please send for that one," said I; and while the messenger was absent I turned my attention to making photographs of the mountains, which as seen from the Plaza—and indeed from the whole town—are superb.

In the centre of the town is the Plaza; a low circular wall of stone incloses a small plat filled with flowers; a round basin filled with water flowing from a fountain in the middle, and a few white stone pillars support a capital and form the entrance, above which, and shading the garden, droop dark green willows. The square surrounding this bit of loveliness is large, bounded on its west side, next the railroad, by a casa municipal, and on the east by the cathedral, large and well preserved. The streets of the town diverge from this centre, lined with low houses of stone and adobe—mostly the latter—and roofed with rough shingles spitted on with long wooden pegs. Water from the mountains runs in little streams through the streets, and is directed by small gutters to the houses for private use. Groups of pine-trees rise above the houses, and all the trees are mainly of the northern zone. East of the town, and, in fact, all around, stretch immense fields of corn and barley, parted by hedges of maguey, and beyond them the foot hills commence, with many a fertile tongue of land running up among them, green and golden with grain. Then they rise higher and higher, covered with black forests of pine, until the grand old mountains are fairly reached, which shake off their garments of trees, and tower above them all, brown and barren; next comes the border of the snow-line, its white robe ragged and patched with brown on its skirts; but, finally, triumphing over all below, it drapes the peaked summit in a glistening garment of spotless white. Facing the east, Ixtaccihuatl—La Mujer Blanca (" the white woman ")—lies above, and apparently nearer the town than Popocatapetl. She covers a long portion of the ridge with her white shroud, and is really suggestive, by her shape, of a dead giantess robed in white for her burial. Far and near this volcano is known as the " White Woman," and from the plains of Ameca-ameca and from the City of Mexico the resemblance to a dead woman lying on her bier, and covered with a white sheet, is most perfect. The neck is a trifle long, and the protuberance of the breasts carried a little too far down, giving an undue prominence to the abdomen; but the dead face is perfect, and the hair streams in silvery locks from the snowy forehead back over the head and down the sides of the bier. Her feet are turned towards her companion giant, grim old Popocatapetl, and between the two lies a long uneven ridge, mainly below the snow-line, brown, and for the most part treeless. Popocatapetl is a solid cone of glittering snow, which appears jagged and sun-bitten at about the same level as is Mujer Blanca, and allows his diadem to lose itself in little streams that trickle down his giant shoulders.

A VOLCANERO,

or " volcano man," one who labours in the crater for sulphur, sought me out as I took my last picture, and offered to conduct me to the summit. His face told me he was faithful and honest, and we closed a bargain at once; he was to furnish me his own services, three horses and a peon, for five dollars a day. Then he took me in tow, and went in search of the one man of Ameca-ameca who spoke English. After much trouble we finally drew up at the door of a little house where two pretty girls were sewing, and, upon learning that papa was out, but would be back soon, I accepted their invitation to enter. They spoke nothing but Spanish, but their father, who had lived in New Orleans thirty years ago, spoke not only his native tongue, but French, English, and Mexican or Indian; his English was, to be sure, a little the worse for his past thirty years' silence, but he patched it up with a little French, and so we hobbled on. "Im speaks" says he, " ze French besser zan de England," and so he did.

Don Felipe was a medico, or doctor, in a small way, and was in great demand. He had one sovereign remedy for all complaints, which was bleeding. He would draw more blood for less money than any physician I ever met. An Indian woman came to be bled while we were waiting for the horses, and he drew from her a pint of blood into a cup, and charged her only a real, or sixpence.

It was said to be fifteen miles from town to the rancho, or
cattle farm, where we should pass the night, and we ought to
have started at noon, but it was four o'clock when we did start.
There is always a vast difference in Mexico between the time you
should leave and the time when you do leave—always. Don
Felipe insisted on accompanying me to the rancho, leaving his
lucrative practice—doctors have always " lucrative practices "—
to the care of his daughters, who were left alone. He was a sad-
faced, quiet man, with thoughtful eyes and grizzled beard; a
grave and courtly Mexican, whose sense of duty to a chance guest
compelled him to climb the mountain with him. Leaving town,
the road winds through great fields planted with corn, and soon
runs at the bottom of a deep barranca, or ravine, ploughed out by
the torrents that sometimes descend from the mountains. Our
peon led a horse with a pack-saddle, and Don Felipe, the guide
and myself had each a small but wiry horse, half hidden beneath
a great Mexican saddle, on the pommel of which was coiled a
lariat, and with large boot stirrups.

As we ascended, we met cattle and sheep, tended by many
children in ragged garments, and donkeys and horses dragging
long · sticks of timber on wooden wheels, a foot or two in
diameter. We frequently met horses with a heavy timber on
each side of them, one end of which was dragging on the ground.
To pass these we had to ride up the steep banks and wait. As
we reached the pine-trees—which do not descend in a body
below a certain altitude—the fields improved, wheat and barley
grew high and thick as far as the eye could reach; over to the
left was a flour-mill, all alone. There are no houses between
the town and the rancho, "only," says Don Felipe, solemnly,
and crossing himself hastily, " only the mountains and God ! "

The pines grew more plentiful, and the air was filled with
their resinous odour; jays and chickadees—birds of the temperate zone—flitted from tree to tree, and reminded me of
northern woods. A high conical hill, rising out of a great field

to the right, is planted with corn to the top, and has rude ruins
on its summit. It is called Tetepetongo, the hill of the round
stones, and was formerly used as an Indian place of sacrifice; at
least, so says tradition. A sister elevation, a mile distant—also
artificial or artificially graded—is known as Tusantepec. As we
go up through immense trees, old Popo seems, at the time, right
ahead, shining golden in the setting sun; again, he is far away,
and we seem travelling from him. Up, still up, the great trees
grow greater, towering away above us, huge hemlocks and pines;
a hill covered with coarse grass is on our left, and, as we reach
its base, it is dark. The night has crept upon us silently, but
has surely wrapped us in its sable folds, and here we are

TEN THOUSAND FEET ABOVE THE SEA,

inclosed in a cold atmosphere and chilled by half congealed rain.
Nothing could compäre for dreariness with that oppressive
silence of those high forests; not even a murmur of wind in the
tree tops, no bird of night to startle us with his cries; nothing
but the hoof-beats of our horses, and the cracking of the twigs
and branches that they stepped upon.

Don Felipe, who had ridden before me silently, wrapped in
his coat, now halted, and demanded abruptly if I were armed. I
said, certainly, and asked him if he had a pistol.

"No," said he, "the people here all know me, and know
that I am poor; but you—they think, of course, that you
are rich."

"But there are no people here?"

"No, but they are passing all the time, and some may have
followed us from town."

"But I have no money; look at me."

"A man can't travel without money."

"Humph! yes, a little, but not enough to tempt them to
kill me."

"Señor, *they would kill you for a dollar.* Señor, there is a black cross on the road yonder, if it were not so dark we might see it; there a friend of mine was killed by the bad men."

"Killed for what?"

"For nothing."

"For money?"

"Si, señor, they shot him there."

It was indeed true; for, two days later, coming down the mountain in the freshness of the morning, I saw the veritable cross, opposite a tangled thicket in a lonely pass; it was of rough wood, painted black, and with an inscription on it, desiring all who passed to offer a prayer for the soul of the murdered man; here Don Felipe paused a moment, crossed himself and murmured a supplication.

That was not the only cross we passed on our way down, when daylight revealed to us the dangers of the road; it seemed as though there was one for every mile. 'In such a country as this the cross is the emblem of death. There is rarely a murderer so hard-hearted and recreant to his religion that he will not breathe a prayer for your soul as he shoots you, or erect a cross above your buried body. I was about to tell Don Felipe I was a dead shot, but I thought that, if I must die that night, I would, at least, be clear of falsehood for that day. So I jogged along in a sullen silence, blaming myself for being led into such a dilemma, and blaming Don Felipe for starting so late, when he knew that we must traverse this dense wood after dark. It was now so dark that my unaccustomed eyes could see nothing but the black trunks of the pinos, and I followed blindly my guide and peon, with Don Felipe behind me. Through an opening in the wood, we obtained one last glimpse of Popocatapetl, standing up like a sheeted ghost against the black sky, and then entered a portion of the forest so dense that I could only follow my peon by his white shirt, and my guide by the glinting silver of his sombréro. We rode over fallen trees, striking limbs and projecting branches, stumbling into holes, jumping gulches, climbing hills, descending hollows—all in a pitchy darkness. Suddenly we were brought to a halt, and the peon darted into the black thicket, I clutched my revolver nervously, and settled myself firmly in the saddle, believing that some foul play was meditated, when Don Felipe told me that he was searching for the trail.

The peon and volcanero held a consultation, and it was agreed to leave all to the pack horse, and putting him in front we went on again, the peon clinging to his horse's tail—all depended upon the instinct of that poor brute.

The cuidado!—"look out"—of the guide became more frequent, as the path was obstructed by fallen pines, and cut across by numerous gulches. A long-drawn howl went through the black forest at intervals, which Don Felipe said was that of a coyote, or wolf; and more rarely we heard the blood-curdling cry of the puma, or mountain lion. Fortunately for travellers, but unfortunately for naturalists, these animals are exceedingly rare. One would have been enough, however, for us that night; he could have demolished the entire party without our seeing him at all. We descended a steep ravine and climbed a high hill, covered with pines, which we went down, and crossed another ravine; and about this time, when I thought it would be the proper thing to despair, we turned a clump of trees and saw a light. Soon we reached a gate, which a servant opened at our knocking, and Don Domingo, the major domo, warmly welcomed us. We had been five hours in the saddle, and were so cold and stiff we could hardly get our legs together when lifted to the ground.

The poor peon, who had walked and run all the way, with only a shirt on, and cotton trousers rolled up to his thighs, had to attend to the horses, though Don Felipe—true caballero that he was—allowed no one but himself to care for his.

It is nine o'clock, Don Domingo tells us; we had thus passed three hours groping in the darkness of the mountain forests.

Made welcome to the roughly-built house, we entered and found a
roaring fire leaping up the open throat of a clay chimney. By
this cheering blaze we thawed ourselves out, and by the time meat
was boiled and coffee ready were in condition to enjoy them. Don
Domingo, a perfect gentleman, of the type so often met with in
Mexico, reads my letters of introduction, and tells me it was not
necessary to present them, as he recognised in me a friend after
his own heart. He then embraced me and patted me on the back,
and set me out his only remaining bottle of wine. There was but
one bed, and in this Don Domingo had been sleeping when we
arrived; but he insisted that I should occupy it, and he and Don
Felipe spread their serapes on the floor, and were soon sleeping
with their heads on their saddles. The " bed " was three or four
boards, raised a foot from the floor, and covered with a thin strip
of straw matting. Drawing my serape over my head, and belting
my knife and revolver about me, I was soon in the land of
dreams.

THE RANCHO AT THE SNOW-LINE.

The rancho of Tlamacas, says Charnay, the archæologist, who
visited it, and found near it some of his most valuable pottery, is
at an elevation of 12,500 feet above the sea !—at an altitude far
above any other habitation in North America. It is in a valley
with high hills on all sides but the north, where the surface slopes
toward the valley of Puebla, about nine leagues distant. The
soil is volcanic, sand and grit supporting a growth of coarse grass
and great pines, hoary with moss and lichens. In about the
centre of this secluded valley is the rancho, its visible portion
being the house and the subliming works where the crude sulphur,
brought down from the crater, is purified. This is done in earthen
jars, which are broken when the sulphur is sublimed. Here then
is a sort of a half-way house for the volcaneros, and a resting-place
for the mules and donkeys that transport the sulphur to the valley
below. Sulphur is not the only product of the volcano; for many

years the only ice used in Mexico was obtained from the ravines seaming the cone above the snow-line.

Even to this day the city of Puebla is supplied from the mountain. The Indians ascend far above the rancho, dig out the ice, where it rests congealed the year through, and carry it on their backs to the donkey trails, where it is packed on the backs of these animals to the valleys. From the fact that the ice is imperfectly crystalised, and more resembles snow, it is known as *nieve*, snow, and this name is yet applied to the ice-cream made in the cities. In the Plaza of Mexico, you will hear every afternoon, the cries of the boys peddling ice-creams, " *Nieve, tome nieve ?* "

The volcano towers directly above the rancho, south-east of it : first a broad strip of pines, then black volcanic sand ; then the snow-covered dome, with the black rock, known as Pico del Fraile, sticking up on its western ridge.

THE ASCENT OF THE CONE.

The peon had been instructed to awaken us at three o'clock in the morning, that we might get well up to the snow-line before the sun rose, but the poor fellow was worn out with cold and fatigue, and when I awoke it was five o'clock, and neither horses nor coffee were ready. The temperature was 48° Fahr. as we started, and the trees sparkling with frost ; the sun peered above the Malinche—the solitary mountain that rises from the valley of Puebla—turning it a fiery red, and bathing the whole Puebla valley in soft rosy mist ; then, striking upon the cone of Popocatapetl, made it glisten like a silver dome.

It was a glorious spectacle, with the sun's rays rebounding as it were from the silver mountain that towered majestically so far above us into the blue ether. It nerved and braced me for a struggle that I had reason to think would be severe. For two weeks before I started I had searched Mexico for some companion, but was successful only in developing some of the most disheartening stories of previous experiences, from the few who had ascended

tho volcano, that over reached tho ears of man. First, I should
be robbed in Ameca-ameca, then murdered on tho road up tho
mountain, as I passed through the forest ; escaping these, I should
certainly succumb to the cold at the rancho, or, if not, then I could
not miss bursting a blood-vessel as I reached the crater. Thus
these pessimistic counsellors pursued me to the very crater, leaving
me not a minute of anticipatory rest in the whole journey. Of
tho many who had attempted tho ascent, few had succeeded ; for
they either became footsore, or fainted, or bled at the nose, eyes,
and ears, or from the lungs, or mangled themselves on the frozen
cone. It was a most discouraging prospect, but, by tho time tho
first story was finished, " my dander "—so tho down-caster would
say—was thoroughly up, and I hoisted my banner with

POPOCATAPETL or—Bust

inscribed thereon. Thus far I had not "busted," and resolved
to push on to tho end. The trouble with nearly all who have
attempted the ascent was, that they were mainly dwellers in
cities, who had not often "roughed it," and who looked upon
tho whole trip as a vast picnic, and prepared themselves accordingly, with great quantities of eatables and liquor. They,
moreover, nearly always carried along their wives and families,
and would drag these frail creatures as long as possible, and
then have to take them back to tho rancho. They told me I
must wrap my feet in rags, to prevent them from sinking in
tho snow, or wear spiked sandals ; but I knew it must be pretty
soft snow that my feet would slump through, and that the only
possible difficulty, when on tho mountain top, would be to find
an area sufficient to place them on ! I strapped on my old
hunting shoes, which had assisted me in climbing many lesser
volcanoes in the West Indies, and buckled on my canvas
leggings ; this was tho only preparation I made for climbing.
My peon furnished me with a spiked staff—not one of those

gaudy "alpenstocks" such as Cook's excursionists use in scaling
the mighty Alps, and then bring home and stick up in a corner
to be worshipped ever after—but a stick little bigger than a
broomstick, with a rigid iron spike in it. From the rancho we
immediately entered the pines, and, riding through them for
half a mile, struck diagonally down the side of a wide deep
barranca, and then climbed the other side in the same way;
here begins the vast stretch of volcanic sand that laps the base
of the cone proper. The horses sank fetlock deep, the grade
was tremendous, and their laboured breathing, as they stopped
every rod or two to get wind, was extremely painful to witness—
owing to the rarefaction of the air, and the great labour of
wading through the heavy sand, it really seemed as though the
blood would gush from their red, distended nostrils. Compelled
to adopt a course of short zigzags, my mozos ranged far a-head
of me, and reached the rendezvous long in advance of the horses.
After about two hours of this work, during which the agony of
the horses seemed so great that I was only restrained from
dismounting by the knowledge that I needed all my strength
for the final climb, we reached a ridge of rocks. It was the
first of a series that cropped up through the back sand, and
ran down towards Puebla with many a fantastic shape, evidently
formed by fire. On the upper rock is a cross, indicating the
death of a man—this time not on the spot, but in the crater.
At this spot—La Cruz—we halted the horses and gladly
dismounted.

THE LIMIT OF VEGETATION

had been passed at a little distance above the barranca, the
pines ending there in a body, as if refusing to advance even
a single straggling sentinel further; and then came clumps of
coarse grass, dwindling finally to little specks, and, at last, all
that remained was the hardly visible blotches of moss or

sphagnum; above, all was sand to the skirts of the everlasting snow.

Here, Don Felipe left me, and turned back with the horses. He had thus far come with me voluntarily and without recompense as my *companero*, but his obligation—like that of the bride who ascended Mount Blanc with her husband and waited half-way up—did not extend beyond the snow-line. Dear Don Felipe! he embraced me as though for the last time, and his serious face assumed an even graver expression as he warned me to return immediately I felt symptoms of giddiness. Then he turned and plodded down the mountain, as we prepared to ascend.

A sublime spectacle was opened to me as I stood by the lonely black cross, wedged into the fire-scathed rock, at this elevation of 15,000 feet. The eye ranged over a vast valley, down the ridges, above the black belt of volcanic sand, across the pines, to La Mujer Blanca, the dead "white woman," now with a wreath of cloud above her, and her snowy breasts upturned, bared to the pitiless sky. A broad table-land lies between the two volcanoes, which appear at a lower elevation, like a narrow gap. Through this gap, which I passed the night before, runs the trail that Cortes took when he first approached the valley of Mexico. From its western slope the future conquerors first saw the wonderful valley, which, says Prescott, "with its picturesque assemblage of water, woodland, and cultivated plains, its shining cities and shadowy hills, was spread out before them like some gay and gorgeous panorama." The same scene of beauty that greeted the delighted eyes of the Spaniards 360 years ago was unfolded to me as I stood at the foot of La Cruz, 8000 feet above the valley of Mexico, where the glimmering towers of the city could be seen, though fifty miles away! The valley of Puebla, away to the north, lay half veiled in vapour, revealing little lakes, a village here and there, white church-towers, and varied hues of hill and vale, of wooded mountains and populous plains. Rising high above it was the extinct volcano, Malinche—Malintzin named by the Indians, in honour of Cortes—and far away to the east the peak of Orizaba, 150 miles distant, its snowy cone glistening like a diamond above the enveloping clouds. A glorious vision! one that I could have looked upon for hours; but the gathering clouds of mist, rolling up from the valleys, warned me that it was dangerous to linger longer.

A wide belt of deep sand lay between us and the solid snow, flecked here and there by little drifts and straggling remnants of former storms. Through this we slowly and painfully waded, falling back at least one step in three, and breathing the first sigh of relief when finally amongst the snow-fields. Simultaneously with our reaching the snow, the threatening clouds gathered about us, and we were enveloped in as dense a fog as any I have ever seen on the Atlantic coast.

ABOVE THE CLOUDS.

We were now fairly above the cloud strata, and walking onward as in a dream, conscious of direction only by the steepness of the incline before us. The only guide-book that describes the ascent of the volcano warns travellers to " provide themselves with overcoats, veils, and alpenstocks, which they drive into the ashes and volcanic sand." It is not absolutely necessary to provide yourself with veils and overcoats " to drive into the volcanic sand," but you must have blue goggles, to prevent the effects of the strong reflection of the sun's rays from this glaring surface of snow. A person with delicate complexion might also feel the need of a green veil, and the moso should carry for him an overcoat or extra wraps.

In the language of a correspondent of a New York paper, writing from Mexico at the time of my ascent, I went up " alone with three Indian guides; " well, so I did, at least there was no *gente de razon*, or "reasonable man"—white man—along with me. There was my peon, in cotton shirt and pants, with only a remnant of a scrape over his shoulder, and only sandals strapped to his bare feet. He carried my tourograph, or camera, and a canteen of nourishment, beside the provisions. Then there was my "guide," now degenerated into a mere *companero*, or companion—who knew nothing, as I ascertained, of the mountain, and the real guide, an old man picked up at the rancho. He also wore cotton shirts and pants, and a broad sombréro, but had his feet swathed in strips of blanket till they looked as though he had an infliction of elephantiasis.

The peon and I soon left the others behind, and plodded on, one step after another, for hours. The snow was just right for climbing over; as there had been no recent fall, it had been softened and compacted, giving quite a good foothold. It had been gnawed by the sun till it lay in great cakes, tilted up edge-ways, forming a great labyrinth of passages, through which we slowly picked our way.

Such terrible stories had been told me of the sufferings endured by mountain climbers of this cone of snow, that I had prepared myself to meet and overcome obstacles requiring almost superhuman strength and endurance. But I had resolved to go on step by step, taking my time, shedding my last drop of blood, if necessary, but to reach the summit by all means. So I took it serenely, following close after my peon, treading where he trod, and letting him take off the wire edge of the trail. He seemed to like that; it showed I had confidence in him, and so I had— confidence that if he fell into a hole and disappeared I should not follow suit. Half-way up, perhaps, my "guides" cried out: "Señor, we can't go any farther; we are lost!" We were surrounded by mist that obscured everything more than ten feet away from us; but I could not see how we could get lost, when, if we went up far enough, we should reach the crater brim, or, if low enough, we should come out on the sand—so I told them.

K

My peon, also, was of my opinion, and, as we combined had the
food, drink, instruments and pistols, I didn't care whether the
others came or not.   In Mexico I had procured a double-handful
of the famous coca leaves, the stay and stimulant of the Indians
of the Peruvian Andes, and to these may be attributed, possibly,
the fact that I made the ascent without fatigue.   Whatever the
reason, I went on, calmly chewing my cud of coca leaves, up, up,
surmounting one snowy barrier after another, for four hours or
more, when my faithful servant turned and said, "Señor, *aquí
está el crater!*"—here is the crater!—Yes! reaching the place
where he stood, I suddenly came upon a

BLACK AND YAWNING GULF,

which even the dense mist could not conceal.   Here, for the
first time, there darted through my temples a severe pain, which
remained for hours, even till I had descended to the rancho.
Overcome by conflicting emotions, and needing no longer any
further stimulus, I sank upon the crater brim, breathless and
panting from excitement.   Then I arose exultantly, and dis-
charged the six chambers of my revolver into the air, creating
such a concussion in the crater that great stones rattled down
its perpendicular sides, and the reverberation nearly deafened
us.   From "crag to crag" leaped the volumes of sound, like
peals of thunder, as though retreating farther and farther into
the entrails of

"OLD TLALOC," THE "GOD OF STORMS,"

whose brow I now pressed beneath my feet, at a height of nearly
18,000 feet above the sea.   The lip of the crater is a narrow rim
of sand, lying above the black abyss, and at the edge of the sea of
snow, like the coral ledge composing an atoll of the southern sea.
Its highest point is at the west, its lowest at the east, and the
crater has somewhat the shape of an ellipse, 4000 or 5000 feet

in its longer diameter, and over 1000 feet deep. The snow stopped abruptly at this wreath of sand, rising to a height of from six to eight feet, and curling over it, but prevented from advancing farther by the heat from the crater. " Thus far and no farther," the heated breath of Tlaloc's vitals belched in the face of the boreal visitor, which rested like a parasitic cloak upon his shoulders. When an opening in the clouds occurred, I descended over the brim about one hundred feet, clinging to the projections of porphyritic rock, to a rocky platform whence the labourers in the volcano were lowered to the bottom of the crater. They had not been at work for a month, and the hoisting winch was dismantled, but by holding by the great beams I could peer over the brink into the horrible pit below. Directly beneath me ascended a dense sulphur cloud, from which, and from various other vents scattered over the surface, arose the strong fumes that suggested to us the infernal regions. It is from these vents that the sulphur is obtained, being sublimed on the sides of the crater. About twenty years ago the present owner of the volcano commenced to work this dangerous sulphur mine, removing the accumulated sulphur at a great profit; at present the only supply is that from the condensed fumes as it is deposited; but originally there was the accumulation of centuries.

It will be remembered that some of the soldiers of Cortes ascended the volcano (much to the wonder of the astonished Indians)—the first to climb it; and that in the years of the Conquest one of his brave captains descended into the crater and procured sulphur for their powder. This latter feat, however, I am inclined to discredit, not believing that the Spaniards of those days had the means for lowering a man one thousand feet into the bowels of the earth. That he might have obtained it from the crevices of the walls, and have imperilled his life in so doing, is possible and probable.

As all the sulphur not furnished by this volcano is obtained from Sicily, there is great demand for General Ochoa's product.

It is difficult for him to obtain labourers, as one would naturally suppose, though there is no special mortality among the men labouring at this altitude. They work in gangs alternate weeks, camping in the crater, beneath rough sheds. A sudden storm or earthquake sometimes makes it uncomfortable for them, but these volcaneros are a hardy race of Indians, and, if well furnished with mescal and aquadiente—rum and brandy—endure their hardships wonderfully well.

Again ascending to the brim, I pitched my camera, and awaited an opportunity to get a view of the crater. Just then a few flakes of snow drifted by, and the next minute a violent gust compelled us to seek shelter under the snow-ledge.

A SNOW-STORM IN THE UPPER REGIONS.

For an hour the storm raged with fury, pelting us with snow crystals till we were half buried in the drifts, and my photographic exposures threatened to be brief. Taking advantage of the lulls in the gale, I crept with my guide to what he called the highest point—" el pico"—hoping to gain a view of the lower regions ; but without avail. We were indeed above the clouds, and on the battle-field of the elements. From the depths of the crater boomed the noise of escaping steam, and detonations that told of the activity of internal forces, while the crashing of falling stones awoke the echoes of this great basin in deafening reverberations. After more than three hours on the mountain top, vainly looking for a clear view over the vast expanse below, we prepared to descend, just, however, taking stock of our provisions and drinking the canteen of cold tea. Wishing to make the ascent as much a test of endurance as possible—as it is certainly a test of lung and vital power—I had not eaten or drank anything since my biscuit and coffee in the morning, having accomplished the ascent in six hours, with nothing in my mouth but the coca.

The most gratifying episode of this trip was the little game I played on my thermometer. For two months previous it had hung against the wall of my room in Mexico, and led an idle life. It would slide up from 70° in a morning to 80° at noon, and then drop back again to 70°, not varying a degree in a week. It had begun to believe that 10° comprised the limit of its range, when I astonished it by taking it up the mountain. It had become so bilious that when it got down to 44° at the rancho, it had not strength enough to get back to its old camping ground in the neighbourhood of 70°. But its severest shock was at the crater; there I hung it up on a stick, and it went down to 34°, which represented the actual temperature. Determined to have full range, I piled snow about the bulb and brought it down to the freezing point, where it stuck for three days; and I had to send to it the coast, where the temperature ranges anywhere from 110° upward, to get it in working order again.

THE 'HERALD' WAY UP.

It is my settled conviction that the 'HERALD' has never attained a higher altitude than that day, when I carried a copy in my pocket, intending to deposit it on the topmost peak. This plan worked all right till it came to the last part—I forgot to leave it. Putting my hand in my pocket, when down among the pines, I found that 'HERALD,' and was almost provoked into climbing back again to carry out the original design. The one soothing reflection in this connection is, that it has been some 17,000 feet nearer heaven than the average New England newspaper, and if any other paper wishes to sing out "Excelsior," it must climb up Chimborazo or Cotopaxi.

At last came the time for leaving; the snow fell thickly, and all hope for clear weather had long since vanished. If the ascent was slow and tedious, going down was exactly the reverse. I believe, on my honour, that I slid two miles at one jump. Down the cone the labourers of the last month had dug a long straight trench, leading from crater to volcanic sand, down which they used to slide the sulphur. Had they been working now I should have borrowed a kind of straw mat, and have slid down on that, as they were wont to do; but, as they were not, I stood up on my broad-soled shoes, and, guiding my course with the alpenstock, sped downward with speed of the wind.

In less than fifteen minutes I had left the zone of storms, and had emerged into the temperate region, the snow-cakes spinning past me in a way that was not at all slow. In less than one minute more I had come near sliding into a zone of tropical heat we sometimes read about, for my toe caught an ice-chunk, and sent me burrowing into a crevice, looking for the centre of the volcano. Fortunately there was not room enough for me and my shoes too, so my peon pulled me out in time to prevent suffocation, and set me down in the snow to recover. With long leaps we sped over the snow, and out upon the sand, and finally reached La Cruz, whence our descent to the rancho was uneventful.

At sunset old Popocatapetl seemed on fire, his peak took on a rosy glow that soon suffused the whole cone; and later, as the sun sank down and spread its warm colouring over the eastern sky, he seemed encased in burnished gold; but, as old Sol disappeared entirely, he relapsed into cold, dead white, standing out like a mountain of marble against the steel-blue sky. The "White Woman" did not share in this afterglow of the sun, but remained resting on her bier, a slight mist draping her, and giving her the livid hue of a corpse—as she is. But when daylight had just faded, and the stars began to twinkle one by one, both the dead giant and the dead giantess were wrapped in the serene white and calm of this upper atmosphere.

That night it snowed at the rancho, and the next morning the whole mountain was covered deep, even down among the pines. All the sand field that we ploughed through the day before was heaped high with snowdrifts, making it impossible to ascend. The

Pico del Fraile was hung with huge icicles; the house-top was white with snow, which dripped off as the sun came up. The day was calm and clear, like early spring in our own mountain region. The valley below was buried in a dull blue vapour, through which lakes and villages barely glimmered. Snow covered the ground in a thin sheet, and sparrows and snow-birds gathered about the yard, to complete the illusion that it was spring. We filed through the valley pass, beneath the silent pines, breathing an air delicious with balsam, brisk and exhilarating, and turned our backs upon Popocatapetl, monarch of Mexico.

* In 'Camps in the Caribbees,' by Mr. Fred. Ober, chap. xviii., there is a most interesting account of the Isle of Martinique, the birthplace of the Empress Josephine. Mr. Ober looked up the archives and registers in Fort de France, and corrects the inaccuracies of several of her biographers, and he also gives a correct drawing of "La Pagerie," where she was born on the 23rd of June, 1763.

CHAPTER XVI.

Travelling by diligence—Dirty state of the town of Pachuca—Our inspection of the silver mines—Method of reducing the silver from the ore—Regla and its hacienda.

SILVER is Mexico's chief product : within her boundaries are found the greatest silver deposits known in the world. Real del Monte, Pachuca, San Luis Potosi, and other of her mining localities, have yielded within the range of statistical data over 3000 millions of dollars—more than six-tenths, in fact, nearly seven-tenths, of all the silver in circulation—and the amount obtained before the Conquest cannot be told. One half the silver in use in the world has come from this locality. To visit Mexico without seeing the silver mines would be equivalent to seeing 'Hamlet' minus the Prince of Denmark. These mines are still producing thirty million ounces annually, and may soon double and treble the quantity, as the country gets settled, railways become extended, and the process of extracting the ore conducted on new and scientific principles. Certainly, after what I have seen, I shall place a greater value on the few silver cups and teapots I possess than I have hitherto attributed to them.

My friend Mr. W. H. Bishop, artist and correspondent for Harper's illustrated publications, and one of the pleasantest companions I ever met, arranged to join me in an excursion to Pachuca and the surrounding mining districts in the State of Hidalgo and we resolved to complete the journey by a visit to one of the largest haciendas in the country, belonging to the Tejira family, to whom Mr. Henry Hope, who married one of the daughters of the house, kindly gave us letters of introduction.

As travelling meant a great deal of saddle-work, we had to limit our respective wardrobes to the capacity of a small bag apiece. The high pommel of a Mexican saddle, originally designed for holding the lariat, or rope with which the vaquero lassoes his cattle, is singularly convenient for carrying anything that may be attached to it by a strap; the article so attached will hang over the horse's forehead without impeding the animal's progress. The spurt of a gallop occasionally bursts a strap or two, and then *impedimenta* fly in every direction; but a Mexican saddle is wisely furnished with long soft leathern thongs, most convenient for repairs, or for tying on extra articles for use on the journey. A Mexican traveller's baggage is not usually cumbersome; the saddles are so made that, though they often weigh, with their heavy silver ornaments, forty pounds, yet they never gall the horse's back, and the Secretary of the Society for the Prevention of Cruelty to Animals would have but a sinecure in looking after them; although, were he to impound the diligence and baggage-mules and *burros*, the country for sore backs and raw places, he would almost put an entire stop to the traffic of the Republic.

Our start was made by rail at an early hour on Saturday, the 16th of July, 1881, to Ometusco, forty-two miles down the line towards Vera Cruz, where *diligencias* are in waiting to convey the passengers to Venta de Cruz, over the usual rough kind of Mexican road; this was so bad, in places, that the vehicles had to turn aside and drive through the cultivated ground, crashing over large maguey plants, and doing damage fully equivalent to what it would have cost to keep the road in reasonable repair. On starting we had a quarrel with a man who persisted in retaining one of the better seats which had been allotted to us, but he carried so many pistols in his belt that we deemed it impolitic further to urge our claim, as the very jolting of the vehicle was sufficient to cause the weapons to explode. There is nothing like travelling with plenty of pistols; had he been unarmed he would undoubtedly have been put through the window without ceremony. After several hours' jolting we were transferred to a horse-car on a tramway, and ran smoothly through a lovely valley to Pachuca, where we arrived at six o'clock in the evening. My note-book contains details of several adventures during the journey, which I regret that I have not space to insert. What Englishman, or any other man, can possibly travel through an unfrequented foreign land without comical, or what he may deem dangerous, incidents almost hourly crossing his path.

The town of Pachuca is situated in a narrow valley, enclosed by steep, rugged hills totally destitute of vegetation. Its present population, with surrounding hamlets, may safely be estimated at 25,000, and this number is daily increasing, as mines are coming into "bonanza," and additional labour is required. From the muddy river, which runs through the town, the houses and mining works on each side rise terrace upon terrace. The church is shabby, the market-place a mound of dirt, the streets narrow and abominable; in a word, it is a mining town in which the high weekly wages of the workmen are gambled away or spent in drink on pay-day, and the women and children are left to starve and struggle through the following six days as best they may. If this be not the case outward appearances are deceptive. Pachuca is the capital of the state of Hidalgo; a once imposing convent has been converted into a mining school, and another has been utilised for the state college. One of the pupils showed me over this latter building, and it was depressing to find some two hundred fine young fellows pursuing their studies in an atmosphere reeking with horrible smells, and in a place whose general filth and dirt must act prejudicially both upon their health and upon their morals. The town of Pachuca presents the worst features of a mining community. I must confess that features of a similar character might be found by

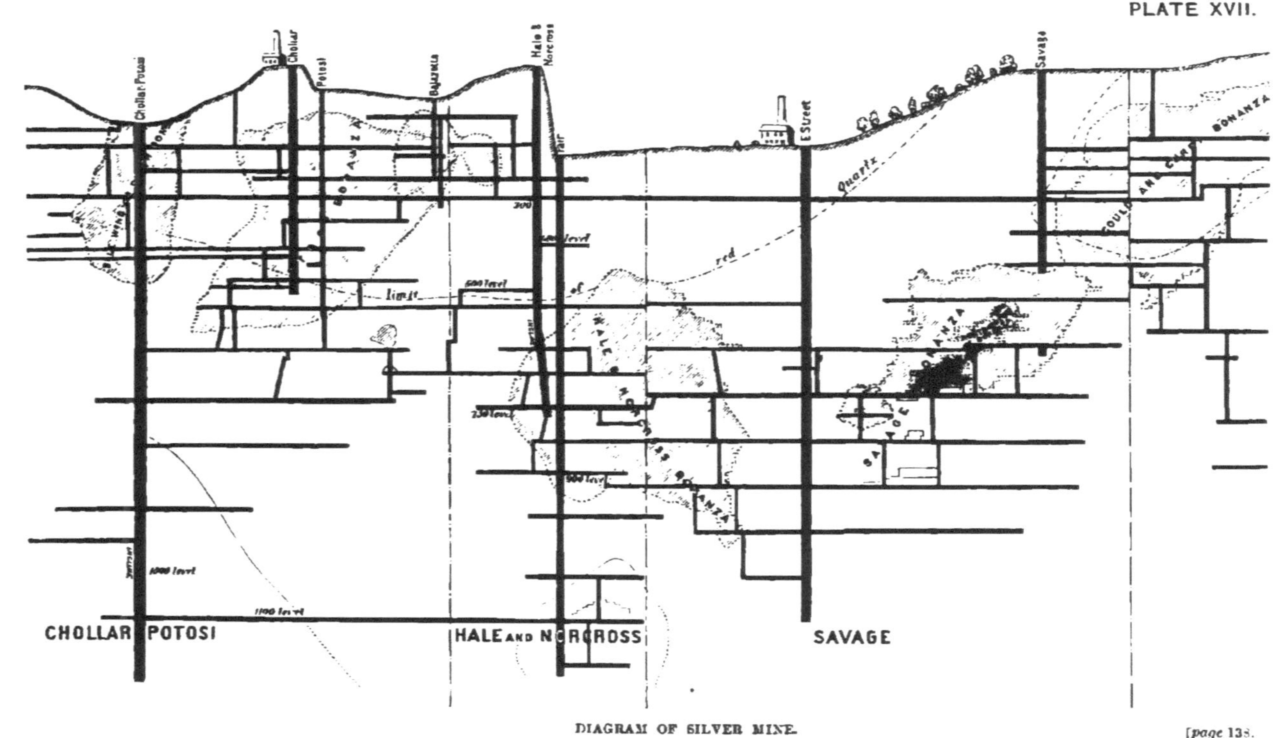

DIAGRAM OF SILVER MINE.

very fastidious and æsthetic persons not far from some of the pleasantest places in dear old England, the gambling perhaps excepted. There were a good many Cornish miners in the town, these gentry being distinguishable from the natives by both appearance and language. I talked to many of them; they were overlookers, and well to do; it was painful to hear them complain of England, and the neglected and uncared-for condition into which they were allowed to fall, before they emigrated from Cornwall; in fact, they used such language against the upper classes of the country that I dread to think there may be even at the present time deserving and suffering workmen in England who consider themselves neglected by those who have it in their power to alter the conditions or laws which affect occasional depressions in trade and commerce.

We had brought letters of introduction to Mr. Landero, the chairman and resident manager of the Real del Monté Company, and we had delivered these on our arrival on Saturday evening, at his semi-palatial house in the centre of the town. He received us most kindly, and placed a guide and riding-horses at our disposal.

As there was only a partial cessation of work in the mines on Sunday, and our time was precious, we made an early start with Mr. Pengilley for a tour of inspection. We rode out to, and descended, the San Juan, Rosario, and Santa Gertrudis mines; although one mine would have satisfied me, as all are similar, and the deeper mines are very wet. At the Gertrudis mine we were shown into a room where we took off all our clothes, and put on flannel trousers and jacket, boots, and a heavy hat to which a lighted candle was adjusted by a piece of damp clay. Before descending the shaft we were taken to be introduced to the head engineer, in order to ask him to let us down the shaft gently, and stop the engines if we signalled from any of the levels; lo, and behold! the engineer was the very man with whom we had had the quarrel in the diligence, and it is difficult to say which of us proved more polite under the present embarrassing circumstances; however, he let us safely down 540 feet to the bottom of the mine, one at a time, in a small, muddy iron bucket. "*Facilis descensus Averni.*" From the galleries of the lowest levels we ascended by vertical ladders to the upper ones; we had to creep through holes barely large enough to admit us. The rock being soft and liable to fall, the sides of the galleries are supported by thick timbers; and, these being very costly, when the ore in a lower seam has been worked out, the refuse from another seam is dropped through trap-doors and slides into the vacant space, and then the timbers are taken out to be used elsewhere. The baulks of timber are from a foot to a foot and a-half square, and eight to twelve feet long. We noticed some of them crushed into powder by the sinking of the rock.

The ore runs in veins through the limestone and serpentine rock in which it is imbedded. It has the appearance of small black grains of sand; when you think you have been taught how to distinguish this, you are shown through a gallery of light-coloured sandy rock, and are told it also is a very rich vein of silver; so you despair of becoming expert enough to obtain a lucrative employment as mine inspector, and only make note of two things, viz.: that the veins run chiefly from N.E. to S.W., and that where any vein divides into two branches the precious metal is found in the greatest quantity. The prevailing form of ore is sulphide of silver, although in some mines native silver is found mixed with the former.

The number of mines now worked in the district are as follows:—

Pachuca	..	..	..	..	..	..	154
Real del Monte	..	..	..	..	..	76	
El Chico	..	..	..	..	..	..	24
Santa Rosa	..	..	..	..	..	..	13
							267

Of these mines seventy-seven are worked by the rich and

powerful company known under the name of "The Real del Monté Mining Company."

From five hundred to a thousand men are employed in each of the mines we visted; they are strictly searched at three different gates on leaving the mine. Any one caught stealing is very severely dealt with; he is imprisoned, or sent to be a soldier. In aggravated cases a man is never heard of after he enters the prison door. An order arrives to transfer him to some other prison, and he is generally shot (by accident!) on the way.

We spent the whole of Monday in what are called beneficiating "*haciendas*," or establishments, where the silver is extracted from the ore. In Pachuca and its neighbourhood the "*patio*" system, which had its origin there in 1557, and was discovered by a Spaniard, Bartolomeo de Medina, is still followed. "*Hacienda*" is the general term for agricultural farms, but "*Hacienda de beneficio*" is used as a mining term; and a beneficiating or ore-extracting "*hacienda*" consists of a large flagged yard, five to ten acres in extent, round which are placed the ore-crushing mills, stables, refinery, retorts, and various workshops.

The water power used for ore crushing purposes is brought in at as high a level as possible on a steep hillside, and passes from the ore-crushing mills on various terraces to the large yard, which is always on the lowest level.

There are three kinds of ore-crushing mills in use: Cornish stamps, Mexican arrastras, and Chilian mills, worked either by water-power or by mules; by these processes the ore is brought to a state of puddle, somewhat softer than clay used for brick-making; it is then spread out to a depth of two or three feet over the paved floor of the patio; to this mass sulphate of copper is added in powder, about 15 lbs. of sulphate to 3000 lbs. of puddle, or half per cent. This is trodden into the puddle by horses; several gangs of old, worn-out horses or mules, about twelve in a gang, are seen in various parts of the patio, being driven round in circles to tread in the sulphate. On the following day 6 per cent. of common salt is added, and in two more days 100 per cent. of pure quicksilver, or as much as the assay of the ore shows to be necessary. The quicksilver is sprinkled over this mass by men who carry it in canvas bags, which they shake or knock against their bare thighs as they walk about. The mass is then trodden up by horses for from fourteen to twenty-one days, when the silver is supposed to be completely mixed with the quicksilver; it is then wheeled in barrows to a large tank, through which passes a rapid stream of water, and in which some dozen nearly nude men keep stirring up the muddy mixture with their feet and legs; they thus cause the clay particles to pass off with the stream, and leave the silver and quicksilver at the bottom of the tanks. This residuum is scooped up in small iron jars and taken to a shed, and poured into long cone-shaped canvas bags, through which most of the quicksilver runs out, and what remains with the silver is passed off in the form of vapour by means of heated retorts. None of the quicksilver is lost or wasted; even the vapour is brought by cold water into its original state, and is again and again made to fulfil its part in the *beneficiating* of silver. The pure silver is finally melted into bars ready for the mint or for manufacturing purposes. The cost of its production from the mine to the bar is about 25 per cent., varying according to the richness of the ore.

The men and children employed in the processes where so much quicksilver is used did not appear to suffer from its effects, but the old, worn-out horses and mules, used in the treading-out process, soon lose their hoofs and become in other ways unfit for service, except perhaps to yield their skins for leather. Indeed, they appeared already half-tanned.

The hillsides are dotted over with little white-washed columns, indicating the extent and position of the mines below the surface. The mining laws are very fair; the government

THE BENIFICIATING HACIENDA OF LORETTO, PACHUCA.

[page 142.

encourages the peaceful working of the mines, and, as a guarantee for this, it retains to itself a share in every mine.

(I have just seen in a local paper a notice that the Governor of the State of Guerrero has issued a new mining regulation for that state, whereby one twenty-fifth of the profit from mines must go to the state.)

We heard many stories of the wealth of some companies and individuals, but there is great uncertainty in the result of every enterprise underground. The present rich mine of Santa Gertrudis had been worked for many years at a loss; it changed hands, and the new proprietors happened immediately to strike a vein of ore in it richer than any in the country.

There was nothing to detain us in Pachuca after our inspection of the mines, and on Tuesday morning we left for Regla by "diligence." After climbing over the tops of the barren hills, we came to a district covered with "*magueys,*" and the road was so bad we had frequent occasion to turn off from it. Of course the horses—we had six in the diligence—do not like travelling amongst the sharp-pointed leaves of the maguey, and the conductor had sometimes to cut a road for us through these with a hatchet. What with the plunging and restiveness of the horses, and some soft boggy places in the ground, we had a more lively time of it on the maguey and cactus fields than upon the road.

The first halt was at an old Spanish "*hacienda,*" called Velasco, which we entered through fortified gates, more fitted for a small town than a single farm. After a hurried breakfast and change of team, during which we saw some comical sights, we sped out through other fortified portals, and up a hill with so sharp a turn that a spill looked more than probable; fourteen mules had replaced the six horses, and most of them required a man with a goad to keep them in their places at starting; at last they dashed through the gate, like a flock of sparrows suddenly alarmed by the firing of a gun.

It is very amusing to watch the *mozo* who attends the driver of a diligence to keep the mules up to their work. This is a performance quite independent of the driver, who flips up the lagging mules with his long whip as they seem to require it from his point of view. The *mozo* has two or three small bags, which he fills with the sharpest-edged stones he can find at any point where the road is under repair. He shies these at the mules from the top of the diligence with much force, and the hit is regarded as a bad one if the stone does not bounce from the back of one mule to the back of another, possibly catching a third in the eye before it falls to the ground. When a stone thuds on the first mule's back, every mule in the team springs to the collar, fancying the same stone may catch him *en passant*.

All the mules had names, the calling out of which was often sufficient, without the application of the whip, to spurt them up a hill. If the harness got entangled, or they got the low loose traces between their legs, they quietly let the *mozo* set it to rights while he ran alongside the team.

Mexican " diligencias " must be under the patronage of some special saint, who builds them strong, keeps their wheels oiled, and balances their leathern springs, so that the malicious demons who have charge of the roads may be foiled in their efforts at destruction.

The small town of Real del Monté—a very favourable contrast to Pachuca—was the next station; and while the mules were being changed we crossed the roadway to the ruins of an ancient castle, built by the Spaniards to hold the prisoners whom they drafted to work in the mines. Regla was reached at four o'clock. It is a large " *hacienda* " belonging to the Real del Monté company, and used solely for " beneficiating " or extracting silver from the ore; and the place has been selected for this purpose on account of a river coming from high ground and supplying power for turning all the stamping-mills in the establishment. The river comes pouring down a gorge which it has succeeded in cutting for itself through a ridge of basaltic columns as fine as any I ever heard of in the world. The hacienda and works are completely surrounded by a wall of basaltic columns some two hundred feet in height; directly opposite the picturesque veranda of the house some of the columns were contorted and whirled into the appearance of a catherine-wheel at the time when their crystallisation was in process.

The works are on the patio system, exactly as I have described those of Pachuca, the noisy stamping-mills working night and day. To me they had a peculiarly musical charm. It happened that in the middle of the night two or three of the nearest stamping-mills stopped on account of something being wrong with the water-wheels, and Bishop and I, who slept in adjoining rooms, both awoke and called to each other, wondering what had happened.

On the following morning we made some sketches, had a bath in the river, ascertained by measurement that the hexagonal basaltic columns were two feet in diameter; and, having remarked the arms and emblazonments on the entrance gates, discovered that the estate in early times belonged to the celebrated Count de Regla, and that the hacienda was built by him in 1792 at a cost of $2,000,000. Count de Regla was the nobleman who established the "Monte de Piedad"—the national pawnshop, or safety deposit place for valuables—of which I have already made special mention in Chapter VI., as being one of the most interesting institutions of the country.

CHAPTER XVII.

HACIENDA, OR MEXICAN FARM.

Thunderstorm—Hospitable Reception—Daily Farm-work—Mexican Farm-life—
Meals—Farm Produce—Departure of the Family—Result of Insurrections.

AT one o'clock our kind host at Regla, after furnishing an extra good breakfast, provided us with horses, and we started to Pulancingo, a city near which the Tejira family were expecting us at their farming *hacienda*, or country residence.

It was a ride of twenty miles, and the afternoon clouds seemed already gathering for a thunderstorm. I rather wished to remain until the following morning, the mornings being always fine; however it was decided that we should start. The road soon debouched upon a grassy plain, over which we had to travel. The storm was coming down from the hills, preceded by lightning such as I never before saw, and hope never to see again; forked flashes were continually repeated above, around, and beneath us, while crashes of thunder caused the earth to tremble.

The only objects visible on the plain were a few wooden crosses, indicating localities where travellers had been struck by lightning. Sometimes we rode close together, then I separated from Mr. Bishop and the *mozo*, fearing we might all three be killed by the same flash; no one spoke, except on one occasion, when, on reaching some rough stony ground, Bishop exclaimed "Keep galloping!" Eventually, about two miles ahead we beheld a building—a barn or shelter of some kind—and, by still harder galloping, we managed to reach it just as the lightning ceased, and the rain

HACIENDA OF TEPENACASCO.

[page 146.

came down in such torrents as to drive pigs, poultry, goats, mules, ducks, geese, bullocks, herdsmen, and two or three travellers like ourselves, under the same sheltering roof.

After a detention of a couple of hours the storm ceased, and the remainder of the journey was delightful. Bishop even wanted to stop on the road to sketch the beautiful belfry of the ruined convent of Acatlan.

When we got to the *hacienda*, Señor Tejira was out, and was not expected back for some hours. Madame, madame's mother, the children and nurses, and several gentlemen connected with the establishment, spoke only Spanish, and if they had but consented to pass us into our rooms, and allow us to rest and be thankful, how happy we should have been! But their politeness took another direction; for three long hours they endeavoured to entertain us; they played the piano, they played the guitar, they sang to us till Señor Tejira returned at eight or nine o'clock. His English was rusty, and we tried French. Supper was served; a prolonged and beautiful supply of piping hot Spanish dishes, and meats of various sorts, winding up with the large dish of *frijoles*, or purple beans, a dish invariably placed upon the table at the conclusion of a meal. At midnight we were at last shown to our sleeping-room.

We spent a most delightful week with the Tejiras. All the family learned to talk English, and we learned Spanish. Bishop and I were allowed to do just as we liked, and were only expected to present ourselves at meal-times. If we wanted to inspect the farm or farming operations, Señor Tejira, or one of the gentlemen, placed himself at our service; horses were prepared for us whenever we wanted to ride; or we were allowed to sketch unmolested, or to lounge away the afternoon on the hill at the back of the house.

The evenings closed in about six, and we generally spent an hour in the office, while the reports of the day were brought in by the head-men, and a portion of the labourers received their wages.

It was a lively hour. The lord of the *hacienda* is " *de facto*," if not " *de jure* " lord of his labourers. He has a prison in the *hacienda*, into which he puts them without ceremony, if he thinks it to their benefit. When the office work is completed, Tejira, or his administrator, holds a short court for dispensing small loans, doles of Indian corn, or advice, or medicine for the sick; for granting licenses for marriage, christening, or other festivities, for settling disputes, and for all such matters as may naturally arise amongst a community of four hundred or five hundred people. At last the day's accounts were balanced, the office closed, and we adjourned to the large reception-room, where Señor and Señora Tejira played and sang till supper was announced at about nine o'clock. This over, the ladies retired, and the gentlemen indulged in cigars, and in singing to the accompaniment of a guitar.

The house arrangements were these: at whatever hour you rose you found chocolate and an immense basket of buns and sweet cakes in the dining-room. A painfully elaborate mid-day dinner was served about noon, and repeated again in the evening at nine. I amused the family one day by asking permission to write down the bill of fare, which commenced with large cups of broth and green aquacaté (*Laurus persea*), a pear-shaped vegetable, which you generally spread in its raw state on bread as you would butter; then followed a thick soup full of vegetables; then a jambalaya of stewed rice and gravy, with hot pepper-pods upon it; a large dish of beef, boiled to threads, and, in place of gravy, a garnishing of roast apples, sweet bananas and fried potatoes—quite an olla-podrida; pigs' feet in sweet white sauce, like custard; mushrooms in gravy; roast fowls and salad; the end of dinner being always the frijoles or beans, undoubtedly the best dish upon the table. Frijoles are to the Mexican what pork and beans are to a Bostonian, macaroni to an Italian, salad to a Frenchman, and caviare to a Russian; but they are better than any of these other dishes, though they look somewhat like a purple-brown mess of oatmeal-porridge. The whole thing wound up with puddings, pies, sweetmeats, and coffee; cigarette-smoking was freely indulged in by both ladies and gentlemen after each course; cigars were handed round at the conclusion of the repast; such was the meal, with variations, which was served twice a day, and we were generally a dozen persons at table. For health's sake, I only partook of one or other of these meals each day, no matter how it might astonish or perplex the family.

The Tepenacasco hacienda estate is some twenty miles long, with a varying width of from five to eight miles, and contains some 40,000 acres. The house is a large one-storied building with two inner courts. On two blank walls of the principal court, round which there ran a handsome corridor, are two large fresco paintings, one representing St. James's Palace with the guards in the dress of George the Third, the other was easily recognised as the garden front of old Eaton Hall, Cheshire. The outer court had a curiously tiled water-tank, and the surrounding buildings were devoted to cheese-making, butter and dairy-work, under the superintendence of Don Daniel, the handsome man who enlivened us after dinner and supper with his guitar and songs. Outside the private dwelling are the fire-proof granaries and sheds. Night and day a sentry is stationed on the flat roof, on the look out for fire and robbers, and the large double entrance-doors are always closed and barred, if the doorkeeper leaves his post; all the windows have strong iron gratings over them, after the Spanish fashion.

Under the Spanish rule this hacienda was magnificently decorated and furnished. It was looted several times during the War of Independence; and down to so late a period as the presidency of Porferio Diaz; it has been heavily fined, both in cattle and money, in successive revolutions, and the remnants of the gorgeous furniture, frescoed walls, canopied beds, and broken couches bear melancholy testimony to its once magnificent condition.

The estate is chiefly in grass; cattle and dairy produce being its main source of revenue.

$12,000 (£2400) worth of cheese, $4000 (£800) worth of butter, is annually sent to market; and 15,000 bushels of Indian corn, 4000 bushels of barley, and 1000 bushels of wheat, are the average yearly produce of the ploughed land. $1200 worth (£250) of pulque is made from the magueys, to be drunk on the estate.

The cattle on the estate are: 834 milch cows, 180 heifers for breeding, 986 calves, yearlings, and oxen, 163 mules for carts and ploughing, 19 mares, 17 horses, 200 hogs, 50 sheep for the use of the table.

The estate contains ten large dams, or reservoirs, for collecting water for purposes of irrigation, which cover a space of two hundred acres; in addition to which there is the Lake of Zupitlan, formed by a wall embankment a mile in length, and shared in by two neighbouring haciendas.

We spent a Sunday afternoon at the ruined convent and church on the edge of this lake. It was a large family picnic, to which we were driven in carriages after Mass, and Edward Tejira and I had some capital duck-shooting, for want of a better Sunday afternoon occupation. I had knelt on a stone floor through a long Mass with the family in the morning, and thought I was entitled to a little recreation with them in the afternoon. The estate boasts of a celebrated spring, San Dionisio, visited by Humboldt during his stay in New Spain. He calls it the best water in America. The water which flows from it belongs to the hacienda seventy hours in the week; the rest of the time it is diverted to two neighbouring villages, the rights of each party being vigilantly guarded.

There are one hundred able-bodied men and fifty boys employed on the farm; these are directed by a major domo, assisted by three captains. There are twenty herdsmen, each accompanied by a joy, who attend the cattle day and night, and there is an aguador, or waterman, who attends to the dams and water-works.

The major domo, the captains, and the overlookers always ride on horseback, this being one of the honours appertaining to their dignified position.

Two days previous to that on which we had secured our places on the diligence from Tulancingo to Ometusco, Señor Tejira was summoned by a telegram to Mexico City, and it was decided that all the family should accompany him, grandmamma and grandchildren included. They were too large a party for the diligence, nor could they have secured any places in it at so short a notice; so they had to make the journey in their own large *char à bancs*. The start was made at five in the morning, and the packing and the departure were most amusing; the baby's bottle being the only one thing needed and of course forgotten. The *char à bancs* had to make a long detour by the road through Tulancingo, and it seemed to be a matter of etiquette and propriety that the *administrador* and other gentlemen left in charge of the establishment, and ourselves, should mount horse and ride across country and bid them final adieu at a certain turn in the road.

When we arrived at the place, it was discovered by the wheel-marks that the carriage had passed; there was nothing for it but to gallop across country to another point to get a glimpse of the carriage as it wound slowly up a hill; in this we succeeded but there was a deep ravine between us and the carriage, so we all fired our pistols to draw their attention, and then, after a great waving of handkerchiefs by both parties, we returned to the *hacienda*, to remain there a couple of days more before following them to Mexico.

It was a very interesting ten days; the weather was perfect, the air dry, the sun not too hot, and occasionally clouded. The time was July. If there were any drawback it was from the 200 hogs which were yarded up every night just outside our bedroom window, and if they were not let out at an early hour their music disturbed our slumbers; in order that they might be counted, a small wicket only in the double doors was opened for them to pass through, one—or at most two—at a time; the strugglings and squealings were awful—first out first served. There were long troughs of whey ready for their breakfast in a distant yard, before the herdsman drove them up to the mountain to pick up a precarious living, or sleep away the day.

All the principal granaries or barns, called "trojes," were inscribed with titles or dedicated to saints, and had quaint entablatures over their portals. Under the belfry and over the main entrance of the hacienda the inscription was—

Eu aquesto destierro y soledad disfruto del tesoro de la paz.

(In this retirement and solitude I enjoy the treasure of peace.)

Some old member of the Tejira family little knew, when he put up the above, how many times his property would be looted and ravaged during the Wars of Independence.

The cottages for the labourers were in a long row, at some distance from the main buildings. Each family had one room, some fourteen feet square. There was a stone for a fireplace in the corner, but no chimney, no windows. The family slept on mats on the bare ground; in the daytime they lived mostly in the open air; a good stream of dashing water in front of their doors enabled the women to do the family washing and keep a bright look out at the same time on the eldest girl at the door of the house, lest she should make the family tortillas " not to the family taste."

CHAPTER XVIII.

Inundations—Enrico Martinez—Difficulties of Spanish Court—The Dyke of
Nochistongo—American projects.

THE drainage of the City and Valley of Mexico has been a subject
of the greatest interest and importance to the inhabitants, at all
events since the days of the Conquest. When the Spaniards
commenced rebuilding the city in 1522, and even some time after
the progress of the work, it was a much discussed question
whether the city should not be moved from its ancient site on
the lake to high dry ground near Tacubaya. Many were the
letters and discussions between the viceroys and the authorities
at home upon the subject; it was finally settled by rebuilding on
the old site.

At the time of the inundation of 1607 the subject was again
slightly mooted. During the last inundation of the City of
Mexico, which lasted five successive years, from 1629 to 1634,
and caused terrible distress, the court of Madrid gave orders a
second time to transfer the city to the high ground between
Tacuba and Tacubaya; but, says Humboldt, "the magistracy
(*cavildo*) represented that the value of the edifices, which in 1607
amounted to 150,000,000 livres, now amounted to 200,000,000
(8,334,000 pounds sterling) so there was a greater objection to
moving the city in 1634 than in 1607. Had the city been
removed, it would no doubt have been healthier and pleasanter
as a place of residence. There is every probability, if the

country continues in the course of prosperity it has entered
upon, that the next generation will live to see the valley drained,
and the city released from inundations. At present there is no
safety, as the city is in the lowest part of the valley, and all the
lakes are on higher levels, except that of Texcoco, which is only
two feet below the city. The surface of the four principal lakes
covers more than a tenth of the land of the valley. The lake of
Tochimilco contains forty-nine and a-half square miles; that of
Texcoco, seventy-seven; San Christóbal, twenty-seven and a-
half; Zumpango, ten. As the valley is entirely closed by
a wall of porphyritic mountains, there is no outlet for these
waters.

The lakes rise by stages a few feet above each other; Texcoco,
the salt lake, is on the lowest level; the Plaza Mayo, or great
square of the capital, being two feet higher than the mean level
of its waters; Chalco is three and a half feet higher than
Texcoco, and Zumpango, which is the most northern lake, is
twenty-nine feet higher than the city. Dating from the arrival
of the Spaniards, the city has experienced five inundations, viz.,
in 1553, 1580, 1604, 1607 and 1629. At a corner of the Calle
Espíritu Santo, at the Secunda Calle San Francisco, a grotesque
carved animal's head marks the height attained by the flood in
1629. Since the last, the city has been frequently threatened.
The catastrophe, however, has been averted by banks and dykes,
and by the canal of Nochistongo, which carries off any unusual rise
of the waters of the *Rio de Quatitlan*, that might otherwise find
their way into the valley and increase the volume of the lakes.
In 1607 the Viceroy employed Enrico Martinez, a native of
Germany, to adopt the best means he could devise to render the
city free from inundations. He presented several plans, and
that for draining Zumpango alone, and so preventing it from
overflowing into the lower lakes, was the scheme which the
Spanish Government adopted. By this plan the flood water of
the river Cuatitlan, instead of falling into the lake Zumpango,

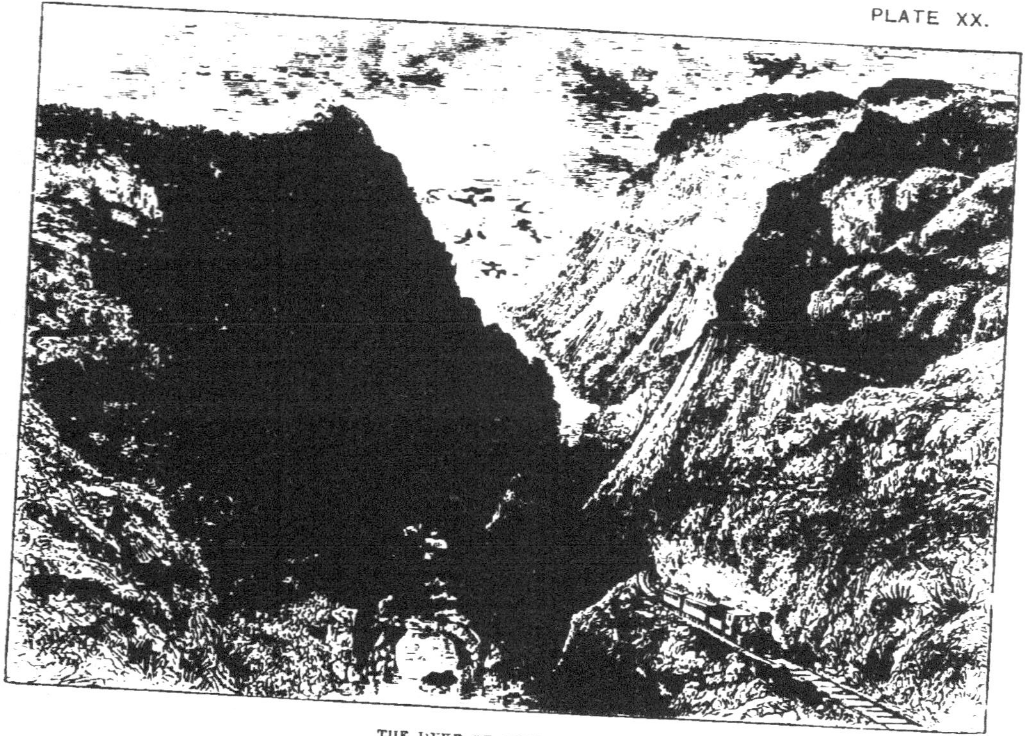

THE DYKE OF NOCHISTONGO.

[page 154.

would be carried off to the Rio de Tula, which runs into the Rio de Panuco, and so to the Gulf of Mexico.

During my stay in Mexico a handsome marble pedestal covered with statistics was erected to the memory of Martinez in the square of Sagrario. As no bust, picture, or counterfeit presentment of any kind had ever been made of him, the pedestal was eventually to be crowned with a figure of Victory or some allegorical device.

His plan involved the cutting of the subterranean gallery or tunnel of Nochistongo, which was commenced on the 28th of November, 1607. The tunnel was found to be too small to carry off the water, and several new schemes were proposed. In 1614 the Court of Madrid, wearied out with disputes on the drainage of Mexico, sent out one Adrian Boot, a Dutch engineer, who of course advised the construction of dykes to keep back the waters of the lakes, similar to those of his own country, a system he was allowed to continue for fourteen years, when a new viceroy, the Marquis de Guelves, arrived. He would not believe the accounts of the floods which were presented to him; he therefore ordered Martinez to stop up the tunnel and let the waters of the upper lake return to the bed of Texcoco, that he might ascertain if the danger were so great as had been represented to him. Having soon received convincing proofs, he set Martinez to work again to improve the tunnel, and it was utilised until the 20th of June, 1629, when, finding that the entire structure was giving way under the pressure of water, Martinez closed it, in order to prevent its total destruction, and on the following morning the city of Mexico was flooded to the depth of three feet, with great loss of life and property, nor did the water subside for five years. During this inundation the wretchedness of the lower orders was singularly increased. Many of the houses tumbled down, and the inhabitants had to resort entirely to the use of boats in the streets, as had been done before the Conquest, when the city was of the same character as Venice.

In the midst of these calamities the viceroy ordered the image of the Holy Virgin of Guadalupe to be brought to Mexico. She remained a long time in the inundated city. The waters, however, only retired in 1634, when, from very strong and frequent earthquakes, the ground of the valley opened and carried the waters off—a phenomenon which was of no small assistance to the miraculous reputation of the adorable Virgin.

At the commencement of the flood, Martinez was imprisoned, under the erroneous belief that he had closed the tunnel without sufficient cause, but, after several years, he was released, in order to assist in the work of cutting a broad open channel down to the tunnel to afford the waters free outlet.

The Spaniards certainly did things in Mexico in superb style: the works they undertook were magnificent. The dyke of Nochistongo is even at this day the greatest earth-cutting in existence. Its length is 67,537 feet, its greatest depth 197 feet, and its greatest breadth 361 feet. It required nearly two centuries to complete, and was not open in its entire length until 1789.

In September I had an opportunity of accompanying the Rev. John Pattison to Tula, to examine the Aztec palace in that locality, lately exhumed by Monsieur Charnay. We travelled by the Mexican Central Railway, the line running through the Nochistongo Pass at an elevation of one to two hundred feet above the channel of the water for the full length of the dyke, a distance of nearly twelve miles.

The present appearance of the dyke (at the time of my visit there was a heavy flood of red-coloured water rushing through it) reminded me of the Avon at Clifton when the tide is low and running out; it resembles also the gorge at Pfeffers in Switzerland; the road in the gorge to the celebrated baths being in the same relation to the surroundings as the Central Railway line is to the Pass of Nochistongo; but the banks of this Mexican cutting are of the softest, most friable earth; and in many places so exactly over the water of the cut is the railway carried that I made a vow in passing, not for any consideration to return by the same route. Here and there at the edges of the torrent we perceived remnants of the stone arches of the tunnel, the making of which, with the later cutting of the channel, cost 70,000 native lives. This tunnel will probably still be utilised for the eventual perfect draining of the valley, and why, after so much expensive labour and loss of life, it is not now used for its intended purpose is one of the mysteries of Mexico. To hear Mexicans talk of the matter, especially when the streets of the city are for several hours a foot deep with water after a heavy thunderstorm, and porters are carrying people about on their backs, you would expect that the work of draining the valley would be commenced in good earnest at once; but as soon as the water has subsided the subject is mentioned no more. When Americans shall have made large additions to the city, of which I saw plans, &c., they will probably undertake the drainage to preserve their property, and by so doing they will contribute as largely to the benefit of the city, and the welfare of its inhabitants, as they are at present contributing to the improvement and opening up of the country by their network of railways. A traveller and visitor in the city soon finds out that better drainage is the one thing necessary for so large and level an area as that on which the city is built. The best method of obtaining a satisfactory result is not easily arrived at; many people feared that the drainage or lowering of the waters of Lake Texcoco would leave a considerable extent of marshy uncultivable ground near the city, and that malaria and other evils might arise, but the clearness and dryness of the atmosphere would probably be an antidote to zymotic disease, should it arise from this cause—one thing is pretty certain, viz., if such an ill-drained city as that of Mexico were anywhere on the coast or in the tierra templada, instead of the tierra fria, the whole of the inhabitants would be swept off by plague and pestilence in a few months.

CHAPTER XIX.

CHINAMPAS, OR FLOATING GARDENS.

Thunderstorm—Dense Vegetation on the Lakes—Mode of making the Gardens—
The Garita—Villages on the Canal—Great Mexican Festival—Mr. George
Carmona—Night in a Ruined Monastery—Polite Padre—Ancient Tlahuac—
Chalco.

On the evening of the 22nd of June, 1881, I sat with Mr. Bishop
on the roof of the Iturbide Hotel from six to half-past seven
o'clock, watching a magnificent thunderstorm pass round the
east of the city. I have never seen nor heard of any scientific
investigation into the character and nature of the various kinds
of lightning flashes, nor the time of their duration. In this
particular storm, the broad flashes of light, which extended across
the heavens, had always a spray of forked lightning, sometimes
resembling a firework, known as a flower-pot or fountain, and
they shot upwards from the earth; another time the light was
scattered from a point high in the heavens, and showered down
on earth, as I have seen it represented in pictures hurled from
the hand of Jupiter Tonans.

During the storm, Señor F. Garay, the engineer in charge of
the drainage of the Valley of Mexico, or, as his card announced,
" Francisco de Garay, Engineer in Charge of the Valley of Mexico,"
called to say that he was going with some friends on a three days'
tour of inspection of the works on Lakes Xochimilco and Chalco,
and politely asked us to join the party. This was just what we
wanted, and we were only too pleased to say that we would be at

the place of rendezvous on the Viga Canal, at six o'clock on the following morning.

What could be more delightful than making investigations into the nature and character of the lakes, in a large, comfortable boat, and under the guidance of a chaperon who was so capable of giving us information about the whole district?

When the plateau of Central Mexico was raised some 7600 feet above the sea, it would appear as if large bodies of salt water had been brought up with the mountains. The numerous valleys, both large and small, are very level, the dry valleys have the appearance of having once been shallow lakes; and the present lakes, of both fresh and salt water, occasionally not half a mile distant from each other in the same valley, are generally but a few feet deep.

The Lake of Texcoco is salt and brackish, but the Lakes Chalco and Xochimilco, adjoining it, are of fresh water, and are covered with a tangled mass of floating vegetation, two to ten feet thick, or even more, and canals have to be kept open and free from vegetation between the shore and various islands for the passage of trading boats.

When a tract of vegetation, composed of reeds, water-plants and bushes, interwoven and laced together, becomes so dense that it will bear a superstructure, strips of turf twenty to thirty yards long, by two yards wide, are cut from some suitable firm place, floated to it down the canal, and laid upon it; this is repeated several times, and thus an island is securely raised two to three feet above the level of the water; a little soil is spread over it, and it becomes a chinampas, or floating garden, on which Indian corn, vegetables, and flowers are grown. The gardens vary in size from one to two hundred feet in length, and from twenty to a hundred feet in width, according to the nature of the vegetation which supports them.

The lakes have a varying depth of ten to fifteen feet, and to secure these gardens in their proper places long willow poles are driven through them into the ground below, where they soon take root. The poles also throw out roots into the bed of the floating gardens, and so hold them steady.

In cases where natives have been followed by the police or by soldiers for crimes, they have frequently been known to elude their pursuers by diving under these gardens and coming up on the opposite side.

The term " floating islands " suggests the idea that the islands floated about, or are easily moved from one place to another on the lakes, but the probability is they were never allowed to move after they were formed. In Southey's 'Madoc in Aztlan,' which is descriptive of the religion and habits of the Mexicans, the lines—

> " Green islets float along,
> Where high-born damsels, under jasmine bowers,
> Raise the sweet voice, to which the echoing oars,
> In modulatic motion rise and fall;"—

indicate the poet's misconception of these islands, and, seemingly in order to prove the truth of the lines in the poem, he states in a note that artificial islands are common in China as well as Mexico, and quotes the following paragraph from Barrow's ' China ':—

" The Chinese fishermen, having no houses on shore, nor stationary abode, but moving about in their vessels upon the extensive lakes and rivers, have no inducement to cultivate patches of ground, which the pursuits of their profession might require them to leave for the profit of another; they prefer, therefore, to plant their onions on rafts of bamboo, well interwoven with reeds and long grass, and covered with earth; and these floating gardens are towed after their boats."

Señor Garay's chief duties seemed to be to keep the canals open and free from weed, and to take care that the islands were attached firmly to the bottom of the lake, so as not to be liable to drift about and block up the channels. Where the gardens become sufficiently firm, the labourers and their families erect huts upon them, the authorities demanding a small rental, which goes to the expense of keeping open the channels. The weed in some districts grows so rapidly that it is with the utmost difficulty it can be kept down, and I took the liberty of suggesting the use of swans, having found in my own experience of them at home that they delight in ripping up vegetation from its roots.

These gardens, which at present are confined to the large fresh-water lakes, Chalco and Xochimilco, were at the time of the Conquest found also on the bitter waters of Lake Texcoco.

In Montezuma's time, so thickly inhabited was the beautiful Valley of Anhuac that the poorer classes were driven to the utmost extremities to win from mother earth everything in the shape of a harvest that she could possibly yield, every patch in the valley and every cleft in the surrounding porphyritic mountains being utilised to the last square inch ; but the valley and its surroundings were unable to meet the requirements, and as the population increased, a trade gradually began with the Indian tribes beyond the mountains, who brought vast quantities of corn, fruit and vegetables into the imperial city. As the Aztecs had no beasts of burden, the ponderous loads were borne by a class of the community known as " tomanes " or porters, whose numbers increased as the demands became greater. It is doubtless to this demand for supplies that the chinampas owe their origin. At the date of the Conquest the name of these chinampas was legion ; one authority, Verytea, says they numbered thousands, while the illuminated tribute-rolls still extant go to prove that a large share of the Aztec monarch's taxes came from the proprietors of them. I must now ask the reader to follow me through the details of our excursion.

At the fine old Spanish bridge at the entrance to the Paséo de la Viga, at the side of which runs the Viga Canal, we found Mr.

Garay, his son Mr. Pancho Garay, and another gentleman, all of whom were awaiting our arrival; we were late, and quietly took our seats in the comfortably-cushioned large boat which Mr. Garay had provided, and were poled swiftly up the stream by four good-looking stalwart Indians, who had white drawers rolled high over the knee, while their necks and breasts were bare, and their heads surmounted by large straw *sombréros*. The sides of the canal, as you leave the city, are lined with beautiful trees. At the end of the Paséo we approached a low arch under a roadway, on which were some pretty red brick buildings; the arch was so low that I scarcely deemed it possible we could pass through, in fact it resembled the entrance to a sewer more than anything else. Here is the *garita*, or local custom house, and we were blocked for several minutes owing to the number of *chalupas* and boats of all sizes, laden to the water's edge with firewood, marsh grass for horses, vetches, charcoal, fruits, vegetables and flowers, waiting to pay toll and pass through to the city. The receipts at the *garita* amount to between three and four thousand dollars a day.

Breaking our way, very much as in a lock on the Thames at Marlow or Cookham, we were rapidly poled through a region of gardens, past the village of Santa Anita, which boasts a small church, good public school, fountain, bridge, and a side canal, blocked with fruit and vegetable boats. In twenty minutes we reached a second village, Ixtacalco, possessing a good-sized church, the altar resplendent with panes of diamond-shaped tinfoil, which reflects light at every angle with marvellous effect. Here meat, eggs and tortillas were being fried on dirty trays all up the sides of the street, for the fête was at hand, and was to be celebrated on that afternoon. We struck a third village, Ixtapalapa, containing a church, schools, pigs, and vegetable gardens; and a little before noon we poled up to Estrella, a village under the famous historical hill of the same name, where the Mexicans held the greatest of their Estrella festivals every fifty-second year. The account of this festival is given by Prescott, vol. i., p. 126, and

HILL OF ESTRELLA.

[page 162.

his description of it is one of the most telling bits of writing in all the three volumes. The following is a quotation : "It was to this hill that a procession of priests led a noble victim, the flower of their captives, to sacrifice on the evening that the constellation of the Pleiades approached the zenith. For five days previous the people of the country had abandoned themselves to despair, broken in pieces the little images of their household gods, and extinguished the holy fires in their temples, and none were lighted in their dwellings. The priests taught them that the world was probably coming to an end. Their wonderful astronomical knowledge led them to adopt cycles of fifty-two years; and (as I have said) it was on the recurrence of every fifty-second year that this fearful ceremony took place. When the Pleiades had passed the zenith new fire was kindled by the friction of sticks placed in the wounded breast of the victim, and a flame was communicated to a funeral pile on which the body of the slaughtered captive was thrown. As the light streamed up towards heaven, shouts of joy and triumph burst forth from the countless multitudes who covered the hills, the terraces of the temples, and the housetops, with eyes anxiously bent on the mount of sacrifice. Couriers, with torches lighted at the blazing beacon, rapidly bore them over every part of the country, and the cheering element was seen brightening on altar and hearthstone for the circuit of many a league long before the sun, rising on his accustomed track, gave assurance that a new cycle had commenced its march, and that the laws of nature were not to be reversed for the Aztecs. The following thirteen days were given up to festivity. The houses were cleansed and whitened, the broken vessels were replaced by new ones; the people, dressed in their gayest apparel, and crowned with garlands and chaplets of flowers, thronged in joyous procession to offer up their oblations and thanksgivings in the temples; dances and games were instituted, emblematical of the regeneration of the world. It was the Carnival of the Aztecs, or rather the national jubilee—the great secular festival, which few alive had witnessed before, or could expect to see again."

The twenty-sixth canto in Part II. of Southey's 'Madoc' is descriptive of this scene; the following lines having reference to the rekindling of the sacred fire :—

> " Meanwhile the priests
> Have stretched their victim on the mountain top ;
> A miserable man—his breast is bare,
> Bare for the death that waits him ; but no hand
> May there inflict the blow of mercy. Piled
> On his bare breast, the cedar boughs are laid ;
> On his bare breast, dry sedge and odorous gums
> Laid ready to receive the sacred spark,
> And blaze, to herald the ascending Sun,
> Upon his living altar."

At this spot, the most noted and sacred place in the whole country of Mexico, we alighted, and through Mr. Garay's arrangement and introduction were most hospitably received and invited to breakfast at a fine *hacienda* on the bank of the canal, where the celebrated hill to which I have alluded formed a fine background to a pretty view, comprising a high arched bridge over the canal, and a gay little general provision shop which seemed cut out of the walls of the *hacienda*. This fine *hacienda* belongs to Señor George Carmona, a gentleman who has a wonderful history. As a boy he sold matches on the coast of Mazatlan, his native place. He entered the army in 1859, when quite a young man, enlisting on the Republican side; during the French intervention joined Marshal Bazaine, taking over with him the forces under his command, and was made chamberlain to Carlotta. Upon the fall of Maximilian he remained in seclusion till about 1869, when the amnesty law was passed. He is reported to be very handsome, and, though illiterate, has a good address. He was afterwards admitted into the best society in Mexico, and married the rich widow Señora Bestique, who subsequently died. He has latterly been in Paris, connected with the household of the ex-Queen Isabella of Spain, and during the week of our visit it was announced in several Mexican papers that he was about to be married to the Princess of Asturias. A strange tale, which is but half told. Let me note that a handsome coffee-pot on the table had the name of a Birmingham maker stamped upon it, and the cups and plates bore a well-known Staffordshire trade-mark. After breakfast, we found horses waiting for us to ride up the hill of Estrella, the boat being sent on to meet us at another point of the canal. The hill is from 400 to 500 feet high, and is of porphyritic sandstone, with here and there a few traces of the ancient masonry and plaster-work.

Going up the hill, a mole-catcher showed us some large moles he had caught; they infest the ground, and have to be destroyed: they are three times the size of the English mole, and have four prominent teeth, two in each jaw, placed outside the lips, so that in cutting their way through roots they can keep their mouths closed and free from dirt.

After parting from our horses, we continued on the canal between lines of brilliant orange, pink, and crimson water-lilies, and towards evening we stopped at a native "fonda," little more than a straw hut on the bank-side. Some men were catching fish with rod and line, and Señor Garay at once proposed we should stop and dine. The men made a charcoal fire on the boat, on which we fried the fish just as they were drawn out of the water; no cleaning, no scaling—three-ounce fish, like trout, so rich and fat that they greased our fingers most offensively, in spite of a judicious use of paper in lieu of napkins. It would hardly be an exaggeration to say they were the most delicious food I ever ate; and we quickly discarded the sardine box and other viands we had brought with us in favour of these succulent morsels.

Owing to a late start in the morning, we were overtaken by darkness before we reached Tlahuac. To make matters worse, a heavy thunderstorm suddenly burst over us ; we got into a hut and waited till the rain ceased; then, with some candles we bought, we had to tramp some distance to the village over a narrow causeway, linked together by a long rope for fear of any one slipping into the deep water on either side.

The only place in the village where we were likely to find a night's shelter was at the house of the curá, and thither, with much difficulty and with the assistance of half-a-dozen guides, we finally arrived ; a lantern indicated a door in an immense wall, on which we thumped and rattled vigorously for ten minutes, when somewhere in the darkness, and at some distance, a woman's voice asked, " *Que, quien ?* " After a long explanation the door was unbolted and fell open, discovering a sheet of water ; it was evident that the yard was inundated by the thunderstorm, no one knew to what depth, or whether there were any deep holes in it. The woman said it was not above two feet deep, and we must cross it if we wanted to get to the staircase ; so we took off our boots and stockings, wet as they were, and waded through it. The building was an immense convent-ruin— a curious sight. We marched down long corridors, passed a large open quadrangle, and were finally shown into a long chamber, formerly the refectory of the convent, where four or five hundred monks were wont to take their daily meals. There was no fire, but it was not cold, and we divested ourselves of some of our wet garments, and laid them on the floor to dry. In a short time the curá came to us, a dark-eyed little Spanish padre, the essence of politeness and good breeding ; he did not even allude to the fact, which was evident, that he and his household were in bed at the time of our arrival. He begged us to make ourselves as comfortable as we could ; he had no beds to offer, but the room we were in, and all that he had, was at our disposal ; he would provide us with supper, which would be ready by-and-by ; and so saying he brought us candles and left us.

The room was some eighty feet long, lofty and well-proportioned. At one end was a daïs with a table upon it, and a large oaken chair. On the whitewashed wall behind the chair was an immense wooden crucifix, flanked on either side by two large oil paintings (Murillos?) quite obliterated by damp and age. On the wall below the crucifix hung a number of small framed photographs of the curá's friends and relations, a few other artistic odds and ends, and on a bracket under the cross a little lamp that was always kept alight. From ten o'clock to midnight we amused ourselves as best we could, thanking our stars we were sheltered from the storm that again raged outside. About twelve o'clock there were signs of supper, a man and two women laid a cloth and spread the table with a bountiful meal of Spanish dishes, also *pulque* and *vino tinto*. When the curá came in, Mr. Garaz introduced us with much ceremony, and we placed ourselves at table around our host, who occupied the large oak chair. The curá proved a charming host; he played his part to perfection. Had he been Lord Chamberlain to the King of Spain, he could not have done the honours of his table in a more courtly manner. The repast concluded and cigars lighted, our host said he would endeavour to soften the hardness of the floor by placing a few carpets for us to sleep upon, and the servants brought in what were undoubtedly his best church carpets, such, no doubt, as were only used on special fiesta days. David eating the shewbread was sacrilegious, but condoned in the New Testament; here the good Samaritan despoiled his church in charity to benighted travellers, and may his offence, if it were one, be also condoned. We arranged the carpets in twenty different ways before we finally lay down upon them. Possibly I might have slept after the fatigues of the day, but the spirits of the old monks lacking the charity of the curá, and possibly scandalised at such profanation of church ornaments, attacked us in the form of mosquitoes, the first I had seen on the high land, and it is needless to say sleep was altogether out of the question.

Soon after six o'clock in the morning we got up, and the curá came to show us his church and such portions of the convent as it was safe to traverse. In the quadrangle were numbers of Aztec remains; two large stones like mill-stones, probably Aztec dials, with the ornamentation too much obliterated for the uninitiated to decipher.

On parting we dared not offer the curá any remuneration for his hospitality; his servants even refused a gratuity; in this emergency, and not wishing to leave without some return of politeness, and noticing he wore a muffler around his throat—Spanish fashion—I offered him a handsome white silk one I happened to have with me, telling him that it had been round the world, and we were all delighted to see with what evident pleasure he accepted the gift.

It is 10 A.M.: the sun is brilliant, but slight traces of last night's storm are visible; we are once again on the lake and passing over the remains of a submerged city, the old City of Tlahuac, which was standing at the time of Cortes' invasion.

The stonework was three to six feet below the surface of the water; we could strike the buildings with the poles, and we saw something beneath us that looked like a pavement; we glided above these buildings for eighty or one hundred yards.

At noon we landed at the volcano of Jico or Xico. It is a peak 500 feet high; the sides are so precipitous that the ascent was very difficult. The lip of the crater forms a complete circle, two miles in circumference, with unbroken edges. The crater is 150 feet deep, and is one large cornfield; we were shown a track on which the mules were driven up the mountain to plough the land enclosed in it. The mules must be as nimble on their feet as the ibex to accomplish such an ascent.

In the evening we arrived at Chalco, where we intended remaining for the night; but hearing the train from Ameca-

ameca was several hours late, on account of a terrible accident on the Morelos road the previous day, we pushed on through Mr. Garay's new canal, which leads to the Chalco station, three or four miles distant, all of us preferring to get back to Mexico City, however late, rather than run the risk of another night on hard boards.

CHAPTER XX.

History of Early Inhabitants—Handbook of Aztec History—The Remains of the
City of Teotihuacan—The Pyramids of the Sun and Moon—Broken Pottery
and Idols—The Ruins at Texcoco—The Pyramid at Cholula—Archæological
Treasures in the Museum of Mexico.

THE problem of the origin of the earliest inhabitants of Mexico
has yet to be solved; the subject is engaging the attention of
numerous savants, and the Americans are making it a special
branch of study.

The archæological and historical societies of most of the large
American cities have sent and are sending their agents and explorers over the country to discover and report upon anything
that may tend to throw light upon its early inhabitants. One
great interest attaching to the matter is that similar remains to
those discovered in Mexico are also found in various parts of the
United States. In addition to the flint and stone arrow-heads,
hammers and implements, which are of about the same character all over the world, the earthenware and pottery exhumed in
both countries are similar; this gives some ground for thinking
that this portion of the world was, ages ago, peopled by races
(possibly nomadic) who had a common origin, and were after-
words more or less connected.

I saw in the museums at Boston and Washington cases of
pre-historic pottery from the neighhourhood of Chicago, from the
state of Iowa, from Texas, New Mexico, Arizona, and California,
so similar in many respects to what I saw, and myself found, in

Mexico, as to convince me that, to a philosophic expert in these matters, there is opened a wide field for inquiry and research. A few additional facts may yet show conclusively to what portion of Asia, and even to what nation of that continent, America is indebted for her first inhabitants.

In the Archæological Museum at Mexico, which is at present being rearranged under the superintendence of Señor Mendoza, at the end of the room in which the Mexican ceramic discoveries are displayed, is a large case containing a number of earthern cups and vases, from a mound near Chicago. It has purposely been placed in juxtaposition to the Mexican vases, that even the casual observer may notice their similarity. On the history of the early inhabitants of Mexico many books have already been written. Lord Kingsborough spent his lifetime, and incurred great expense, in publishing voluminous illustrated works upon Mexico, with the object of proving that the inhabitants were part of the lost tribes of Israel. My friend Mr. Vigil, the chief of the National Library in Mexico, showed me several learned works on the subject. He himself compiled one of great merit, with a copy of which he kindly presented me. It is in Spanish, and would take me some time to translate, as it is full of difficult technicalities. Mr. Vigil's idea is, that there is sufficient resemblance between the roots of many Mexican words and the roots of Sanscrit to warrant the supposition that there was originally an emigration to Mexico from India.

Interested as I was in what I saw, and in the discoveries that were being made almost daily during my stay, I had to remain temporarily satisfied with a simple account from the 'Historia Elemental de Mexico, por Tirso Rafael Cordoba,' published in Mexico, in the year 1881, and adopted by the government as the history to be used in all the public schools. The rising population of Mexico are thus instructed as to the pre-historic history of their country.

The book is divided into four parts :—

No. 1. Ancient history, from the earliest people of the country, or their first political existence, about 500 A.D., down to the last Aztec emperor.

No. 2. The history of the events of the Conquest in 1521.

No. 3. The 300 years of Spanish domination.

No. 4. The revolt of the Mexicans in 1811, and their first republic, with an account of the events which have since occurred.

Young Mexico is taught that the first inhabitants of America came from Asia, either over a piece of land which once united the two continents, where are now situated the Aleutian Islands, or by a long succession of islands in the Pacific Ocean, which existed in remote times.

After a variety of speculative propositions as to nomadic tribes wandering over the country, the history is reduced to the fact that the first inhabitants of whom there is any certain knowledge were a race called the Toltecs, who, after founding a great nation, and building cities in the northern part of Mexico, and finding the subsistence in that part of the country insufficient for the population, migrated southward about the year A.D. 607, or more than a hundred years before the time of Charlemagne's empire in Europe.

After various wanderings, the Toltecs settled at Tollam, or, as the city is now called, Tula; this was about the year 713, from which date the country and the people were called Analhuac.

It is clear that these people had been an enlightened, stable nation for several generations, as, at the time to which I refer, their principles of government, the hereditary succession of their princes and chiefs, their laws and their worship, had assumed settled forms

The names of the nine kings who ruled up to A.D. 1097 are well ascertained.   The first king was one Chalchinhtlanctzin, and the names of the other eight were equally long.* It was the fourth king who built the city of *Teotihuachan*, which signifies "the habitation of the gods;" nothing of this city now remains but the two great Pyramids of the Sun and Moon, which I describe later in this chapter.

The kings were allowed to reign only fifty-two years; if one outlived this period, he handed over his kingdom and government to his eldest son, or other successor.

All the kings are represented as wise, and doing great things for their country!

King Tepancaltzin's reign, commencing in 1042, is noted for the discovery of pulque by his relative Papantzin, in reward for which the king gave him his beautiful daughter Mochitl. This celebrated lady played the part of a Helen of Troy, which led to many serious state troubles. War ensued, and finally a famine and pestilence, and the desertion by the Toltecs of Tula and of the country.

This part of the school history concludes with the reflections that the Toltecs were the fathers of civilisation in Anahuas, and that they advanced agriculture by the cultivation of maize, the pulque, maguey plant and cotton.

They discovered gold and silver, and the mode of cutting precious stones. Architecture, painting, and the regulation of time are attributed to them. All the pyramids found in the valley of Mexico date from their era, and are authenticated by maps and hieroglyphical manuscripts still in existence, of which a few samples are seen in the National Museum.

The majority of this strange people, after extending their sway over the remotest borders of Anahuac, seem to have disappeared from the land as silently and mysteriously as they entered it; and are supposed to have travelled south, leaving an

---

* In reference to long Mexican words, Torquemada quotes "Tlacochcalcoat-lyacapan," the name for arsenal, as a specimen of Mexican sesquipedalianism—himself using a word almost as long.

evidence of their greatness in the present ruins at Palanque and Metli. Those of Yucatán are attributed to branches of the Toltec nation in later times.

For two or three hundred years from this date the country was divided up amongst kings or chiefs ruling petty kingdoms, of various nationalities (admixtures of the remnants of the Toltecs and other tribes), and the city of Texcoco, on the eastern border of the Mexican lake, became noted for the civilisation of its people and the refinement of its princes. The fact that several of the tribes, wearied with the tyranny of their kings, adopted republican and free constitutions, which can only be formed after a long period of popular struggles, indicates a certain degree of cultivation, but the great question has still to be asked, where was the source of this cultivation? and where is the country from which the Toltecs and Mexicans issued? Humboldt says that the Toltecs in 648 A.D., had a solar year more perfect than that of the Greeks and Romans. It was not till the year 1325 that a new emigration of several northern tribes came down into the plain of Mexico, and settled at Mexitli, from which we date the present race of Aztecs or Mexicans, who under emperors called Montezumas* rapidly brought the country to the height of powerful and barbaric grandeur in which the Spanish found it.

I have before alluded to the fact that the country of Mexico, previous to the Conquest, was densely populated; and the visitor to the high plateaux of Central Mexico can have little doubt but that such was the case, from the archæological remains which the eye can discover wherever it chooses to search. The soil on the fields in and around the City of Mexico is filled with broken

---

* There are various ways of writing the names of the Mexican kings. In the preface to Humboldt's 'New Spain' it is remarked that the Spanish, French and Italian writers write Motezuma; the English, Montezuma; the proper orthography being neither Motezuma nor Montezuma, but Moteuczoma. I have adopted the English mode of writing the name.

PYRAMIDS AT TEOTIHUACAN

stone implements and pottery. And a visit to Tula and San Juan Teotihuacan compels the most casual observer to believe that sometime there must have been living on these very spots citizens of a nation not far behind the Egyptians in the magnificence, if not in the stability of their pyramids and buildings.

Teotihuacan is about thirty miles north of the City of Mexico, on the line of railway to Vera Cruz; it is the site of what was once a city twenty miles in circumference. Three layers of concrete floors have been found over this extensive space; the lowest floor being five or six inches thick, upon this is a layer of from one to two feet of earth, again covered with two floorings of concrete of less thickness and but a few inches apart. Explorers seem quite undecided as to the object of these three floorings; the only conjecture my companions seemed to have formed was, that the city may have been a favourite burial-place, and that the bodies were laid under the lowest layer; but I heard of no bones being found to corroborate this.

Most of the ground has been disturbed by the plough, other portions have been covered with trees and shrubs; but we could trace large patches of the three floorings wherever the ground was bare, and particularly on the sides of the roads and watercourses; an archæologist has yet the opportunity of discovering the use and intentions of these three floorings.

Any one visiting this locality might possibly ride over it without being aware of the vestiges of the city under his feet; the general appearance is very similar to that of any other part of the plain, except near the centre, where stand the Pyramid of the Sun and the Pyramid of the Moon, and under them a space a mile or two square, on which are smaller mounds of broken brick or stone; these indicate the positions of ruined palaces and other buildings. A long road or street, starting from a square at the front of the Pyramid of the Moon, appears to have had on both sides flights of steps on which, in the days of the city's prosperity, thousands of people probably stood watching, magnificent processions passing from pyramid to pyramid. This street is called "The Path of the Dead."

On Tuesday, the 24th of May, 1881, I spent a day amongst these ruins with Mr. Frederick Ober and Mr. Campbell, who were engaged in excavations and investigations for the benefit of some institutions at Boston. We were on horseback all day, riding over various parts of the site, and we climbed both the pyramids on foot, while the horses were left in charge of the *mozos.*

Prescott gives a short description of this wonderful place (vol. ii., page 387), commencing with the statement that "the monuments of San Juan Teotihuacan are, with the exception of the Pyramid of Cholula, the most ancient remains probably on the Mexican soil; they were found by the Aztecs, according to their traditions, on their entrance into the country, when 'Teotihuacan,' the habitation of the gods, now a paltry village, was a flourishing city, the rival of Tula, the great Toltec capital."

From the summit of the Pyramid of the Sun the outline of the surrounding ruins beneath is easily traced. This pyramid has a base of 682 feet long, and is 180 feet high. That the reader may compare it in imagination with the Pyramids of Egypt, the great Pyramid of Cheops is 728 feet at the base, and 448 feet high. The Pyramid of the Moon is rather less, and is due north from that of the Sun. The principal road or street before alluded to runs in a south-westerly direction some four or five miles to the hills; it is cut nearly at right angles about its middle point by the Vera Cruz Railway.

In moving from one part of the ruins to another we passed over several fields from which some crop had lately been cut, and where the land was being ploughed for maize. We soon discovered it might be worth our while to dismount from our horses and follow the plough for what it might turn up. The ground was a mass of broken pottery and small clay heads of idols, some with ornamental head-dresses, and others quite plain, *a*

b

b

d

c

*d**

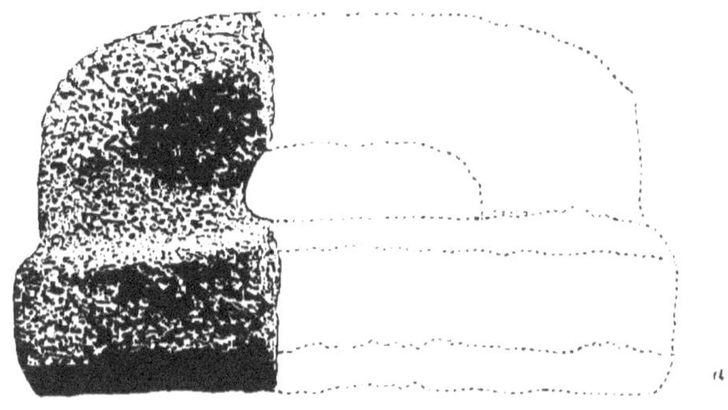

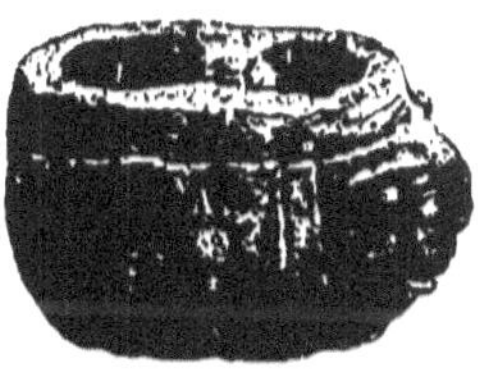

a. PLASTERER'S TROWEL, 6 inches long.
b. LAVA HEADS, 5 inches high.
c. PHALLUS? 5 inches high.
d. PASTILE HOLDERS.

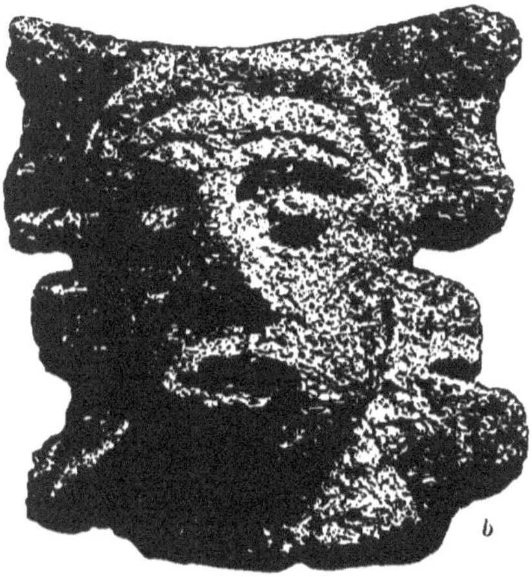

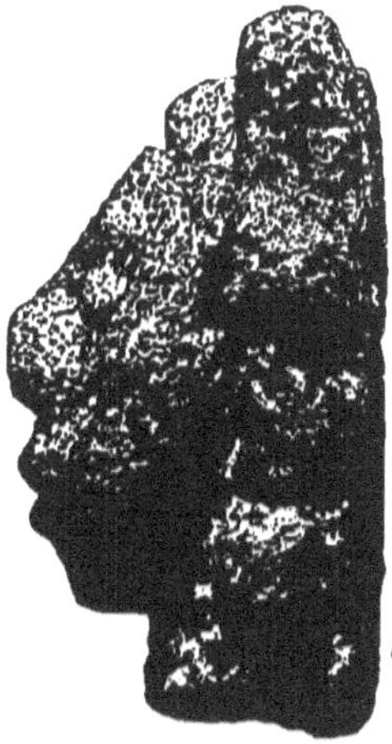

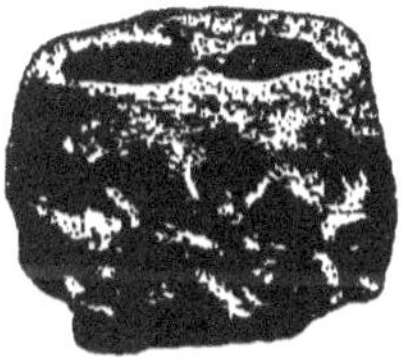

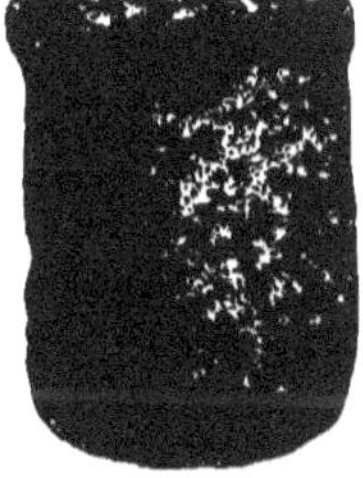

[*page* 176.

with some admixture of obsidian knives, arrow-heads, stone
pestles, and broken plastering trowels. I have given several
plates of the objects I found on the ground. Perhaps the little
human heads of clay, plain, or with ornamental head-dresses,
turn up in the greatest quantities. [See Plates XXIII., XXIV.,
and XXV., at end.] As no one could give me any information
about them, I make the suggestion that the plain heads were
types of certain nationalities or clans, and those with ornamented
head-dresses represent chiefs to whom they were attached, or
possibly deities whom they worshipped; if the latter, they were
probably made by the priests and sold to the people on the
occasion of deaths or some great religious ceremony that they
might be kept by them as protection for the household.
These clay heads were of various sizes; the two largest I
found are given in Plate L. [at end of volume]. Some of the
heads were perforated, so as to be suspended, like the two on
Plate LI. [at end of volume]; these two heads have curiously
shaped bases on which they may be set up. All the clay heads
appear to have been cast in moulds, but I also found a few
broken portions of heads carved out of fine stone, indicating
very good workmanship; these, broken as they are, were more
appreciated by Mr. Franks and the authorities of the British
Museum than any of my clay ones. There was another object
in great abundance on the ground, which is figured on Plate
XLIX. *d*; it is a lump of clay, generally of the rudest workmanship, though I found one slightly ornamented, XLIX. *d**.
None of my friends could say more about them than that they
were known in common parlance as inkstands, and were occasionally sold in the shops set upon a little slab of Puebla
marble for this purpose. Some of them have holes, through
which a cord might be passed, in order to hang them against
the wall. Will some one corroborate my idea that they were
made for the purpose of holding joss-sticks or incense-sticks,
to be burned before the household deities? Broken pieces of

pottery were strewed about in all directions. Plates LII. *a, b, c*
[at end of volume] represent the three best pieces I picked up.

It was not likely that perfect specimens of pottery would be
found on the ploughed fields, but the cottagers occasionally
discovered them, and hid them under some bushes, ready to be
offered to a treasure-seeking traveller. The one given in Plate
XXVI. is a fair specimen, and has a good polish; the five little
bosses near the grotesque head probably indicate the measure of
the quantity this vase would contain; such bosses or spots were
the common indication of the numbers up to twenty, for which
number a symbol, often a flag, was used, each successive ten
having a different symbol.

Some very curious and grotesque black clay vases were
occasionally offered for sale, but, being informed that these were
mostly modern imitations, I only bought one or two as curiosities.
On comparing them closely with similar vases in the museum
in Mexico, the museum authorities could not distinguish any
difference between them and those they supposed to be ancient.
I have given two on Plates LIII., LIV. [at end of volume]. Señor
Mendoza said they were considered to be ordinary domestic Aztec
ware. The market price of these vases was only from four to
eight shillings, apparently a very small sum for the amount of
workmanship. It was further supposed that if these black vases
were imitations, the workman had probably an original vase
somewhere in reserve from which the copies were made. There
are a number of these grotesque vases in the cupboards of the
British Museum, which I have examined. Mr. Franks and his
friends intend to place them amongst the Christy Collection, if
they satisfy themselves as to their authenticity.

Obsidian is a vitrified volcanic matter having the appearance
of jet or black glass; it is found in large and small beds traver-
sing volcanic rocks; its structure is compact, brittle, colour a
brownish-black, lustre vitreous; opaque, but translucent on the
edge; it fuses into a transparent glass before the blow-pipe; it

AZTEC JAR FROM TEOTIHUACAN
(10 INCHES HIGH)

may be called melted silica crystallised. Whether the Aztecs found rocks of it in the volcanic regions of the plain or depended upon boulders of it in the rivers and streams I could not learn. I found many small boulders of it a few inches in diameter in the brook or river that meanders through the plains of Teotihuacan. It was of this substance that the Aztecs made masks, vases, ear-rings, lip-rings, many ornaments, knives, and arrow-heads— the two latter are to be found probably in every ploughed field in Mexico. I have engraved a few; Plate LV. *a* [at end of volume] is called a core, from which the knives are sliced off. In the Christy Collection of Mexican objects in the British Museum are some excellent specimens of obsidian ornaments; also some rings in the process of manufacture, indicating the immense labour required to work this brittle substance into delicately fine ornaments. The Aztecs' lip ornament of obsidian was a diminutive representation of an Englishman's "stove-pipe," or Sunday hat, the rim being inserted inside the lip; there are specimens in the British Museum well worth inspection, though there is nothing in the Christy Collection to be compared with a small obsidian vase five inches high in the Museum at Mexico; this is ornamented with the outline of the human figure, the arms being adapted as handles, and as supports to the lip or spout; the polish on this little vase is so bright and the substance so delicate that it impressed me as a work of art, ranking equal to the Portland vase in the British Museum. How it was made and fashioned by people who had no knowledge of iron instruments, but used a bronze of tin and copper, adds much to the marvel of its production. In the museum in Mexico are some obsidian masks of the size of the human face. These ornaments were used at the obsequies of great people. Another object very common on the plains of Teotihuacan was a stone in the shape of a smoothing iron, of which I have given a drawing in Plate XLIX. *a*. I only found broken specimens, and have filled up the outline from examples I saw in the Museum of Mexico; these were no doubt in very

N 2

common use, as all the buildings as well as the floors that have been excavated appear to have been thickly covered with smooth cement. Another object is very common on the ground; it is given in Plate XLIX. *c*, and I must leave it to the learned to say whether it is simply a pestle or has anything to do with phallus worship, though Chavero, in his essay on the calendar stone, says: " The Aztecs could not have received any of their religious ideas from the Asiatic nations, as there is no indication of this worship." Schliemann, in his 'Ilios,' page 276, represents a similar object, and alludes to many others as found in the sacred city, but adds that this cultus was not mentioned either by Homer or by Hesiod, or by any of the other poets. Perhaps next to arrow-heads and stone implements found in any part of the world, whorls or spindle-tops, indicating progress in civilisation, are the most plentiful. The sites of the ancient cities in Mexico yield an abundant supply of these rudimentary domestic machines; there are plenty on the ground in Teotihuacan, they seem to be identically similar in shape, and more or less so in ornamentation, to those found in such quantities on the plains of Troy. I give a plate of two I picked up, one with a much higher class of design on it than any figured in Dr. Schliemann's book; it has a highly polished brown glaze surface upon it. At the time I was gathering these curios, Dr. Schliemann's work had not yet reached me, or I should have been more interested in my search, and not have despised the broken fragments, as the ornamentation on them might have been useful to archæologists. No doubt the American explorers will soon crowd on to this happy hunting-ground, and give the world the benefit of their researches. May they do it with the same speed that their engineers are projecting railways all over this country, and may I live to know more from them about the hidden treasures of Cholula, Texcoco and Teotihuacan.

We soon filled our provision satchels, our pockets, and any sort of bag we could improvise, with them; it was very hot, and

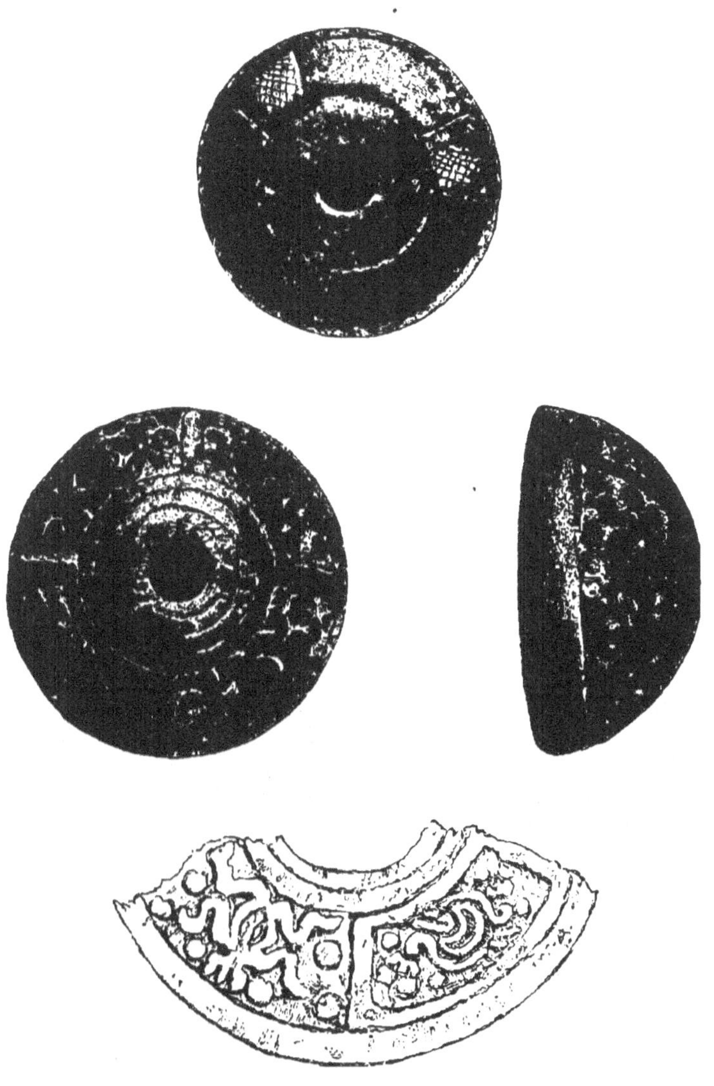

WHORLS, OR SPINDLE-HEADS IN CLAY.

EXACT SIZE.

[page 180.

one of the party took off his coat and utilised the sleeves as well as the pockets for holding them. It was merely a question of selection of the most perfect specimens; it is a matter of surprise that, as most of the objects are of clay and many of them un-glazed, they are in the perfect state in which they are found.

I paid a second and third visit to Teotihuacan. After alighting at the station you have nearly two miles to walk to the village, in which there is a shop and *fonda*, where the traveller can procure excellent food and wine. Mine host provides horses and a guide; the latter, having assisted Monsieur de Charnáy in making his excavations on the ground a year or two ago, is a very fair cicerone to all the most interesting portions of the ground. I made my last journey to the spot in October, hoping to find another bagful of treasures, but, alas! the ploughed fields we had traversed in June were now covered with Indian maize from six to ten feet high, and we were obliged to confine our attentions to the pyramids, and take another look at the only carved figure now on the ground; it was a colossal ornamented head, cut on a single block of stone some eight to ten feet high. This head is said to have been rolled down from its original position on the Pyramid of the Moon into the hole where it now stands. The excavation was suggested by Maximilian in order to show the whole stone. It is probable that the same Catholic bishop Zumarraga whose hand is described by Prescott as falling more heavily than that of " time " itself on the Aztec monuments, has been the cause of much disappointment here as elsewhere to the modern traveller. While on the subject of ancient ruins, I must allude to a visit I paid to the city of Texcoco, on the opposite side of the lake from Mexico City. Mr. Ober and I agreed to accompany the Rev. John Butler, who was obliged to go there to see after one of the rural native Methodist ministers who had been thrown into prison.

Future visitors will find a railway to the place—we had to do the thirty miles on horseback. It was the 20th of June, and rather warm at 10 A.M. The road, for the most of the way, was overshadowed by an avenue of trees, and for some miles was good for galloping along the turf on the wayside.

The first thing to be seen at Texcoco was a section of an immense broken bas-relief, that had lately been discovered by Mr. Evans, the correspondent of the *Chicago Times.* I occasionally met him in Mexico. He was not in any way an archæologist, but a clever newspaper correspondent, and was much elated by his discovery, which was spoken of in Mexico at the time as "the great find." It appears some brickmakers were utilising an old small pyramid or mound of old *adobe*, "unbaked bricks," for present purposes, and struck this broken piece of sculpture; it is supposed to represent a prince or king, said to have been Nezhual-coytl, one of the most refined and cultivated princes of Texcoco.

In the afternoon we rode out ten miles to the hills to see some extensive flights of steps cut in the solid rocks, bathing-tanks, vestiges of temples and other architectural remains, that quite corroborate the description of the magnificence and luxurious tastes of this prince given by Herrera, who styles his reign the Augustan Age of Mexico.

One more visit and I have done. The Pyramid of Cholula, near Puebla, is perhaps better known than any ancient ruin in Mexico, as it is specially connected with the history of the country, and Prescott's description (vol. ii., page 22), of the terrible massacre Cortes committed on the Cholulan chieftains is a chapter easier to be remembered than any in the three volumes. At the time of the Conquest, Cholula was undoubtedly one of the principal cities of the plain. It is described as the great commercial emporium of the country. It is said that the inhabitants excelled in various mechanical arts, especially that of working in metals, the manufacture of cotton and agave cloths and of a delicate kind of pottery, rivalling, says Herrera, that of Florence in beauty.

I can only refer to the present aspect of the place. In the

PYRAMID AT CHOLULA.   REMAINS OF A SMALL PYRAMID.

[*page* 182.

centre of a lovely plain, at a distance of from six to eight miles from Puebla (from which place there is a horse train to it), stands the Pyramid of Cholula. Four terraces are distinctly visible. Its vertical height is 177 feet; its base, which is square, is 1423 feet long, covers forty-four acres, and is solidly built of *adobe bricks.*

There is a wide winding path from the bottom to the top, where stands a modern-looking Spanish church, and from the terrace and graveyard in front of this there is, as might be expected, a lovely view. The snow peak of Popocatapetl is directly opposite; it conceals its rival; Ixtaccihuatl is unseen, being behind it. The peak of Malinches is a little on the right, Puebla and the hill of the Cinco de Mayo, on the extreme right; on the left a plain spreads out until it is lost in bluish mist.

I mentioned in my chapter on churches that I counted thirty-four from this position; some five or six were in the village at our feet, two or three of them large enough to remind one of our St. Paul's, London. These churches give evidence of the great number of inhabitants in the valley at the time of the Conquest. "Teocalles"—temples or sacred places—probably then stood upon the same sites, as it was the rule of the Spaniards, whenever they destroyed a heathen temple, to compel the natives to build a Christian church, and conform or perish.*

* "The Christian fanaticism broke out in a particular manner against the Aztec priests, and the Teopixqui, or ministers of the divinity, and all those who inhabited the Teocalli, or houses of God, who might be considered as the depositaries of the historical, mythological and astronomical knowledge of the country, were exterminated: for the priests observed the meridian shade in the gnomons, and regulated the calendar. The monks burned the hieroglyphical paintings by which every kind of knowledge had been transmitted from generation to generation. The people, deprived of these means of instruction, were plunged in an ignorance so much the deeper as the missionaries were unskilled in the Mexican languages, and could substitute few new ideas in place of the old. The better sort of Indians, among whom a certain degree of intellectual culture might be supposed, perished in great part at the commencement of the Spanish Conquest, the victims of European ferocity. The natives who remained consisted only of the most indigent race—poor cultivators,

Interspersed amongst the churches at our feet are the remains of two smaller adobe pyramids, around which were some newly-ploughed fields, where we found a few obsidian knives and relics. In examining the smaller pyramid, which has been almost cut away, doubtless for the making of bricks, I noticed it had been erected in distinct solid blocks of about thirty feet by fifteen feet in thickness, and the blocks not in any way tied together. In some cases rain had washed the sides so as to separate them for several inches. This gave me the idea that these pyramids were originally built in blocks by contract, or that every village or district contributed a block to the construction.

Señor Mendoza is publishing a very interesting illustrated book on the archæological treasures in the National Museum. He gave me several numbers which are already printed, and promised to send the others as they appeared. He certainly had some treasures of Aztec mosaic work, and beautifully embossed golden plates, which once ornamented the statues of Mexican deities. When I say embossed, I think I should say cast, for we concluded that the gold had been run on to exquisitely engraved moulds. My journal is quite full of the many objects of archæological interest which I saw. I hope I have not wearied the reader with this long chapter, half of which he may consider might better have been omitted.

If any English archæologist has time on his hands and will visit Mexico, he will be well repaid. He might even find *dolmens*, which so much exercise the minds of archæologists at the present time.

artisans, weavers—porters who were used like beasts of burden. How shall we judge, then, from these miserable remains of a powerful people, of the degree of cultivation to which it had risen from the twelfth to the sixteenth century, and of the intellectual development of which it is susceptible? If all that remained of the French or German nation were a few poor agriculturists, could we read in their features that they belonged to nations which had produced a Descartes and a Clairault; a Kepler and a Leibnitz?"—Humboldt, vol. i., p. 117.

CLAY MOULDS FOUND AT TEOTIHUACAN.
(EXACT SIZE)

Professor Morse, of Salem (Boston), lately gave me a description of the *dolmens* he had discovered in Japan, and also the pamphlet containing his diagrams of them ; these show that they are just like those found in England and parts of Europe. No doubt they are to be found in Mexico for the trouble of searching.

I often longed to have at my elbow Professor Boyd Dawkins, or Dr. Sainter, of Macclesfield, when I saw anything like a small mound, or a cavern of the pleistocene period.

CHAPTER XXI.

MEXICAN ANTIQUITIES.

Aztec Calendar Stone—The Sacrificial Stone—Idols in the Museum of Mexico—Skulls used as Ornaments—Teoyamiqui, the Idol of Death—Aztec Vases and Maps.

AFTER a chapter on the ruins of ancient cities, let me give the reader who is interested in such matters a short account of some of the things well worth his inspecting in the City of Mexico.

In the first place the Aztec Calendar, fixed in the wall of the cathedral tower, directly opposite the Monte de Piedad, is assuredly the most striking curio that will attract a stranger's attention. Its position in the plain smooth plinth of the tower is excellent as inviting inspection, and to remove it, as is proposed, to the Museum, where it will be comparatively lost among surrounding objects of similar character, would be a mistake—unless such removal is positively necessary for the preservation of the monument. I saw several small circular stones less elaborately carved, but of similar character, in other places ; the fragment of the large bas-relief supposed to represent the Texcucan monarch, luckily found by Mr. Evans, of Chicago, during my stay, had a large dial mixed up with the figure ; the dial had a date upon it which was indicated by a finger. There were some smaller dial-stones of similar character in one of the courts of the ruined convent at Tlahuac.

The hieroglyphics on the calendar stone in the church tower are supposed to indicate the astronomical knowledge of the

THE AZT

WRIGHT 25

Mexicans at the time it was sculptured. Many learned treatises have been written upon it, notably by Señores Orozeo, Herrera and Gama; in the 'Anales del Museo Nacional de Mexico,' published by the government under the superintendence of the curator, Señor G. Mendoza, is a special article on this subject, "La Piedra del Sol," by Señor Alfredo Chavero. As I had the pleasure of making Señor Chavero's acquaintance in Mexico, and was told that this, his last treatise on the subject, is considered the best authority, I give the reader a short resumé of it.

Señor Chavero tells us that it was made in honour of the sun, in the reign of King Axayácatl in the year 13 acátl, which corresponds to 1479 of our era; it was originally placed horizontally in the grand temple of Mexico, in the part called Quauhæilco. When the city was taken by Cortes, on the 13th of August, 1521, and the grand temple destroyed, the calendar stone was left in the great square until Friar Alonso de Montufar, Archbishop of Mexico, ordered it to be buried, somewhere between 1551 and 1559; the monument was found during the repaving of the great square in 1790, and the canons, Don José Uribe and Don Juan José Gamboa, petitioned the Viceroy for it, and placed it against the tower, where it still remains. The stone is a block of traquita, or basalt, weighing twenty-five tons, and its diameter is eleven feet. The circle on the stone has been carved upon a block of irregular shape, as taken from the quarry; that the form is unaltered is proved by some hieroglyphical marks being carried over the edge that appears to be broken. The irregularities of the broken part were not visible when it was on the floor of the round temple of the sun. There is a manuscript extant, a translation of which is found in Duran (vol. i., chapter 36), in which the inauguration of the stone is described in the following terms:

Tlacaelel (the high priest?) turned and spoke to the King Axayácatl thus :—

"My son, thou hast just partaken of the feast in which thou hast made thy name great, and traced it with the colours and pencil of fame for ever; it now remains for thee to still further extend that name, and the greatness thou hast acquired; thou knowest that the sun-stone is now finished, and it is necessary that it should be put in its place with the same solemnity that has been gone through for this one [probably referring to the large sacrificial stone once in the temple and now in the Museum garden]. Therefore send thy messengers to Texcoco and to Tescuba, with messages to the lords of those provinces, that they may come and build the place in which they are to sit, which is to be twenty arms round, and in the middle of which is to be placed this stone."

Señor Chavero goes on to say: "This monument is a votive stone dedicated to the sun, on which are sculptured the different phases of the star of light, astronomical and cosmographical, and also those that relate to the ceremonies and the custom or customs (?) of the ancient Mexicans. The face in the centre is the god-star throwing his light over the earth, which is represented by the tongue projecting from his lips; he has the pupils of his eyes turned upwards, and they are seen through the sacred mask that covers the upper part of the face. The hieroglyphics on the diadem encircling the head represent the division of time and the Mexican method of numbering the years; the civil year, like ours, was 365 days. Each four years had different emblems repeated successively, without reference to other chronological arrangements. The first year was called Tochtli or rabbit, the second, Acátl or reed, the third, Técpatl or flint, the fourth, Calli or house.* In addition to these periods, the years were arranged

---

* I see Señor Don Joaquin Garcia Icazbalceta in his essay on "Computation of Mexican Time" in the 'Anales del Museo,' places these four signs in a different rotation from Señor Chavero's, viz.: first, Tecpatl the flint, the symbol of sacrifice, being the instrument with which the heart of the sacrificial victim was cut from the

by the number of thirteen, four of such periods making fifty-two years, or a Mexican age, when the festival of fire, a most serious event for the Mexicans, occurred, as the priests taught the people that the world might come to an end, and that the Tzitzimines, who were very ugly and terrible demons, would descend from above and eat up mankind."

With reference to the ceremonies that took place on these occasions, I have given an extract from Prescott in the chapter describing the ascent of the hill of Estrella, near Mexico. Señor Chavero's essay is very interesting, but too long and full of technicalities for me to give more than a brief outline of it. I hope at some future time to give a correct and full translation, as he alludes to the earlier races who preceded the Aztecs, and their methods of computing time, and also the changes that they adopted from 1091 A.D. until a perfect computation of time for 365 days, that is a solar year, was correctly ascertained.

The two claws represented on the dial on the sides of the mask have their meaning. The hand and fingers are used to denote certain computations of numbers, which are lengthily described by Chavero. The various positions of the fingers indicated the numbers up to five. Señor Chavero gives the following table up to twenty :—

1, 2, 3, 4, 5, the open hand in various positions.

6, 7, 8, 9, 10, the fist, or closed hand, in various positions.

11, 12, 13, 14, 15, the hand in the form of a claw in various positions.

16, 17, 18, 19, 20, the hand with the four fingers and the thumb joined by their tips.

It will be noticed that these two claws have spots or rings on them, plain or ornamented. Such spots or rings were in common

still living body; and Calli, Tochitli, and Acátl in later succession. When they came to the thirteenth year, they called it the great year, four times thirteen making fifty-two, which was the ending of their epoch, and the beginning of a new era inaugurated by their great festival.

use in computations; thus the five spots on the vase on Plate XXVI. probably indicate the measure or quantity the vessel might contain, and the spots on the claws refer to a date. Señor Chavero in his essay compares the Mexican computation of time with those of Asiatic nations of the older periods, from which the Egyptians and Greeks derived their inspirations; and he gives the early people of the New World the credit of having worked out their own wonderful and correct system by their own unaided efforts, or if they derived them from an Asiatic origin, then only from such data as might have been brought by an uncultivated and savage tribe from the outskirts of what was probably in early ages a continent or islands on the east of Asia, now covered by the waters of the Pacific Ocean.

Señor Chavero explains all the engravings on the stone, giving to every part a special signification; for instance, the four larger reversed-V shaped ornaments denote four equal divisions of the day; the smaller V's indicate a further division of the day into eight portions; the intermediate ornaments between the V's represent eight divisions of the night. Again, the twenty various ornaments in panels in the circle inside the V's are symbols of twenty days, the number of days in a Mexican month; these twenty symbols are found on earlier calendar stones of the Nahoas, a nation preceding the Toltecs.

The two crowned faces at the lowest extremity of the circle as engraved are those of the dual god, creator and fire, the protruding tongues being, as I before said of the face in the centre of the stone, symbols of life and light.

After an examination of the Calendar Stone the visitor should cross the Plaza and stroll into the court-yard and new hall of the National Museum, where he will find an abundant variety of objects illustrating the worship and history of both Toltecs and Aztecs. The famous Sacrificial Stone at present stands in the centre of the garden, and certainly ranks next in interest to the Calendar Stone, if not before it. It is likewise a single block of porphyry, over three yards in diameter and five feet thick. It originally stood in the great temple in Mexico, probably about the spot where now stands the high altar and baldacchino in the cathedral. The bas-reliefs on the sides represent conquerors holding captive foes by the hair of their heads, and reminded me of the triumphs of the Egyptians, as sculptured and painted on the walls at Karnac and other temples on the banks of the Nile.

In the 'Anales del Museo,' Señor D. M. Orozco y Berra gives a long description of it, from which may be gathered that this magnificent relic was discovered on the 17th of December; 1791, while some alterations were being made in the repaving of the Plaza; and that, had not Canon Gamboa happened to be passing when the workmen discovered it, it would have been broken in pieces to faciliate its removal. Thanks to the canon, it was preserved, and placed in the cemetery of the cathedral, where it remained till the year 1824; thence it was removed to what was then the garden of the University, and is now in the "Museo Nacional." The place where it was found in the Plaza is marked by a stone erected by Señor Don Fernando Ramirez, Minister for the Home Department, under President Arista, in 1852. The stone bears an inscription certifying the spot and date.

The Mexican name for the stone is Cuauhxicalli de Tizoc. The bottom of the stone is level and smooth, the top and sides being covered with sculpture in relief. The ornaments on the upper surface of the stone are very similar to those on the calendar stone. The Λ triangles and circles have reference to epochs and division of time; all the rings or other figures are in fours, or multiples of four, to which I have already alluded as a special chronological arrangement on the calendar stone.

The bas-reliefs that encircle the block are fifteen in number, and represent fifteen victories gained by the Emperor Tizoc over so many neighbouring states. The victorious figures holding the captives by the hair were generals who for their valour were created Knights of the Sun, no doubt an honour coveted as greatly as a G.C.B. in the present day. There is a cartouche or small ornament in the upper right-hand corner of each panel, which indicates the name of the conquered city or district ; copies of five of these panels are given on Plate XXXI.

g represents a walled town, Tetenauco; *h*, a district of flowers, the present Xochimilco; *i*, a necklace of jewelry— Tozxiuhco, supposed to be a place where such necklaces were either made or much used; *j*, a frog, is a symbol of the state of Oaxaca; *l*, a hand, signifies a place that was taken by the Acolhua.

All the Knights of the Sun are uniformly dressed, one figure only having a much more extensive head-dress of feathers, and some other insignia; this figure probably represents Tizoc himself. Some of the captives are nude, others wear a sort of skirt; they are less ornamented than their conquerors, the Knights of the Sun, who delight in the name or title of Cuacuauhtin.

Tizoc died in the year 1486, about the date when the stone is supposed to have been made; but whether by his own or his successor's order is uncertain.

The next prominent object in the museum is a large stone deity, that at first sight appears composed of heads, claws, and hands. I have given an engraving of it, but can give the reader very little information about it, other than that every portion of the ornamentation is said to have had a special signification. I was told it represented Huitzilopochtli, the Aztec god of war, but it was easily to be seen that the monster represented a female, and according to Señor Chavero, whom I have before quoted, it represents Coatlicue, the translation being the Earth at night, or Death; she was the mother of Huitzilopochtli, the god of war, and of Quetzalcoatl, the evening or the morning star; and from Señor Chavero's essay in 'Los Anales de Mexico' we learn that this monument was found in the great square at the same time as the Calendar Stone. It is about ten

OUTLINE DRAWING ON AZTEC SACRIFICIAL STONE.
SEE PLATE XLVII. FOR SKETCH OF STONE.

[page 192.

feet high, and has a skirt of snakes. The goddess represented
was considered the progenitrix of mankind; she was worshipped
in the grand temple of the City of Mexico, in a part of the
building called Atlaulico, which is derived from Atlauhtli, signifying a large figure in the earth; a woman was sacrificed to her
every year in the Tzacualli, which means "the place of snakes;"
she appears to have had several different names, in accordance with
her various attributes; and parts of the ornamentation of the
statue were always introduced in the statues of Huitzilopochtli,
Quetzalcoatl, and other deities descended from her. The number
of hands on the statue are symbols of the creative power of the
earth; the skull ornament on the waistbelt represents Mict-
lancihuatl, the deity of death, as she was supposed to receive the
bodies of all who died, and to keep them in her bosom till the day
of general resurrection. The teeth of Tloloc, the god of the
waters, are introduced as signifying that the greater deities of
earth, life, creator, and fire were thought to repose on water,
and the feet of these deities are generally ornamented with shells
of the sea.   In further illustration of the symbolic character of
the ornamentation, I will mention that the feathers on the back
are arranged in thirteen glyphs, or symbols of the days of the
thirteen years of the period Flalpilli; the seven small points or
spots give us Chicomecohuatl, another attribute of the deity;
finally, there are in the hem of the skirt twenty-six spots, which,
in their different combinations, give us the days of the sacred
year, and the years of the cycles of fifty-two years, at the end of
which the sacred fire was extinguished and relit; it is to be
presumed that they wished to represent the earth on the night
of death, or last night of the epoch; this is shown by the
union of the years with the image of Tzontemoc, who, as his
name expresses, fell head foremost from heaven (as represented
on the stone of Tuxpan), and will come forth from the house
of death with the sign Omeacátl, or the sun of the new epoch.
     The skull, representing the deity of death, seems to have

been a prominent feature in the religion of the Aztecs; I saw some curious representations of it in Mexico, and there is a notable specimen or example of this sacred skull in the Christy Collection in the British Museum, of which I give a coloured drawing; it is a natural human skull, which has been covered with alternate bands of black obsidian and blue turquoise; the eyes are formed of two iron pyrites, and the nose is inlaid with scarlet shell-work. The jaw is not fixed, but movable, and there are two thongs of leather attached to the skull, by which it could be tied on to a figure or idol; the effect of its appearance is in reality more hideous than the coloured plate suggests. There are several smaller heads and knife-handles in the British Museum, inlaid with obsidian and turquoise in the same manner as in the plate above referred to.

Masks made of stone or obsidian seem to have been much used in the ceremonial and religious worship of the Aztecs, and I regret I did not purchase some undoubtedly authentic specimens, which were occasionally offered for sale in the Portales. The obsidian masks were of life size, the back being quite flat and smooth; I saw them used as letter weights in one or two houses; and I was told their original use was to be placed on the breasts of the bodies of nobles or priests during funeral services.

In the museum of Mexico there is a small stone idol, three feet ten inches high, named Teoyamiqui, or the goddess of death. She has a skirt of plaited snakes, and I give a sketch of her general appearance on Plate XXXIV., at the end of the volume. Look at her hands, they are disproportionately large, and have corns on them; these indicate her greed and strength. The idol was once painted; the nose is inlaid with scarlet shell, like that of the human skull before alluded to in the British Museum. The small holes round the skull were used for holding on a wig, probably a frightful one, making her as hideous an apparition as imagination could desire.

COATLICUE, THE CHIEF AZTEC DEITY.
10 FEET HIGH.

SKULL ORNAMENT.

We will now turn to a prettier object. The vase, Plate XXXV., also at the end of the volume, ornamented with the emblems of Centeotl or Ceres, is twenty-one inches high, and nineteen inches in diameter on the top. There were in the museum several equally large earthenware vases of Aztec workmanship, and highly coloured, but the gem of the whole collection up to the present time is undoubtedly the small obsidian vase of which I have spoken.

Next in order of interest to the idols, vases, and musical instruments in the museum (not omitting the feathered shield and dress of Montezuma), are undoubtedly the small collection of Aztec maps and charts, and the series of coarsely-drawn hieroglyphical coloured pictures, representing the immigration of the Aztecs into the country in the thirteenth century. The line of route is indicated by the outlines of men's feet, and if the pictures are in any way truthful, they corroborate the story that the Toltecs fled before the invaders, and gave up their cities without any struggle to defend them.

The museum is being greatly enriched from day to day, since archæological treasures are continually unearthed, one of the principal additions being the serpents' heads in front of the cathedral already alluded to as found during my visit. Every treasure trove belongs to the National Museum or state museum of the country. I saw several private collections that had been made some years ago, before the Government interfered, the owners of them being very polite, and apparently much pleased to exhibit their treasures to a visitor. In all the collections there were curious stone yokes in the shape of large horse-shoes and horse-collars, some much ornamented and engraved; there are specimens of these in the British Museum, but neither the authorities there, nor Señor Mendoza, nor any of the savants in Mexico, could explain their use, the only supposition being that they were used in holding down the victim on the sacrificial altar; but this is only a supposition, as in none of the ancient drawings and pictures of human sacrifice are there any representations of this mode of binding; all the pictures of such scenes represent the victim as being held by cords from the feet and hands.

During my visit a large and handsome hall was being constructed on one side of the museum, for the reception of the most valuable pieces of ancient Aztec sculpture, and it is possible that the large sacrificial stone, now so beautifully embowered in shrubs, and the large idols, which are also in the garden, will eventually be moved under cover for their better preservation.

CHAPTER XXII.

INNER LIFE.

Spaniards—Pure Indians—Courtship—Music—Dancing—Tortillas—Murillos.

OUTSIDE of the families of the diplomatic circle in which I had the pleasure of visiting, my friends were Spaniards rather than Mexicans; while their ancestors might have been in Mexico for several generations, they still retained all the characteristics, customs and manners of the old country. Many gentlemen in official positions, and some deputies in the House of Congress, were pointed out to me as being of pure Indian descent. They were generally handsome men, and I should have imagined them Spaniards, had I not been informed of their origin. The present president, Gonzales, is of pure Indian descent, and not darker in complexion than many Spaniards; and Benito Juarez, who may in some ways be considered the father of his country, as he fairly acted the part of a Washington through the perilous times of the birth of the Republic, was also of pure Indian descent, and was acknowledged by foreign diplomats who came in contact with him to be one of the ablest men they had met. In speaking, therefore, of the inner lives of the families whom I visited, it must be assumed they are of Spanish descent and Spanish in almost every particular. The Mexican Spaniards have preserved all the exquisite politeness of their Spanish ancestors. If they are a little distant at first, so much the better; they are cautiously taking your measure, but when once you have been admitted to their acquaintance you will find them charming, and the oftener you visit them the more they will be pleased, increasing at each visit the cordiality of their reception.

Families generally occupy a whole flat or floor of one of the large houses, which have each a quadrangle ornamented. with flowers, and a common staircase. The reception rooms are elegantly furnished, except perhaps the *salle à manger*, which is generally a dark room at the back near the kitchen, and used as a pantry as well as a dining-room. Cake and wine are in most cases offered to visitors, and if you are sufficiently intimate you are pressed to stay to dinner or supper, *sin ceremonias ;* and wherever I stayed, in compliance with such an invitation, there was no sign of extra preparation or apology for shortcomings, but I was made to feel perfectly at home and at my ease.

I have made mention that the men salute by embracing one another, while hugging, each taps the small of the other's back. The ladies meet each other in the same way, and kiss a good deal. The children kiss the hands of their parents, and a well-bred child will say to a grown-up person of distinction, "I kiss your hands." To a lady you say "I kiss your feet," and you end your letter to them with the same expression.

A Mexican is almost as polite as a Japanese. The latter people in every grade of society seem to possess this charming attribute naturally; whereas in Mexico, special lessons in urbanity are given in schools, and little children are taught to utter all sorts of pretty phrases.

Wooing in Mexico is said to be a serious matter, the ladies are so shut up that it is difficult for a gentleman to get an introduction to them. But I suspect the churches, the theatres, and the *zocalo* afford the necessary opportunities for exchanging glances and little notes, which are probably sufficient, though Juliet has to sit behind the barred window of her balcony, and poor Romeo is denied admittance to the house. These sighing cavaliers will be found in the streets at all times, and the more constant the gentleman, the more haughty is the lady. I was told of a case of a gentleman, now one of the divisional magistrates of the City of Mexico, who wooed for seven long years without ever speaking to the lady.

I had the pleasure of meeting a considerable number of Mexican ladies. As an Englishman, I believe I was frequently introduced where a Spaniard would have found the *entrée* forbidden.

The piano is an institution with the Mexicans. They play anything and everything: the violin, the concertina, and the guitar; in the Tejira family I have known the music of a whole opera, vocal and instrumental, to be rendered in one afternoon by various members of the family, a succession of callers not interfering in the slighest degree with the performance.

Mexicans are not by any means crazy on the subject of dancing, but when they do dance they do so with a grace of which people who have not visited the country have but little conception; the Spanish dances—especially *La Danza*—are slow and stately in movement, except perhaps the Fandango, which is only danced by the lower classes. I attended a ball given at the Spanish Club, a very gay and crowded affair. A number of Germans were present, whose boisterous style of dancing caused the Mexican ladies to shrink back into their seats, and express themselves as surprised and horrified at such rough and uncouth movements. The *danza*, as performed in the "*venta*" and the drawing-room is a very different dance; in the one it is bacchanalian, in the other very graceful and elegant, but an Englishman or an American might vote it consummately slow.

There is a good deal of sociability in Mexico, but their dinner-parties and breakfast-parties are too elaborate to indulge in frequently; pot-luck is good luck, and I have enjoyed a most delightful meal by being taken in by mine host in this way, though I never could be induced to eat the *tortillas*—a little hot soft cake, made out of Indian corn, which is baked hot and hot for the different courses of every meal. Tortillas are the daily food of the people, they are the only bread food of the poor, and they seem never to be omitted from the tables of the rich. The labour of making tortillas is enormous. In a poor man's house the wife is occupied most of the day in preparing a few tortillas for her husband's supper on his return from work, and she has no time to attend to her children or any other household duty. In the mansions of the rich, an expert woman is retained for the sole purpose of making the tortillas for the family. The process is as follows: a quantity of maize is put into a jar of lime and hot water overnight; there must not be too much lime nor too little, if there is not exactly the right quantity, the grain is not properly softened, and the cakes will not come out right. The grain is taken from the jar and placed upon a small stone bench, at which a woman kneels, and with a long stone roller reduces the grain to a kind of paste; when this paste is at a proper consistency she, or possibly the eldest girl of the family, pats pieces of it between the palms of the hands until it assumes the appearance of small pancakes, these are then slightly baked or dried on a large tray or flat earthenware pan over a small charcoal fire, and, lo! you have the tortilla.

They are very tough eating; you tear them to pieces almost as you would a piece of leather. I pronounce them execrable, and, until the Mexicans turn from tortillas to grinding their corn and making bread, the drudgery of manufacturing tortillas will prevent their women from rising in the social scale, and keep them in their present overworked and degraded condition. So long as they have to go through this daily operation, so long will they keep neither themselves nor their houses clean; so long will they be unable to attend to their children, or perform that high characteristic duty of woman's civilisation, the running of an American sewing-machine.

In the diplomatic circle, and in the society of the foreign residents in the city, it is whispered that, although the Mexicans will come to their entertainments as often as asked, they very

MAKING TORTILLA CAKES.

[*page 200.*

seldom return the compliment. If this be so, it no doubt arises from the privacy in which the Mexican and the Spaniard enshrouds his family.

The wearing of mourning in a family is very strict, and is much prolonged by the ladies, who remain in complete retirement, even for some time after the gentlemen have re-entered society and may be seen dancing gaily at all the balls.

I was taken by Mr. Bandelier, an American archæologist, to the private houses of several savants—I may mention Señor Icazbalceta and Señor Chavero—where I saw very fine libraries, valuable books, and also many beautiful oil paintings. Señor Icazbalceta had a famous collection of manuscripts, and he showed me many original letters of Cortes. He said he believed that Sir Thomas Phillips had the best collection of Mexican manuscripts in England; he was greatly desirous of seeing a catalogue of this collection, and I promised to do my utmost on my return to England to procure one for him.

I had the good fortune to obtain an *entrée* into some dozen houses where picture-galleries, libraries and old Spanish ornaments were the special attractions; the kind hosts being delighted to show and explain their treasures. I was rather amused at one feature in these collections. Every gallery possessed a Murillo! and each owner questioned the existence of any other Murillo in the city, always excepting the ' Madonna ' which used to hang in the cathedral, but which now, for greater safety, hangs in the archbishop's palace.

In these houses, where I was unacquainted with the family, and merely taken as a stranger, the elderly ladies often came forward, and were charmingly polite, even to showing me the arrangement of the *cuisine*, if I happened to profess an interest in it. No young ladies were ever presented. I fancy they lead very secluded lives, the balcony and the church being their only recreation, for it cannot be much pleasure to drive in the Paséo in a very close carriage.

In concluding this short chapter upon a glimpse of Mexican private life, it would be an oversight not to mention the two beautiful houses of Señors Barron and Escandon at Tacubaya, to which Don Pablo Escandon drove me. These two mansions and their lovely gardens are occasionally opened to the public by ticket. They may be regarded as the Chatsworth and Eaton Hall of the country, but it would be drawing a long bow were I to lead the visitor to expect similar splendour and proportions; the residences at Tacubaya are modern buildings, whose beautiful surroundings are in perfect order, and which bear no similarity to the older houses of Spanish character in the neighbourhood, where a broken pane of glass or an unhinged shutter almost invariably indicated neglect, if not decay.

CHAPTER XXIII.

AMUSEMENTS.

Bull-fights—Gambling—Theatres—The Circus—Marionettes.

THE *Corrida de toros* is almost as fashionable in Mexico as in Spain, and the *Plaza de toros* is as attractive to the multitude as Epsom Downs on Derby Day. The sporting men have their stock and betting-books; and each *ganaderia* (the farm on which bulls are raised) is as well known to them as Mr. Blenkiron's Middle Park is in England.

The bulls for fighting are in charge of *vaqueros*, or herdsmen especially trained, and when young, each *novillo*, or bull, is branded with a hot iron.

The *toros de muerte*, or bulls that are to fight to the death, are judged ready for the corrida, or arena, when they are from three to five years old. When they are being brought from the farm where they are raised, they are led by *cabestros*, or tame bulls, and travel by night, always reaching the *plaza* the night before the fight, where they are immured in the *apartado*, a strait and dark pen, from which they are one by one driven into the *toril*, their last prison, before leaping forth into the arena for the fight.

Sunday is the great day for this cruel amusement, and during the week previous the City of Mexico exhibits on all the advertising walls flaming placards announcing the particulars. This *programa de las funciones* is headed with an attractive woodcut of the

arena, and generally announces five or six events, commencing with
" *Cuatro Escogidos Toros*, from the unrivalled *hacienda* of Atenco."
Number two, *Segunda Corrida*, announces, " *Dos magníficos Toros
à Muerta!* " Number three, " *Cuatro arrogantes Toros* from Cuba,
con monedas de plata en la frente. Price of entrance ; shady side,
4 reals [or 2*s.*]; sunny side, half-price."

For some reason—possibly the assemblage of too great a
crowd—bull-fights are not allowed within the city limits, and the
world has to journey out to one of the neighbouring towns or
villages to enjoy its favourite pastime. Bull-fights are prohibited
by law in the Federal District, but the State of Mexico does not
prohibit them, hence the bull-rings are built just on the edge of
the Federal District. The first and only bull-fight I went to see
was on Sunday, the 24th of April. It was at Cuatitlan, two
hours distant by rail from Mexico City. Train upon train conveyed the enthusiastic multitude to the place.

The interior of the bull-ring is always the same, a roofless
amphitheatre. The arena is called *El Redondel*, and round it
runs a wooden barrier, painted red, of about the height of a
man, against which are fixed three or four little boxes, called
burladeros, behind which the *toreros*, or bull fighters, can hide
away from a maddened or revengeful bull, the entrance being too
narrow to allow of the bull following them.

The *tableros*, or barriers, are pierced with four doors ; the
principal communicates with the *toril*, and through this the bull
darts into the arena. One door is used for admitting the *picadores* on their horses, another door for the *matadores*, and the
fourth door, with a pair of wide gates, is used for the team of six
richly caparisoned mules that is driven in to drag out the bodies
of bulls and horses that have been killed. All round the arena,
outside the *valla*, or boarding, runs a passage called the *callejon*,
so that if a bull jumps the *valla*, which he occasionally does, he
does not hurt but only alarms the spectators, who are ranged in
tiers outside it.

The *gradas* are the seats next to the *callejon ;* higher up are the *tentidos ;* higher still the *tablincelos ;* then come the *palcos* or covered boxes.

The scene as you enter is very animated ; people are in holiday attire, and a brisk use of fans by the ladies, the cries of the boys selling programmes, the shouts of the vendors of ices, *dulces* and *toros* toys, all tend to enliven the exhibition, while the gold and silver on the sombréros and jackets flash in the brilliant sunlight.

The corrida commences with a procession of the bull-fighters ; the *espadas* come first, leading in miserable horses, only fit for the knacker's yard ; the poor beasts are bandaged over the left eye to prevent their seeing the bull too readily ; after the *espadas* come the *banderilleros,* then the *chulos* or *capeadores,* followed by the *picadores* on horseback. The fools and jesters at the side of the procession dance and cut capers.

The dress worn by the bull-fighters is a tight-fitting one, of gay-coloured satin or velvet, and covered with silver buttons.

The *muchachos* are smart, active men attached to the stables, who run in and assist the prostrate *picadore* to rise and to remove the saddles and trappings from such horses as may be slain.

The procession marches round the arena, the band plays, the *aguacil* asks the *juez* or judge, who occupies a special box, for the key of the *toril ;* this is flung to him, ornamented with a great knot of ribbons, and he gallops off. The instant he disappears the *mozos* open wide the doors of the *toril,* and out the bull darts into the arena, the *divisa,* or his stable colours, consisting of a rosette of the known colour of his trainer stuck in his shoulder ; all round are grouped the fighters. The *capeadores* are ready with their loose scarlet cloaks, on the alert to be the first to attract the bull's attention ; the *picadores* are moving round the ring on their horses, keeping a watchful eye on the bull. A silence, such as we experience for one brief instant after the cry "They are off!" at the Derby, falls on the spectators, and every one is in the highest state of tension.

Reader, have I wearied you? You must witness the remainder of the fight to be able to enter into the spirit of it, or to express your disgust, according to your mood. By all means go to see one bull-fight, if you have a chance; you can please yourself whether you go to a second. I saw five good bulls killed after they had shown tremendous pluck and rage; I saw as many or more horses killed.

Perhaps the only interesting feature of the performance was the manner in which, when the bulls were nearly exhausted, the *matador* stepped into the arena and gave his *coup de grâce*, by placing his sword in such a position that when the bull made his final, but weak charge, the point of the sword entered near the shoulder, and went straight to the heart, and the brave baited beast rolled over on the sand.

Another amusement in which the Mexican frequently indulges is cock-fighting. I never saw it within the city boundary, but whenever there was a *fiesta* in any of the neighbouring towns or villages, the cock-pit was the principal attraction. It is one means of pampering the gambling proclivities for which Mexicans are so noted. Public gambling and gambling-tables are not allowed in the city—at least I never saw nor heard of them; but at certain *fiestas* in the neighbouring villages, gambling-tables, at which *rouge et noir, monté*, and *keno* are played, are set out, and these games are indulged in in the most public manner. Piles of silver dollars, heaped upon the tables, indicated the extent of the play; the whole scene reminded me of Monte Carlo, for here also were seated round the tables, for the two days of the *fiesta*, eager ladies, as well as anxious men.

This national vice pervades all classes, from the gentle dame, who has her lottery-ticket placed every morning upon her breakfast table, to the poor peon, who risks his last *medio* on the turn of a card at *monté;* and the children get their *dulces* at a common wheel of fortune at the corner of a by-street.

Milder and less harmful amusement is to be obtained at shooting galleries, where pistol practice is preferred to rifle practice, and the smashing of eggs at ten to twenty yards' distance is considered a necessary accomplishment for a gentleman; nor is this very difficult, as I soon got into the knack of it.

The theatres are not so numerous as might be expected. I heard some operas fairly well performed, but the ordinary play was to my fancy utterly ruined by the loudness of the prompter's voice, every sentence being distinctly audible before the actor delivered it. The excuse made to me for such an objectionable feature in the play was that a Mexican audience required so rapid a succession of new pieces that the actors had no time to learn their parts by heart; two new pieces per week were often demanded. The ticket-office in a Mexican theatre is admirably managed; the whole side of the wall is guarded by iron bars, with half-a-dozen officials behind them, and thus a rush of business can be met at once without any crowding or hustling. A plan of the house is exhibited to you, on which little pegs mark the places; if you engage a seat, the peg is withdrawn, and handed to you as a voucher, which you in turn are to deliver to a stall-keeper. You can purchase a ticket for one act, or for two or three acts, as it pleases you, and you come out between the acts for the cigarette and the *Cognac con seltzer*, while the ladies munch *dulces.*

The mildest form of amusement was an *al fresco* breakfast, or an evening entertainment at one of the numerous and delightful "*Tivolis*" in the suburbs. The grand *Tivoli*, the *Eliseo*, the *Ferro-Carrill* and the *Petit Versailles*, were those to which friends occasionally invited me. These gardens are some of them extensive, and well planted with shady trees; and as for flowers, they appear in masses of most vivid colours. Miniature lakes, rivers, and rustic bridges are crowded into a small space. There are grottos and kiosks in which meals and refreshments are served, and in case of damp weather there are large and small rooms in a substantial building. The *menu* is very extensive, and particularly French. The *Tivoli Eliseo* is situated on the spot where Don Pedro del Alvarado made his desperate and celebrated leap on the " *noche triste*." All the gardens or *Tivolis* are reached by tramcars; and a meal in a summer-house in the delightful climate of Mexico is a pleasant change from the soup-reeking *comedor* of the hotel proper.

The circus, such as we know it in England, I found in every part of the world I visited, nor do I see why the arena of a *Corrida de toros* should not be utilised for the purpose of circus exhibitions. There was a first-rate circus in the square of the Sagrario, just under the cathedral walls, during the whole of Lent. It was held in a large tent, and was crammed full every night by every class of society. Most of the performers were English, and had well-known English circus names. Never was a better clown than Mr. Henry Cook, and his effort in making a comic speech in Spanish every evening was received with deafening applause.

In a building near the cathedral there was an entertainment which drew together several hundred people of the lower class every evening. During Lent the exhibition was announced as *Los Procesiones;* a long procession of ecclesiastical devices, represented by small figures two to three inches in height, passed at a slow rate along a narrow stage arranged lengthwise in the room. At other seasons of the year it was a regular marionette theatre with a stage at the end of the room; one of the representations being that of a bull-fight, and so inimitably carried out in all its detail, and withal so comical, as to be much better worth seeing than the reality.

I did not omit visiting some of the minor theatres and

singing places, and found them to be what they are in other large cities.

In the variety shows, the native dances proved a source of considerable attraction; the *fandango* is nearly as amusing as the old can-can dances used to be at the students' ball in the *Quartier Latin*, or the now happily defunct *Mabille*.

CHAPTER XXIV.

COURTS OF JUSTICE.

The Belem and other Jails.

NOTHING has afforded me more interest or amusement in every country I have visited than the procedure in the petty criminal courts, where the magistrates deal with the ordinary street cases of disturbance amongst the lower classes.

In such a court you obtain an insight into the mode of life, the misery, the immorality, the troubles of a class of whom the traveller would otherwise know nothing, save what he sees of it in the streets or reads of it in the daily press. It is ever a matter of difficulty to find these courts; few of the people whom you meet in society can give you any information about them. They sometimes say: " Ah, Mr. So-and-so is a magistrate, but I have no idea where he sits, or where any of the courts are, as I have never been to one." You have need of endless inquiries, and some difficulty in making people understand what it is that you really want to see, before you can get any information; and even then the first effort generally results in your being taken or sent to the higher courts, where long-winded cases are being heard, of no interest to a stranger.

In Mexico the administration of justice appears to be carried on in so different a manner from what an Englishman is accustomed to, that I, for one, could not quite comprehend the proceedings. I cannot, therefore, give a very trustworthy account of them, but only report what I actually saw.

There is a large and handsome building over the colonnades, apparently of ancient date, in one corner of the Plaza Mayor; this is the municipal palace, and is called La Deputacion. At a large portal, opening to a handsome stone staircase, some dozen soldiers were always to be seen lounging about, one of them being occasionally in an attitude of mounting guard. At the top of the staircase is a fine long gallery, with old-fashioned wooden seats against the walls, and with five or six large windows giving upon the square. This is a waiting room for those who have any business in the criminal court. Passing through passages in the back, you see several smaller rooms, in some of which are two or three gentlemen seated at a table, and you are told that one is a magistrate, and the others are attorneys laying the pros and cons of a case before him for decision. No prisoner, no witness, no police are seen. You come out of the building, and turn down a narrow side street, in which a large open gateway admits a view into a yard, and you see soldiers, police, and rough-looking men, whose appearance indicates that they are the prisoners of whom you want to get a glimpse. Everybody is smoking, not a few are eating, and there is a general fraternisation all round.

As far as I could learn, the magistrates whom I had seen upstairs decided as to whether a case should be dismissed, a small fine imposed, or the delinquent sent to the large prison at Belem, on the outskirts of the city. In order to follow up my investigation, I pressed into the service Señor Cesar Diaz, who kindly took me to Belem.

The large gateway was so crowded with rough people (the prisoners' friends who came to see them, or bring them food), that the police had difficulty in passing us through them to the inner door a formidable barrier with grated openings. We were admitted into a room where some judges or officials were seated at tables, investigating and deciding cases reported to them in the same way as had been done at the municipal

court in the Plaza. In this room there happened to be one of
the officials of the Central Railway whom I knew. He said he
had come down on account of one of their engine-drivers, who
had been thrown into prison for running over a man, and he was
anxiously waiting for his case to be brought on, or the man
liberated, as the company stood greatly in need of his services.
While we were waiting, he was informed that the engineer's case
was immediately coming before a magistrate in another chamber,
and if he wished to be present he must go thither at once. He
asked us to accompany him, and we gladly complied. A railing
divided a very small room; on the inner sides of the railing sat
the magistrate, a very nice-looking, intelligent man, and near
him was seated his "escribano," or clerk. For ten minutes or
more these worthies carried on a conversation in a whisper, or
conversed in too low a tone for us to hear, the result being that
the railway official was told the case would be decided as soon as
possible, and so we left the room.

We were afterwards shown over the prison; and this was a
sight that recalled the description given by Mr. Gladstone thirty
years ago of the prisons in Italy. After passing through several
iron-gated corridors, we saw some cells, very lofty, with a
glimmer of light from somewhere near the roof; better-class
prisoners were lying about in these cells, and a barber was exercising his art on the smooth chin of a smart-looking young man.
We afterwards went through several corridors in which the
doors of the cells were closed; thence into another corridor,
where the prisoners had fairly comfortable rooms, for which they
paid handsomely, their friends being allowed to visit them.

Then we went into a gallery surrounding an open court,
where a sight of rather a startling character presented itself.
There were 1200 prisoners in view. The yard was crowded.
The first corridor and all the rooms opening upon it were
thronged, and the upper corridor was equally full of human
life.

I learned that the prison dietary was as follows: twelve ounces of bread per diem, corned meat at *almuerzo* or mid-day meal, half a pound of meat at supper, and a bowl of rice or broth. Three times a week at the evening meal the prisoners get *frijóles* or beans. Those prisoners that work for the prison are allowed double rations, or a better quality of food. I saw that the bread and meat for the prisoners' dinner was carried in bags made of the fibre of the maguey plant, and the prisoners in the yard appeared to help themselves.

In another part of the prison we saw other prisoners muster for dinner in a large room, and pass out through a narrow doorway, each carrying a pannikin, which he extended as he passed the spot where two superintendents ladled soup, while two others stood at the doorway, and popped a roll of bread into the hand of the passing prisoners. Prisoners sentenced for from one to eleven months are compelled to work. The government pays 3 reals per day for skilled labour, the least pay being $1\frac{1}{2}$ reals, or ninepence. Some skilled prisoners can earn \$3 per day; one half of the savings goes to the prisoner's family, the other half being kept by the prison authorities until the term is expired, when the sum is handed over to the departing prisoner.

When a prisoner is wanted to appear before the magistrate, or for any other purpose, a warder keeps howling out the name at the top of his voice, and others take up the cry. These howls are perpetually resounding through the prison, which is a very Babel. The main dormitories are about fifty-five yards long; three hundred prisoners sleep in each, on mats arranged in three rows of one hundred each. There is nothing in the room but the mats. At six in the evening roll is called, and the prison is surrounded by extra guards, especially on the roof. At nine o'clock the watchman's bell is rung; from that hour the bell is rung every five minutes during the night; there are three bells, each being in a different section of the prison.

The prison opens at 6 A.M., when work commences. The

prisoners who do not work are compelled to go to school. The school hours are from 7 to 12, and from 1 to 3.30 o'clock. I saw about 200 in the school, and was told that this was about the average attendance. There is no library, but books, papers, and pamphlets of any description are allowed to be sent in from outside, as also are clean clothes and other luxuries. There is a special department of the prison for police agents who have gone wrong.

I will take the statistics of one month, as an illustration of the commitals and crimes at Belem Prison. In the month previous to my visit there were 1278 male prisoners; these were classified thus: thefts, 198; fighting, 109; stabbing (serious), 518; stabbing (slight), 313; wounding with sticks, 140; total, 1278. Amongst this number were many who had been committed from the police-courts and were awaiting trial.

A prisoner is allowed to make a verbal declaration before the magistrate who finally disposes of his case.

There are six magistrates presiding over the city police-courts. They sit from 8 A.M. to 1 or 2 P.M. every day, and are paid each $3000 per year; one sits all night at the Deputacion. The superintendents of the Belem get $25 per month, and the turnkeys $15. There have been but three organised attempts to escape in ten years; twenty-two prisoners escaped in the first two attempts; the third attempt proved a failure. I was told that the hospital was pretty full of prisoners who had suffered from the *machete* or knife; about ninety per cent. of the prisoners are in jail for the too-free use of this handy weapon.

There was a buzz of conversation, mingled with various louder sounds. A few of the prisoners were employing themselves in cigarette-making, shoemaking, tailoring and mat-making; the rest moved restlessly about; they were not in any prison dress. There was a large stone tank down the centre of the yard in which men were bathing and drying themselves in the sun, or washing clothes, and no one took any notice of their perfect nudity.

Our conductor led us not only round the corridors, but through the crowded yard, and pointed out to us at least half-a-dozen men who were under sentence of death, and perfectly aware they might be sent for any morning to undergo the penalty of their crime. Upon being told this, I noticed they appeared as gay and reckless as any of their numerous companions. Round the parapet wall on the roof half-a-dozen soldiers were stationed with loaded rifles; they stood sentry over the prisoners below, and would no doubt have fired upon the inmates in case of an *émeute.*

This motley crowd was composed of prisoners waiting their trial, as well as those undergoing their sentences. Men who had only committed slight offences were thrown into company with men who had committed many murders. A not bad-looking young fellow was pointed out as having at different times killed seven men in cold blood. He was one of those under sentence of death. Some of the male prisoners were very elegantly attired and gentlemanlike-looking men. Cards seemed to be very much in vogue, and the players were so deeply absorbed in their game that they never looked up or took so much as a glance at us; all the prisoners having anything to sell of their own manufacture importuned us to buy, offering their wares at very high prices. Dogs, cocks, hens, and turkeys are allowed in the prison, and roam about at will in search of the offal food which lies about everywhere. From the male wards we were taken over the roof into the quadrangle in which the women were incarcerated. On the occasion of my visit there were reported to be ninety women within the walls, classified thus : Sentenced to work, 10 ; in kitchen and laundry, 16 (7 of these were paid); tortilla makers, 19 (13 of these were paid); better class, 7 ; in hospital, 6 ; miscellaneous, 39 ; total, 90.

Women are allowed to keep with them their children up to

three years of age, provided that they have no home and no one
to protect them.　Solitary confinement is the heaviest punishment for women.　When a prisoner commits an offence in prison
she is locked up in the solitary cell, and remains there until the
board of superintendents meets and decides the punishment.
Little altars are to be seen everywhere in the women's quarters,
some of them with lights burning on them.　There appeared to
be about thirty women in the open court, some with babies
lying about on mats on the floor of the yard, some were engaged
in washing, others in cooking.　They were very quiet, and really
cleaner and more comfortable than many I have seen in the dirty
huts on the roadside.　The guide said stabbing was their principal crime.　One woman, who had been committed for murder,
had managed to bring a knife into the prison, with which she
stabbed one of her wretched companions in misfortune, thus
committing a second murder.　No woman is executed in Mexico.
The men who are sentenced to death are led out into a grim dank
yard, overgrown with grass, and then placed kneeling with their
backs to a wall, blindfolded, and shot.

I passed along a gloomy passage which leads to this field of
blood through a great rusty iron door, that grated harshly on
its hinges, and is seldom open save to permit a murderer to pass
through to his doom.　We descended some broken stone steps,
covered with a green slimy plant, passed through another iron
door, and stood in the place of execution.　It was a square yard
open to the sky, surrounded by walls thirty feet high ; the wall
against which the malefactors are placed is riddled with bullets,
some of them still sticking in the mortar.

A Mexican prison is a very hopeless sort of place ; you might
write on its portals the celebrated "Leave ye all hope behind who
enter here."　A prisoner who has committed a grave offence
never knows, nor can his friends discover, at what date he may
be led before the tribunal of justice.　He knows that, when he
enters he may languish for weeks, months, years ; hence his

apathy, or rather cheerfulness, for apathy yields to the latter feeling when the prisoner gets accustomed to his surroundings. Indeed the whole scene was worthy of the best efforts of a modern Hogarth. The prison diet, as I have mentioned, is ample, but the prisoners rely upon their friends outside for dainties. At noon, the hour of *almuerzo*, a train of women may be seen standing in line, each with at least one dish containing some toothsome morsel for the hapless relation or friend within the grated windows.

At Puebla I tried to get into the magistrates' court, but without success. However, at Cholula (a small town six miles distant from Puebla), while walking round the square, I passed an open portal which gave evident signs of being the entrance to the court-house and prison of the district. Mr. Bishop, my companion on the occasion, assisted me, through the medium of the politest Spanish phrases he could muster, to an introduction to the magistrate, who happened to be sitting in open court; and this functionary very graciously gave us permission to visit the prison situated at the rear of the building.

Passing through a double series of iron-barred gates, we entered a courtyard some twenty-five feet square, in which were fifteen prisoners employed in making mats, and weaving bright scarlet-coloured cotton sashes. In a vaulted room opening from this yard were a dozen more convicts busily engaged in the same work. The majority of these, we were informed, were terrible fellows, incarcerated for twenty years or for life, for robbery with violence. The prison was perfectly clean; some fig-trees and pretty bushes were growing in the yard, and the prisoners looked healthy and well fed. Our visit must have been a red-letter day to them, for both Bishop and myself at once sat down and sketched them at our ease. We were not allowed to speak to them, and they had to maintain strict silence. A portion of the produce of their labour was given to them for the purchase of luxuries to add to their ordinary prison fare. With the pretty trees in the court, and the bright, hot sun shining down upon them, their lot in life was preferable to that of an English convict under the same sentence.

The only other occasion upon which I saw Mexican prisoners was when they were working in gangs on the public roads. Their legs were chained together in such a way as not to impede them in their work, but close enough to prevent their escaping from the guards who had charge of them, and who, no doubt, had orders to shoot them down at the first sign of outbreak or attempted flight. The prison vans conveying prisoners from the municipal offices already described to the prison at Belem were closed, and in all respects such as are used in England. Why are they known as Black Marias? Several armed men rode both in front and in rear of these conveyances. It is a curious fact that surrounding circumstances produce distinct crimes, which are peculiar to certain communities and countries. In Mexico City theft is such an ordinary matter that it is jocularly said, "If you drop a coin it is caught before it reaches the ground"; whereas in Yucatan, one of the Mexican states, people are so honest that Consul-General Aymé told me if you accidentally dropped a coin on the floor the housemaid would leave dust around it rather than disturb it, and theft of any kind was a thing unknown.

There was a good tale told in society during my stay against the senior magistrate in the City of Mexico. It happened that a friend accosted him in the *portales*, and in the course of conversation asked him what o'clock it was, when he replied, "*Dios mio!* I have left my watch in my watch-pocket over my bed at home." A thief having overheard this remark, bought a turkey and took it to the house of the magistrate, sending in word to madame that master had sent a turkey, and requested that she would send him his watch which he had left in his bedroom; this, in her simplicity, she did. On the magistrate's return in the evening his wife observed: "Thank you for the turkey, but I

PRISON AT CHOLULA.

[page 218.

have not ordered it to be cooked to-night, as another dinner was prepared." The explanation revealed the loss of the watch. But this was not all. On the following day an accomplice of the thief called at the house and said: " The magistrate has had his watch returned him, and he begs you to send him the turkey, that it may be offered in evidence against the prisoner." Of course, when the magistrate arrived at home in the evening he found that he was minus both watch and turkey; and, moreover, the tale got bruited about, and both he and his household lost the credit which should attach to one in his important position. As the Italians say, *se non è vero è ben trovato.* But I heard it from half-a-dozen persons, and have no doubt that it is substantially true. For my own part, I found the servants in my hotel, and the servants at the Concordia Restaurant, and at the Hotel Bazaar, where I occasionally dined, perfectly honest; everything that I left about in my rooms at the hotel was as safe as if in my own house, and my note-book, which I accidentally left both at the Concordia and at the Bazaar, was returned to me intact when on the following day I asked for it. I may also mention, to the credit of the country, that some loose coin I left in the pocket of a canvas coat sent to the wash was returned to me with the clean clothes, and folded up in paper upon the top of the basket, without a word being said. Such experiences are proof sufficient that there is really more honesty in the country than remarks commonly made by strangers would lead a traveller to expect. Possibly I was under a special providence, as a native servant in the employ of the Palmer-Sullivan Railway Company one day during my stay walked off with most of the clothes of some of the clerks whom I knew; but such things occur in the best-regulated communities.

CHAPTER XXV.

VISITS TO NEIGHBOURING CITIES AND OTHER PLACES.

Caves of Cacahuamilpa—Teocalles—Toluca—Tula—Puebla—The Cathedral and
Churches of Puebla, and those at Cholula.

In addition to visiting the villages near the City of Mexico, so
easily reached by tram-car, the traveller should not omit making
journeys to some of the large cities and other places of interest
on the plateau. At the time of my visit, Puebla, the second most
important city of the country, was accessible by rail; the other
places had to be reached either on horseback or by the uncomfortable and jolting diligence, the railways to them not being then
completed.

The caves of Cacahuamilpa, formed by two branches of the
river San Geronimio—two days' journey from Mexico City—are
probably the finest limestone formations of the sort in the world;
their stalagmites and stalactites assuming fantastic shapes of
every description. Many of the galleries and halls of these
caves have not yet been explored.

If the traveller likes to turn aside *en route* to them he will be
repaid by seeing several artificial mounds; and also the remains
of pyramids and teocalles, or Aztec temples; these are so often
referred to in these pages, that I give (Plate XXXIX., at end
of volume) a drawing of one that is still standing in a very
perfect condition. All the teocalles were of similar character,
viz., a solid building of pyramidal form, with a steep flight of
steps leading to the platform on the top; there was a small

[page 220.

ENTRANCE TO LIMESTONE CAVE AT CACAHUAMILPA.

dark temple on this, in which was a figure of a deity, and in front of which stood an altar. The teocalles were of various heights and sizes, varying in proportions as do our own chapels and cathedrals. The great temple in the City of Mexico, on the site where the present cathedral stands, and which was only completed in 1486—about forty years previous to the coming of the Spaniards—was encompassed by a wall about eight feet high, ornamented on the outside by figures of serpents,* in *basso relievo*, and pierced on its four sides by gateways opening on the four principal streets. Over each gate was an arsenal; and barracks near the temple were garrisoned by 10,000 soldiers. The temple itself was a solid structure, the base was of adobe brick, coated externally with hewn stones. It was square, its sides facing the cardinal points, and was divided into five stories, each of which receded so as to be smaller than that below it. The ascent was by a flight of 114 steps on the outside, so contrived that to reach the top it was necessary to pass four times round the whole edifice; and the base of the temple is supposed to have been 300 feet square. The summit was a large area paved with broad flat stones. On it were two towers or sanctuaries, and before each was an altar on which a fire was kept continually burning. The top of this remarkable structure must have commanded a superb view of the city, lake, valley, and surrounding mountains.

The cities that I visited were more or less of Spanish character in their construction. Pachuca has been described in the chapter on silver mines. Toluca prides itself upon its Portales, a handsome corridor running round a large block of buildings in the centre of the city, and under the arcades of which are some very fair shops. I made the journey to Toluca with a party of gentlemen who were proceeding to some silver mines a farther day's journey to the north. My note of this

* Two of these stone serpents were found by workmen during the time of my visit, as described at page 60.

journey to Toluca may convey my rather unfavourable impressions of the place.

Note.—*Friday, Sept. 2nd*, 1881.—Returned from a three days' visit to Toluca. The journey by diligence is over so bad a road that no vehicle but a Spanish diligence drawn by some dozen or fourteen mules could accomplish it ; the road had been made worse than usual by the heavy carting upon it involved in bringing wood and material to the railway which was being constructed parallel to it.

People had praised Toluca to me rather too much. With the exception of a fine arcade running round a block of houses in the centre of the city there is nothing attractive. The three large churche's I visited were dirty and tawdry. I happened to be at the cathedral one day at noon ; the organ was out of repair, and a large musical box was rattling away the tunes from ' Madame Angot ; ' as the clock struck twelve, the church suddenly filled, some three hundred boys from a college and school hard by were marched to seats in the centre of the nave, and a short mid-day Mass was celebrated while a string band in a side gallery rendered the well-known airs of ' La Favorita.' My three companions devoted themselves entirely to the billiard-table ; I got, with much difficulty, a horse, a wretched animal, and rode up a neighbouring hill to get a general view of the locality, the principal feature of which is a very fine extinct volcanic mountain, about five miles from the city, and said to have a well-defined crater. I was told I should find the people very clean and interesting as compared to those of Mexico City, but it was not so. The hotel and the restaurant were noisy and bad. Several diligences left the hotel very early in the morning, the mules for them being brought from the stables and harnessed in the courtyard where the diligences stood all night. The row commenced about 4 A.M., after which time sleep was out of the question, as our bedrooms were on the corridor which overlooked the yard. Toluca

TOLTEC PALACE AT TULA.
(LATELY EXCAVATED BY MONS. CHARNAY.)

contains about 12,000 inhabitants, and is famous for its hams and sausages; a dirty river runs through the centre of the town at the bottom of a barranca or deep ravine, on the banks of which were innumerable pigs, thin, long-snouted, and almost wild; apparently living but poorly on what the stream afforded! They would require much better feeding before they could sustain the character of the place for its celebrated commodity. To say the broad well-paved side-paths on both sides of the streets were the best feature of the town is, perhaps, the highest compliment a casual visitor can pay its inhabitants.

The return journey by diligence to Mexico City was worse than the going out, and we had a heavy thunderstorm, on the highest part of the mountain-pass, which drenched us outside passengers to the skin, to say nothing of the terror we suffered from lightning.

Tula is a small town, having from 3000 to 4000 inhabitants; it boasts of a large market square, with a garden in the centre, and a very fine church, built of well-jointed and smooth blocks of white stone; whereas most of the country churches are built of rough stone and plastered over with cement. Tula, formerly known as Tolam, was the ancient capital of the Toltec nation about the seventh century, and had necessarily a palace for its king, and many temples. The palace stood on the top of a neighbouring hill, and its foundations and ruins have been lately excavated by Mons. Charnay; it appears to have consisted of a great number of small rooms, narrow passages, steps and little courts; in these latter there were, probably from the present aspect of the ground, tanks of water; the walls were thickly plastered and painted red; scrubby bushes and vegetation cover most of the buildings; near the foot of the hill are the remains of two temples, the walls of the one which I visited, still standing and forming three sides of a hexagon, are twenty-five feet high, and turreted; and there appears to have been a chamber or platform at about three-

fourths of the height, judging from a ledge and some rafter holes
in the masonry; there was a large amount of stone débris round
the base, through which trees had forced their way, and had
grown up so as almost to hide the temple. Our guide said the
other temple had still a perfect roof, and I made an effort to visit
it; but our horses got stuck in some swampy ground, and we
could not reach it. I therefore exchanged the archæological
amusement for an ornithological one, trying to shoot some
curious-looking large vultures (not zapilotes) which were wise
enough, however, to move continually out of range of my gun.
In the market-place of Tula are four colossal pieces (one prostrate) of ancient Toltec statuary; strange to say, the legs and
feet only are standing; their height is eight feet, and we were
told they were originally brought from the palace excavated by
Mons. Charnay. But what has become of the busts and heads of
these monsters I was unable to find out. I give a drawing of the
extant portions in Plate XLI.

Before visiting the minor towns of Toluca and Tula, the·
traveller will probably find his way to Puebla; should he
happen to be in the City of Mexico during Lent, or at the time
of any great Church festival, he will find the Plaza and
principal streets placarded with notices to the effect that excursion trains are running to that city, offering to convey people
at cheap rates to witness the Church processions and religious
ceremonies, which are carried out on a grander scale at Puebla
than elsewhere.

The journey takes from six to seven hours; you have
Popocatapetl and Ixtaccihuatl on your right all the way from
Mexico to Puebla; at Apizaco, which is a junction, refreshments
are served. An English engineer conducts the train, and from
him I learned that an engine-driver between Esperanza and
Vera Cruz (170 miles) is paid $125, or £25, a month, and the
fireman $60, or £12.

He also told me that from Esperanza to Mexico (eighty

miles on the level) the driver has £18 a month and the fireman £12.

Puebla strikes you from a distance as all domes and steeples, surrounded by a vast plain of wheat on a dead level, nothing breaking the monotony but the clouds of dust raised by trains of donkeys on the roads. Go to the Hotel de Diligencias; it is better than anything I have found anywhere in Mexico; the meals are served at little tables in a large open upstairs corridor which runs round the court of the hotel; this corridor is ornamented with shrubs and flowers and cages of singing birds; the landlord, Mons. Canni, besides being young and handsome and having a very pretty wife, was exceedingly attentive and polite; the charges were two dollars a day for bed and board—just half of what I had to pay in Mexico for much worse accommodation and fare.

The city contains 84,000 inhabitants. It slopes to a stream that runs through its centre, the drainage is good, and the streets are wide and beautifully clean. The Plaza round the cathedral is well planted on one side with fine trees; the shops under the colonnades are lively and full of quaint articles of merchandise; one side, the north, is exclusively devoted to the sale of tiny little figures in wax, representing the national customs and costumes of the country; bull-fights are to be had for any price, from a peso upwards, and the modelling of the animals is simply perfect. Here I found a novel mode of caricaturing the prominent men, in the shape of scarf-pins, the head of the individual being grotesque and the likeness always admirable. I understood these grotesque pins were worn by people of the opposite party; the Gladstone and Forster pins, if the plan were adopted in England, would be seen in the scarves of the members of the Carlton, while those of Lord Salisbury and Sir Stafford Northcote might adorn the manly breasts of the members of the Reform.

The cathedral is a most imposing pile, and dates from

Q

1665; a statue of Pio IX. stands in front. The towers still bear marks of balls fired during the siege from the French guns, in May, 1862. The Episcopal Palace on the right is an intensely interesting building; its roof-tiles are blood-red, faced with white. The stone of which the cathedral is built is a dark grey, inferior in effect to the white stone of the cathedral of the City of Mexico; but the interior is singularly handsome, the side chapels being gaudily gilded and the altar a blaze of gold. The onyx pulpit is a very marvel. The crypt, where the Archbishops of Puebla lie urned, is built of onyx, and the cicerone makes you stand outside while he enters with a lighted candle, that you may see how transparent the onyx or Mexican marble is. This marble is obtained from quarries in the neighbourhood, and is worked up into table-tops and ornaments of every description—brittleness is its only fault; the cicerone's light can be distinctly traced through the thickness of the wall, which is six feet. There is one objectionable feature in the cathedral. Under all the altars in the side chapels are glass cases containing life-size effigies of martyrs in wax, scantily clothed in bright-coloured silks and satins; a bone of the martyr, from whatever part of the body it may have been taken, is exposed by not having any wax over it; a knuckle, knee-joint, or cheek-bone so exposed being painfully hideous to any one unaccustomed to such sights. These relics are chiefly those of Roman martyrs, and were sent as presents from the Eternal City; the figures are much jewelled and overdressed—a Roman centurion, for instance, being draped in a pink satin tunic, embroidered with pearls, and having sandals and armlets to match.

We ascended one of the towers, first of all arranging with the custodian not to jingle the bells while we were near the belfry; the view repays the climb. The city presents no outskirts, the streets ending abruptly on cornfields or broken ground. Near the railway station were two large cathedral-like churches, partly in ruins; one had been utilised as an iron-foundry, and the other

as a cotton-weaving and cotton-printing establishment. It was
an unusual sight to look upon tall red-brick factory chimneys,
puffs of steam from the ends of tall iron pipes, and long lines of
freshly-printed pieces of calico hanging up to dry, all intermingled with domes and towers and vaulted church roofs.

There are many other churches in Puebla worth visiting. In
the Church of Concordia the altar railing is of glass, and was the
first glass manufactured in Puebla—in 1818. There is a 'Calvary'
in this church, the figures being all life size and very painful to
gaze upon. In the Church of San Francisco the frescoes are
particularly fine; the side chapels are devoted to scenes from the
life of the saint; over the high altar a 'Christ with the Virgin in
clouds' is a remarkable picture.

One afternoon, in the course of a ramble in search of an
encaustic-tile manufactory, one of ten in Puebla, we came upon a
rather nice-looking new church, called El Corazon de Jésus, to
which was attached a large Capella Maria; the walls of this
chapel were panelled with paintings of the Virgin, kit-cat size,
representing her in more than four hundred different characters
as mediator or reliever in cases of so many sicknesses or distresses.
Inscriptions are written under each picture, referring to a complaint or trouble; as, good for sore eyes, good for a bad wound,
good for the loss of a valuable article, preservation against
robbery, preservation against ringworm, and four hundred such
evils.

In 1869 the city contained sixty churches, thirteen nunneries,
nine monastries, twenty-one collegiate houses; to-day there are
twenty churches, no nunneries, and but two monasteries, which are
more probably hospitals or almshouses for infirm priests. Some
of these confiscated ecclesiastical buildings have been utilised and
adapted to secular purposes, such as hospitals, schools, libraries,
etc.; several of these I visited. The nunnery of Santa Rosa is
now used as the Hospital de Dementes, or as an asylum for the
insane. I was conducted by the doctor over this building, which

is decidedly the most beautiful of the kind I have ever seen ; the exterior walls of the courts are covered with scarlet-coloured tiles, generally diamond-shaped, with pretty patterns upon them in blue and white tiles ; the courts, fountains, corridors, were all ornamented with tiles ; the bath-rooms of the nuns and some of the principal apartments formerly used by them, and even their kitchens and cooking-stoves, were as beautiful as coloured tiles could make them ; where the walls were plastered, they were decorated with birds and flowers painted by the hands of the nuns in most brilliant colours; surely no other madmen in the world live in so beautiful a place, and it is much to be regretted that the monastery has not been adapted to some educational purpose, so that the public could be admitted to it.　There were forty-two male patients in the hospital, and some females whom we did not see; all the men were harmless and middle-aged. Debauchery and drinking adulterated spirits were given as the chief causes of disease ; the doctors have lately reported to the government that the latter cause is increasing the number of patients, and the legislature have just passed a law instituting analytical investigations and severe penalties for the sale of adulterated drinks.　There were also some private patients.　I gathered that about 1 per cent. of a population of 300,000 in the district were occasional or permanent inmates of this establishment.　The general hospital, another institution in a fine range of old ecclesiastical buildings, over which I was shown by Dr. Dias, was interesting from the fact that one half of the hospital was devoted to allopathic treatment and the other half to homœopathic.　I tried to get a report of the result of the two systems, but without success, and I was obliged to content myself with noticing that the rooms in which the homœopathic patients were established were cleaner and sweeter than those of the opposition.

I had a letter of introduction to a Mr. Dias, an uncle, I think, of the doctor, requesting permission for me to see his picture-gallery. One afternoon Mr. Bishop and I went in search of the house; after some trouble, we found it. It often happens in Mexican cities that the entrance to a palace is through a hovel; such was the case in the present instance; we passed the door several times before we ventured to inquire if the dirty little corn-chandler's shop was the object of our search; finding this to be really the case, we presented our letter, and were most politely welcomed by one of the shopmen, and immediately conducted through a door at the back of the shop into a beautiful court filled with flowers, and thence up an outside staircase leading to a corridor and a suite of elegant rooms. These were filled with first-class pictures by old masters, principally of the Italian schools. There were four pictures in the collection by Rubens, or, I should rather say, three, the fourth (to make up the set) having been painted by an inferior hand. Many pictures by Rubens seem to have found their way to Mexico, most private galleries containing one or two examples. The view from the windows was perhaps prettier than any of the pictures; a church and some ecclesiastical buildings embowered in trees formed a foreground to an open view of the hill and fortresses of Guadalupe, from which the Mexicans expelled the French in an unexpected manner on the 5th of May, 1862, a victory they always commemorate on its anniversary by a national holiday celebrated with great parade. Puebla is a beautiful and interesting city. It is the capital of the state of that name, and its full title is "La Puebla de los Angeles." It is seventy-six miles from the capital, and no visitor to the country should omit visiting it, and running out by the tram-car to Cholula, the site of one of the chief cities of the Aztecs at the time of Cortes' invasion. It was here that he was obliged to perpetrate one of his most terrible massacres of Cholulan nobles, as described in the seventh chapter of Prescott's 'Conquest.' At present all that remains of this once most sacred city is the pyramid on which the temple stood, and several other large mounds, built of adobé or sun-dried bricks, which I have described in the chapter on ruined Aztec cities. To those who are not interested in Aztec antiquities the churches in the village may be more or less an attraction; the journey by tram-car is under an hour, and the car starts for the return journey sufficiently late in the afternoon to have allowed the visitor time enough to inspect all the places of interest. There are three large churches near the great square in the village, more or less in ruins, though used for occasional services. In one of them was a large coarsely painted fresco on the wall representing a martyrdom of priests in Japan; also a large fresco, quite newly painted, representing the Calvinists mutilating Catholic priests in Holland, a most terrible picture of tortures, under which was written in large Spanish characters :

" St. Nicholas and his eighteen companions, martyred by the Protestant Calvinists on the 9th of July, 1576, in Holland, for defending the Real Presence of Our Lord in the Holy Sacrament, and the supreme authority of the Roman Pope. (Canonised by Pio Nono, on the 29th of July, 1867.) "

We met a very pleasant padre at luncheon at the Fonda in the Square. Seeing my collection of obsidian arrow-heads, etc., he quaintly asked if I were in search of Montezuma's treasures, shook his head, and said I should have to search a long time; it is a common belief in Mexico that at the time of Cortes' invasion Montezuma ordered all his treasures to be hidden, and afterwards put to death all that assisted in the work of hiding, leaving himself and his high priest the only two persons cognizant of the hiding-place. The padre also told us that some fifty years ago a Catholic priest, receiving valuable contributions to his church from the poorest of his congregation, obtained information through the confessional to the effect that the valuables were procured from a cave, and were supposed to be part of Montezuma's treasures; the priest prevailed upon a man to lead him to the cave, but it was required that he should be blind-folded; the clever priest took several rosaries with him, and

contrived to drop the beads one by one on the road ; after seeing
the treasures in the cave and returning home blindfolded, his
conductor said : "I have kept faith with your reverence, but you
had the misfortune to break your rosary, and drop the beads on
the way.   I have, however, picked them all up, and now return
them to you ; you will not find any missing."

Of the town of Ameca-ameca with its Sacra Monte and magic
grotto I have spoken elsewhere.   Orizaba has been alluded to in
the second chapter, as passed on the railway route between
the capital and Vera Cruz. This latter city is so entirely
different from all the others in this part of the country, that the
visitor should not miss the opportunity, if it presents itself, of
visiting the place.   I was not able to stop long enough to have
more than a glimpse of it, and I was more than disappointed that
my time did not permit of my visiting the coffee plantations and
tobacco fields by which it is surrounded.

By the time these lines get into print, railways will undoubtedly have brought other cities and places within easy
distance of the capital, and thus have added to the resources
available for the traveller's amusement.

CHAPTER XXVI.

General Grant—List of Railways in Mexico—Cost per Mile—Navvies—
Small Pox—Sea Routes.

I TRUST that my general remarks about Mexico will lead the
reader to believe that at the present time the country is passing
with rapid strides from a state of anarchy and confusion to a
condition of devolopment and improvement.   My observations
have led me to a firm conviction that such is the case.   Happily
for tho future prosperity of Mexico, the aspirations of the government and of the people towards so desirable a result are being
furthered and assisted by their neighbours in the United States.

The American raid upon Mexico in 1847 originated in the
desire of Texas and California to separate themselves from
Mexico and join the United States; the result of the war and
the taking of so large a slice of Mexico by Brother Jonathan has
been to render the people of the latter nation a little nervous as
to the Americans exhibiting so serious an interest in them at the
present time.

During my stay, however, General Grant, and several other
leading Americans who were in the city, made notable speeches
on public occasions, dwelling upon the friendly relations existing
between the two republics; and their addresses tended in a very
great degree to allay the fears and misgiving of the Mexicans.
But foreign capital pouring into the country may well make the
the Mexicans exclaim, " *Timeo Danaos et dona ferentes.*"

In order to afford my readers an idea of how Uncle Sam is about to assist in developing Mexico through the medium of railways, I shall mention in brief the various iron roads for which charters have already been granted by the Mexican Government. Many of the roads are approaching completion, while others are in an advanced stage of progress.

The first thing to develop and open up a country in these days is good railway communication. The very nature of the country has hitherto rendered the rivers unnavigable, and canals an impossibility, while until lately the only railway in the country was that which runs from Vera Cruz to the capital. Ex-President Diaz, President Gonzales, and all the enlightened public men of Mexico, agreed that to further the construction of railways to the utmost limit of their power was the very best policy, since wherever they could be constructed the value of all the neighbouring property would be quadrupled; silver mines would be worked with double activity, and an outlet would be afforded to the products of the labour of the agricultural community.

It is a geological fact that silver ore is found only in very rough, rugged, hilly districts, where the soil is sterile and unproductive. The railways that would transport silver from the mines to the capital could carry back provisions of all sorts from the rich valley of the City of Mexico to the mining districts.

The thousands of muleteers on all the high roads, whose labour must be considered unproductive, could turn to employment that would yield its quantum to the general wealth of the nation. It is not unlikely that the signs of a lively feeling shown by all civilised communities as to the necessity of a ship canal or a ship railway across the Isthmus of Panama may have an influence with the Mexican Government in stimulating a wish on their part to develop the resources of the country by the time when these great highways shall have been completed between the eastern and western hemispheres.

I was present at the state opening of the sessions on the

1st of April, 1881, and heard President Gonzales read his message to the House. It was chiefly composed of flattering allusions to the national prosperity, the blessings of peace, and the extension of railways.

The map placed opposite gives a general idea of the lines surveyed, in progress and completed.

The Americans, in their go-ahead impetuosity, propose not only to join Mexico to their system of railways, but also to carry two great trunk lines, one down the east and the other down the west coast of South America, even to Patagonia, and it is more than probable that some of the youngsters of the present generation may live to see this "big thing" in railways an accomplished fact.

For more easy reference I have numbered the lines on the map.

No. 1. Vera Cruz to Mexico, with branch from Apizaco to Puebla, Ferro Carril, Mexicana. English Company.

No. 2. "Mexican Central," from Paso del Norté to Mexico City, and across Mexico from Tampico to San Blas.

No. 3. "Mexican National," from the City of Mexico to Manzanillo, and from a point on this line at Acambaro to Laredo on the Rio Grande. Narrow gauge.

No. 4. "Sonora" Railway, ending at Guaymas, on the Gulf of California.

No. 5. "The Topolobampo," Pacific branch of the "Great Southern Pacific," from the Rio Grande at Eagle Pass to Mazatlan on the Pacific.

No. 6. "Oriental" (Jay Gould's), from Laredo to the City of Mexico, passing the hot country, *viâ* Pachuca.

No. 7. "Mexican Southern" (Grant's Road).

No. 8. "Morelos" Road (Mexican), on which there was a terrible disaster during my visit.

No. 9. "Tehuantepec." Mr. Eades' proposed ship railway.

Many small branch roads radiate from all these trunk lines.

Agnana

In order to encourage the construction of railways, not only does the government readily grant concessions, and admit into the country all railway stock and plant free of duty, but it grants out of the public treasury subsidies varying from $7000 to $9000 per kilometre (1093 yards, or a little more than half a mile) of road when completed and accepted as in working order by a Government Inspector.   In mentioning the word kilometre it may be as well to state that President Juarez adopted the French metric and decimal system, in order to put an end to the confusion arising from the use of innumerable European and native measurements which prevailed.

Some of the railways are broad gauge, four feet eight and a-half inches, others are narrow gauge, three feet.   The tramways in and around the cities are of both gauges, the carriages being so constructed that the mules can be detached, and the carriages transferred to the railway lines without the passengers being subjected to the inconvenience of changing their seats.   The average cost per mile, for a broad gauge, is estimated at about $30,000, and for narrow gauge $20,000 ; the latter gauge is preferred in a mountainous district.   All the carriages and rolling-stock on these railways are built in the United States on the American plan ; the carriages on the Vera Cruz line alone being built on the English plan.

I spent several of my Saturdays while in Mexico on the line of the Mexican National Railway (Palmer-Sullivan), to see the labourers at work on the line, and to watch the payment of the week's wages in the afternoon.

It was a very pleasant excursion, and I was indebted to Mr. Clinch, the head-cashier, for being included in the party ; no doubt he was glad to have companions, and he seldom had any difficulty in getting five or six gentleman to accompany him.   We assembled on horseback in the courtyard of the company's buildings at 5.30 o'clock in the morning, where we saw the loading of some ten mules with from $10,000 to $15,000, in silver and copper. Ten of the company's most trusted servants, mounted and armed to the teeth, took charge of these mules; and, as a further safeguard for so much money, a troop of the Rural Guard, under the command of an officer, further augmented the party. We also were armed. The route to St. Estevan and Rio Hondo was changed a little every Saturday, in order to throw any would-be robbers off the scent, and Mr. Clinch and the Railway officials who accompanied us exhibited signs of lively anxiety if any of the party lagged behind or straggled from the cavalcade.

After our arrival, at whatever place the wages had to be paid we had breakfast, and afterwards spent an hour or two in riding down the line where the works were in progress.

The tunnels and culverts being constructed under the road seemed perfectly inadequate to the task of carrying off any heavy fall of water, and that such falls occasionally occurred there was ample evidence in the deep watercourses on the neighbouring hillsides. The accident on the Morelos Railway was entirely owing to a heavy flood having washed away a bridge; and a similar accident may any day be expected on the Palmer-Sullivan Road unless the water-culverts are enlarged.

In the afternoon it was a work of four to five hours to pay the wages of the navvies, who came up in gangs under charge of their gangsmen, and passed under an open window, through which each man's money was slid down a groove into his hat, which he held out to catch it.

The general demeanour of the men, their smiling faces (the Mexican seldom smiles or laughs, and has a melancholy expression), their patience, jokes, and good humour while waiting for their turns, were indications of their happiness at receiving such high wages. They are paid five cents per hour, and double for extra work, or if working in wet places or during the night. No doubt railway labour is more continuous and harder work than they are generally accustomed to, but they come from homes situated at great distances, some even twenty miles, to obtain it.

Their general occupation is irregular farm labour, and the burning and carrying of charcoal into the towns and villages. It was amusing to hear residents in Mexico complain bitterly that the prices of wood, charcoal, poultry, eggs and other things had been raised, and that these commodities had become more scarce since the railways had commenced to monopolise so much labour. There were some 30,000 or 40,000 men reported working on the various lines, led by some 600 American and English engineers and "bosses."

Usually for most of the afternoon I watched the men receive their money; it was a capital opportunity for studying the physiognomy of, perhaps, the lowest class of native; they had broad, flat, heavy Mongolian faces, bright eyes, and a forehead that receded from a little above the eye in such a way as to give the head a sugar-loaf appearance; their thick black hair was cut short, and usually grew down to an inch above the eye. Very few were marked with the small-pox; I counted several hundred, and in all that number only noted one in two hundred bearing any marks, and these but slight, of that terrible disease. The vaccination laws have been rigidly enforced by the government for the last twenty years. The ravages of this disease are described by Humboldt as appearing at very marked intervals in the country, and as fearfully fatal. It was unknown before the Conquest, but since 1520 it has returned every seventeen or eighteen years. In 1763, 1779, and 1797 it carried off thousands.

In 1779 nine thousand people in the City of Mexico alone are reported to have died of it. Inoculation was introduced in 1804 by Mr. Thomas Murphy, and vaccination by Don Antonio Valmes a few years later. Humboldt relates that vaccination was known in the Peruvian Andes before the eighteenth century, that those engaged in the milking of cows had often a sort of cutaneous eruption, which the Indians said came by the contact of certain tubercles sometimes found on the udder of cows, and that those who had this eruption never took the small-pox. These remarks on the disease are perhaps a little out of place in connection with a description of railways; but the subject is one of vital interest, in whatever country a traveller finds himself. By this short notice I have possibly saved the reader a special chapter on the question, as I made many notes in reference to it on several occasions.

Before concluding this account of railways, I must note that amongst the numerous Americans and Englishmen who crowded the hotels in Mexico, and who seemed all more or less engaged in railway matters, Mr. Eades and his proposition for the Ship Railway attracted the most public attention. There were pictures of his scheme in many of the shop windows, representing a great ship propelled up an incline by a couple of locomotives on either side. Taking into consideration the shortness of the distance from sea to sea, where it is proposed to construct the road, the vessels need never know that they have been out of the water till they get into it again. Nevertheless a ship canal would be a more practical work, and I would invest money in that rather than in a ship railway. I hope M. de Lesseps may add another laurel to his crown by having his scheme eventually adopted.

Personally I regret that the Americans have not undertaken this system of railway lines for joining Mexico to the United States some years earlier, that I might have been saved the disagreeable passage by sea. At present the only mode of getting to Vera Cruz is by the Alexandra steamers from the port of New York, or the Morgan Company's steamers from New Orleans.

The voyage from New York takes eleven days, the steamers calling at Havana, at Progresso, and at Campeachy, on the peninsula of Yucatan, as well as at Frontera, which is in the Mexican State of Tabasco; the passage costs $85, or £17. From

New Orleans to Vera Cruz, (the route I selected and have described) takes only four or five days, and costs $50 or £10.

Steamers also ply regularly from San Francisco and other places in California to Acapulco, calling at Mazatlan, Manzanillo, and other Mexican towns on the Pacific coast.

These sea routes will probably be little used, except for freight, when travellers can go to Mexico by rail. This feat will be capable of performance in less than two years hence, when people will board the train at New York and reach the halls of the Montezumas within five days.

CHAPTER XXVII.

COINAGE, INSURANCE AND OTHER MATTERS.

Different Mexican Moneys—Nickel Coin—Gold Coin—Banks—Utilisation of
Ecclesiastic Buildings—Advertisements—Insurance Companies.

TRAVELLERS coming to Mexico should be prepared to speak a few words of Spanish, or they will find a little difficulty at first in procuring food or lodging, or in asking any question in the streets. Ordinary cloth dress, exactly such as would be worn in England or America the greater portion of the year, is suitable for the City of Mexico. A light overcoat for evening wear is absolutely indispensable.

Mexican money should be obtained immediately on entering the country. Although the United States dollar was at seven per cent. premium at the time of my visit, I found neither the paper dollars nor silver coin of America would be taken at any of the shops or restaurants, and the street car conductors invariably refused American money.

The moneys in ordinary use are one, two, and five dollar notes issued by the Monte de Piedad, and by a private bank, the *Banque de Londres*. The metal coinage of the country is—

	s.	d.
Peso, silver, dollar, equal to	4	0
Toston, silver, half-dollar, equal to	2	0
Peseta, silver, quarter-dollar, equal to	1	0
Real, silver, 12½ cents, equal to	0	6
Medio, silver, 6¼ cents, equal to	0	3
Cuartilla, silver, 3⅛ cents, equal to	0	1½
Tlaco, copper (64 to the dollar, 8 to the real), equal to	0	0¾
Centavo, copper, 1 cent, equal to	0	0½

There are 8 reals to the dollar.

The medio, equal to 3*d.*, is the coin in most ordinary use. There was often a difficulty in procuring small coin, sometimes necessitating a visit to a restaurant or pulqueria before a purchase of some trifling article could be effected. Since writing these lines I saw in a Mexican paper, *Boletin del Ministerio de Fomento de la Republica Mexicana*, October 4th, 1882, the following paragraph :—

" NICKEL COIN.

" A portion of the machinery, including several presses, for the nickel mint which is to be established in this city has arrived from Vera Cruz. This machinery was all manufactured in England. The scarcity of small change is so great that the nickel coin will be very welcome."

The peso, or dollar, is very heavy and cumbersome to carry about in one's pocket when travelling; Mexicans generally carried the coins distributed in a belt which they wore round their waist; and the lower orders had a breast-pocket inside their shirts, in which they carried their small coin, carefully wrapped up in a handkerchief or in a canvas bag.

One day I visited the Mint, where all these various moneys were being coined by a process exactly similar to that in any other mint. The clerks and workmen were evidently a selected class of men. Here I saw four, eight, sixteen and twenty dollar gold pieces being coined, though I never happened to see them in circulation. The Mexican dollar is preferred to the American in China and Japan, as also in the Sandwich Islands, and possibly all over the Eastern Archipelago, but it gets so stamped with Chinese private marks, and consequently deteriorated in value, that when it finds its way back to Mexico, which very seldom happens, it is recalled into the Mint.

During the Government of the Spanish Viceroys the exportation of gold and silver was only permitted to Spain. There is now a duty upon the exportation of bullion, viz., five per cent. on silver coin, two per cent. extra on uncoined silver, and only one-half per cent. on gold. On account of this difference, European banks gather in the gold coin as soon as it leaves the Mexican Mint, which fully accounts for no gold coin being seen in the country.

The Mexican dollar, though of purer silver than that of the United States, will not pass there at its full value, being a little lighter in weight, and worth only 85 to 95 cents. A Mexican dollar weighs 864-thousandths of an ounce, but it is called an ounce, and I saw it used as an ounce weight on several occasions, of course to the detriment of the buyers. There were also in circulation a few old Spanish dollars, coined as far back as Ferdinand and Isabella's reign, some weighing more and some less than an ounce.

There was nothing in the nature of a bank in Mexico during the period of Spanish rule; a few private individuals banked, but it was generally left to the clergy to act in this capacity, and they lent money at six per cent. per annum. The Monte de Piedad only lent money upon deposit of an article. At the seizure of the church property by President Juarez of course the clergy were stripped of their wealth, and could no longer act as the bankers of the country.

The English were the first to establish a bank in the modern acceptation of the term, the Bank of London and South America being the first to issue notes, which have had a good reception from the outset. This bank has done an excellent business, and pays very large dividends. The example of the English Bank was soon followed by the Monte de Piedad, which now issues notes, and does a banking business. Lately a charter has been granted to the Franco-Egyptian Bank, which has started with a capital of $8,000,000, one of its charter privileges enabling it to increase its capital to $30,000,000. This bank was organised in France.   The Spanish in Mexico have also started a joint-stock bank under the name of "Banco Mexicano Comercial."   This is composed of some of the wealthiest private merchants and bankers of Mexico, and is said to have a bright future before it; it was started because the Franco-Egyptian Bank would not allow the Mexican bankers to take as much stock as they desired.

There is still room for banks in Mexico.   I am told that in some parts of the country the rate of interest is scandalously high, and will continue to be so until there are enough banking facilities to supply the wants of the people.   As I have said before, Mexico is entering a new era.   Railways will cause a development that will surprise the world.   She will have produce to export as soon as these roads are finished.   Hence the necessity of larger banking facilities.   Until within the last twenty years anything like joint-stock companies did not exist, mines being the exception, and even the mines were rather of the nature of a partnership than anything else.

Whichever way the traveller turns he sees changes and improvements taking place; in the cities many of the deserted convents and churches are crowded with workmen and builders, who are altering and adapting them to secular purposes, mostly for hospitals, libraries, and educational institutions; this is paralleled in the country districts by the extension of farm buildings, the improvement of high roads, and the railways already alluded to.

The press of Mexico is filled with paragraphs and advertisements having reference to trade, agriculture, and commerce. Notices such as the following are found in all the daily journals: "The block of traffic at Leon!" "Progress in Hidalgo!" "The steamer *Hewes* has commenced running from Tlacotalpam to Havana, her first cargo being 500 head of beef cattle in prime condition."

The National Telegraph and Telephone Construction Company

announce in capitals that, "having just completed a large contract, they are ready to contract again for anything," heading a long list with "the lighting of cities," and ending it with "burglar alarms." No advertising page seems complete without a print of an agricultural steam-engine and boiler on wheels, illustrating an announcement of "Maquinas de vapor de todas clases y dimensiones;" then come pictures of pumps, rams, and the latest inventions of the plumber's trade, followed by sewing-machines with the newest improvements. The Ameria Americana of Wexel and De Gress supplies steam-engines and plant for the manufacture of cotton, woollen, and paper, for brass and iron foundries, for breweries, and for sugar refining, and they announce they have "unicos agentes para la Republica." Indeed, the Mexican newspapers have caught the American *furore* in the matter of advertisements; and, in soft and smooth-running Spanish, some of them are pleasant reading, especially when they end with "tenemos efectos Ingleses en general."

Another feature of progress which attracted my attention is that in the City of Mexico several life and general insurance companies have been lately established by Americans, and I was introduced to some of their principal agents, who said that they had come into the country in order to ascertain what business could be done in this particular line. These companies were of course branches of well-established wealthy associations in the United States.

I had the pleasure of frequently meeting Colonel A. G. Dickenson and his family in the City of Mexico, where he had established himself with office and residence, and where he extended his hospitality as freely as he extended his policies of life insurance. Colonel Dickenson was an interesting man; he had lost an eye and had been severely wounded in the American Civil War. He and his family were Southern people, and had fought on that side. He himself had taken part in many engagements, and had undergone great hardships, which had been shared in by Mrs. Dickenson, who had followed him through the war, and had saved his life by good nursing on several occasions. His was not the only case where I found men, deeply engaged in professional or mercantile pursuits, who had during the terrible Civil War suffered all the hardships that fall to a soldier's lot, and I always feel the greatest respect for such men. Colonel Dickenson had only lately arrived in Mexico for the purpose of founding a branch of the New York Life Insurance Company, and in the first year the business had been about $400,000 of insurance; and he was engaged in extending the organisation of the company throughout the entire Republic, with, he said, every prospect of increasing operations. The classes who insure are not slow to comprehend the principles of insurance, and it is surprising to find that the Monte de Piedad Company have not added this to the other ramifications of their useful business.

I had also the pleasure of an introduction to Mr. F. S. Winston, president of the Mutual Life Insurance Company of New York, who after a visit to Mexico published a report to the board of trustees which was rather of a gloomy character than otherwise, intimating to those gentlemen that policies could not be satisfactorily arranged on account of the high rate of exchange and the difficulty of issuing policies in the interior of Mexico, especially as regards restrictions to parties visiting or residing for short periods on the sea-coast, a district subject to yellow fever and other tropical diseases; and this class of persons would doubtless be more likely than others to apply for insurances.

Mr. Winston in his report also referred to the difficulty of approaching the people of the better class without having any acquaintance with their language and customs. He admits there is a great deal of wealth and capital at present buried or concealed for safety, but this he thinks would, in the first place, be brought into circulation in business yielding profitable returns rather than in insurance. As a proof of Mr. Winston's being right in regard to treasure being locked up, I may mention the case of the worthy don who died· lately leaving the mother-in-law of Señor Riva Palacios, Minister of Public Works, over five million dollars. Out of this sum two millions were found in specie in old trunks and boxes in the bed-chamber of the deceased.

THE CASTLE OF CHAPULTEPEC.

[page 216.

CHAPTER XXVIII.

FAREWELL.

North Wind across the Gulf of Mexico—Last Rides round the City—Dr. Jose
Gonzalos' Garden—A Humming-bird's Nest—Outline of the Country—The
Cathedral by Moonlight—Last Look at Sacrificial Stone—Adicu to Señor
Romero—Crowd of Friends at the Station.

OCTOBER the 6th.—In walking about the city this morning I
met several friends, who said, " Have you heard the good news ?
They have had the first Norther across the Gulf, and it will clear
off every vestige of yellow fever from Vera Cruz." In the
afternoon General Strother, the American Consul, showed me a
telegram confirming the morning's report. He said he was on his
way to the packet office to secure berths for himself and family
in the next steamer, which left Vera Cruz on the 12th, for New
Orleans. Hearing from him that the Misses Townsend and some
other of my friends intended leaving by the same steamer, 1
accompanied him to the office, and secured a berth for myself. It
was short notice to quit, and I returned to the hotel to consider
how the arrangements could best be made. A number of people
would have to be called upon, and "P.P.C.'s" dropped at several houses where I had received more or less kindness. There were
half-a-dozen places I should like to take a last look at, and before
I sold my horse, for which luckily a man was waiting, I wanted a
few more rides. Engagements would be certain to crowd in the
nearer the time approached for departure, so the sooner I set to
work to fulfil the parting duties the easier things would be at the
last hour.

On the following morning I rode out to Guadalupe with Mr. Neyt. We scrambled our horses over the rough hill-side at the back of the shrine, and descended on the side where the muleteers who did the traffic on the road to Vera Cruz before the railway was opened had once a large and prosperous village, of which only a few huts and deserted roads now remain; the muleteers and their families left the neighbourhood when their employment ceased. My last ride was to the castle of Chapultepec, where I lingered several hours, riding up and down the hill and through the cypress groves at its base, hoping that when the government could give time to take in hand ornamental work they would restore the ruined portion of the castle and relay the terraces, from which there is so magnificent a view in every direction. Nature and art have already done so much for this favoured spot that very little restoration is required to render it one of the most ornamental pleasure grounds possessed by any city in the world. When the new avenues of eucalyptus-trees on both sides. the Paseo de la Reforma have had a few more years' growth, and the commemorative monuments—for which the foundations are already laid—are completed, the approach from the city to the castle—a distance of three miles—will be as perfect as any art-loving people can desire. The coloured sketch (Plate XLIV., *Frontispiece*) which I made early one morning may give the reader a faint idea of the beautiful view which is seen from the terrace of the castle on the side in which are the rooms once occupied by the Emperor Maximilian.

Soon after my arrival in the city I had called upon Dr. Jose Gonzales, the leading homœopathic physician, to tell him if ever I were in need of his services he must kindly attend me. He appeared to be a prominent and much-respected man: his photograph was one of the very few in the windows, and one morning a biography of him filled the whole side of a newspaper. His town residence was nearly opposite the Hotel Gillow in the Cinco de Mai, and he had a beautiful country house and large

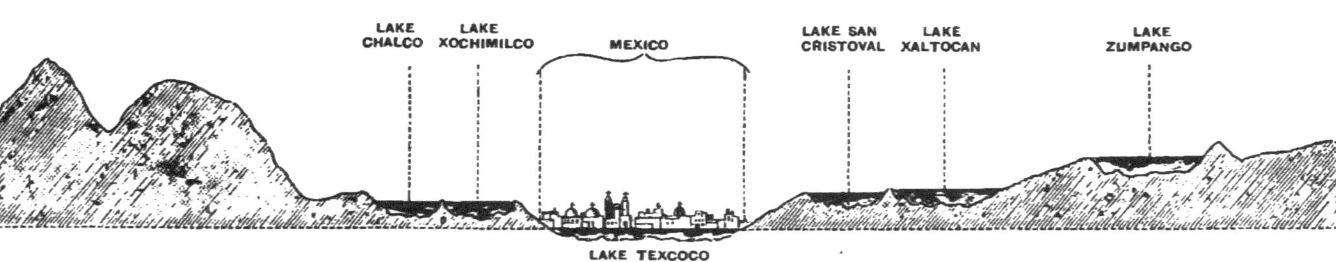

a.—SECTIONAL PLAN OF MEXICO, FROM THE PACIFIC TO THE GULF.

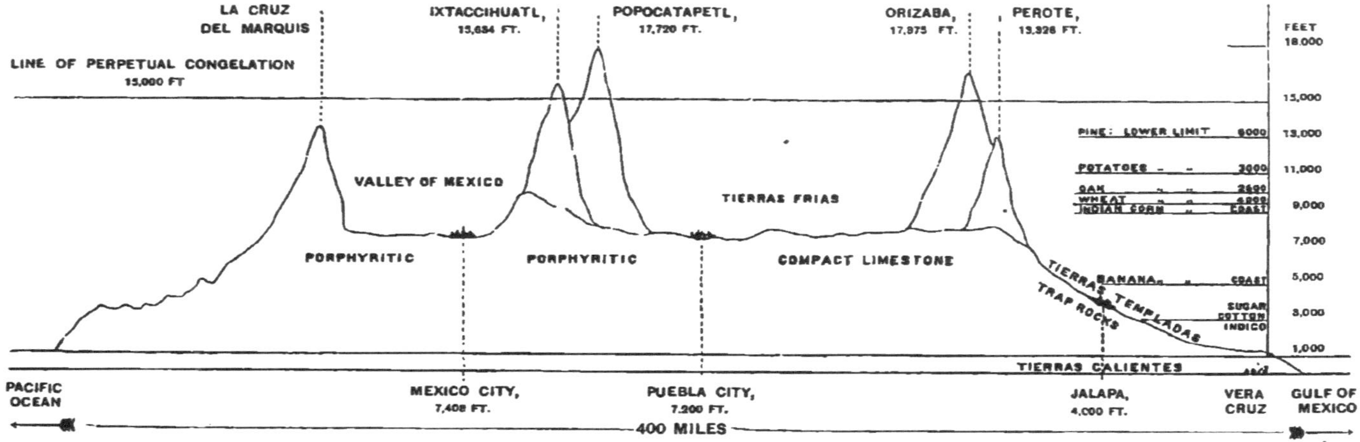

From Map by S. A. MITCHELL, 1847.

b.—ELEVATION OF THE LAKES IN THE VALLEY OF MEXICO.

[*page* 248.

garden near Popotla, to which he drove out every afternoon; he took me with him once or twice, and it was probable he would ask me to go out with him on one of my last days, the afternoon being the only time he was at liberty from professional duties. His garden was three or four acres in extent, and was filled with rare trees and shrubs, including European fruit-trees. The doctor showed me some coloured prints of plums, cherries, and pears which had been sent him from Paris, and he thought the seedsman had not sent him the same trees as ordered, the fruit not proving nearly so fine as in the drawings. I told him that I knew many people who had bought trees and seeds in Paris from exaggerated coloured drawings, and who were equally disappointed with the result. Dr. Gonzales was a naturalist as well as a botanist, and he allowed no one to disturb the birds and insects in his garden. Curious nests of bees, wasps and hornets were shown to me; and he allowed me to take a peep at three eggs, each about the size of a small pea. They were in a humming-bird's nest in a rose-bush, and he first ascertained that the old birds were not looking on, as he said they would desert the nest if they found us close to it. There were two houses in the garden—one occupied by his daughters, the other by himself, where he could have all his scientific papers and apparatus unmolested. An old map of Mexico hung in one of his rooms; and in searching amongst the maps of the London Geographical Society in Savile Row, I found a copy of the same map; it appears to have been drawn by an engineer at the time the railway from Vera Cruz to the capital was proposed. By the kindness of the secretary I was allowed to take a tracing of it, and have added an outline of the country to the Pacific coast; it will give the reader a general idea of the conformation of the country, and show why the valleys of Mexico and Puebla have so mild and equable a climate, varying but a few degrees in temperature throughout the year. Many of my friends expressed surprise that I should remain so close to the equator through the summer months, but the elevation above the sea and the snow upon the mountains tends to render the climate delightful. There is a freshness and briskness in the air, however hot the sun may be, that I have never experienced in any other country. At the edge of the map the different heights are given at which certain trees and plants flourish, and although only one or two classes are mentioned, it may be taken as a rule that most trees, cereals and vegetables that grow in any other country where those that are mentioned flourish, may be found at various altitudes in Mexico. I have also added a plan of the lakes near the city, showing their various elevations above Lake Texcoco, which is the lowest.

There was a pavilion in Dr. Gonzales' garden, in which was a collection of ancient Aztec curios; and on my examining some small clay heads, similar to those on Plates XXIII., XXIV., and XXV. (at end of volume), he told me that there were special characteristics, both on the plain and on the ornamental heads, which enabled experts at once to decide at which ruined city or in what district they had been found. In this collection were a number of small idols and heads, sculptured from very rough red lava-stone, similar in character to two I picked up at Teotihuacan (see Plate XLIX.). Why so much art was expended on so rough a material is extraordinary; it may be the cells of the lava were once filled with a softer stone, which time and weather have worn away—they surely would not have been so finely chiselled if they were intended to have a coat of plaster. Whatever I admired the doctor politely requested me to consider as my own—if I am not mistaken he really meant me to take one or two things; but my politeness in refusing was, I hope, equal to his in giving. There was one drawback—he only spoke Spanish, so our conversation was rather restricted; nevertheless, two last precious hours could not be better spent than in his company.

It was happy luck that during my last few days in the city the moon was coming to the full, and I saw the Plaza and the surrounding buildings by night as well as by day; for several

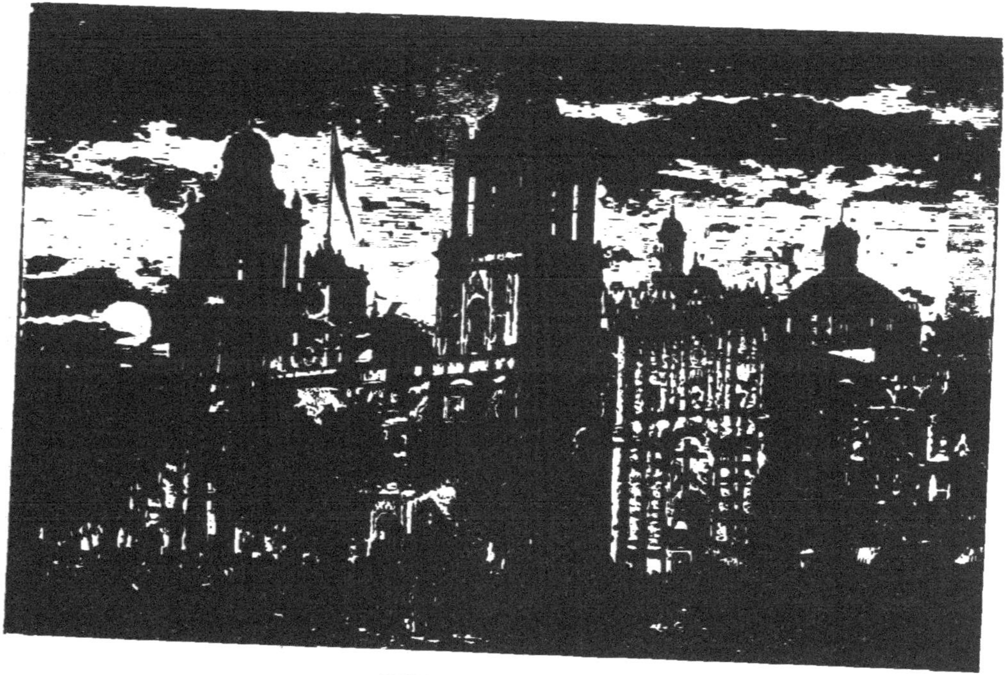

CATHEDRAL BY MOONLIGHT.

[*page* 250.

nights I did not leave the garden in the Plaza till long after the band had played its last piece. The lines of the cathedral, as seen above the trees, were never more beautiful than by moonlight; and the rich stucco tracery of the Sagraria Church was softened down into shadowy confusion, and looked like white lace curtains. I have seen the square gaily illuminated several times, and red and green Bengal lights burnt in the open campaniles of the cathedral towers, showing the outline of the bells in a very effective manner,* but the moonlight view was most beautiful and natural; and when the quarter chimes were jingled on the bells, the eye and ear were both charmed. It is perhaps better to walk under the shadow of a cathedral or under the roar of a waterfall on special occasions than to live in close proximity to so much grandeur.

" *October 9th.—Journal.—*I have walked eight times round the Zocola. The hands of the illuminated clock in the palace turret are close upon the hour of midnight, the bugler of the watch in the palace-yard is breaking the silence of the night with his trumpet; and before the clock strikes, half-a-dozen bugles will be heard answering the call from the different barracks at the gates of the city, and this will be followed by the shrill whistles of the policemen in every direction. In passing the restaurant of La Concordia on my way home I saw a few late loungers enjoying coffee and tobacco-smoke, and I have now only to thump the huge knocker on the massive double doors of the Gillow Hotel, and the doorkeeper, who sleeps on the mat within the portal, will open one door just wide enough for me to pass in, and he will conduct me with the politest Spanish compliments to the foot of the staircase."

* At the Falls of Niagara the water is illuminated for an hour each evening by brilliant colours from several electric lights placed in various positions. The first effect is startling; but our party at the Falls agreed that the descending mass of water looked the best under the soft silver rays of the full moon.

The day before leaving I had a last look at the rubbish exposed for sale in the Portales, but I had no time to turn the things over, and see if there were anything worth buying. No one can buy curios in a hurry; the broken Spanish fans, the damaged pictures, and the rusty swords and stirrups, had no attraction for me. The old bookseller who had a stall at the corner of the cathedral did his best to tempt me, knowing it was his last chance, as I told him I was leaving, and wished him good-bye. I treated him to a glass of pulque at the pulqueria close handy, while his boy watched the stall, and then I passed on to the post-office, to see if my name were on any lists of persons for whom uncalled-for letters might be lying in the office. These lists are written out every week, and the names want closely scrutinising, as the clerks are not always particular in writing out the address correctly. I left a commission with a friend to look at the list for a week or two, and claim and forward to me any letter that might possibly arrive.

The next gateway to that of the post office is the *porte-cochère* leading into the garden of the National Museum. Here I took a last look, and made a sketch of the sacrificial stone which stands embowered in tropical plants. In my description of it at page 191, I did not mention what from the first view caused me to arrive at the conclusion that the stone was not originally intended for sacrificial purposes: the bowl in the centre and the groove from the bowl to the outer edge is cut through the ornamental sculpture, and greatly damages it (see Plate XXXI., facing page 192). Had it been intended in the first instance for human sacrifice the ornamentation would have been arranged accordingly. I give this second plate of the stone as it at present stands (Plate XLVII.), because later travellers will probably find it moved into the large hall of the Museum.

As I expected, I had not time to call on all the people to whom I ought to make my adieus. My last spare hour was spent at Madame Romero's. Señor Romero told me his physicians had

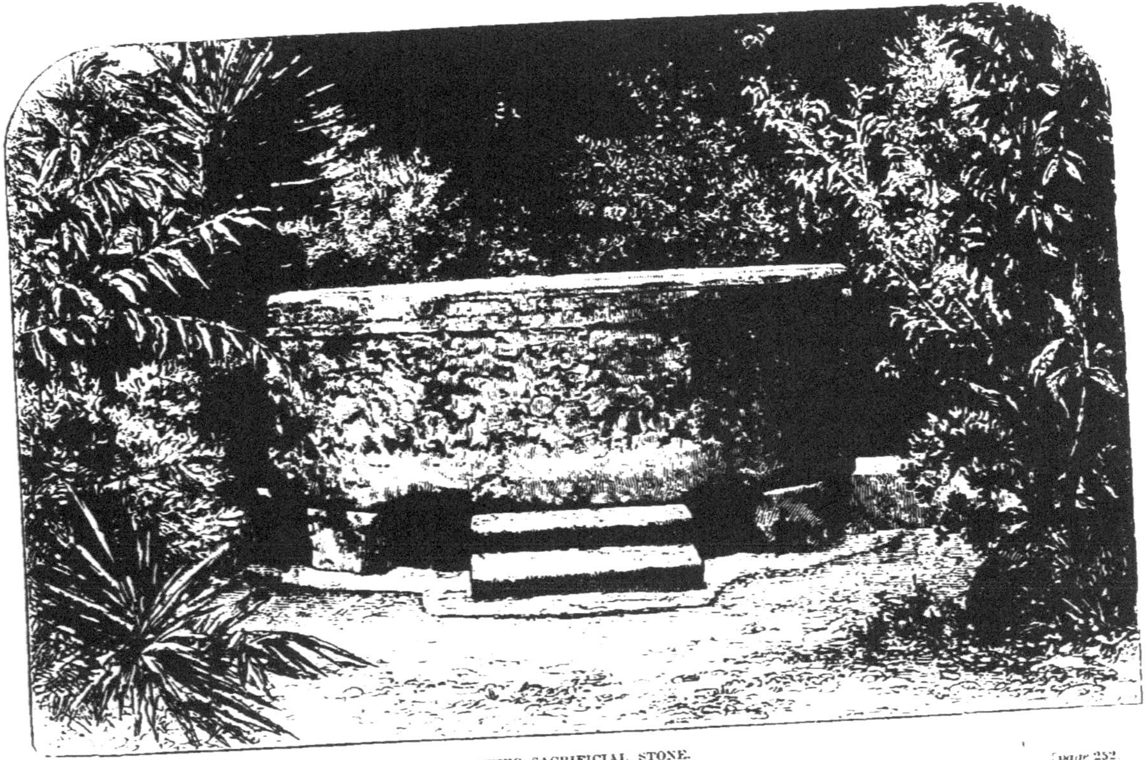

AZTEC SACRIFICIAL STONE.
9 FEET 6 INCHES DIAMETER, 5 FEET THICK. See PLATE XXXI

[page 252]

recommended him to leave Mexico for a time, so he had just accepted the appointment of Mexican Minister at Washington, in which city I had afterwards the pleasure of seeing him again. The train left the city a little after midnight, and before starting for it I wrote a few lines to the editor of the Spanish and English newspaper, requesting him to insert a letter full of the politest expressions of farewell he could compose. Many friends came — as it is the custom—to see us off at the station; and when we had passed the shrine of Guadalupe we all settled down to our several reflections.

I awoke up at the first dawn of light to look at the various portions of the scenery I had missed on the journey up on account of the night overtaking us; and I broke the journey at Orizaba, to get an idea of its position and the quaint architecture of its houses.

CHAPTER XXIX.

CONCLUSION.

The Rainy Season—National Progress—Clerical Obstructiveness—Female Drudgery —Immigrants—The President's Message to Congress in October 1882—Desirability of English Diplomatic Assistance—Hospitality to Strangers.

I QUITTED the City of Mexico on the 12th of October, 1881. I had spent seven months there, including a few weeks occupied in the excursions to neighbouring cities which I have already described. No rain fell from the time of my arrival, in March, till near the end of May, and people occasionally complained of the dust; but in the cities there was no inconvenience from this cause, as the inhabitants were compelled by law to water the roadways twice a day, each householder being responsible for half the width of the road opposite to his property, while the principal rides and drives in the outskirts of the city were well watered by order of the authorities. From June to September is the rainy season, but during this period the rain only fell in the year of my visit two or three times a week, and always in the afternoon or evening, freshening the verdure, and adding to the beauty of the mornings. Occasionally the afternoon thunderstorms were terrific. It seemed to be a matter of question among visitors and inhabitants whether the dry or the rainy seasons were preferable. I think on the whole the rainy season was preferred.

A traveller, having only seven months' experience of a new country, may perhaps hardly be qualified to express opinions on the habits and customs of the people, and the method of government; perhaps he should confine himself to recording simply the ordinary sights that come under his observation day by day. If the traveller in Mexico points to anything in which the country is notably behind-hand, he should add that there is a promise of immediate amendment.

The post-office service, for example, is, I learn, to be immediately reformed. At present no postage-stamps can be obtained beforehand, and every sender has to take his letters to the central office and wait while they are stamped, and post-office orders are unknown. The expectation of better arrangements which I found were entertained during my visit is confirmed by a paragraph in the President's speech at the opening of the session in October 1882. He says: " The Commission that was appointed to study the reforms to be introduced in the post-office department has just finished its labours, and submitted to the Executive a radical reform of the said department—a matter which was imperiously demanded both by the imperfections of our actual system and by the increasing development of our postal communications. Cheap postage, and the security, rapidity and frequency of our communications shall have an immediate realisation."

A nation that has adopted compulsory education, and provides that the education given shall be fairly practical, will have to march with the times in everything else. Even the priesthood will ere long have to replace the realistic form of religion which they put before the present generation by something of a more spiritual character. The children of the present ignorant and fanatical population, when educated, must have religious matters put in a very different light by the priesthood than is done to-day, or blind devotion may be followed by utter rejection of the doctrines of their Church. The clergy of this or any other country if they uphold doctrines at variance with the well-ascertained facts of science, have only their own indiscretion to thank if the people generally turn from their teachings.

I have already dwelt at some length on the beauty of the climate, the scenery, and the flora of the country, the every-day sights of the capital, and, indeed, of all the people with whom I came in contact. I may in some cases have spoken too favourably of the mass of the population. Other travellers, who have had perhaps a more extended field of observation, by proceeding to greater distances from the capital, may have seen things from a different point of view. One thing I will here allude to is, that no one ever solicited alms from me anywhere, except on one occasion, when a poor cripple in a church mutely held out his hand.

One or two American journalists, who were in the country at the same time as myself, wrote letters, which were published in Boston and New York newspapers, in which the people generally were spoken of in terms with which I cannot agree; with the exception of a few vagabonds—the remnant of the late civil wars who are still at large—all the natives of the labouring class appear about as quiet and industrious as those of any other country.

One of the worst features is the terrible drudgery to which the women are subjected, in making the *tortillas* for the daily food of the family, in addition to performing much of the labour on the farm. You meet numbers of them on the roads, as heavily laden with market produce as the men; and this in addition to their babies. The condition of the women ought to have been ameliorated under Spanish rule, but the Spaniards exacted for themselves the labour of all the men, so that the women had to take more than their share in providing for the households. At the present day the Mexican army, 25,000 strong, has no commissariat; crowds of women follow the troops wherever they are moved, and provide the soldiers with food.

There are very large tracts of land in the country—not the most fertile or productive, I imagine—which are held by the government; and the question of encouraging immigrants to take up these lands has been before the House of Congress. On one occasion when I was present the subject was under discussion, and it was proposed to offer certain facilities for the immigration of Italians, as it was considered the climate, the style of agriculture, and the general surroundings were more adapted to the working men of this than of any other European nationality.

The speeches which I heard delivered in the Congress House in reference to immigration seemed to have forced the question on the government, as in the last presidential message, delivered in October, 1882, and before referred to, I notice the following paragraph :—

"The Executive has devoted all its attention to the important branch of colonisation, as it well deserves, and has recently established a new colony in the district of Cholula (State of Puebla). This colony has been formed with some of the Italian families previously established in some of the other colonies, they having expressed a desire to be taken to a milder climate. Fifty more families about to arrive from Italy will be established in this new colony. As regards the other colonies already established, the necessary works are going on in them in order to secure the well-being of the families that compose them. Every day new facilities present themselves for the coming of immigrants, and the acceptance of propositions to bring colonists from different countries has been delayed, because the Executive desires to first secure convenient localities for their settlement under the best possible conditions."

All immigrants in Mexico will have to acquire the Spanish language, because it is the language of the civilised portion of the community, and that used in all the schools. The Italians will very easily acquire Spanish ; and already the number of Spanish-speaking people in Central and South America comes next to that of the English-speaking people in North America, all of whom have come from the Old World to the New.

So long as the Northern States of America offer such advantages to emigrants from Europe, it will require something more than ordinary inducements to bring a good class of people to try the unknown waste and arid lands of Mexico. There is no doubt that an admixture of any energetic European people, such as would leave their homes in the Old World to strike out a new path of life in a distant land, would tend very much to the prosperity of such a country as Mexico.

The proposed routes for the passage of ships across the Isthmus of Panama will exercise some influence on the immigration of the future. And it is within the range of probability that a good immigrant population would soon attain comfort, if not wealth, in a land offering every product of the earth.

I have every confidence that the favourable terms in which I have generally spoken of the country will not hereafter be found to be exaggerations; that my ideas as to the future prosperity of Mexico being early realised are true, and that such ideas are held by most of its leading men. The President's Message to Congress in October 1882, already alluded to, opens with a paragraph quite in accordance with the above remarks. "The brief period of time elapsed since the closing of your last session has been remarkably fruitful, and events of the greatest importance, both for our international relations and for our home affairs, have taken place. Were it not for the fear of being suspected of intentionally exaggerating the picture of our prosperity, I would at once and unhesitatingly declare that every day that has passed away has witnessed the realisation of some decided progress—of some positive improvement. The rapid sketch I am going to trace, of the actual state of the different branches confided to the Executive's management [*confiados á la direccion del Ejecutivo*] will show you the improvements achieved, as well as the public wants which most urgently claim your attention; and the same shall unfold to your eyes the bright future in store for our country, if, as it is hoped [*si, como es de esperarse*], it continues to steadily advance through the path of order and improvement on which it has entered with so much faith and confidence."

The concluding lines of the message are rather prospective: " It shall perhaps not be hazardous at all to predict for the tender generation, scarcely capable at present of attending our schools, or even of pronouncing Mexico's beloved name, to celebrate, in 1921, the first centennial of our independence [*el prima centenario de nuestra independencia*], with similar legitimate pride as our northern neighbours celebrated theirs in 1876."

As soon as the English Government find it in their power to resume diplomatic relations with the country, it will be the dawning of a brighter day for Mexico, and more auspicious for the land of the Montezumas than any other event that could occur for her welfare. England should lose no opportunity of bringing about a reconciliation with a country in whose aid her influence and power could be so beneficially exerted.

I shall never regret my stay in Mexico, nor cease to remember with pleasure the generous hospitality extended to me there. I can only express my earnest goodwill towards the people, together with the officials of the government whom it was my pleasure to meet; one and all they seemed to have at heart the object of elevating their nation from the misery in which it had been left by Spanish rule and its own late civil wars to a front rank in the community of nations.

LONDON:
PRINTED BY WILLIAM CLOWES AND SONS, Limited,
STAMFORD STREET AND CHARING CROSS.

CLAY HEADS FOUND IN GREAT QUANTITIES.
ON THE SITES OF ANCIENT AZTEC CITIES
(EXACT SIZE)

CLAY HEADS FOUND IN GREAT QUANTITIES,
ON THE SITES OF ANCIENT AZTEC CITIES
(EXACT SIZE)

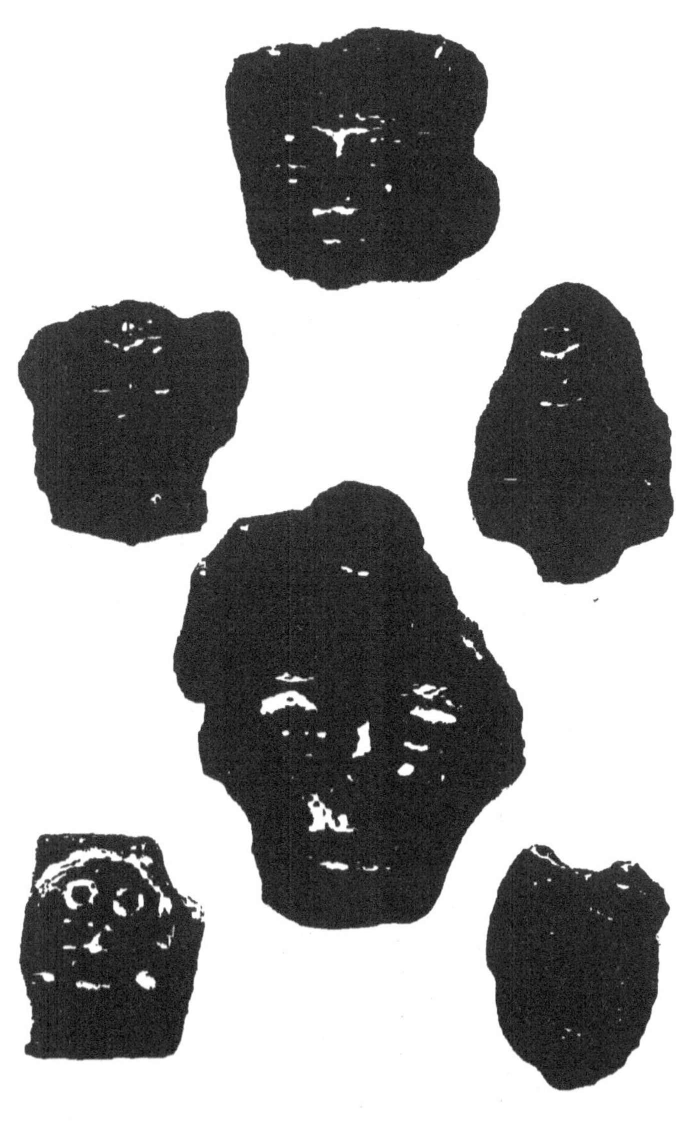

CLAY HEADS FOUND IN GREAT QUANTITIES,
ON THE SITES OF ANCIENT AZTEC CITIES
(EXACT SIZE)

TEOYAMIQUI, GODDESS OF DEATH

VASE OF CENTEOTL OR CERES

TEOCALLE, OR AZTEC TEMPLE.

[at end of vol.

CLAY HEADS FOUND IN GREAT QUANTITIES.
ON THE SITES OF ANCIENT AZTEC CITIES
(EXACT SIZE)

CLAY HEADS FOUND IN GREAT QUANTITIES.
ON THE SITES OF ANCIENT AZTEC CITIES
(EXACT SIZE.)

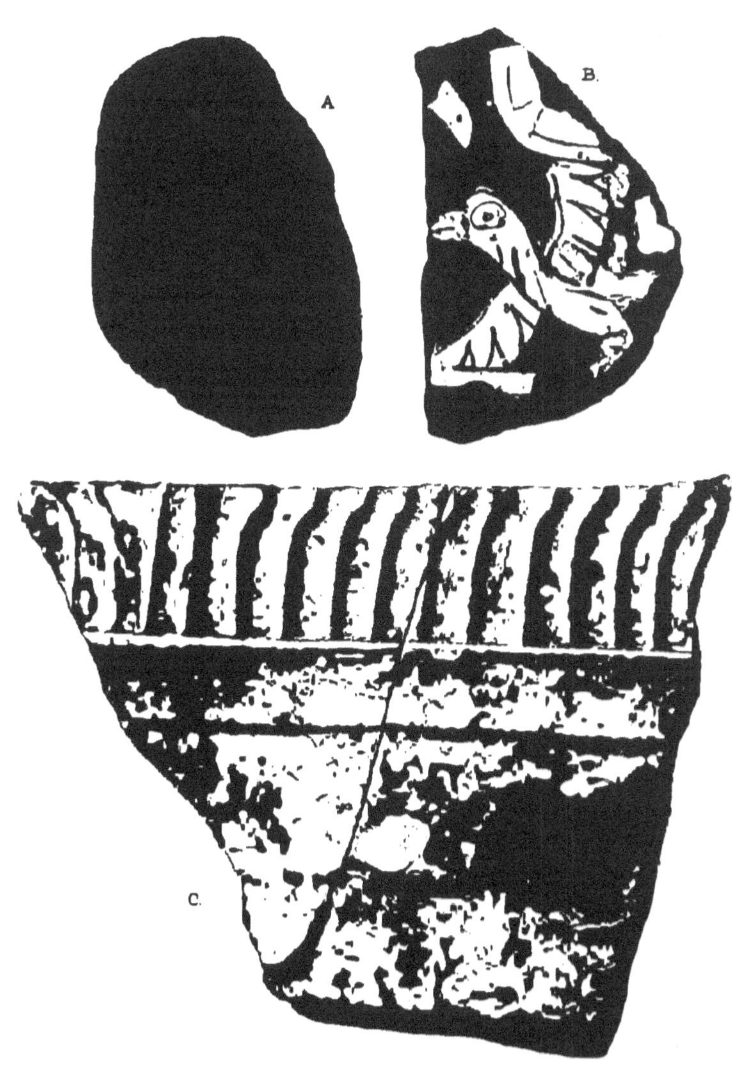

BROKEN PIECES OF POTTERY.

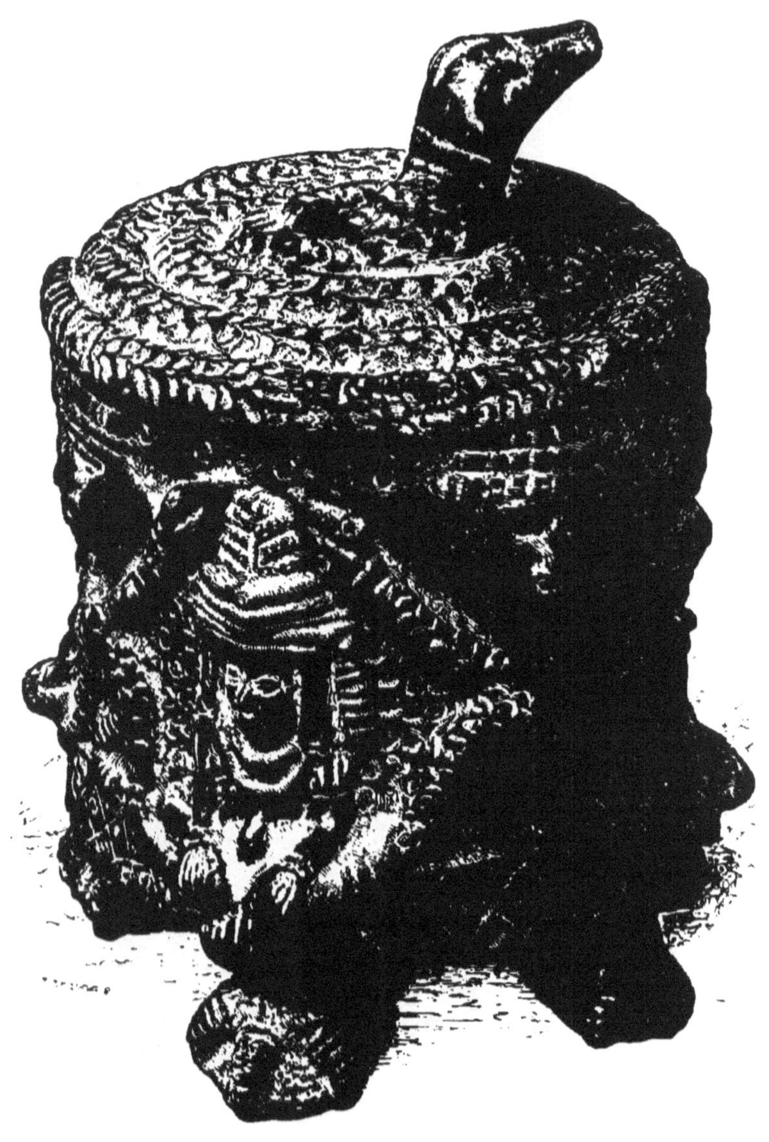

AZTEC VASE IN BLACK CLAY,
12 INCHES HIGH.

[at end of vol.

AZTEC JUG IN BLACK CLAY,
10 INCHES HIGH.

[at end of vol.

OBSIDIAN KNIVES AND ARROW-HEAD.   (at end of vol

a. THE CORE FROM WHICH THE KNIVES WERE CUT.

4 INCHES LONG.   OBSIDIAN ARROW-HEADS.

[at end of vol.